From *London: Kit & Robin*

I stared, awestruck, at the gems on display in the Tower of London. The gold, the diamonds, the sapphires, the emeralds, the silver.

As the group continued the tour, I avoided standing close to Kit. He was too cute, too English, too intimidating, too male, and too unexpectedly nice and funny. *I can't like him,* I warned myself. *He would be horrified by the real me.*

From *Paris: Alex & Dana*

I darted a quick glance at Alex. I imagined his hands caressing my cheek, massaging my neck and shoulders—*whoa!*

The last thing I wanted was for someone from Mustang, Texas, to fulfill my fantasies for a romantic year in Paris. And I absolutely did not want Alex Turner running his hands over my back. No. I wanted someone else. A French guy.

From *Rome: Antonio & Carrie*

He strode toward the kitchen, leaving me standing there with a song of love humming through my veins. No one had ever told me my name was beautiful, and no one had ever spoken it with such a harmonious cadence.

I thought that I could definitely fall for this guy, fast and hard.

a Year in Europe

Three Novels

Rachel Hawthorne

LAUREL-LEAF BOOKS

Published by Laurel-Leaf
an imprint of Random House Children's Books
a division of Random House, Inc.
New York

This omnibus was originally published by Bantam Books in separate volumes
under the titles:
Love Stories Year Abroad Trilogy 1: London: Kit & Robin
© 2000 by 17th Street Productions, an Alloy Online, Inc. company,
and Jan Nowasky.
Love Stories Year Abroad Trilogy 2: Paris: Alex & Dana
© 2000 by 17th Street Productions, an Alloy Online, Inc. company,
and Jan Nowasky.
Love Stories Year Abroad Trilogy 3: Rome: Antonio & Carrie
© 2000 by 17th Street Productions, an Alloy Online, Inc. company,
and Jan Nowasky.

Produced by Alloy Entertainment
151 West 26th Street
New York, NY 10001

www.randomhouse.com/teens

Educators and librarians, for a variety of teaching tools,
visit us at www.randomhouse.com/teachers

RL: 6.0
ISBN: 978-0-375-84073-9 (trade)
ISBN: 978-0-375-94073-6 (glb)
September 2007
Printed in the United States of America
10 9 8 7 6 5 4 3
First Laurel-Leaf Edition

Contents

London: Kit & Robin

Prologue

From: U.S.Robin
Sent: Friday, September 1 . . . 8:03 P.M.
To: BritishKit
Subject: Me and London

Hey, Kit:

In less than twenty-four hours I'm gonna be in London! Is that the coolest thing or what?! I can't wait to meet you and your family. I can't wait for the first day of school! (Whoa—did I really just say that?? No one here in Mustang, Texas, would believe it!)

Thanks for offering to pick me up at the airport. Seven-thirty P.M. at Heathrow Airport, baggage claim. Here are my vital stats: short, blond hair, blue eyes, tallish, jeans, and a red down vest. Just look for the incredibly excited American! My two best buds will be with me too. It's gonna be so hard to say good-bye to them. Well, I'd better finish packing and then hit the sack.

—Robin Carter

P.S. Do you say "hit the sack" in England? Guess I'll find out soon enough!

One

Robin

TEEN, SEVENTEEN, JANE, Cosmopolitan. All the mags said: *Be bold. Be brave. Girl power and all that. Ask him out. He'll like it.*

Yeah. Uh-huh. Right. They weren't talking about Jason Turner. Or me. Maybe all those articles about getting up the guts were for girls who didn't have any guts to start with. I'd always had too many guts.

Because asking out Jason Turner was the dumbest thing I'd ever done. It was pretty much the reason why I was on this airplane—and about to change my whole stupid life and my whole unsuitable self.

Okay, okay. Just because I asked out Jason and he turned me down (in front of everyone, mind you) didn't mean my life was stupid or that I should change everything about myself. But you have to understand—I asked him out, like, *ten* times. Okay, maybe more like *twenty*. And he kept saying no. But I kept asking anyway, thinking I'd wear him down and he'd say yes.

Turned out I wore him down and he said no. Twenty times.

He didn't say the big, fat *no* (in front of everyone) until I got sort of pushy. And that was when I finally got the message. About how incredibly unappealing I was as a girl. *Uncouth* had been one of the words Jason used in his megaphone-esque *no,* actually. I had to look it up in the dictionary. *Uncouth* meant—

"Stop thinking about Jason!"

I turned to the left and stared at my co–best friend, Carrie Giovani. She was twisting her long, brown hair into a low bun. "How'd you know I was thinking about him?"

I heard a fake laugh to my right. Dana Madison, my other co–best friend, gently clasped my chin in her hand and turned me to face her. "You're always thinking about him! So cut it out and look out the window. We're almost there!"

I smiled. "Well, then move that head of yours outta the way so I can see!" The three of us had drawn straws, and Dana had won the window seat. Carrie had gotten second-best—the aisle. I was stuck in the middle. But being stuck between my two best buds for eleven hours wasn't so bad. Especially considering that I wouldn't see them—except for a few scattered weekend vis-its—for a year!

"Robin, we're serious," Carrie added. "We can always tell you're thinking about that jerk when you get quiet. Forget Jason! He thought he was so cool just because he moved from Dallas to Mustang. *Hello!* Big *whoop.* *You're* going to *London!* In, like, half an hour you're going to be on the soil of your heroine!"

Princess Diana's face floated into my mind. Carrie was right. I had to stop obsessing about Jason Turner right now. Why was I wasting my time thinking about that gorgeous, smart, funny, irresistible—

You're hopeless, I told myself. "Okay, okay. You guys caught me. I won't think about him once while I'm in London. I swear—"

The pilot cut me off as the overhead speaker buzzed on. "Ladies and gentlemen, this is Captain Ron speaking. We are beginning our final descent into Heathrow Airport."

"Yeehaw!" I shouted, then clamped my mouth shut. On this plane, which was flying di-rect from Dallas, Texas, there were a lot of loud women with big, blond hair and men in cowboy hats and really tight jeans. This was a *yeehaw* kind of environment.

But they didn't say *yeehaw* in London. Which was one of the main reasons I was heading there. Princess Diana didn't say *yeehaw* to express her excitement. I wonder how she would have reacted to having a loudmouth tomboy from some tiny town in Texas idolizing her. She'd have probably been really nice about it and said something like, "How lovely." After all, the princess had been a true lady. The meaning of the word *refined*. She was exactly what I wanted to learn how to be.

So I had better remember to say "how lovely" in response to everything everyone in England said to me. Or I'd be laughed out of London the way I'd been laughed out of Mustang High School.

Carrie crowded against me to peek out the window, and I crowded against Dana. The three of us stared out, unable to speak as a million tiny, twinkling lights suddenly came into view. I had never seen anything like it before in my life.

For a moment I couldn't believe this was really happening. I pinched myself again—and felt it. So this wasn't a dream. I—Robin Jo Carter from bump-in-the-road Mustang, Texas—was actually about to arrive in the coolest of cities.

London!

I grabbed Carrie's hand and then reached for Dana's. "Can y'all believe I'm gonna spend a whole year in London?"

"I still can't believe you guys didn't pick Paris," Dana said, returning her attention to her *French for Travelers* handbook. The girl was a total Francophile, which meant she was really, really,

really into all things French. Paris was cool, of course, and so was Rome, which was where Carrie was heading, but nothing beat London. After all, Princess Di had lived there.

Before Carrie or I could wax on about why our cities were the coolest, the plane bumped through the air, and the pilot announced we were flying through a bit of turbulence, not to worry. My stomach almost dropped to the ground—which was still thousands of miles below. But the sensation only added to my excitement. I'd never been on a plane before. Heck fire! I'd never even been out of *Texas*. My dad was a farmer, a full-time, year-round job that didn't give my family many opportunities to travel.

"Don't worry about the bumpiness," Carrie re-assured me. (She'd been on planes many times before.) "It's totally normal."

I smiled. "I don't mind a ton of bumpiness as long as I know I'm headed to London. Gosh, I owe y'all big time for this," I said to both of them as I pressed harder against Dana and strained to see if the tiny lights had turned into visible forms of the city.

"Remember how dead set against this your dad was?" Dana mused.

I suddenly envisioned Daddy, in his work overalls, hat, and big boots, telling me I could go on the program with his blessing. That had taken some doing. My mom had been reluctant too, but my daddy had been the absolute worst. My folks had grown up in tiny Mustang, Texas. They'd spent their honeymoon at Six Flags, for goodness sake, and the flags of Mexico, Spain, and France that snapped in the breeze at the entrance to the theme park was the closest they'd ever come to traveling abroad.

Carrie and Dana were from Mustang too, but they lived in *town*—not on a farm way out in the middle of nowhere, like I did. Carrie's parents were involved in the local theater and were really big into activism, like getting folks to vote and enter raffles. Carrie's mom was Mustang's liaison to the Year Abroad program (the Giovanis went to Italy for a vacation every year to visit their relatives). So the Giovanis worked on the Madisons, and both families worked on my mom, and then my mom worked on my dad, and suddenly I got the okay to go. Mr. Giovani had told my dad I'd return from London a sophisticated young woman. My daddy had said that was what he was afraid of—I was a farm girl, not Eliza Doolittle!

I knew who Eliza Doolittle was. Mustang High had put on the play two years ago. And I could really relate to the character. As a matter of fact, I sorta saw myself as a Texas Eliza Doolittle—thanks to the not-so-kind words of Jason Turner.

Yep, I was Eliza Doolittle, all right. Only a

little worse. I carried pigs around instead of flowers.

Returning to Mustang as a sophisticated young lady was exactly what I intended to do after my year abroad. More than anything I wanted to be elegant, reserved, and proper, like Princess Diana and the English girls I'd seen on TV and in the movies. After a year in London, I'd never again be the loud, brash big mouth who embarrassed herself all the time. I'd be a girl who I and others would approve of. And it was my English host "sister," Kit Marlin, who I intended to study and imitate.

"Daddy can't comprehend how embarrassing it is to be a farm girl," I said, trying to explain my parents. But as we all knew, sometimes you just couldn't explain adults. "I'm so *uncultured*. He doesn't understand that I want to be different from the way I am."

"I don't get that part either," Dana told me. "Why do you want to be someone you're not when who you are is so great?"

"Great?" I scoffed. "If I'm so great, then why wouldn't Jason Turner go out with me?"

Dana raised her finely arched eyebrows. "Because he's a jerk?"

Dana had short, chic red hair and the greenest eyes I'd ever seen. She looked like an aristocrat. I knew she couldn't understand why I hated coming across as though I'd just fallen off a turnip truck.

"*I* was the jerk," I said. "I've got a loud voice. I talk without thinking. I embarrassed Jason. I embarrassed myself. I've been embarrassing myself forever—without even knowing it. All the times I thought people were laughing with me, they were really laughing at me."

Dana shook her head. "I think you're making a big mistake to use this year abroad to become something you aren't." She leaned forward slightly. "You're just fine the way you are. Tell her, Carrie."

Carrie shrugged, making her dangling earrings jangle. Her olive complexion and dark hair made her look exotic. She credited her Italian heritage with what we called her *allure*. "I think her plan sounds like fun. We're supposed to use this year to experience new things. Stores, clothes, food—"

"Guys!" we all said at once, and laughed.

I definitely planned to experience guys. As soon as I lost my slow Texas drawl and learned to talk like a cultured person, I knew I'd have guys knocking on my door. No more *y'all* for me!

I leaned toward the window, practically smushing Dana against it.

"Come on." Dana unbuckled her seat belt. "This is your city. Let's switch seats."

"City! Not *town*. Incredible!" I knew I was being small townish by getting excited about a city, but I couldn't help myself. These last few minutes before the plane actually touched down would be my last as Texas Robin. Once those wheels hit the runway, I would be well on my way to becoming London Robin.

Dana and I giggled as we squeezed past each other. There wasn't a lot of room in an airplane. You most definitely did not want to sit by someone you didn't like for hours on end. I dropped into the window seat and quickly refastened my seat belt. I'd promised my daddy that I would follow all the rules. He was such a worrier.

I touched my fingers to the smooth glass and stared out the window. I desperately wanted to catch my first glimpse of London but could only see thick, white, billowing clouds. I wondered if Kit was already at the airport. Was she staring up at the white clouds, waiting to catch a glimpse of the plane?

Kit and I had e-mailed each other a couple of times. It was a little strange e-mailing someone I'd never met. I didn't really know what to say to her, so I kept the e-mails fairly brief. I didn't want to give too much away because I planned to alter my personality while I was in London, and I didn't want to confuse Kit.

Like me, Kit Marlin was an only child. I had always wanted a sister. Someone to share the house with. We could swap clothes, jewelry, perfume, and makeup. We could talk late into the night any night we wanted. I wouldn't have to wait for a sleep over.

I would have a year-round sleep over with my new sister.

It was going to be the most wonderful year of my life!

There was a wispy break in the clouds. Buildings, land—a mosaic of brown and green—and water came into view quickly and then disappeared. My breath hitched.

"Did you see that?" I asked breathlessly.

"I saw it," Dana and Carrie said at the same time.

"It was awesome," Dana told me.

I latched my gaze past the window, searching for another glimpse of the city I had dreamed about for months. The plane broke through the last barrier of clouds. I marveled at the domed roofs, spires, old buildings and new reaching toward the sky. And a castle. I could actually see Windsor Castle.

"Oh my gosh, y'all," I whispered in awe. "We're definitely not in Texas anymore."

After getting our luggage, we'd had to go through the passport inspectors and then the customs inspectors. I was beginning to think we'd never get out of the airport. After what seemed an eternity, I stood in the public lobby and waiting area with the backpack and laptop I'd carried on the plane plus my three pieces of luggage at my feet. The night before, I had tied bright purple ribbons around the handles so that I could find them quickly. Now I wished I hadn't been so efficient. I had way too much time to look around.

English accents surrounded me. People whizzed by, looking ever so sophisticated. I was struck dumb for the first time in my life. I was suddenly hit with reality and fear: I was in a foreign country, and my friends were about to abandon me! Carrie and Dana had a layover in London until tomorrow, so they were staying in a hotel. They would be so close, but so far away at the same time.

My stomach was tied up in one big knot tighter than the bows on my luggage. Standing here, waiting for Kit, was worse than waiting on the judges at the county fair to place ribbons on the winning livestock.

Carrie and Dana stood beside me. They had piled their bags on a nearby cart. Miss Lawrence, the YA sponsor, walked over to us.

"Did you get all your luggage?" she asked.

"Yes, ma'am," we answered in unison.

"Wonderful. As soon as Robin gets picked up, the rest of us will head to the hotel. I'm going to check on the best way to get there." She narrowed her gaze. "Stay put. You're not allowed to go off on your own until you've hooked up with your host family." She walked toward the glass doors at a brisk pace.

"Stay put?" Carrie retorted. "Like there's

some trouble we can get into before our host family picks us up that we can't get into after they pick us up?"

"She's responsible for us," Dana explained.

"What an important job! Fly around the world and drop off students." Carrie's voice dripped sarcasm. She had always been the most independent. I figured that happened when you had five brothers and one sister. Carrie was accustomed to taking care of herself.

"If it wasn't for Miss Lawrence, Robin wouldn't be here at all," Dana pointed out. "Her parents wouldn't let her fly all the way to London by herself. Isn't that right, Robin?"

Dana was Miss Logical, always watching out for the underdog.

"Right," I replied, distracted.

Where is Kit? I wondered. My host sister should have already been here. I glanced at my watch. Somewhere over the Atlantic Ocean, I had set it to London time. *Over the Atlantic.* I'd even slept over the Atlantic. Not bad for a small-town girl.

"Where's your host family?" Carrie asked.

"Only Kit is coming." I searched the crowd like I knew who I was looking for. But I only had a vague idea of what Kit looked like. In the few e-mails we had exchanged, we'd never gotten around to exchanging pictures. I knew Kit was tall. She had blond hair and blue eyes, like me. I also knew that Kit and I would get along well. After all,

I had a great-aunt named Kit, so I saw that as a good sign. It made being thousands of miles from home seem not quite so scary.

"So far I'm not impressed with your host sister," Dana said. "She should have been here on time. She must have known you'd be nervous."

"I'm not nervous," I assured her. *Terrified* was a better word. *Frightened*. *Scared*. Either of those would work too.

There were so many people. They all looked confident. They spoke briskly, walked briskly. They knew where they were going. What had I been thinking to want to travel thousands of miles from home? The airport was as big as Mustang.

"Okay, listen," Carrie began, and I turned my attention to my friend. Carrie always had a plan. And she always talked with her hands drawing pictures in the air. She said it was the Italian in her blood.

"We have one day together in London tomorrow," Carrie continued. "What do we want to do?"

"Something touristy," Dana replied. "I promised Mom that I'd send her a postcard from London."

Carrie smiled. "Tower of London? We can take a gander at the crown jewels. Maybe they even have some that we can try on. What do you think, Robin?"

"Sounds good," I murmured. I started searching the crowds more diligently, my worry increasing. If my host sister didn't show up, I would have to go to the hotel with Miss Lawrence. Not a good way to begin my year of adventure.

Where in the heck was Kit? She'd written that she'd wear a red sweater.

My wandering gaze slammed to a halt as I spotted a red sweater. Then my hopes sank deeper than a Texas oil well. I was looking at a guy leaning against the far wall. A very cute guy.

I barely managed to tear my eyes off him to look around for another red sweater. But I could feel the guy's eyes on me. I sneaked a glance back at him. He *was* looking at me. He was tall, with blond hair that fell across his brow.

He shoved himself away from the wall and ambled hesitantly toward me. He stopped in front of me, angled his head, and narrowed incredible blue eyes. He looked like someone who was trying to solve an extremely difficult problem.

"Red vest, short, blond hair, blue eyes, with two American friends—are you by any chance Robin Carter?"

I froze. His elegantly spoken words slammed into me with the force of a stampeding bull. They were the exact words I'd written in my e-mail when I told Kit what to look for. Horror swept through me.

Kit Marlin was a *guy?*

Two

Robin

KIT MARLIN HAD the most cultured voice I'd ever heard—warm and gentle, sort of like Hugh Grant's. Mine was more like a herd of cattle, which was exactly how Jason Turner had described it.

My mouth grew dry, and my chin tingled. I thought I might be ill. No, no, Princess Diana would never have thrown up in the middle of an airport.

I swallowed to get rid of the stuffed-cotton feel in my mouth. *Remember, you're in London now. Speak like Princess Di.* "I was expecting a female person," I said formally, in a very low voice to disguise my accent.

He leaned forward slightly. "Sorry?"

For what? I wondered. *Keeping me waiting?*

Then it dawned on me. That wasn't what he meant. I'd watched Hugh Grant in enough movies to realize that Kit meant, *Excuse me? What? Come again?*

I cleared my throat and said a little louder, "I was expecting a female person."

He smiled warmly. The most beautiful, welcoming smile I'd ever seen. "Kit is short for Christopher."

My scared-spitless smile evaporated as the reality hit me. Not only didn't I have an English sister to study and imitate, but I had to live in the same house with a guy for the first time in my life. I mean, I'd lived with my daddy, but that didn't count. He was a father. Kit was a . . . Well, Kit was a *guy!*

Sure, he was English and he was cute—to-die-for cute—but he was still a guy, and we'd be sharing accommodations!

If Jason Turner from no-big-deal Dallas thought I was a hillbilly, what was Kit Marlin going to think once he got to know the real me?

"Will you please excuse me a moment while I converse with my companions?" I asked Kit in a low voice.

He furrowed his brow. "Pardon?"

I reined in my impatience. I was certain that talking in a low voice would work once we got out of the bustling airport. Raising my voice just a little bit, ever mindful to keep my words clipped and

18

even, I repeated, "Will you please excuse me a moment while I converse with my companions?"

"Oh, right," he said, nodding. "I'll watch your baggage."

Walking like I was balancing a book on the top of my head, I escorted Dana and Carrie to an area out of earshot. With my back to Kit, I contorted my face into an expression of hopeless despair. As much as I wanted to, I couldn't very well scream in the middle of the airport. "What am I going to do? He's a guy!"

"A cute guy," Carrie pointed out. "And that is so totally not fair. Your first night in London, and a dream guy walks right into your life."

"You're missing the point here! Didn't you hear him talk? He's too English. What do I do now? How am I gonna live in the same house with him? He's gonna think I'm a freak if he hears how I talk and sees how I act." I knew I was rambling, something I did when I was totally nervous—and at that moment I was more nervous than I'd ever been in my entire life.

"He won't think you're a freak," Dana assured me. "He'll like you just like we do."

I shook my head fiercely. "No, no, he won't. Can I stow away with one of you guys and go to Paris or Rome?"

Carrie put her hand comfortingly on my shoulder. "Hey? Aren't you dare-me-to-do-anything Robin?"

19

"I've only ever lived with my parents," I blurted out. Why couldn't they see what a disaster this was? "Don't dare me to live with a guy!"

"I've got five brothers," Carrie reminded me. "All you have to worry about is making sure that you get a good heaping amount of food on your plate before he sits down to eat because guys wolf down everything in sight. And you just need to check the toilet seat because they always leave it up. Always. It's disgusting."

"I can't do this," I insisted. "He was supposed to be a girl. Kit is a stupid name for a guy."

"As in Kit Carson?" Dana asked.

I glowered at her.

Dana shrugged. "I'm just saying . . . he seems okay with you being a girl. So you can handle this, Robin."

I glanced over my shoulder. Kit was watching me. He quickly looked away.

Carrie leaned close and whispered in my ear, "And he is so totally hot."

I glared at Carrie. "That's one of the things that makes this so hard."

But neither Dana nor Carrie was listening to my pleas for understanding. Instead their eyes were flashing silent *dare yous*. Sometimes it's not a good thing to have friends who know your weakness. I gave a brisk nod. "All right. I can do this. It's not a whole year. It's just a whole school year, which is what . . . one hundred and eighty days?" Wasn't that how Henry VIII counted the time he spent with his wives before he beheaded them—in days instead of years?

"You can do it," Carrie assured me.

"But you're going to have to stop whispering," Dana told me. "And the formal talk? Where did that come from? *Companions?* My grandmother has a *companion*. We're *friends*."

Carrie nodded. "I have to agree with Dana on this one. You sound too bizarre." She looked past me to where Kit was standing. "He, on the other hand, sounds just like Hugh Grant." She sighed dreamily. "You are so lucky!"

I felt anything except lucky, but I knew that Dana and Carrie were right. I had to stay. Convincing my parents had been a difficult task. If I changed plans now and went to Paris or Rome, they'd have a cow and tell me to come home.

"I'll cut back on the formal words, but not the low voice." I hated to admit it, but *female person* had been a little out there now that I thought about it.

"Oops, there's Miss Lawrence waving at the door. We've gotta go," Carrie said. She gave me a tight hug. "You're gonna do just fine."

I nodded, blinking back the tears stinging my eyes.

Dana hugged me fiercely and kissed my cheek. "Don't cry yet. We're still in the same city, and we'll see you tomorrow." She drew back and smiled. "And tomorrow night we'll all cry when we say good-bye."

Carrie grabbed Dana's arm. "Come on. Let's see if we can talk Miss Lawrence into taking us to a pub tonight."

"She's not going to take us to a pub," practical Dana responded.

"Simply for the cultural experience," Carrie assured her with a laugh.

"Y'all be careful," I called softly after them as they hurried to the cart holding their luggage. So softly that I didn't think they heard me. But I couldn't risk calling out, couldn't take a chance that Kit would hear my real voice.

I watched them say good-bye to Kit before pushing the cart toward the door. I felt like my lifeline was cut when the doors closed behind them.

I wanted to scream, *Wait, take me with you!*

But I had come here to change my screaming ways.

I pasted a smile on my face and walked toward waiting Kit.

I tried not to stare at Kit as he pulled my larger bags into the parking garage. I had my small bag, my laptop, and my backpack. Thank goodness my luggage had wheels. I never would have been able to haul it through the airport otherwise.

"I'm terribly sorry about making you wait so long," Kit said. "But I made the same mistake you

22

did. I expected you to be a guy. Robin as in Robin Hood. I stood there for the longest time looking for a chap in a red vest."

Great! Now he's thinking of me as a boy.

In a low, twang-free voice I said, "I expected you to be a girl, as in my great-aunt Kit."

He paled and quickened his step.

Great start we're off to here, I thought glumly.

He came to a stop beside a black sedan. "Well, here we are. I'll put your things in the boot."

The boot? What was he talking about?

He opened the trunk. I felt like such a fool. "Oh, you mean the—"

My loud southern voice echoed around me. Thank goodness he'd just ducked his head into the trunk to shift some stuff around, so he didn't hear me. He grunted as he lifted my first suitcase. With a thud it landed in the trunk—the boot.

He rubbed his arm and stared at me. "Blast it all! What have you got in there? It must weigh ten stone."

Ten stone? Did he think I'd packed rocks?

They obviously had different words for things over here. I was going to have to remember that.

He obviously hadn't expected me to tell him what was in my suitcase because he went back to arranging my luggage inside the boot. He had broad shoulders. I didn't have any trouble imagining him working my daddy's fields.

I shivered because of the chill in the air. It was

ninety-eight degrees when I left Texas. I'd felt silly carrying a coat into the Dallas airport, but I was glad I had it now.

"Come on. Let's get you inside where it's a bit warmer," he said. He slammed the trunk closed and walked around to the left side of the car.

Panic surged through me as he unlocked the driver's-side door and held it open for me. I shook my head briskly and stated in a level voice, "I'm not driving."

He furrowed his brow and took a step toward me. "Pardon?"

"I'm not driving," I repeated a little more loudly, trying to keep my voice evenly clipped.

He gave a quick laugh. I liked his smile and the way his blue eyes twinkled.

"Of course you're not. You're sixteen, right?"

I nodded.

"You have to be seventeen to drive over here." He tilted his head slightly. "This is the passenger side."

I eased up slightly like I was approaching a cantankerous bull. I peered inside. No steering wheel.

I felt my face turn bright red. I grimaced and looked at him. "I forgot that you drive on the wrong side of the road here."

He laughed again. "It's you Americans who drive on the wrong side."

I almost barked out my laughter. Wouldn't he

find that charming? The way I brayed like a donkey.

I climbed into the car and took a deep breath. He got behind the steering wheel and started the car. This was weird, sitting on the driver's side without a steering wheel. I felt like I needed to wrap my hands around something, namely a steering wheel, but since there wasn't one in front of me, I balled up my hands and put them on my lap.

Whoa, boy! my mind screamed as he pulled into the left lane of the highway. Even though I knew he was going to do it, my reflexes kicked in. I stiffened and reached for a brake that wasn't on my side of the car.

He chuckled. "I suppose it's a bit strange— driving on the right side of the road for a change."

Only he wasn't on the right side. He was on the left side, so he was on the wrong side! I wanted to yell at him. Instead I glanced out the window at the gray sky.

"Does driving on the motorway make you nervous?" he asked.

I jerked my head around and looked at him. Was he talking about the highway we were driving on? He had to be. "No," I answered succinctly. *No* was a good, safe word with no extra syllables to accidentally draw out.

"Did you have a good flight?" he asked.

"Yes." Another safe word.

He cast a quick glance my way before turning his attention back to the highway. The motorway? He furrowed his brow. "I suppose it was a long flight coming all the way from Texas, as you were."

Silence. Was I supposed to respond to that? I didn't hear a question.

"My mum should have dinner ready by the time we get home," he told me. "The drive's a half hour. To give you a sense of where Hampstead is in London, it's about twenty minutes or so from Buckingham Palace."

I was still on *mum*. Wasn't that a flower used in homecoming corsages? Not that I'd ever had one, but I'd heard rumors.

"I think she's planning on a bit of bubble and squeak for tonight." He darted a quick glance my way. "Do you like that?"

What in tarnation was he talking about? I was getting more confused by the minute. He'd mentioned supper, but that couldn't be food. It had to be a game. That's what it was. We were going to play some sort of game to get better acquainted. His question required only a one-word answer, and that's all I was going to give him. "Yes."

"Oh, good. Mum will be pleased to hear that. She wasn't quite sure what to cook."

My stomach roiled. Bubble and squeak *was* food! Oh no. I'd told him that I liked it, so I'd have to eat it now—whatever the heck it was.

"So where are your friends going to school this year?" he asked.

"Paris and Rome."

"The one with the dark hair . . . her name would be?" he prodded.

I closed my eyes on a silent sigh. In my shock over his gender, I hadn't even bothered to introduce my friends. He probably thought I was the rudest person west of the Atlantic. My parents had raised me better than that. I opened my eyes. "Carrie."

"And she's the one going to?"

"Rome."

He smiled slightly. "And the girl with the short red hair?"

"Dana."

He nodded. "So she must be going to Paris. I feel rather like Sherlock Holmes with that deduction." He released what sounded like a nervous laugh. "It won't be much longer now."

I stared out the window. He was so formal and polite that he was scaring me to death. The longer we drove, the queasier my stomach got, and it didn't have anything to do with the speed of the car and the way he had to keep swerving in and out of traffic. I was going to a new house. A house I would live in for a whole year. A house I would live in for a whole year with this guy.

My stomach was knotting up so tightly that I didn't know how I'd eat supper. I wanted to ask him what bubble and squeak was, but then I'd have to confess that I had lied earlier, and wouldn't I look stupid?

A heavy silence wedged its way between us. I wanted to fill it with questions. I had at least a hundred. Was his mother like Queen Elizabeth? Not with the crown, of course, but regal? Was I supposed to salute his dad? Curtsy? Did they ever eat regular food like hamburgers and barbecued chicken?

I opened my mouth to ask Kit what his folks were like, but I didn't know if that was proper in England. I snapped my mouth closed.

It was better if we drove in silence anyway. After all, I didn't want him to ask *me* any more questions.

I couldn't imagine what his reaction would be if Mr. English City Boy learned that I had pet pigs and won the last hog-calling contest at the county fair.

Three

Robin

"MARVELOUS! I'VE ALWAYS wanted a daugh-ter," Mrs. Marlin said as she hugged me.

I was having a hard time believing that I was standing inside a house in London. When Kit had pulled the car to a stop in front of the house, I could only stare. Brightwell Street was a row of two-story brick buildings lined up side by side like soldiers. The house looked narrow from the front, but inside it seemed larger. *Well laid out,* my daddy would say.

"Haven't I always said that, Nickie?" Mrs. Marlin asked. "That I'd like to have a daughter."

"Indeed you have, love," Mr. Marlin said as he stood smiling beside his wife.

Tall, with wavy, blond hair, Mr. Marlin re-minded me a lot of Kit. Mrs. Marlin, on the other hand, was short and round, with black hair peppered with silver.

"We must not have paid much attention to the papers that they sent us, eh, Kit?" Mr. Marlin asked. His smile grew broader as he leaned toward me like he wanted to impart a national secret. "We thought you were a lad."

"I explained that to her, Dad," Kit said.

The heat of embarrassment scalded my face. Okay, so everyone had made an idiotic mistake. I wanted to forget it.

Mrs. Marlin slipped her arm through mine. "Let's give you a quick tour so you'll feel completely at home here. After all, this is your home now."

My home! Omigosh. A wave of homesickness washed over me. Staying here was quickly becoming a reality.

Although the downstairs area had a different feel to it that I couldn't quite identify—old English charm, maybe—it wasn't that much different from my house in Mustang. Except all the walls had flowered wallpaper on them. All the walls. At home we only had wallpaper in the kitchen and bathrooms.

A swinging door separated the kitchen from the dining room on one side of the house. No breakfast area like we had at home. A huge living room sat in the center of everything. Mr. Marlin's office was to the side. Kit's parents' bedroom was at the back. My parents' bedroom was at the back of the house, and my dad did all his paperwork in the room next door. Of course, his office didn't have leather books lining the bookshelves like this one. He had farm manuals and tattered farm-supply catalogs.

"It's a very nice house," I said quietly, politely.

Mrs. Marlin beamed. "Thank you, dear. And now, my prized garden."

I wondered what kind of vegetables she grew as we stepped through French doors onto a pebbled patio. Beyond, I could see flowers lining the house and trestles with ivy clinging and weaving its way up. Mrs. Marlin must have been referring to her flower garden. There wasn't anything else in the yard except for a small white gazebo and some stone benches.

"We're quite pleased with the garden," Mrs. Marlin told me. "Kit helped his father make the gazebo for my birthday a few years back. I think it really adds to the beauty of the garden."

Garden. Yard. They had to be calling the yard a garden even though they were mostly growing grass. I felt like these people were speaking a foreign language. But Mrs. Marlin was completely elegant and regal as she daintily pointed to her flowers. Her speech was refined and proper. And soft without being a whisper.

I can learn from her, I thought. *I can study her and imitate her proper, sophisticated ways. Then I'll be exactly what I want to be.*

31

"Tell us about yourself, dear," Mrs. Marlin prodded.

I swallowed the knot rising in my throat as we strolled back into the house. Mr. Marlin and Kit were dogging our heels. I felt like I was walking to my execution. What could I tell them about myself that wouldn't make me sound like a country bumpkin? My mind was in an unnatural state—it was absolutely blank.

"We're your family now, dear," Mrs. Marlin said. "So you mustn't be shy. What sort of things do you like?"

I smiled at the simple question as the answer popped into my head. "I really like Nick Lachey."

Mrs. Marlin's face brightened. "Oh, so you have a boyfriend back home."

I stared at her. She was joking, right?

Kit cleared his throat. "Mum, Nick Lachey is a pop star."

His mother blushed. "Oh, of course. I probably knew that."

No, she didn't, I realized. Imitating Mrs. Marlin might turn me into a proper *nerd*.

"Although I'm sure Robin *does* have a boyfriend back home," Kit added.

Now I stared at him. *That* was unexpected. Why would anyone think *I* had a boyfriend anywhere?

"Come along, dear," Mrs. Marlin said. "I'll show you your room. It's on the first floor."

I watched her head up the stairs. The woman was insane. I was going to live a whole year with a crazy woman. Hadn't she said my room was down here?

"Go on," Kit said behind me, nearly making me jump out of my skin.

"She said my room was on the first floor," I explained in my low, twang-free voice.

"It is," Kit assured me.

"But she's going to the second floor," I muttered.

Kit shook his head and grinned. "She's going to the first floor." He pointed at his feet. "This is the ground floor."

I raised my finger toward his mother. "And that's the first floor?"

He nodded.

Great! I was going upstairs to the first floor. That made no sense.

"Nickie! Will you and Kit bring up Robin's things, please?" Mrs. Marlin called down in a lovely singsong voice.

I caught up with her at the top of the stairs.

"Here you are, dear," Mrs. Marlin said.

I stepped into the coziest room. The walls were decorated with pale lilac wallpaper adorned with bouquets of lilies. The room had a small fireplace, although no fire burned in the hearth. Beside the fireplace was a four-poster bed with a lavender lace canopy.

"I'm ever so glad you turned out to be a

lass," Mrs. Marlin whispered conspiratorially. "I wasn't quite certain how a lad would take to this room."

"It's wonderful," I murmured, breathtaken. A small TV sat on a little table in the corner. It looked new, and I wondered if they'd bought it just for my visit.

The window had a violet padded bench seat beneath the windowsill. Perfect for curling up and looking out on London. Simply perfect.

"Kit's room is directly across the hall," Mrs. Marlin told me.

Not so perfect.

"You'll share the bathroom," Mrs. Marlin added.

Absolutely imperfect.

I stepped farther into the room. A small desk sat near the window. Above it on the wall hung a framed poster of the Dallas Cowboys. "They're not English," I blurted out.

"Kit put that up," Mrs. Marlin explained. "He thought it would make our new American guest from Texas less homesick."

He did? Hmmm. Maybe Kit wasn't quite the staid and proper guy that I thought he was.

If only Kit were a girl. I could throw myself at a girl's mercy and plead with her. *Help me! Change me! Make me just like you!*

But a guy? Way too embarrassing.

Especially one who lived right across the hall.

★   ★   ★

I was probably seriously suffering from jet lag, but I was too excited and too nervous to close my eyes for a second. So, I unpacked my bags. I placed my neatly folded clothes into drawers scented with lavender sachets. Hung my sweaters in a closet that smelled of cedar. Mrs. Marlin had told me to freshen up a bit before dinner—which would be in one hour.

What did that mean? Freshen up. On the farm it meant wash the dirt off your hands and the dust off your face, brush the tangles out of your hair. But this was London. And as I was quickly learning, the same words meant different things over here.

Boy, howdy. Freshen up. They'd given me an hour to do it. It had to mean dress up.

I was certain it did. Mrs. Marlin had said she was making a traditional English meal to welcome me. Was that a fancy meal? It had to be. Like I saw in the movies. The long table, the flickering candles, ten forks, and a dozen knives. Formal.

I had brought one formal gown. Should I wear it? Was it that kind of a dinner? Dinner, not supper. It even sounded fancy.

I needed some serious help.

I went to the phone on the small, dainty desk and dialed the hotel where Carrie and Dana were staying. The ringing took me by surprise—short, quick staccato bursts. When the hotel clerk answered, I asked for their room. I sat carefully in the

35

elegant chair, fearful of breaking it. I listened to the phone ring, ring, ring. *They must have talked Miss Lawrence into taking them to a pub,* I thought glumly. A cultural experience.

How's this for a cultural experience? I have no idea what I'm doing here!

I hung up and began to pace. I desperately wanted to call my mom, but we'd agreed to call only once a week to cut down on the expense of this trip. Calling about what to wear to dinner seemed trivial. I had no idea what other crisis would erupt before the week was out—and I might really need my mom then.

Better to save the phone call. I could set up my laptop and e-mail my mom, but she would be busy with chores right now. It might be hours before I got a reply, and that would be way too late.

Admit it, Carter. You are totally alone here, and you don't know how to do the simplest things!

How countrified is that?

A bundle of nerves, I plopped onto the bed, fell onto my back, and flung out my arms in hopeless frustration. I stared at the lace canopy. The web of tiny threads made me feel trapped.

How in the heck am I gonna handle the first day of school the day after tomorrow? I can't even handle going to dinner. How am I gonna talk to anyone if I have to hide my accent?

Things were really getting bad. Now I was rambling to myself. Why couldn't Kit have been a

girl so he could have helped me out? He'd probably already changed into his clothes for dinner.
How much trouble was it for a guy? Slacks, shirt,
jacket.

"Robin!" Mr. Marlin called. "Dinner's almost
ready!"

Omigosh! I wasn't ready. What had I been doing
for an hour? Worrying. That's what! What had it
gotten me? Nothing.

I grabbed a black skirt and a lacy white blouse
from the closet. If I worked really quickly, I could
make myself presentable for dinner.

I felt like a total fool.

No candles. Only one fork, one knife, one
spoon. No long, elegant table. No one dressed in
finery.

Everyone else had done exactly as Mrs. Marlin
suggested. They had simply freshened up. They
hadn't changed clothes. Kit was still wearing jeans
and his red sweater.

"You look lovely, dear," Mrs. Marlin said as she
passed me the leg of lamb.

I wished the floor would open up and swallow
me whole. Or better yet, where was a good tornado
when I needed one?

"That's the first thing I'd do after a long flight,"
Kit announced.

I looked at him, sitting across the table from me.
"What?"

"Change into some other clothes," he answered almost innocently, but his eyes twinkled with mischief.

Did he honestly think that was the reason I had changed clothes, or was he making fun of me?

"Dad, you need to pass Robin the bubble and squeak. She fancies it," Kit explained.

"Fancy that," Mr. Marlin murmured as he picked up a bowl. "Have you eaten many British foods?"

With trepidation, I took the bowl and peered inside. Cabbage and potatoes. I almost laughed. Cabbage wasn't my favorite, but I could tolerate it, especially when the alternative was admitting to a lie.

"No," I said in a low voice as I scooped a heaping onto my plate.

All three Marlins leaned toward me and said, "Pardon?" at the same time. I almost choked, trying so hard not to laugh. I was definitely going to have to speak a little more loudly.

"No," I repeated, and they all settled back into their chairs.

"Well, then, you're in for a lovely treat. Maude made trifle for dessert," Mr. Marlin told me.

"Mum doesn't make it often," Kit added. "It's a lot of trouble to cook."

The heat warmed my face. "You shouldn't have gone to any trouble," I told Mrs. Marlin.

"Nonsense, dear. Kit is just giving me a hard

time because I only make it for special occasions, and he'd gobble it down every night if he could," Mrs. Marlin said.

Watching the refined way that Kit ate, I couldn't imagine him gobbling anything. He ate precisely, his fork in his left hand, his knife in his right. Glancing around the table, I realized I was the only one who cut the meat with my right hand and then put the fork in my right hand to bring it to her mouth. Were they all lefties, or was this a British ritual?

"So tell us a bit about Texas," Mr. Marlin urged me.

I almost choked on my lamb. I drank some milk, anything to dislodge the food stuck in my throat. I glanced across the table. Kit studied me as if I were something from another planet. I couldn't tell these classy people that I came from a farm, had pigs and goats, and could milk a cow really well.

"Mustang is a small town," I told them, glancing nervously around the table. "Everyone knows everyone."

Relatively small words, low voice. I hadn't detected any twang in my speech.

"The school we'll be going to is rather like that," Kit explained. "Only those students preparing to go on to the university will be there."

He looked like he expected me to say something. But what?

"What do you do for fun?" Mr. Marlin inquired.

"Fun?" I repeated.

"Yes. In America. What do you do?" he repeated.

Mud runs. Tractor pulls. Rodeos. Wouldn't that impress the heck out of them?

"Movies," I responded quietly.

"What sort of movies?" Mr. Marlin asked.

He wasn't going to let me get off with a one-word answer. What was he? A lawyer?

"Probably the same sort of movies that we watch, Dad," Kit said as he reached for some bread. "I don't imagine that the kids over there are that much different from us over here."

"That's what we're supposed to find out this year, isn't it?" Mr. Marlin asked. "We share our culture, she shares hers."

"Speaking of culture," I said quietly. "I promised my friends that I'd meet them at the Tower of London tomorrow. Is there a bus stop near here?"

"The tube would be better," Kit told me. "You can catch it right down the street."

I stared at him. The tube? Why did sliding down water-park rides flash through my mind?

Mrs. Marlin chuckled. "You look confused, Robin."

"Uh, no," I lied, determined to make this year work if it killed me. "Which end of the street?"

"Kit will take you tomorrow," Mrs. Marlin said.

Kit and I both groaned low and then jerked our gazes to each other. Okay, so Dana had been wrong.

He wasn't any more thrilled with me than I was with him.

He slid his gaze to his mother. "You mean just walk her to the end of the street?"

"No, I mean take her to the Tower. For goodness sake, we can't have her getting lost after only one day. You need to show her how to use the tube and get around a bit. Tomorrow will be perfect for that, don't you think?"

Kit's gaze darted back to me. I knew he wanted to say no. It was in his eyes. Instead he nodded.

"Sure, Mum. I didn't have any plans," he muttered with an edge to his voice. It was sharp enough that I could have used it to cut the lamb.

"I'm glad that's settled. Robin, you must realize this is your home. Just let us know what you need," Mrs. Marlin told me.

I need to feel sophisticated. I need a sister, not a brother who has the most intense blue eyes I've ever seen.

"Anything. Anything at all," Mr. Marlin said. "By the way, what does your father do for a living?"

My heart slammed against my ribs. I felt Kit watching me as I slowly chewed the broccoli, taking a moment to collect my thoughts. I loved my dad, but I didn't want to tell these people he was a farmer, a small-town farmer at that.

"Dad, I thought I heard the car make a strange rumbling noise on the way back from the airport," Kit declared.

I didn't remember hearing anything, but then,

I'd been in semishock at discovering I had a brother instead of a sister.

"Mmmm," Mr. Marlin mumbled. "I'll look into it tomorrow."

Kit gave me a little wink. So Brits lied too. I wanted to thank Kit for steering the subject away from me. He seemed to realize I didn't like talking about myself because he began asking his dad questions about his plans for the week. And when he was finished with his dad, he started asking his mom questions.

I sat there, my stomach settling, so I was actually able to eat. And I thought the food might stay down. I loved listening to their accents. I had a hard time keeping my eyes off Kit. He was amazing to look at. I wanted to brush the lock of blond hair off his brow and watch it fall back into place. He had the cutest smile, a little on the shy side.

I thought about the poster in my room. About him explaining Nick Lachey to his mother. He wanted me to feel at home. And now he'd cleverly put a stop to the inquisition so I could relax.

He was much kinder and more thoughtful than I'd originally realized. And so incredibly hot looking.

How was I going to be able to sleep with him right across the hall?

Four

Kit

THE NEXT MORNING I rolled over in bed and slapped off the buzzing alarm. I squinted at the red numbers on my clock. 7:20 A.M. I groaned. It was my last day before school started up again, and I'd planned to sleep until noon. Why had I set the alarm?

Ah, right. The American.

I'd promised to take her and her friends on their tour of the Tower. What a drag that would be with soft-spoken, reserved Robin!

I flung myself onto my back and glared at the ceiling. Where was the brash American brother that I'd expected to be living with me when I had begged Mum and Dad to host a foreign-exchange student?

Robin was so prim, proper, and reserved—utterly boring!

I had figured that anyone who went on the Year Abroad program had to be gutsy, but Robin was more like a timid mouse waiting for the cat to pounce. She talked in such a quiet voice that I constantly had to ask her to repeat herself. *I might have to get a hearing aid for the year.*

As if that wasn't bad enough, she acted like her face would crack if she smiled.

How was I supposed to learn to loosen up and let go from Robin Carter? I had been counting on my American "bro" to help me figure out the best way to break up with Brooke and still remain friends with her. It had to be an American experience because actors in Hollywood seemed to have great success at doing it. I really didn't want to hurt Brooke. She was a lovely girl, but she was rushing our relationship along like it was a train going downhill without brakes.

We'd gone on two dates before she left for holiday two months ago. She had spent the summer touring the continent, sending me e-mails from different countries. I had thought it would be exciting to hear of her adventures. Instead I discovered she was scared of everything: foreigners, trains, eating ethnic food. She hated doing anything new and complained about anything unfamiliar.

She wasn't at all what I wanted in a girlfriend. I wanted someone who dared to take chances, who wasn't afraid of her shadow, who was willing to experience new things.

I furrowed my brow. Maybe I was judging Brooke too harshly. E-mail couldn't always convey a person's true personality. I thought about Robin's e-mail. She had certainly sounded enthusiastic and excitable. Exclamation marks everywhere. She hadn't spoken one exclamation-mark sentence since I'd met her at the airport. She was incredibly boring. Not at all what I'd expected—not to mention that she was a "female person."

So maybe the real Brooke was the girl I'd dated a couple of times. I hadn't meant to become her steady so quickly, but based on her letters over the summer, I realized she thought we were a hot item. I decided I should probably give her a chance.

Brooke wasn't supposed to get back from holiday until late tonight. I wouldn't be able to see her until we arrived at school tomorrow morning. Maybe I'd just read the tone in her letters wrong.

Well, I would have to worry about that tomorrow. I threw off the blankets and sat up in bed. Right now I had to get through what promised to be a really dull day in my as usual dull life!

I needed to hit the shower. Maybe the hot water beating on me would cheer me up. Not likely, but you never knew.

I knew seeing Robin certainly wouldn't cheer me. I had so looked forward to having a sibling, but not one who was so meek and mild mannered that she blended in with the wallpaper.

Wearing nothing but my underwear, I dragged myself into the hall—and stopped dead in my tracks.

Robin stood in the hallway—wearing nothing but her bra and panties!

My mouth dropped open. My eyes widened. The heat of embarrassment scalded my face. But my feet wouldn't move.

She stared at me. I stared at her.

Then she shrieked and darted into her room, slamming the door.

I rushed into my room, closed the door, and leaned against it. Right. That was embarrassing.

A grin spread across my face. But also incredibly funny! At least I'd finally managed to get an exclamation mark out of her.

Obviously Robin wasn't used to sharing a bathroom with someone of the opposite sex either. With my parents' bedroom downstairs, I was accustomed to living alone upstairs.

I dropped back my head. Robin definitely had cute curves. Truthfully, I hadn't seen anything that I wouldn't have seen if she were wearing a bikini. I just hadn't expected to ever see her in a bikini—at least not in my hallway. That had made the moment seem so personal, so intimate.

It shouldn't have because I didn't even like her. I chuckled low. At least I hadn't had any trouble hearing her shriek. Maybe I should suggest she think of me standing in the hall in my underwear whenever she needed to talk. Maybe then she would talk loud enough that I could hear her.

I combed my fingers through my hair and took a deep breath. I needed to tell her that she could have the shower first.

I grabbed my jeans off a nearby chair and jerked them on. Then I slipped a T-shirt over my head. This time I opened my door slowly and peered into the hallway. The bathroom door was open, and her bedroom door was closed.

In bare feet I crossed the hall and knocked softly on her door. I heard a very low, strangled, "Yes?"

"You can have the shower first. I'll just stay in my room until I hear you go downstairs."

Silence. I pressed my ear to the door. Did she say something, and I just didn't hear her? "Don't use all the hot water," I teased.

All I got back was another low, strangled word. "Okay."

With a deep sigh, I headed back to my room. *Maybe I* had *better invest in a hearing aid,* I thought glumly.

I quickly discovered it was a lot more awkward than I'd imagined possible to sit across the breakfast table from a stranger who I had seen in her skivvies.

I'd seen girls in bikinis before, some bikinis that revealed more than Robin's underwear had. But it wasn't the same. Bras and panties, by their very nature, hinted at intimacy.

Robin wouldn't even look at me. She talked quietly—naturally, very quietly—to my mum. She completely ignored me.

So I'd seen her in her underwear. So what! So what? She was cute in her underwear. Very cute. Soft curves. Flat stomach. She even had tan lines. That's what.

I could see the red flush that was still on her face.

At least she was dressed normally today in jeans, a jumper, and trainers. An image of what she was wearing beneath all that clothing flashed through my mind. I felt the heat warm my face. I wished that my dad were sitting at the table so I'd at least have someone to talk to. But my dad always slept in on Sunday morning. Which I had really wanted to do as well.

I pushed that thought aside before my irritation with this whole situation got out of hand. The tension at the table was thick enough to cut with a butter knife. My whole last day before school started was ruined because I had to take her to the Tower, and she was treating me like I had the plague. I needed to get out of here, cool down, and decide what to do.

"Mum, I'm done. I'll be waiting by the front

door for Robin," I said, addressing the table at large.

My mum glanced over her shoulder as though only just noticing I was there.

"Certainly, dear," she said quickly before turning her attention back to Robin.

Great! Now not only could I not walk into my own hallway in my underwear, I was being ignored by my mum.

I strode to the entryway, leaned against the front door, and crossed my arms over my chest. So far, hosting a YA student was nothing like I expected it to be. Was I going to have to live the whole year walking on eggshells just because I'd stepped out of my room without thinking, out of habit? Not likely.

I'd apologize to Robin. A very straightforward apology. Simple and clean. It would put the horrid shower incident—as I was beginning to think of it—behind us. We could then move forward. Knowing how formal Robin tended to be, I decided that I needed to be equally formal in order to gain her attention.

My dear Miss Carter, my humblest apologies if I offended your sensibilities this morning when I unwittingly stepped into the hallway in my just-crawled-out-of-bed attire as I had every morning for as long as I can remember.

Right. That one was fairly sickening. She would no doubt love it.

She came into the foyer. I opened the front door and watched her trudge outside, her head bent. Her face was set in an expressionless mask. I wondered briefly if I should just skip the apology. Forget this morning ever happened.

No, no, it was best to face things head-on.

I followed her out and waited until I'd closed the door firmly behind us. I had to hurry to catch up to her, and her apparent embarrassment was making me feel a tad awkward. "Er, sorry 'bout before," I offered. So much for my formal apology.

She plastered a frozen smile onto her face but kept marching forward like a determined soldier. "It's okay. Let's pretend it never happened."

I almost asked her to repeat what she'd said, but I thought I'd caught the gist of most of it.

"It could have been worse. We might have been wearing nothing at all," I teased, trying to chip something off the iceberg building between us.

She jerked her head around and glared at me.

I felt my face turn red. "Best to forget about it," I agreed as I fell into step beside her and directed her toward the tube.

Fantastic. She didn't have a sense of humor. She couldn't speak above a whisper. And she'd seen me in my underwear.

I had a whole blasted year with her to look forward to. I could barely contain my excitement at the prospect.

Five

Robin

THE SUBWAY! THE tube was the subway.

I sat on the seat beside Kit as the train flew between stations. I sneaked a peek at him as he stared at the advertisements plastered on the side across from us. Could this morning get any worse? I was beyond mortified.

At least my natural shriek had been appropriate. It hadn't contained an ounce of twang. Just pure one hundred percent humiliation.

How could I have walked into the hall wearing nothing but my underwear and a blush? Only one explanation made sense. Between the jet lag and waking up forgetting where I was, I had walked out of my room thinking I was at home!

I have got to stay alert and keep my guard up, I reminded myself.

I couldn't let Kit distract me. And he had certainly done that in the hallway, standing there in nothing but his briefs. I wouldn't have freaked out if he'd been standing in sand, on a beach. In that situation I would have even admired his body.

Okay, I had admired it in the hallway as well. But that was beside the point. He had remained calm, while I had totally freaked out. He'd even had the presence of mind to come and tell me I could shower first while I'd been trying to decide how to take a bath using only the water that was in the pitcher on the bedside table.

And he seemed to have a sense of humor. It would have been worse if we'd been wearing nothing at all.

Without looking at me, he murmured, "Sorry my dad put you through the grand inquisition last night."

I shifted on the seat. "He was just being curious."

He grimaced. "Only because curiosity is his job. He's a solicitor."

"Ah, a telemarketer," I commented softly with a nod.

He leaned toward me, his brow creased. "Pardon?"

Oh gosh. Now I didn't know if he hadn't heard me or he didn't know what a telemarketer was. Trying to hide my accent was almost more trouble than it was worth. He was so cute and seemed really nice. I was almost tempted to be myself.

But then what would he think? That he had

Dr. Jekyll and Miz Hyde living in his house for a year?

Nope, I'd set my path, and now I had to follow it. Besides, who knew what he'd tell kids at school?

I decided to speak a little louder and give a little more explanation, so I covered all my bases. I cleared my throat. "A telemarketer. An individual who solicits people on the telephone and attempts to convince them to purchase items such as neon headbands."

He gave me his shy grin. "That's what I thought you meant. I think in the States that you call my dad's profession being a lawyer."

I felt the heat flush my cheeks. I was riding the tube with a bloke whose dad was a solicitor. I absolutely wanted to scream. It was like talking in a foreign language—only worse because I knew the words. I just didn't always know what they meant.

"You never did tell my dad what your dad does," he said over the din of rumbling tracks.

No, I hadn't. If Kit was asking me a question, I didn't hear the question mark. When would we get to our stop?

"What does he do?" Kit asked.

Question mark. Dadgum it. It was there loud and clear, and I couldn't very well ignore it.

"He's into agriculture," I said evasively. That wasn't a lie, although my dad would have said it was pretentious. "Honey, I'm just a farmer," he always said, like it was no big deal that he worked seventy hours a week for less than minimum wage so people would find food in the produce section of their grocery stores.

I felt the train begin to slow. *Please be our stop. Please be our stop.*

Kit stood. "Here's our stop."

I let out a great gust of air and got to my feet as the train halted. We stepped onto the platform.

"It's just a bit of a walk," he said, shoving his hands into his jeans pockets.

When we strolled out of the station, I knew how the country mouse felt when she went to the city. I wanted to grab Kit's arm and point at the buildings and ask him what they were. Instead I balled my hands into tight fists and shoved them into the pockets of my jeans. I knew my jaw had dropped to my knees and my eyes were as big and circular as a harvest moon, but I couldn't help it.

"Right, here we are," Kit said, and I felt like I'd been thrown back in time.

I had been expecting a solitary tower like the one Rapunzel sat in. I wasn't expecting this huge stone complex with turrets and towers.

I saw Dana and Carrie at the entrance. My pulse picked up its tempo. What a relief! Everything didn't seem so overwhelming now. I almost shouted to them but caught myself just in time. As long as Kit was beside me, I had to be sophisticated and very low-key. Ugh! Why couldn't he have had some plans for today?

Carrie and Dana greeted me with wide grins. I offered them a small smile. Ladylike and sophisticated.

"I'm so pleased you could make it," I said softly.

Dana rolled her eyes, and Carrie gave me a slap on the back that nearly sent me staggering forward.

"We are too," Carrie said loudly. Her drawl, not quite as pronounced as mine, echoed around us. I never thought I'd welcome the sound of a Texas twang.

"We went to Covent Garden last night," Dana told me. "We sure missed you."

"I would have liked to have shared the experience with you," I said. "But I needed to get accustomed to my new home."

"And your new brother," Carrie announced with teasing laced in her voice.

Kit cleared his throat and looked at me, his eyes twinkling. "We both had some things to get accustomed to."

I knew he was thinking of our close encounter in the hallway on our way to the shower. How could he joke about it?

"Today is my parents' treat," he said. "I'm going to pop over and get the tickets."

As soon as he was out of earshot, Carrie and Dana closed ranks around me.

"Okay. Give us the entire scoop," Carrie demanded.

"You seemed to have survived your first night living with a guy," Dana mused.

"Barely," I declared. I felt my body blush from the top of my head to the tips of my toes. "I had a close encounter of the most embarrassing kind! This morning I, like, forgot that I wasn't at home. You know that I don't wake up quickly. So I headed for the shower wearing only my bra and panties. I staggered into the hallway—and there he was, on his way to the shower, wearing the same thing!"

"He wears a bra?" Dana inquired, clearly startled.

"No, goofus," I said, feeling like I was completely losing my ability to communicate. "He was only wearing his briefs! I was totally mortified. It was the single most humiliating experience of my entire existence."

"Oh my gosh." Carrie sighed dreamily. "What did he look like? I want details."

"Like any normal guy wearing a bathing suit— only it was his underwear," I explained.

"I've seen my brothers in their underwear. It's no big deal," Carrie assured me.

"No big deal? I shrieked at the top of my lungs and hightailed it back to my room. I wanted to die," I muttered dejectedly.

"Your reaction was normal," Dana assured me.

"Yeah, for someone from bump-in-the-road Mustang, Texas. I should have remained calm and poised and just turned around and walked back into my room as though I saw guys in their briefs all the time," I murmured.

Dana shook her head. "That was probably the first time he actually saw you as yourself."

"That's what I'm afraid of," I confided. "I almost ruined my cover."

"Oh, Robin, you need to be yourself," Dana insisted.

"Oh yeah, right. Jason was from big-city Dallas, and he thought I was a backwoods hillbilly farm girl. What do you think Kit would think of the real me? The dare-me-to-do-anything Robin Carter who has the worst twang, worst way of speaking, and most embarrassing loud, brash personality?"

"I think he'd like you as much as we do," Dana told me.

I had a lot more I wanted to say, but Kit returned with our tickets.

"Thank you," I said as I took my ticket from him. "I appreciate your parents' thoughtfulness."

"Right," Kit said in a clipped British accent.

"Let's head for the crown jewels," Carrie suggested. She slipped her arm through Kit's. "Do you think they'll let me try them on?"

Kit's laughter echoed around me as Carrie led him toward the entrance. I felt an unexpected pang of jealousy. Carrie was always comfortable with guys, but then, guys liked her.

Following them, Dana leaned toward me and whispered, "You sound completely unfriendly and unfun talking in that low, formal voice without your accent."

I stared at her, unable to believe that Dana still didn't get it.

"That's how I'm trying to sound."

"Can y'all believe these crowns?" Carrie asked. "I've never seen so many different jewels. And they're huge! Huge!"

I couldn't believe it either. The gold, the diamonds, the sapphires, the emeralds, the silver. Like Carrie, I was completely in awe. I turned to the guard standing nearby. "Are these jewels real?"

He wrinkled his nose as if he smelled something foul and looked down at me. "Yes, miss. After all, this is not Disney World."

I wanted to die of mortification. I heard snickers from the tour group behind me. Would I never learn what to say and not to say in front of people?

I glared over my shoulder at Carrie and Dana and said with my eyes, "See, I *need* help!"

Carrie and Dana just rolled their eyes toward the snobbish guard. But then, they weren't the ones who had experienced the humiliation of being told in front of a crowd of students near the guy they liked that they were uncouth and obnoxious.

"This isn't Disney World?" Kit whispered to me. "One look at the guard's Mickey Mouse–like ears, and I thought that's where we were!"

I couldn't help myself. I burst out laughing. The guard glared at me, but he had lost his power over me because of Kit's comment.

I wanted to sling my arms around Kit's neck and thank him for coming to my rescue. But I couldn't do that. I had to remain demure, even though I'd slipped for a moment there.

As the group continued the tour, I avoided standing close to Kit. He was too cute, too English, too intimidating, too male, and too unexpectedly nice and funny. *I can't like him,* I warned myself. *I absolutely cannot! He would be horrified by the real me. I would never be able to talk above a whisper if I liked him. I'd never be able to be myself. Don't like him!*

That order was a lot easier to give than to obey. But obey it I would or risk humiliation far worse than I had suffered that morning.

My feet were aching by the end of the afternoon, and my enthusiasm was waning. How could anything that housed something as beautiful as the crown jewels also hold Traitor's Gate and the Bloody Tower? I hated hearing about the young princes who had probably been murdered. Richard of Gloucester had taken them to the tower, and they'd never been seen again. He was later crowned king.

As though sensing that we were saddened by the Tower and its woe, Kit took us to see the ravens next. They were only black birds, but I thought they looked somewhat majestic.

"Legend has it that if the ravens ever leave the Tower, Britain will fall," Kit explained.

I wished I didn't enjoy the musical cadence of his voice so much.

"And they never fly away?" Dana asked. "That's amazing."

Kit cleared his throat and shifted from one foot to the other, looking extremely uncomfortable.

Carrie plopped her hands onto her hips. "All right, Kit, out with it. What aren't you telling us?"

He grimaced. "They clip their wings so they can't fly."

My stomach rolled. I loved animals. Had rescued fallen birds and nursed barn owls back to health.

"Sorry," Kit said, and I knew he meant it. For some reason, I wished that he hadn't meant it.

"Well, on that cheerful note," Carrie said, "we're gonna have to go."

"So soon?" I asked. The afternoon had passed so quickly. When Kit wasn't standing nearby, I had been able to be myself, laughing, joking, groaning. How would I survive this year without my two best friends?

"We're supposed to meet Miss Lawrence at the entrance at five," Dana explained.

"Let's say good-bye here," Carrie suggested. "Then when Dana and I walk away, it won't seem like we're really leaving."

I felt the tears sting my eyes. "It's gonna feel like you're leaving no matter what we do."

I slung my arms around my closest friends, and tears slid along my cheeks. I wasn't only saying good-bye to them; I was saying good-bye to myself. It was only around them that I could ever be the true Robin.

"Y'all had better e-mail me every day or else," I ordered.

"You'd better e-mail us," Carrie told me.

"I will as soon as I get home. . . . Well, not home." I released choked laughter. "Not my real home. My home here. You know what I mean. I'm babbling."

"You're babbling," Dana repeated.

"Watch out for those guys in Paris," I warned Dana.

Dana wiggled her eyebrows. "I plan to watch them very closely."

I laughed again while the tears continued to fall. I knew Dana wanted to fall in love in Paris.

"Carrie—," I began.

"I know, I know, watch out for the Italians." She smiled brightly and looked past me. "Kit, you take care of our friend."

61

"I will," he said quietly.

My heart slammed against my ribs. I'd forgotten he was nearby. Gosh, he'd seen and heard everything. I wiped the tears from my face and tried to recompose myself. I threw back my shoulders and lifted my chin.

"Have an amazing year abroad," I said in a low, accent-free voice.

Dana leaned close and whispered with a cunning look in her eyes, "Too late."

My heart sank. I was afraid that might be the case.

I watched Dana and Carrie loop their arms around each other's waists and head for the entrance. Oh, it hurt. I wanted to call after them, but I had to try to repair any damage I might have done while saying good-bye.

As it was, Kit probably thought he was living with a total freak!

Six

Robin

SITTING ON THE window seat, hugging my bent knees against my chest, I stared out my bedroom window while the lights of London glowed against the black sky. Saying good-bye to my friends had been so hard. Riding home on the tube with Kit in silence had been so hard. Eating dinner with the Marlins tonight had been so hard. And now being alone in my room was so hard!

I wished I could call my friends, but I couldn't. I hadn't really considered all that was involved in the YA program when I'd accepted Dana and Carrie's dare to join them in the program. Until this moment I hadn't truly realized that I was on my own here, so far from home, from anything familiar. Where were my pigs when I needed them? I knew my dad was feeding them, but I still worried about them. Did they miss me?

Someone knocked on the door. My stomach knotted tightly. Keeping up this facade of a demure, sophisticated Robin was suddenly too much. Tears started to sting the backs of my eyes.

I cleared my throat. Irritating tears were hovering there too.

"Come in," I croaked, hardly sounding sophisticated. I tried to blink back the tears, but they were stubborn and refused to go away. Instead they seemed to be inviting all their friends to a party. *Join us, and the party can spill out of her eyes and onto her cheeks.*

Kit walked into the room. I'd really been hoping for Mrs. Marlin. She would understand the tears. But a guy? No way.

I stared down at the hardwood floor so he wouldn't see the sign of my weakness. His feet came into view. Well, not his feet, exactly. The socks covering his feet. I'd never seen a guy without shoes. But then, I'd never seen a guy without clothes either. It looked like this year I was going to experience a lot of firsts—and not all of them pleasant.

"I'm creating a schedule so we won't be caught again in something like what happened this morning," he explained.

A corner of my mouth fought to lift into a smile. He'd said schedule wrong. *Shedule* was what it sounded like instead of *skedule*. The English. Didn't they know anything?

"Did you want the bathroom first or second in the morning?" he asked.

"I'll take the bathroom first," I whispered.

I felt him studying me. I pressed my knees hard against my chest, wanting to curl into a ball of misery. Why wouldn't he leave so I could let the tears fall?

"Are you from a different part of Texas than your friends?" Kit asked.

Huh? What was he talking about? I wondered.

Not daring to look at him, I watched his toes wiggle up and down in his socks.

"I was just curious because you don't sound like they do," he explained.

Disappointment reeled through me. I slid my eyes closed. So much for trying to disguise my voice. He'd seen right through me.

"I mean, they actually talk like cowboys in old Western movies," he went on, "but your voice has hardly any trace of accent."

My eyes flew open. He hadn't noticed my accent. I was pulling it off! I was really pulling it off. Now to keep up the illusion, all I had to do was reverse the truth.

"They're, um, from a farm, and I'm, um, from town," I murmured in my low, accent-free voice. It was almost becoming second nature to talk like this. Before long, I wouldn't have to think about it.

I would talk this way naturally. "We townspeople have less of an accent."

"I like their accents," he told me.

"You do?" I blurted out in my deep Texas twang. I slapped my hand over my mouth and glared out the window. So much for second nature. Who could have missed that loud, brash question?

He dropped down on the window seat beside me. I drew myself more tightly into a ball. What a lame thing to do! Two words had totally blown two days' worth of effort.

"Why are you hiding your real way of speaking?" he inquired, clearly confused.

Into my silence he added, "I find your accent charming, especially when you said 'y'all' as you were threatening your friends, telling them they'd better e-mail every day or else."

I scoffed and continued glaring out the window.

"Do you plan to whisper for a whole year?" he asked.

Being mute would have been better. I was afraid I was going to break down into heart-wrenching sobs. As much as I hated to admit it, Kit was so totally right. Today had been a nightmare, talking normal around my friends, talking low whenever he came near. Now Dana and Carrie were gone, and I'd never be able to talk normal again—at least not for a year anyway.

Overwhelmed by that realization, I jerked my gaze to his and blurted out exactly what I was feeling, even if it wasn't the answer to the question he'd posed. "I'm as lonely as the last star before sunrise."

He smiled tenderly, and I felt more tears surface. I dropped my gaze quickly before he caught sight of them.

"Of course you're lonely," he said gently. "You're really far from home and your friends. But you'll be fine. You've got me for a brother, after all."

I glanced up at him, unable to believe how nice he was. I swiped the tears from my eyes. "Some people don't like small-town Texas accents," I explained, thinking of Jason's comment that I sounded like I was putting on the slow drawl.

"Then they're idiots," he told me. "Your accent is charming."

He was the one with the charming accent. I sniffed. "It's embarrassing."

"It shouldn't be. It's part of who you are," he explained.

I didn't figure now was the time to tell him that my accent wasn't the only thing I'd been hiding. I was hiding my entire personality. Texas Robin would have been pacing by now. But I had my arms wrapped around my legs so tightly that I was in danger of cutting off my circulation.

I gave him a shaky smile and a promise. "I won't whisper anymore."

He released a deep breath. "Am I ever glad to

hear that! I thought I might go hoarse saying, 'Sorry?' all the time."

I released a small, self-conscious giggle.

"You do realize that I was afraid I was going deaf, don't you?" he asked.

He was making me feel completely silly for ever trying to hide my voice, but he was doing it in a way that didn't make me feel . . . as ungainly as a cow. He wasn't ridiculing me for trying to hide my accent, but he'd managed to coax me into revealing it, and I figured he might not laugh if I confessed something else.

"About school tomorrow . . . I'm as nervous as a long-tailed cat in a room full of rocking chairs," I confided.

"Don't be. You're going to be a huge hit." He leaned close as if to impart a secret. "As long as you don't whisper," he whispered so low that *I* almost said "pardon!"

So much for not liking him. I was falling harder for Kit than I'd ever fallen for anyone, even snot Jason.

He stood and stretched. "Well, I'd best be off to bed. Just give a brisk knock on my door in the morning when you're done with the bathroom."

I watched him stroll casually across the room. He stopped at my door and glanced over his shoulder. He smiled warmly. "Good night, sis."

Sis? Huh? He thinks of me as a sister?

Ugh. That figures.

But there was totally no way I could possibly think of him as a brother.

Seven

Robin

NERVOUS WRECK. THAT was an apt description for how I felt sitting at the breakfast table the next morning. My first day of English school! This was ten times worse than the first day of school at Mustang. At least there I had Carrie and Dana for moral support.

Even though I had slathered butter on my English muffin, it felt like sawdust in my mouth. And I absolutely could not dip my spoon into the boiled egg that was sitting upright in a tiny cup—its top lobbed off. The yolk was still shimmering! I liked to make sure my eggs were dead before I ate them, and this one looked like it had only recently been plucked from the henhouse.

I gulped some milk and glanced at the clock on the wall. If a watched pot never boiled, maybe the hands on a clock wouldn't move if they were watched.

I really needed more time to adjust before going to school in London. Just a little more time. Like . . . a year, maybe.

"Don't be so nervous," Kit ordered.

It had been so quiet at the table that it was like his voice came out of nowhere. My body jerked, each limb working on its own. I thought of that cat in the cartoons that shrieks and ends up hanging upside down with its claws digging into the ceiling. That could have easily been me at that moment.

How could he sound so calm?

"You'll probably find that my school is a lot like your own," he added.

Uh-huh, I thought. *Right. So far everything has been exactly like Mustang, Texas. Not!*

My stomach felt like it was a tangle of string creating Jacob's ladder by the time Kit told me that we needed to leave. I grabbed my backpack off a side table where I'd set it earlier.

"You'll probably want to take your mac," he said as we walked toward the door.

"Oh, great!" I exclaimed before hurrying up the stairs. Taking computers to school was definitely not the way it was done in Mustang. Cool! I'd be able to take notes in class—notes I could actually read later. I dashed into my room, unplugged my computer from the socket and the phone jack, and quickly packed it into its small case.

I rushed back down the stairs. Kit was waiting by the door. "Got it!" I cried, holding up my laptop.

He furrowed his brow. "Your mac?"

I nodded.

A corner of his mouth lifted as if he was on the verge of finally understanding the punch line to some joke. "Your mackintosh?" he asked.

I held my computer higher. "My Macintosh!"

He lifted his coat off his arm. "Raincoat."

I felt like a total idiot. So much for being able to read my notes. I made another quick dash upstairs to put away my computer and grab my raincoat.

Everything's called something else in England, I realized glumly. What if I made a total fool of myself in school? That possibility was looming before me as a definite reality.

I couldn't even enjoy the walk to school. I was too busy studying my feet, trying to make sure that they kept moving forward—instead of going off in the direction that they wanted, which was back.

"Sorry?" Kit inquired beside me.

I jerked my gaze up to his. He wore this incredible heart-stopping smile, and his eyes held this teasing glint in them.

"I thought you said something," he explained.

I shook my head, baffled. "No."

"Ah, that's right. I forgot. From now on, you're going to talk loudly enough for people to hear you, right?" he teased.

It felt good to laugh. "Right," I agreed, smiling brightly.

He slipped his arm around me and gave my shoulder a quick squeeze. "You're going to do just fine," he assured me.

He dropped his arm to his side, and my lungs started drawing in air again. I told myself that it had been a . . . brotherly hug. No big deal. Just because his touch made my heartbeat double . . .

We reached the school, and I had to admit that Kit had been right. From the outside, it wasn't that much different from Mustang High. Brick building. Windows. Doors. Concrete walks.

The difference was the people. I didn't know anybody!

My nervous level shot up like the mercury in a thermometer that was placed in boiling water.

"Hey, Kit!" a guy yelled, and hurried over.

"Hey, Peter," Kit greeted him.

"New love?" Peter inquired.

Kit laughed lightly and put his hand on the small of my back, a comforting gesture, I told myself, because he knew I was nervous. Plus he was probably trying to quiet the thudding of my heart.

"Robin is our Year Abroad student," Kit explained.

Peter wrinkled his entire face as if it helped him think. He had spiked blond hair, and when he wasn't talking, he could easily pass for a guy from Mustang High.

"Thought our YAS was a guy," he mused.

"Right, but in my excitement over being selected to host the YAS, I didn't read the information packet closely enough. Robin's our girl," Kit said.

I liked the thought of being someone's girl. Especially since I'd never been anyone's girl. It gave me a warm, snuggly feeling.

Peter grinned broadly. "So what do you think so far?"

The moment of truth had come. Kit's hand moved to my shoulder, and I knew I could do this. All I had to do was answer as demurely as possible, toning down my accent while still being audible. "It's different over here."

Kit squeezed my shoulder, and I knew I'd pulled it off.

"In what ways?" Peter asked.

I was spared answering when a girl with long, black hair that had one purple streak down the center approached.

"Is she the YAS?" the girl queried.

Kit's hand moved back to my waist as he introduced me to Zoe. It was so reassuring to have the pressure of Kit's hand on my waist, my back, my shoulder. I felt like I wasn't alone here.

Zoe was bouncing questions off me, one right after the other, like she was conducting an interview, only she never let me answer. Even when more people circled us and she was eased aside, I could still hear her asking questions.

Kit was making introductions left and right, and the questions were coming fast and furious. I knew students from other countries were popular at Mustang High, but I'd always figured it was the novelty of something different in a town that should have been named Boredom. I hadn't expected sophisticated Londoners to take more than a passing interest in me.

I was actually beginning to feel like I was smothering with all the attention.

"All right, all right," Kit finally cut in. "You all have a year to ask your questions. Right now, I've got to get Robin to the main office."

He put his hand on my back and propelled me forward through the crowd.

"Welcome, Robin!"

"Save me a place at lunch, Rob!"

"See you in class, Robin!"

"We're glad you're here!"

I wanted to laugh with complete and absolute joy. They liked me. They actually seemed to like the new me that I was striving to become. I had held my accent at bay.

"Shouldn't you call back that it was nice meeting *y'all?*" Kit asked once we'd moved beyond the maddening crowd.

I shook my head. "I'm really trying to tone down my accent."

"Why?" he asked, sounding completely baffled.

"Because it's so utterly country."

He opened his mouth to say something, but before he could speak, a girl stepped out from behind a pillar, swept in front of him, and planted a major doozy of a kiss smack-dab on his lips. Sorta like she owned those lips of his.

Shock waves rippled through me as I watched him fold his arms around her.

He drew back and bestowed upon her a hundred-megawatt smile. "I didn't realize how much I'd missed you."

"It was the most miserable summer of my life, and all because you weren't there." She spoke in a soft, cultured voice.

I thought I was going to be ill. Had I actually thought that Kit could be more than a brother? Of course a guy as cute as he was had a girlfriend. What was I thinking?

With one arm still wrapped possessively around the girl—who happened to be more beautiful than any girl should be—Kit turned toward me. With a cute laugh, he introduced me. "Brooke, this is my sister, Robin."

Brooke gave me an icy glare and snapped, "I thought the exchange student was a guy."

Kit laughed a little self-consciously and rubbed

the side of his nose. "Actually, so did I. It's been quite an adjustment."

That was an understatement.

"Listen, I've got to get Robin to the main office, so I'll catch up with you later." Kit brushed a quick kiss over her upturned cheek.

She smiled, and I thought of a witch out of a Disney movie.

She flicked her flowing blond hair over her shoulder. "I'll just tag along."

And she did, wedging herself between Kit and me. The absence of his nearness caused my nerves to go on full-scale alert. I suddenly felt incredibly alone even though this brazen blond babe was walking beside me.

"So, have you a boyfriend back in the States?" she inquired.

At that moment I considered fudging the truth and telling her that I did have, but we'd decided to date other people during our year apart, but I was already being so unfaithful to my true self that I decided I should opt for the truth. "No, no boyfriend."

"Someone you like?" she prodded.

I couldn't figure out where she was going with this. There seemed to be a little more to her tone than "inquiring minds want to know."

"There's a lot of people that I like," I pointed out.

"I was thinking of someone specific, someone you fancy, someone you're pining after, who you're hoping will miss you so much while you're away that he'll fall at your feet when you return," she said.

She'd hit a little too close to home with that scenario. "No, no one."

"Mmmm. Well, maybe that'll change here. The YAS is usually an instant smash. Appearance, personality, being hip really don't come into the play because the YAS is so absolutely novel," she purred.

I had the feeling that I'd just been insulted.

"Here's the main office," Kit said as we rounded a corner.

Through the wide, double-glass doors I could see a long counter and two women standing behind it. Just like the office at Mustang High.

"Did you want me to go with you?" Kit asked.

"No, I'll be just fine," I assured him, smiling brightly.

I turned and headed for the doors. The truth was, I desperately wanted to get away from Brooke.

Her cold shoulder was giving me frostbite.

Eight

Robin

I WAS INCREDIBLY relieved to see Kit when I walked into my creative-writing class. One friendly face!

He smiled at me and tipped his head toward the empty desk beside him. I returned his smile. I didn't want to be anywhere else.

As I took a step forward, someone brushed by me. I watched in stunned silence as Brooke gracefully slid into the chair that I had planned to drop into. I halfway expected Kit to explain to her that seat was taken.

He lowered his head as she whispered something to him. He gave her a soft smile. Then he looked at me and pointed to the desk behind him.

I shook my head and sat at a desk in the front. No way did I want to be in a position to watch them making goo-goo eyes at each other during class.

All morning my classes had distracted me, so that I'd almost forgotten how surprised and surprisingly hurt I'd been to see another girl kiss Kit. But that hurt hit sharply now like a stab to my heart. I glanced over my shoulder. Brooke gave me a cold look. I wondered how she washed her face. Water must freeze the moment it touched her skin.

The teacher rapped her ruler on the desk to gain attention. I shifted in my seat. *Mrs. Lambourne* was written in bold, purple script across the white dry-erase board.

"I expect this term to be an amazing experience for all of you. We are fortunate enough to have our Year Abroad student in this class." She pierced me with her gaze and raised her hands, palms up, like she was a magician levitating a prone body. "Stand up, please."

Inwardly I groaned. I'd gone through this ritual in every class so far. I stood. I still hadn't figured out where I was supposed to look. Should I focus on the teacher? Should I sweep my gaze around the room? Maybe I should just stare at the floor or ponder the pattern on the ceiling.

"Robin Carter has traveled all the way from Mustang, Texas, to be with us this year," Mrs. Lambourne said, as if she were personally responsible for my being here. "Turn around so everyone can get a good look at you."

Now I knew how criminals in a police lineup felt. I could sense everyone gawking at me and imagined them pointing fingers. "That's her! She's the one! She did it! Off with her head!"

I turned, and my eyes immediately fell on Kit. He winked and gave me a thumbs-up signal. Such a little thing, but it really restored my confidence.

Mrs. Lambourne gave me permission to sit, and it was only when I sat that I realized I was trembling. I'd had no idea that being popular could be so nerve-racking.

Mrs. Lambourne went into a spiel on the dynamics of creativity. I furiously took notes only because it distracted me from the fact that Kit sat at the back of the room with Brooke. I wondered briefly why he hadn't mentioned her, but when I thought about it, I realized we hadn't really talked, hadn't really gotten a chance to know each other. My low talking had managed to put a wall between us, and I regretted that I'd taken that approach in the beginning.

"Your first assignment," Mrs. Lambourne announced in a way that reminded me of drumrolls, "will be an oral presentation to be delivered next Monday."

My heart very nearly stopped beating, and I found myself staring at her. Oral? This class was creative *writing!* I had specifically avoided signing up for any classes that even hinted they might require someone to speak.

"The topic I selected will allow you to share yourself with your fellow classmates—'My Goal for This Semester,' whether it be to get better marks, learn to play the guitar, sleep more, what have you."

This assignment was the worst I'd ever been given. My goal was to go from hillbilly farm girl with the heaviest southern drawl to sophisticated, reserved Princess Di type. There was no way that I could admit that openly to my fellow classmates! Maybe I could talk about hoping to learn about English culture or finding my way around the roundabouts or something.

But how was I gonna get through an oral presentation and hide my accent and my usual way of talking? I could handle it a few words at a time, but we were talking paragraphs here, possibly pages!

As soon as the dismissal bell rang, I approached Mrs. Lambourne. She smiled brightly and swept her fist through the air in a silent, jolly-good-show movement.

"I'm so pleased you're in my class," she said enthusiastically.

"I thought this was a writing class," I admitted.

"Of course it is. First you write the essay, and then you present it orally," she explained.

"I don't mean to be obtuse, but wouldn't it be better just to let everyone read our essays? You know? Writers write so people can read their words," I pointed out, hoping she'd see the correlation.

She shook her head. "It's necessary to expose the essence of yourself to the class. The more vulnerable you become, the more deeply you will write." She patted my shoulder. "I look so forward to hearing your presentation. I shall no doubt let you go first."

Was that supposed to make me look forward to Black Monday, as I'd already dubbed that dreaded day? I walked out of the room, dragging my feet and my expectations. I had seven days to get rid of the accent. A crash course was in order.

Popular was not a word that I usually associated with myself. So it was a little unnerving at lunch to find myself surrounded by people I didn't know—who were incredibly anxious to know me.

My plan had been to casually eavesdrop on a table of English girls here and a table of English girls there. But that was not to be.

The table I sat at seated six, and five girls quickly joined me. They were an excitable group.

"Your jumper is smashing," Zoe said. I remembered meeting her that morning.

I had no idea what a jumper was, so I simply smiled and faked it. "Thanks. So is yours."

Her eyes grew wide, and she barked out her laughter. "I'm not wearing one."

Did I feel foolish! I offered her a sheepish grin. "Sorry."

The girl sitting next to me, Beth, pulled on the sleeve of my pullover sweater. "Jumper."

I grimaced. "Ah, sweater."

"Why does it have a horse embroidered on the shoulder?" Zoe asked.

I touched the emblem. I'd worn the pullover so I wouldn't miss my old school so much. "It's a mustang. My school's mascot." My explanation probably made no sense to them, but they all smiled brightly and nodded. I figured we were all faking it. Maybe we weren't so different after all.

I really wanted them to talk more so I could learn to imitate their speech. I needed a question that required a detailed explanation. "What did everyone do over the school break?"

"I went on holiday to the seaside," one girl said.

"Tamara always goes on holiday to the seaside," Zoe explained. "She likes to see the fellows in their bathing trunks."

"You'd better believe it," Tamara said.

"My dad took me up to Scotland in his lorry," a girl named Lizzie told me. "I enjoyed seeing the countryside." She grinned and glanced mischievously around the table. "But I'd rather see the lads at the seaside."

I had no idea what a lorry was. How was I supposed to emulate these girls with their sophisticated, elegant ways when I couldn't understand half their words? I was beginning to think I needed a British-American dictionary. I was never gonna make it here!

Zoe tapped my shoulder with a perfectly manicured finger. I bet she'd never tossed manure onto her dad's fields to ensure that they had a good crop come fall.

"What are the lads like in Texas?" she asked.

What I had wanted to avoid was suddenly dropped in my lap. A question directed at me. "Not that much different than the guys here."

Zoe leaned forward on her elbows, zeal in her gaze. "Oh, come on. Give us a bit more than that. How do they kiss?"

"Yes, how do they kiss?" a very cultured voice asked behind me.

I looked over my shoulder, and there stood Brooke, her eyebrows raised. The bloodred lipstick on one corner of her mouth was slightly smudged, and I wondered if she'd been kissing Kit again. Until I'd seen her in a lip lock with him, I hadn't realized how much of a lifeline Kit had become since our talk last night. Or how much I liked him.

He suddenly appeared beside Brooke and grinned. "How's it going?"

I offered him a smile of bravado. "Interesting."

"I'll just bet. You'll have to tell me all about it when we get home. You gonna eat your biscuit?" he asked.

I glanced at my plate. I didn't have a biscuit. I

85

didn't even have a roll or a slice of bread. But I knew he wouldn't deliberately try to embarrass me, so something on my plate was a biscuit. I looked back at him and shook my head. He snatched the cookie off my plate. "Got to get to class."

I watched him walk off with Brooke. I was alone in a strange country, and he had reached out a friendly hand when I most needed one. But it wasn't like I could ever hope to win his heart.

A proper, reserved English guy like Kit going for a girl who had to hide her personality? Ha. He had thought it was charming that I had felt the need to hide my cute li'l accent. What would he think if he knew I'd been voted Queen of the Dare and Most Talkative every year in school?

Well, I wouldn't win those awards next year, I vowed as I stood, slung my backpack over my shoulder, and picked up my tray. Next year I'd win Most Changed for the Better!

Nine

Robin

I HAD HOPED that the second day of school would be easier than the first. But no such luck. If anything, it was harder. The rumor had circulated. I was the YAS.

I actually had a fan club. Well, it wasn't the Robin Carter fan club, exactly. It was the YAS fan club, and I was by default the official mascot. Before class started, after class started, in the hallways, in the cafeteria, in the atrium—girls stopped to ask me questions.

I was afraid that my conversion to sophisticated Robin was going to be limited to sentences that ended in a question mark. It was hard to grab the right inflection on normal sentences when all I heard were questions. The upside was that most of the questions could be answered with one word.

Fortunately, guys were not enamored of my special YAS status. Most looked at me as if I were a five-legged calf, and they couldn't quite decide if that fifth leg was interesting or just plain weird.

That was fine with me for the time being. Until I had nurtured my changed image and felt comfortable with it, I really didn't want any guys talking to me.

Well, that wasn't exactly true. I craved Kit talking to me the way I craved chocolate. It was a fact of my life that I needed chocolate to survive.

And I was beginning to realize that I needed Kit too.

Strolling home with him yesterday had been the best part of the day. His reassurance that I was a hit had gone a long way toward giving me the courage to walk through the school doors today.

Yesterday I had also learned that afternoon tea was a British ritual. Sitting at the table, drinking tea, and eating chocolate digestive biscuits with Kit and his mom had been . . . well, perfect. I'd felt like such a lady with the dainty teacup and the china saucer.

I thought classes today would never come to an end. When the final bell rang, I released a grateful sigh. I had somehow, through no fault of my own, managed to survive without disclosing my deep, dark twang. A true miracle, considering all the questions I had answered.

I sauntered into the hallway, almost feeling invincible. I noticed a banner slung across the top of the doors.

Get Acquainted Social, Monday, September 11, 7 P.M.

Black Monday. After giving my oral presentation, unless I could tame this wild accent, I didn't figure I'd be welcomed at any social. The thought left me rather glum.

But I cheered up considerably when I caught up with Kit at the atrium. My heart did a little tap dance when he smiled at me.

"How was your day?" he asked.

I decided to try out a word that I thought, when spoken just so, sounded terribly British. "Lovely."

He chuckled. "What would you have said if you were in Texas?"

I shrugged. "Awww right." I really drew out and exaggerated the first word.

He laughed and casually put his arm around my shoulders. "I don't know why you don't share that *lovely* accent with everyone."

"It doesn't sound lovely to me," I admitted.

"I suppose beauty is in the ear of the beholder," he remarked.

A bubble of laughter rose in my throat. "I thought it was the eye of the beholder."

"Depends on the beholder and what he's looking for," he teased.

He squeezed my shoulder. My mind said it was a brotherly squeeze, but my heart . . . Well, it seemed it had a *mind* of its own, and it wanted his touch to be so not brotherly.

"Listen, I hope it's okay if you have tea with my mum alone this afternoon. I'd like to spend some time with Brooke," he announced.

Brooke. Oh, I felt like such a fool. Of course. He liked Brooke. Elegant, graceful Brooke. He'd probably wanted to spend time with her yesterday, but he'd had his host sister to contend with.

I shrugged out from under his arm. "No, I don't mind. Go on. Have fun."

He looked guilty, shifting from one foot to the other. "It's just that she was a bit miffed yesterday—"

"Go on," I interrupted. "I understand completely." And unfortunately I did. I could never compete with someone as sophisticated as Brooke.

"I'll see you home first," he offered.

I waved my hand through the air. "Don't be silly. I remember the way, and I'm a big girl. I can get myself home."

"Are you sure?" He had the cutest way of wrinkling his brow. And I really hated for him to feel bad about abandoning me.

"Yeah, I'm sure. I mean, I have to learn my way around sometime. There's no time like the present. You can't rearrange your whole life just because I'm here," I pointed out. Babbling. I was babbling.

He backed up a step. But he didn't look relieved. "Then I'll see you at home later."

"Later," I repeated as cheerfully as I could.

But watching him hurry off to be with Brooke, I'd never felt more miserable.

"Brooke is such a lovely girl," Mrs. Marlin said.

There was that word again: *lovely*. I decided I was going to erase it from my vocabulary.

I had tried to show proper enthusiasm when Mrs. Marlin taught me how to make scones, but the truth was that I wanted to retreat to my room and brood. What was the advantage to living with a cute guy if he had a girlfriend? And as a guy, he wasn't much help when it came to teaching me to be a proper English girl.

"Try the strawberries and cream," Mrs. Marlin suggested.

The cream was actually whipped cream. I took a bite of the scone and shoveled a strawberry and some cream into my mouth. Pretty tasty. I swallowed and smiled. "It's good."

"I've always enjoyed my afternoon tea with Kit," Mrs. Marlin remarked wistfully. "I suppose I need to get used to his wanting to spend the afternoon with a girl other than his mum."

Using my spoon, I made little mountains with the whipped cream in my bowl. "I guess he and Brooke have been going together for a long time."

Mrs. Marlin wrinkled her brow in a way that reminded me of Kit. "Not so long, really. They went out a few times before she went off on holiday, and he seemed rather fond of her then."

Rather fond? I thought of the knee-melting kiss I had witnessed the day before. They were more than fond of each other.

Mrs. Marlin tapped the table. "All done here. I'd best see to dinner."

I helped her clean up before retreating to my room. Sitting at the dainty desk, my laptop humming, I read the e-mail from my mom, really disappointed that I didn't have anything from Dana or Carrie waiting for me.

From: FarmLady
Sent: Tuesday, September 5, 2000, 5:34 A.M.
To: RobininLondon
Subject: We miss you

> Hi, sweetie. Your dad and I sure do miss you. It's so quiet around here. Your dad is still worried that you'll change, but, well . . . It's okay if you do. A farm life isn't for everyone. Robin, I want you to experience everything you can this year. Grow into the girl that you want to be and know that we'll always love you.
>
> —Mom

I could picture my mom sitting at my dad's computer in his untidy office. Her tears would be hitting the keyboard. My mom cried more than anyone I knew. She cried when a horse foaled. She cried when my pigs got first-place ribbons at the county fair. She'd cried at the airport when we said good-bye. And I knew she'd cry the next time I saw her. She was just like that.

My computer spoke to me. "You have mail."

I clicked the mailbox icon. I was thrilled to see that I had mail from Dana.

From: ArtsyDana
Sent: Tuesday, September 5, 2000, 5:00 P.M.
To: RobininLondon, PizzaGirl
Subject: Paris

Robin and Carrie:

You're not going to believe who's in Paris at my school. Alex Johnson! That's right. The same boring Alex Johnson from Mustang High. I'm constantly running into him. He is rapidly becoming the bane of my existence. How can I meet a French guy and fall in love when Alex keeps getting in the way?

And the French guys are to die for. Cute, cute, cute. I've already branded a couple as potential boyfriend candidates. Paris is the most magical place ever. Did you know they have bakeries on almost every corner?

—Au revoir, Dana

I sympathized with Dana. The whole point in joining the YA program was to get away from people we knew. I couldn't remember much about Alex Johnson, so he must not be a guy who made much of an impression. Although Dana was complaining about him, it didn't seem like she was going to let him ruin her year abroad.

My laptop interrupted my thoughts. "You have mail."

I clicked the icon, and there was Carrie's response.

From: PizzaGirl
Sent: Tuesday, September 5, 2000 5:03 P.M.
To: RobininLondon, ArtsyDana
Subject: An experiment in Rome

Alex Johnson? What's he doing there? Never mind. But boring? Alex Johnson? I always thought he was cool. Good luck with the French guys!

Italy is amazing! I've got a little experiment going with an Italian guy. Let's just say that he needed to learn a lesson, and I decided that I was the one to teach it to him. Details to follow.

Hey, Robin, how's that hot "brother" of yours? Any more close encounters? If so, send us the details!

—Ciao, Carrie

I could actually hear Carrie laughing when she wrote the letter. Oh, that felt good, to read letters from my mom and friends. Even though we were in different countries, we were still close. The power of the Internet.

Carrie and Dana sounded so happy, like they were fitting in. Why couldn't I?

I missed home: the farm, my pet pigs, my family, school, the warm Texas weather. And I missed something else, something I couldn't put my finger on.

It was almost as if I missed me, but that couldn't be it because I was here.

I knew I needed to e-mail everyone back, but I didn't want anyone to read any unhappiness into my tone, especially my mom. Before I replied to their e-mails, I needed to work off some tension. Usually I rode my horse, Dreamer, when I was feeling all knotted up like this. Gosh, I missed that mare. Guess I'd have to settle for a walk.

When I strolled into the hallway, I noticed the door to Kit's room was open. I glanced inside, hoping he was home already. But no such luck. He and Brooke were probably caught up in the whirlwind of a heavy make-out session. I spotted a soccer ball in the corner and decided that was exactly what I needed. Something I could kick and vent my frustrations on.

I snatched up the ball and headed out into the garden. I'd played a little soccer with Carrie and her brothers, so I knew to use the side of my foot instead of my toe to dribble the ball. I couldn't do the impressive moves that they could, but my skill was passable enough that her brothers fought over which one would have me on their team.

Carrie was always complaining about her brothers, but I thought they were neat. They were always throwing their arms around my shoulders and rubbing their knuckles on top of my head. I guess it could get old if I was around them and they did it all the time, but it still made me feel special.

Just like Kit had this afternoon. Based on my experiences with Carrie's brothers, however, I should have definitely recognized a brotherly hug when I got one.

Dribbling the soccer ball up and down the garden didn't take much concentration.

Brooke's regal face popped into my mind. I thought about the icy glare she'd given me today when I walked into creative-writing class. Much colder than the one she'd given me yesterday. For a minute I'd been tempted to come home and get my parka. What was it with her and the chilling looks? Why was Brooke being so unfriendly?

It wasn't that the girl could be jealous or insecure that a girl was living in her boyfriend's house. After all, it was just me, hardly someone to inspire jealousy!

I supposed I could ask Kit what Brooke's deal was, but asking obnoxious questions just because I was dying for the answer wasn't appropriate. I'd learned that lesson over and over with Jason. Especially on that most humiliating day of my life, the day I'd realized how embarrassing my real personality was. I shook my head to clear it of the painful memory.

But it didn't work. Why couldn't the brain function like an Etch-A-Sketch? A good, hard shake and everything was erased forever.

Unexpectedly the soccer ball was snatched away, and I staggered forward because I'd set myself up to kick something that was no longer there.

I spun around. Kit stood nearby, holding the ball, a watchful expression on his face.

"Did you have a nice time with your girlfriend?" I asked in a formal tone. He angled his head slightly, and I thought of the look my golden retriever gave me at home—as if he couldn't quite figure out what humans were all about.

Why couldn't I sound like other people when they spoke formally instead of coming across as someone trying to speak formally but failing?

Suddenly Kit smiled, a challenging glint in his eyes that I didn't quite trust. He ignored my question and bounced the ball off his knee. "Let's have a go at a game." He pointed. "That end of the garden is your goal. All you have to do is kick the ball against the fence to score." His smile broadened.

"After you steal it away from me, that is."

With one quick movement he dropped the ball to the ground and began dribbling it toward the other end of the yard—garden. The sneak!

I released a shriek and hightailed it after him. Since he was taller than me, his legs were longer and he could cover ground faster. But I wasn't going to let that little advantage stop me from scoring. Somehow I managed to get in front of him. He turned. I scrambled. He turned again, and amazingly enough—I was ready.

I shot out my foot, hooked my instep around the curve of the ball, and was off.

"Hey!" he yelled, clearly incensed at my agility.

I laughed as I neared the other side. I could feel him bearing down on me, and I gave the ball one hard kick.

It bounced off the fence, the echo of victory reverberating in the air.

"Yeah!" I leaped in the air, and then I did a little dance around the ball like the St. Louis Rams' players did when they got a touchdown, pointing my index fingers at the ball.

Kit picked up the ball. "Let's see you do that again."

"No problem," I goaded, feeling good. Oh, so good.

He dropped the ball to the ground and nudged it forward with his foot. I sidled around. He twisted first one way, then the other, apparently not in any hurry to get it down to his end.

I was impressed with the fancy footwork that always managed to snatch the ball just beyond my reach. I was also highly aggravated by it. It seemed Kit was as competitive as I was. I figured he hoped to wear me out. Only he didn't know the kind of stamina a farm girl built up over the years. My advantage: He didn't know I was a farm girl.

I quickly dodged in front of him and made contact with the ball. But before I could actually say I had possession of it, he had it back.

He darted to the side. I stayed as close as his shadow. My foot hit the ball. His foot hit the ball. Then somehow we both hit the ball, it spiraled upward, our feet got tangled together, and we both lost our balance with a flailing of arms.

Kit groaned as he hit the ground. I yelped when I landed on top of him.

I was certain that I'd had the wind knocked out of me. That was the only logical explanation for the fact that I couldn't breathe. My inability to draw air into my lungs had nothing to do with the fact that I was lying on top of Kit, staring into his deep blue eyes.

"Sorry for tripping you," he mumbled.

"No problem." I was surprised that he was breathing as harshly as I was. But we'd been running, kicking the ball. It was only natural for us to be out of breath.

My hand was pressed to his chest, and I could feel his heart thudding. I wondered if he could hear mine. It was the exercise, not the closeness of each other, that had our hearts racing. At least, that's what I tried to convince myself of.

"Interesting way to play football," a feminine voice announced.

I jerked my head around. Brooke stood over us, her hands planted firmly on her hips.

And she didn't look happy. "Or what do you Americans call it, *soccer?*"

Ten

Kit

I T WAS BAD form when you had a girlfriend to be caught lying on the ground with another girl in your arms. Unfortunately, at that moment I found myself sort of wishing that I didn't have a girlfriend.

I hadn't quite figured out yet exactly how I felt about Brooke. I'd really been surprised by how glad I was to see her that first day at school. And spending time with her after school, looking through the photos she'd taken while she was in Europe, had been interesting.

Although not as interesting as playing football with Robin.

Awkwardly, Robin and I managed to untangle ourselves. My heart went out to her. Her cheeks were burning a bright crimson. I knew she was embarrassed, and she really had no reason to be. We'd both gotten carried away, playing quite aggressively, which had surprised me. I had never expected Robin to be so . . . animated.

As soon as I was standing, Brooke moved up against me and plopped my Texas Rangers baseball cap on top of my head. "You left this at my house."

I grabbed the bill and settled the cap more firmly into place. I enjoyed watching American baseball and had ordered the cap through the Internet. I didn't wear it often, which was the reason I'd forgotten it. I wasn't even sure why I'd stuffed it into my backpack this morning. Maybe to be closer to my American sister?

"If you'll excuse me," Robin announced formally, "I need to get started on my homework."

I watched her walk into the house with her back straight as a board. I was baffled by the abrupt change in her attitude. She was extremely stiff and distant once again. While we had been playing football, she was exactly as I'd expected an American to be—yelling at me, laughing loudly. And her little tribal dance around the ball had been incredibly cute. Her excitement had been contagious and part of the reason we had gotten tangled up and ended up tripping over our feet.

I hadn't been paying attention to what I'd been doing. I'd been paying attention to her, thoroughly enjoying a girl who was an absolute stranger.

It was almost like there were two Robins—the

one who lived in my house and the one who played soccer. Was it possible her accent wasn't the only thing she wanted to hide?

Robin had barely disappeared into the house before Brooke kissed me. Unexpectedly, just like she had at school. The odd passion almost seemed forced, desperate, not real. I couldn't explain it.

Brooke leaned back and looked up at me. She really was pretty. Blond hair, every strand in place.

"Let's set up Robin with a guy and double-date," she suggested, a twinkle in her green eyes. "Wouldn't that be fun?"

I was incredibly confused. Two different Robins. And now two different Brookes. The one I'd come to know through e-mails this summer and this one standing beside me.

This Brooke was suddenly acting more interesting: kissing me in a very PDA way, suggesting blind dates for Robin, and coming over unexpectedly to return a stupid cap.

Maybe it was wrong not to give her a chance. That sounded rather like an excuse, I realized. But for what? It wasn't as if I was interested in Robin. She was like my sister, for goodness sake. I wasn't really "allowed" to like her.

Still, I didn't want to fix up any of my friends with Robin. If she kissed as passionately as she'd played soccer just then, I didn't want any of my friends to know it.

*   *   *

After Brooke left—which wasn't until she'd sold me on this crazy double-date idea—I bounded up the stairs, grabbed my BlackBerry, and went to Robin's room. The open door beckoned me inside, so I didn't bother to knock. She sat on the window seat, a textbook balanced on her knees, but she was looking out the window, a wistful sort of expression on her face.

As I stepped closer, she must have heard me because she turned and gave me a smile that nearly knocked me over. It was like the smile she'd worn when she'd played football. Only it was warmer. Had I really thought when I first met her that she was afraid to smile?

I realized now that she had probably only been nervous that first night. And that was certainly understandable. A new home, new people, new country.

I'd never realized before how quickly I judged people. First Brooke and now Robin. I hadn't given myself a chance to really get to know either one of them. I was glad now that Brooke had suggested the double date. It would be fun.

I thought about sitting on the window seat, but after getting so close to her when we had played football earlier, I thought it would be best if I kept my distance a bit. So I just stood where I'd stopped when she flashed that beautiful smile at me. "I hope I didn't hurt you earlier when we fell."

Her smile deepened, and her cheeks burned a bright red. "Naw, I'm pretty tough."

Her accent reminded me of a slowly sung ballad. When she spoke naturally, it was as if the words weren't in any hurry to get anywhere. I found it incredibly appealing.

"Right. I'm glad to hear that." I held up my BlackBerry. "I thought we'd double-date Sunday afternoon. I need to compile a list of your likes and dislikes so I can accurately match you up with one of my friends."

The smile abruptly left her face, the blush turned a deeper red, and she stared at me with large, round blue eyes. "I'm not ready for a date. I—I won't be ready for months," she stammered.

Huh? What did she mean by that?

She set the book aside, scrambled off the window seat, and began to pace agitatedly. "You see, I feel it's important to acclimate myself to London first, become one with the culture, make friends, then maybe worry about dating."

She was moving her arms through the air like a Dutch windmill.

"I just got out of a relationship back home, and I need the break anyway." She gave a quick nod, and her hands stilled.

She's lying, I thought. I wasn't sure about which part, but I could sense from her body language and the way she'd rushed around like she was trying to escape from her words that she was lying.

I rocked back on my heels. "All right, then. How about if Brooke and I, plus you and one of my mates, all go out Sunday? Just chums getting together?"

She hesitated. I was fascinated, watching her. I thought I could actually see her carrying on an argument with herself. She finally nodded. "Okay."

I was surprised by the depth of my relief. She wasn't into dating! Great! Any of my friends would be crazy about her: She was so pretty, caring, and fun.

I'd seen that from a distance when she was at the Tower of London with her friends. There seemed to be so many facets to her personality. Suddenly I realized that if she wasn't into dating, she'd also not be interested in dating me.

I crashed for a second, then realized that didn't matter because we were like brother and sister. We lived in the same house.

We couldn't date, could we?

The next day at school I studied my friends. Which one should I ask to be Robin's nondate?

I wanted someone on the good-looking side, but he didn't have to be movie-star handsome. He needed to be fairly intelligent. Based on the snatches of conversation I'd overhead at the Tower, I knew Robin was no slouch in the intelligence department. Besides, the YA student was expected to make certain marks in school, so I figured she did well at her studies.

I thought of the way she'd gotten upset over the ravens' wings being clipped. Her nondate should be compassionate.

I remembered the absolutely terrific way she'd laughed when I'd made my comment about the guard's Mickey Mouse ears. She did have a sense of humor. It just didn't surface often, so I wanted her nondate to have a sense of humor as well.

Using my BlackBerry, I ticked off the traits I thought would appeal to her. Unfortunately, the most practical choice wasn't the best choice: me!

Right. So I probably wasn't going to be able to settle on one of my mates who had all the traits I thought she'd admire in a bloke, but surely someone had most of the traits.

Throughout the morning, in the hallways and in our creative-writing class, I noticed that lots of guys checked her out and seemed interested in getting to know her. Several of them asked her questions, but she always shied away. It was a cute maneuver she'd perfected. Ducking her head slightly, smiling shyly, and scurrying away as soon as she'd quickly answered whatever the question had been. Good. It didn't seem like anyone had caught her fancy.

I knew I shouldn't be glad, but I was.

When I sat beside Brooke at lunch, I was no closer to selecting the perfect nondate than I had been when I began this mission. I brought out my BlackBerry and studied my list of requisites.

"What are you doing?" Brooke inquired.

"Still trying to determine who would be a good date for Robin," I replied.

She scoffed. "What's to decide? Ask the next guy you pass in the hallway."

I scowled at her. "She's my sister, Brooke. You don't set your sister up with just anyone."

Richard Wiggins dropped into the chair across from me. We'd been friends forever. "How's it going with the YAS?" he asked.

I glared at him. "She has a name. It's Robin."

He looked taken aback, and I immediately regretted my outburst.

"What's wrong with you?" Brooke demanded. "He was just being polite."

"I'm sorry, Richard." I truly was. "It's just that everyone keeps calling her the YAS as though she's a thing. And she's a person with thoughts, feelings, fears, dreams—"

"Whoa!" Brooke interrupted me. "This is getting a little too heavy."

"Again, I apologize." How could I explain the responsibility I felt as Robin's brother? "I've never been a brother before."

"Sounds like you're taking the role way too seriously, man," Richard informed me.

I released a nervous chuckle. "Probably."

"How about Richard?" Brooke asked.

"Richard?" I stared at her, flustered.

She nodded. "As a possible date for Robin."

I jerked my gaze to Richard. With his brown hair and eyes, he was really better looking than what I had in mind. On the other hand, I did enjoy his company, so it was likely that Robin would too.

Hmmm. Why did that thought bother me? It shouldn't. After all, this wasn't really a date.

Brooke reached across the table and took Richard's hand. I didn't know if I'd ever seen a guy blush before.

"We're looking for someone to date Robin," Brooke explained.

"Not a real date," I hastily added.

Brooke snapped her attention to me. "What?"

"Well, Robin doesn't feel that she's acclimated enough for a real date, so all we really want is someone to sort of serve as her escort Sunday afternoon," I clarified.

Richard shrugged. "Sure. Sounds like it might be jolly good fun."

Of course it would be, I thought. And I could trust Richard. He wouldn't come on overly strong or make Robin feel uncomfortable. Besides, Robin would be too shy and reserved to attract Richard anyway. Right?

Plus Robin wasn't into dating. No problem.

Eleven

Robin

B Y SUNDAY AFTERNOON I was an absolute basket case about my first date, unofficial or not. Brooke hated me, Kit was probably hoping I'd hit it off with Richard so I'd take the pressure off him to be my "host brother," and Richard would probably be unable to hear a word I spoke because I'd be trying to hide my stupid accent!

I pulled a soft-knit, light blue turtleneck sweater over my head. I wished I could just go out with Kit and talk to him about what I was trying to do and why.

I looked in the mirror and used my fingers to fluff up my hair. Kit was so easy to talk to, and he wasn't judgmental at all. But then in order to explain what I wanted to be, I'd have to admit what I truly was.

I moved closer to the mirror and applied a light layer of lip gloss that was almost the shade of my lips. It didn't really add a lot of color, but it managed to highlight them a little. I didn't even know why I was so worried about the way my lips looked. It wasn't as if any guy was dying to press his mouth to mine.

Suddenly images flashed through my mind—like previews of past attractions.

I thought about those heavenly moments when Kit and I had been lying on the ground together, entangled in what could have so easily turned into a kiss. Our eyes had been locked on each other, our mouths scant inches apart. I'd felt his warm breath whispering over my cheek. If he'd just shifted a little, the kiss would have become reality instead of just living in my imagination.

Yeah, right. While we'd been playing soccer, I'd practically blown my cover. My face burned every time I thought about that ridiculous dance I did around the soccer ball. He'd laughed, and I'd loved the sound of his laughter. But no guy wanted to get involved with a girl that he laughed at.

So forget it. I couldn't let Kit know the real me. Even though he had a perfect girlfriend, and Kit and I were just friends, I still couldn't bear for him to think of me the way Jason had.

I sat in the movie theater, grateful for the darkness. Richard was on my left. Kit on my right. And elegant Brooke was on the other side of Kit.

I was certain that my face was still red.

When we were riding the tube, Brooke had suggested that we go to Piccadilly Circus. I'd gotten really excited at the prospect of seeing animals perform. I had actually thought that I might have something in common with these people.

"I love the circus," I'd announced in a moderate but stately tone. "We always go see Ringling Brothers' when they're in the area."

Brooke had stared at me, obviously in shock that I had spoken. "You're kidding us, right?"

Richard had looked like he wished he was anywhere but sitting next to me.

Kit had given me an embarrassing kind of grimace as though he hated to break the news to me. "Piccadilly Circus is what we call the entrance to the entertainment district."

I had tried to salvage my pride and make light of my ignorance. "No high-wire acts, then?"

He had grinned. "Sorry."

So now I sat straight and tall in the theater when I really wanted to slouch down in my seat until I was invisible. But in the back of my mind, I heard Carrie and Dana daring me to see this through to the end.

I cast a sideways glance at Richard. His brown hair was spiked in the front, short on the sides, and long in the back. He was cute, and even though this was a nondate, he'd bought my ticket and popcorn.

Unfortunately, I only remembered he was here when I thought about it. Kit—I was constantly aware of him sitting beside me.

He shifted in his seat, and his arm touched mine where it lay on the armrest. I thought about how wonderful it would be if he turned over his hand and wrapped his fingers around mine.

Like he would ever want to hold my hand. Especially when he was sitting next to gorgeous Brooke. I slid my gaze past him to Brooke. From the moment we'd arrived at her house, I'd been watching her closely. I pretty much had her I-can't-believe-you-actually-said-that look down pat. She must have given it to me at least a half dozen times. Pretty much any time that I spoke.

When she wasn't looking at me with a frigid glare, she was actually worth studying. Her walk was kinda slinky, seamless. And she did this little flip with her hair that made her shoulders roll. She spoke softly but was still audible. I realized that was where I'd made my mistake. Trying to talk quietly. I just needed to talk softly.

Yeah, right. Breaking Brooke down into parts was like missing the forest for the trees. Overall, she was like a national forest—not just a solitary oak tree.

Brooke was so perfect that she was intimidating. And she did it without trying.

★   ★   ★

As we stepped out of the theater, I was again hit by the life that pulsed through Piccadilly Circus. It was late afternoon, but bright neon lights advertised Coca-Cola, McDonald's, Sanyo, and other products—British and non-British. It was amazing. It was like a melting pot of products. We had nothing like it in Mustang, and I was awestruck as we passed restaurant after restaurant.

My traitorous gaze kept returning to Kit and Brooke, walking in front of Richard and me. K & B—as I was beginning to think of them—were holding hands and talking with their heads bent and close to each other. Then Kit laughed. The sound washed over me, and I remembered how much he'd laughed during our little soccer game.

He hadn't laughed much since. But then, being funny wasn't what I wanted.

I glanced over at Richard. He was shuffling along beside me, his hands shoved in the pockets of his baggy jeans, his eyes focused on K & B too. I wondered what he was thinking. I thought about asking but figured being nosy wasn't too sophisticated.

Kit turned slightly, grinned broadly, and jerked his thumb toward a restaurant. "Fish-and-chips?"

"Sounds good," Richard replied.

I thought of cornmeal-covered catfish fried in huge barrels of grease at family reunions. I'd avoided American foods since I'd arrived, but something with a back-home taste appealed to me as we walked into the restaurant.

We sat in a corner booth. I could look out the window and see everyone hurrying by. I saw a lot of couples, and I wondered how long it would take for me to learn everything I needed to capture a guy's attention.

I certainly didn't seem to have Richard's. He was studying the tines on his fork like he wasn't quite sure what they were used for.

The waitress came over to take our order.

"Fish-and-chips all around," Kit told her. "And cola."

When she had walked away, Kit tapped his fingers on the table and looked at me. "Did you enjoy the film?"

"What I could understand," I admitted. It had been a British movie.

"There was a lot of cockney in it," Kit explained. "There are a variety of accents in Britain, and you can usually tell where someone is from based on their accent."

"Texas is like that," I told him.

Brooke did that little flip of her hair and settled her gaze on me. "I thought you'd sound like J. R. Ewing, but you don't have any accent." One night Kit and I had watched reruns of the old *Dallas* series. It seemed a lot of American shows were in syndication over here. "All your words sound exactly the same, a steady sound," Brooke continued.

116

I couldn't have been more pleased that I'd managed to effectively eliminate the twang in my words.

Brooke wrinkled her nose. "You know. Like the constant beep on a heart monitor after the patient has died."

That stung. "I don't have much of an accent because I'm from the city." And I was working like crazy not to reveal my drawl.

"Her friends are from the country and have really cute accents," Kit told Brooke. He looked at Richard. "They actually say y'all."

Brooke shook her head. "I'm sure they were putting that on."

"No, they weren't," Kit insisted. "When we were at the Tower, they were saying it all the time, and I knew they weren't thinking about it."

Thank goodness, the waitress arrived with our orders right then, so the subject of accents got dropped. She set my plate in front of me. I picked up a big, fat, juicy french fry. I smiled at the waitress. "I was expecting potato chips."

She rolled her eyes.

Brooke shook her head in agreement. "That's so typically American."

"That makes sense since I'm a typical American," I shot back. I was getting fighting mad. I couldn't understand why Brooke felt this need to throw constant jabs my way. What had I done to her? Other than move in with her boyfriend, that is.

We ate without talking. Instead of ketchup everyone soaked their fish-and-chips in malt vinegar. It gave it a certain tangy taste that appealed to me.

But the heavy silence weaving itself around us was enough to ruin my appetite. I ate only half the food on my plate.

I glanced at Richard. He was staring at Brooke. He shifted his gaze to me and, with a guilty look, he went back to munching his fries. When he was finished eating, he patted his stomach. "That hit the spot."

He cast a quick glance at Brooke again.

I wished I knew how to liven up the group. I thought about all the times Carrie, Dana, and I went out to eat. The conversation and laughter were nonstop.

Kit reached across the table and jabbed Richard lightly on the shoulder. "Why don't you and Robin go put on some music?"

Richard looked at me and shrugged. "Sure."

He scooted out of the booth. Without giving a backward glance to Brooke, I followed. I wondered if Kit wanted to get rid of us so he could tell his nasty girlfriend to be nicer on the trip home. Or were they going to laugh at me?

We got to the jukebox. Richard slipped some coins into the slot. "Punch the ones you want."

He cast a quick glance at our table. I figured he

wasn't looking at Kit. *Why would any English guy like uncouth me?* I thought sadly.

Even though this was a nondate, I felt like a zero. "Which ones do you like?" I prodded.

He looked surprised that I'd spoken. Then he gave me a small smile. "You know? You do have an accent when you're angry."

"I'm not angry." I leaned my hip against the jukebox. "This whole nondate thing is just kinda awkward."

He nodded. "Yeah. I've never gone out with a girl before that I wasn't supposed to like."

I stared at him. "You're not supposed to like me?"

"Well, you know, not in a date kind of way," he explained.

I laughed. "Yeah, right." I looked at the list of songs. "Why don't you pick them?" It only seemed fair since it was his money.

"All right, I will."

He went to studying the songs, and I cast a quick glance back at our table. Kit's eyes were glued to Brooke's face. It sure didn't look like he was giving her a dressing-down. As they talked, he tucked a strand of hair behind her ear.

Okay, so he just wanted to be alone with her. I felt like the third wheel on a bicycle.

Shakira began singing "Hips Don't Lie." I remembered Carrie's excitement the day she got her *Oral Fixation* CD. She'd had a sleep over, and she'd played the thing all night.

Suddenly I wanted to be back home, curled up on my bed, talking to my friends, staring at a room that was all me with county-fair ribbons hanging on the wall.

I had been crazy to think hillbilly, country-hick-farm-girl me could survive in London.

Richard slapped his palms against the jukebox. "There we go. You pick the last one."

Without looking, I just punched a number. I was really starting to hate this whole nondate idea.

Richard and I returned to the booth. Brooke was snuggled against Kit now. His arm was along the back of the booth, his fingers toying with her blond strands. I felt pathetic noticing all this and wishing I was sitting on the other side of the booth exactly where Brooke was.

"What's everyone planning for their oral presentation for the creative-writing class?" Brooke asked.

I'd been doing all I could to avoid thinking about the presentation. Having it slapped in front of me, plus the whole horrible nondate, made me really queasy. I broke out in a light, cold sweat, and I actually thought I might throw up.

Richard touched my shoulder. "Hey, you look a little pale. Are you okay?"

I forced myself to give him a shaky smile. "I'm not used to pouring vinegar on my food. I think I used too much. I'm kind of nauseated. I hate to be a party pooper, but maybe I should just go home."

Great. Now I'd just told everyone the state of my stomach. That was real sophisticated.

I thought the ride home on the tube would never end. Everyone was silent, and I was reminded of deathbed scenes from movies. I just didn't think this night could get any worse.

I was wrong.

Kit and Brooke stood at the end of the sidewalk while Richard walked me to the door. In silence.

I couldn't believe it when he leaned forward and kissed me—a small peck on the cheek. I imagined he was Kit, and that was so totally unfair to Richard.

But I was feeling miserable. Physically and emotionally.

"I'm sorry I ended the night so soon." I glanced at my watch. "It's barely six-thirty." We'd caught an early afternoon movie.

Richard shrugged. "Don't worry about it. It's not a problem."

"Guess I'll—I'll see you around," I stammered, trying to find a way to make a quick getaway.

"Sure thing. Cheerio, then." He turned and hurried to join his friends.

I watched Kit, Brooke, and Richard start walking away. I figured the three of them were going to go back out for a night on the town now that I'd made it easy for them to get rid of the hick.

Twelve

Kit

I DIDN'T SAY much as we walked Richard home. Brooke was between us, her arms linked around mine and Richard's. I felt rather like the characters out of *The Wizard of Oz,* trudging down the yellow brick road.

Brooke was telling Richard that he was really a good sport to suffer through an afternoon excursion with the American.

"She's not half bad," Richard commented.

Not half bad? Then why bother to kiss her!

I was surprised how much I had disliked watching Richard lean close and give Robin a kiss. Even though it was just on the cheek, he'd gotten closer than I'd thought he should. I wanted to ask him if her cheek was as soft as it looked. If her breath had caught. If her eyes had twinkled or darkened with passion.

Passion for a kiss on the cheek? I was totally losing it. I shouldn't even care.

Brooke leaned into Richard and laughed lightly. "You're so gallant."

Richard latched his gaze onto hers with something close to adoration—like she'd just knighted him or some such. Then he looked at me, and his face turned red. He shrugged as if he was suddenly embarrassed. "I'm not gallant. I was just doing my good mate here a favor."

What was going on? I had noticed him looking at Brooke a couple of times, but I couldn't fault him for that. I'd seldom been able to keep my eyes off Robin. It was a natural guy thing to compare your date against the other guy's. Only this hadn't been a date!

I'd kept telling myself that I was just watching Robin to make sure she had a good time. Brothers are supposed to do that. Although I felt guilty because if I was honest with myself, I really hadn't wanted her to have a good time. Not with Richard anyway.

We finally arrived at Richard's house. He worked his way out of the pretzel twist Brooke had on his arm.

"Thanks for going with us," I told him.

"Sure, it was fun," he commented. "See you around."

He disappeared into his house, and I chalked up the afternoon as one of the most miserable of my life. Now I just needed to get Brooke home, and then I could go check on Robin. I felt bad that she wasn't feeling well, like it was somehow my fault.

Brooke leaned her head against my arm. "Why don't we go back to your house to watch a video on the telly?"

Although I wanted to look in on Robin, I didn't want to do it with Brooke there. Yet Brooke was my steady, and it wasn't right to make her play second fiddle just because I suddenly found myself with a sister who intrigued me.

"Why don't we go to your house?" I suggested.

She wrinkled her nose and tightened her hold on my arm. "My parents have people over. We wouldn't have any privacy."

Privacy. We definitely needed some privacy. Most of the time I liked Brooke a great deal. But sometimes . . . I couldn't quite put my finger on what it was about her that bothered me. I hadn't liked some of the things she'd said to Robin, but I chalked it up to an overly protective brotherly instinct. I was, after all, new at this being-a-brother stuff.

As we turned toward my house, I felt funny taking Brooke back over there with Robin not feeling well upstairs, but maybe time alone on my own turf with Brooke would be a good way to determine exactly how I felt around her.

If I could figure out how I felt about Brooke,

maybe I'd understand why I spent so much time thinking about Robin.

I sat on the sofa with Brooke snuggled against my side.

I figured it was because I'd watched *The Ring Two* close to a dozen times, trying to discern all the subtle hints in the movie, that my mind wandered now. It just couldn't hold my attention any longer since I could practically recite the dialogue line by line.

I'd wanted to pop upstairs to check on Robin, but Brooke was being very possessive. She'd explained to me that when a girl wasn't feeling well, the last thing she wanted was for some guy to see her. Only I wasn't *some* guy. I was her brother.

But Brooke convinced me that it just wasn't done. Since she had two sisters and no brothers, I wasn't certain how she'd learned this bit of information, but the last thing I wanted to do was offend Robin. She had somehow, amazingly, in a short time become very important to me. I wanted everything to be absolutely wonderful for her. And I just didn't know how to make that happen.

Brooke wiggled against me as if we didn't fit together quite right and she couldn't find a comfortable spot. I really liked the way she felt against me, though. I liked her soft perfume and the way her silky hair felt as I toyed with it.

"The double date was an absolute disaster,"

Brooke announced. She'd seen the movie before as well, but it was her idea to watch it again. "Could Robin have done anything else to make it so not fun?"

What I didn't always like were the words that she spoke. The condescending tone of her voice. The way she said Robin's name like it was something to flush down the toilet. I was overwhelmed by the jumble of images her comment caused.

"You don't like Robin, do you?" I accused.

"What's to like? She is so weird. One minute she's a quiet, timid mouse, and the next she's blurting out some dumb comment. Her accent is ridiculous, and you'd think someone would learn the customs and language of another country before coming for a year. She's so embarrassing!"

Red-hot rage surged through me. I'd never in my life felt this angry. I was totally prepared to tell Brooke off and break up with her, but I needed some distance between us so she could feel the full effect of my wrath.

I jumped off the sofa, my arms flailing. Unfortunately, my glass of cola caught the impact of my anger. I sent the glass and its contents flying, and it landed with a thud on my mum's intricate oriental rug.

Blast it all!

That certainly served to quench my fury. My mum was particular about how things looked.

I rushed into the kitchen to grab a dishrag. I stumbled to a stop.

Robin was standing there. Tears welled in her eyes, and her bottom lip trembled. The depth of sadness in her eyes was enormous, and I could envision only one thing that would make her this sad.

She'd heard Brooke.

A tear plopped onto her cheek, and I thought my heart was going to break. I remembered the girl who had tried to talk quietly so no one would know she had such a wonderful accent. An accent she was ashamed of for reasons I couldn't begin to comprehend. I remembered the hurt in her eyes when the guard at the crown jewels had looked down his nose at her.

And somehow I knew instinctively that people saying cruel things to her wasn't new. And Brooke must have listed everything about Robin that she doubted within herself.

But those were just Brooke's words, not my feelings.

I opened my mouth, but before I could utter a word, Robin burst into tears and rushed past me.

"Robin!" I called after her as she ran through the living room and out the front door.

The door slamming echoed around me as I walked into the living room.

Brooke stood and crossed her arms over her

chest. "I'm so glad the crybaby ran away. Maybe she'll learn a lesson about how to act."

At that moment I absolutely lost it. Something I'd never done. Cool, calm Kit faded into the wallpaper, and someone I hardly recognized stood in my shoes.

"You're the one who needs to learn how to act!" I blasted out.

Brooke dropped back down onto the sofa, her eyes and mouth forming large, perfect circles as I marched toward her. With my hands balled into fists at my side, I towered over her. She had to bend back her head to look at me, which I found extremely gratifying.

"Robin is different, yes," I concurred. "Absolutely! No question about it. She's pretty, refreshing, and fun. She looks at London as if everything is wonderful and exciting. She's brave. She's in a foreign country, living in a house with strangers, going to a new school where she doesn't know anyone, and trying her hardest to fit in. I wasn't what she was expecting, but she kept her chin up and accepted it. I would think you would understand. You were in foreign countries this summer. Robin doesn't complain about every little thing like you do. She's loads of fun when you're not around."

Brooke narrowed her eyes and slowly came to her feet like a panther about to strike. "Fine!" she spat. "If she's so wonderful, then date her yourself."

"Maybe I will, but one thing is for certain—I'm not dating you any longer. You and I are through." The words just came out and with them, a sense of relief.

Brooke stormed out. I was left standing alone in the living room, the angry words echoing around me.

Full-blown, out-of-control panic was taking hold of me with a vengeance. Night was settling around me, and I couldn't find Robin. I had this horrible vision of her getting lost in the maze of tubes, never finding her way home. Or worse yet, getting off the tube and getting lost in the maze of London streets.

Standing in front of my house, right back where I'd started, I took a shuddering breath. Panic was so totally unlike me. I was literally running around like a chicken with my head cut off. I didn't know where to look. As far as I knew, I was the only friend Robin had in London—and some friend I'd turned out to be. Subjecting her to Brooke's vicious tongue and icy glares.

I wouldn't be surprised if she packed her bags and joined her true friends in Paris or Rome.

That thought caused the panic to recede and sadness to sweep in. I simply couldn't stand the thought of her leaving. Of never again seeing her sit in the window seat or watching her kick a ball around in my mum's garden.

My mum's garden!

Of course. It had to be Robin's favorite spot in London. It was the place where she'd most been herself. She could have easily gone out the front door and circled around to the back.

Sure enough, that was where I found her. Sitting on a bench inside the gazebo, sobbing quietly.

Just like her accent, she wanted to hide her sorrows. And just like I wanted to hear her accent, I wanted to share everything that was bothering her.

I stepped beneath the latticed archway. She glanced up and quickly swiped away the tears on her cheeks. Unfortunately, there were enough left in her eyes to roll over and dampen her cheeks again. I handed her my handkerchief.

"Thanks," she rasped. She wiped her tears and delicately blew her red, swollen nose. Why I would think that nose was cute at this moment was beyond me.

I shoved my hand into my jeans pocket. "I'm sorry you heard all that," I murmured.

She just shook her head, and I saw more tears surface. I felt wholly inadequate at being a brother or being a friend to this American.

"I told Brooke off. I explained in no uncertain terms that everything she said was so far from being right that it made her look petty and—"

"Everything she said is true," Robin interrupted me. "Everything. I've only been in London a week, and already I'm a laughingstock. Even when I try to tone down my accent and be more proper, I come across as *embarrassing!* Maybe I should just go home."

My heart lurched at the thought of her leaving.

"Maybe I'm not cut out for a year abroad," she continued. "Maybe I'm incapable of ever being more than a loudmouth hillbilly."

She released a heart-wrenching sob that made her shoulders quake. I dropped onto the bench beside her, slid my arms around her, and drew her close. It was uncanny the way that her face fit perfectly within the hollow of my shoulder.

"You're not a loudmouthed hillbilly," I reassured her.

"Yes, I am. Jason Turner said so," she lamented.

"Who is Jason Turner?" I wondered aloud. He sounded like a complete idiot.

"He's a guy that went to my school back home." She glanced up at me quickly, then lowered her gaze. "I had a major crush on him. He'd moved to Mustang from Dallas. I figured he didn't know anyone since he was new, so I asked him to go to the county fair with me. He had some excuse, something to do that weekend. But I kept asking him out to other things, and he kept saying no."

"He didn't tell you why?" I asked gently.

She shook her head, burrowing the side of her face more deeply into my shoulder. "Not until I went too far."

"However did you manage to go too far?" I was

132

definitely confused. All I could see was someone trying to help a stranger feel at home, not unlike what I'd tried to do. Although I'd certainly failed at every turn.

She sniffled. "I approached him in the cafeteria. He was sitting at a table with some people. I asked him if he wanted to go to a mud run with me."

"A mud run?"

She released a tiny chuckle. "You watch big-wheeled trucks race through an obstacle path that's mostly mud and bogs. It can get really exciting."

"It sounds as if it would be," I lied. I decided it was one of those things you had to be there to appreciate. Even though at first mention I didn't find it particularly appealing, I thought attending anything with this girl I held in my arms would be delightful. I would have given it a go had she asked me. "So what happened?" I prodded.

She moved away from me and studied her hands, balled in her lap. "He snapped. He stood up and yelled in front of everyone that I was an obnoxious, annoying, loud, brash pest. He was sick of being embarrassed by me all the time. That he wasn't interested and I'd better get it through my thick skull! That's when I realized how I came across to people. I'm not fun to be around after all. I realized how everyone I dealt with must see me."

I was dumbfounded. "You're only seeing yourself through the eyes of one stupid guy."

"No, he was more than that. He came from the city, had seen so much of the world." She shifted on the bench until she faced me. Her eyes held such earnestness. "That's when I came up with my plan to come to London. Everyone here is so sophisticated, so refined. I wanted to spend a year here so I could return to Texas a changed girl: an English girl."

An English girl. I'd just broken up with an English girl—because of this American girl. This American girl who was trying so hard to hide her true self.

"I wish you'd let me see the American girl that you truly are," I pleaded. "The girl you just described sounds like a lot of fun."

She scoffed. "You're just being nice."

"No, honestly, ever since you got here, I've been so intrigued by the girl I've glimpsed those times when you forgot to hide your true self. That's the girl I wish I could have living in my house."

Robin bolted off the bench. Having experienced this same response from Brooke earlier, I knew this action wasn't a good sign. Robin began to pace, her arms flailing about in circles. This was the true Robin, I realized. A girl so enamored of life that she couldn't be still.

"I'm not the girl you caught glimpses of. You haven't seen the real me since I've been here because I've kept her hidden. Believe me, you would detest her as much as Jason did." She stopped pacing and faced me squarely, her hands planted on her hips. "If you were my friend, you'd coach me on the lingo and teach me how to act."

That she wanted to thrust this desire for a transformation on me angered me beyond reason. I stood. "If you really want to turn into a boring, reserved, prissy girl who's unenthusiastic and no fun to be around, I'm not going to help you."

I spun on my heel and headed inside.

Thirteen

Robin

FURIOUS WAS TOO tame a word for what I
was feeling as I stomped up the stairs to my
room.

Who did Kit think he was?

How dare he say such ugly things to me!

I stopped beside his room and glared hard at the
closed door. I was surprised that it didn't burst into
flames.

I jerked open the door to my room, stalked inside, and slammed the door behind me. The one
advantage to my anger was that it had driven away
the hurt I'd been feeling earlier.

I began formulating a plan. If Kit wasn't going to
help me, I'd just help myself. Besides, who wanted
the help of a guy who had absolutely no idea what
he was talking about?

He'd like to get to know the real me? Yeah, right. When pigs could fly.

He liked Brooke, for goodness sake! How could he ever like the real me?

I plopped onto the bed, picked up the remote, and turned on the small television that sat on a little table in the corner. I hadn't watched it much while I'd been here. No time, really. While I was running around crazily trying to absorb all the culture, it was sitting right here, waiting for me.

I began flicking the channels. *There are a lot of American TV shows here,* I realized in annoyance.

I finally found an English show. Okay, so the subject was gardening. The host was a woman who spoke with a very charming accent. All I had to do was mimic her.

There was absolutely no way I was going to embarrass myself during that oral presentation tomorrow. I was going to learn to speak and act the way I was expected to: in a reserved, accent-free, proper, elegant way.

The first thing I had to do was lose the twang.

"When pruning roses, you want to make sure that you avoid pricking your fingers on the thorns," the woman said, smiling gently.

That was probably a sentence that I'd never use in my entire life. Even so, I tried it out. "When prunin' roses, you wanna make shore that you avoid prickin' your fingers on the thorns."

I repeated the sentence, listening carefully. I

realized I was dropping the *g* when I spoke. While her words ended in a nicely ringing *ing,* mine came to an abrupt halt with *in*. Disgusting. No wonder I sounded hick. I spoke the words in a slow drawl but still managed to cut off part of them. Worse than that, some words like *want to* ended up being one word with no *t* sound whatsoever. I was pathetic, but teachable.

"When prunin' . . . pruning roses, you wanna make sure that you avoid prickin' . . . pricking your fingers on thorns."

I felt like that sentence was filled with thorns. But I repeated it over and over, listening intently to each word until it finally came out: "When pruning roses, you want to make sure that you avoid pricking your fingers on the thorns."

Jolly good show! I thought, knowing now how Eliza Doolittle had felt. I skipped around the room, singing, "The Rain in Spain."

Then I stopped and looked at the girl on the TV. Only the program had changed. Based on the canned laughter, I was watching a comedy, but I couldn't understand most of the words. They spoke so quickly. Was it cockney they were using? I definitely didn't need to pick up another accent.

I switched off the TV and simply recited words I knew that ended in *ing*. As long as I stayed focused, I could speak clearly, succinctly, without a twang reverberating against my eardrums.

I was feeling the panic ebb away.

Now all I needed to do was write out my oral presentation and start practicing in front of the mirror. As much as possible, I needed to avoid including words that ended in *ing*. Sure, I'd mastered not dropping the *g*, but why take chances?

I decided to write about my goal of learning all the English words that are different from American words, like *jumper* for *sweater* and *tube* for *subway*. That way I'd show everyone that I was trying to become a Londoner while in London. Then they could accept me as one of them.

I turned on my laptop and began typing away, carefully wording my presentation so I didn't fall into any hidden traps, words that could foul me up. I spoke out loud as I typed, testing the words, concentrating on no twang.

Preparation was the key.

The phone rang, and I nearly jumped out of my skin. I caught myself just before I picked up the receiver. There was no one here to call me. I went back to working on my presentation. I was actually getting into it. It would help ensure my metamorphosis from Texas Robin into London Robin.

A knock on the door had me hitting the keys so that a string of *z*s flew across my screen. I really wasn't in the mood to talk to Kit.

"Robin?"

Ah, it was Mrs. Marlin.

I jumped up and opened the door. "Yes, ma'am?" Inwardly I cringed. Definitely a drawl on *ma'am*.

"Phone call for you."

Joy surged through me. It had to be my mom. "Thanks."

I closed the door and hurried to the phone. "Howdy!"

"Robin?" a deep voice inquired, definitely not my mom. I grimaced. My greeting had been about as Texas as I could get.

"Yes," I replied very succinctly.

"It's Richard."

Knock me over with a feather. I dropped into a chair. "Hi."

"Listen, I was wondering if you'd like to go to the school social with me tomorrow night," he announced.

Whoa! This was a total shock. I'd gotten the impression that Richard didn't even like me. Why would he invite me to the social? Still, I wanted to experience London life, so I said, "Sure. I'd love to."

"Great! I'll drop round your house at seven," he said.

Then he hung up. *Bam!*

That was weird. *Maybe I did okay tonight after all.*

Yeah, that was it, I thought. I did okay, and maybe Richard was surprised. After all, they told him not to like me as a date, but obviously he did.

141

That just went to show how wrong Kit was. Thanks to me trying my hardest to be different, I now had a date to the social.

Feeling better about everything, I began working to finish my presentation. But I kept getting distracted.

The guy I really wanted to go to the social with thought I was a total idiot—without even seeing the real me at work!

Kit just didn't get it, I thought sadly.

I wondered if he'd apologize to Brooke for giving her what for and take her to the social. Probably. Now they could both laugh at how ridiculous I was.

Fourteen

Kit

Lying on my bed, I stared gloomily at the ceiling and wondered if Robin was still talking to Richard on the phone.

I really owed Richard one.

After that horrible argument with Robin downstairs, I'd called him.

"Hey, Richard, I've got a major favor to ask," I'd told him as soon as he answered the phone.

"Ask away, buddy," he responded.

I took a deep breath before I blurted out, "I need you to take Robin to the school social tomorrow night."

"You're kidding, right?" he scoffed.

"I'm serious. I know things didn't go splendidly today—"

"That's an understatement," he interrupted. "I

can't hear half of what she says. And when I can hear her, what she does say is just plain weird."

"It's simply because she's nervous, being in a strange country and all," I tried to explain. That was partly true, although Robin would be nervous no matter where she was. That much had become obvious in the gazebo. I thought it was a real shame too.

"Ask someone else," Richard responded.

"Come on, Richard, be a good sport. She's the YAS. Taking her to the social will elevate your status in the school," I pointed out. Not that Richard needed his status elevated. Everyone pretty much liked him, and I figured he could really go out with any girl he wanted. I could almost hear the wheels turning in his head as he mulled that over. I needed to strike quickly and deadly. "I promise I'll do any favor you ask in the future."

"Any favor?" he asked, skepticism evident in his voice.

"Any favor at all without hesitation," I promised.

"All right, then, I'll do it."

Two minutes after we hung up, the phone rang for Robin, and I knew Richard was inviting her to the social.

I knew that Richard was the kind of guy Robin wanted or hoped to impress with the new her. I might not agree with what she was doing, but I did want her to be happy.

144

It's not like she'd go with me, I reminded myself. *She pretty much hates my guts now.*

I'd never felt so much internal conflict. I wanted her to like me, but I knew that I could never like the girl she wanted to become.

All in all, though, by calling Richard, I knew I'd done a good thing by Robin. I rolled over in bed, pounded my fist into my pillow, and tried to fall asleep.

But that wasn't likely to happen.

The next morning I sat on the edge of the mattress and hung my head.

I had no idea what sort of reception I'd get from Robin. I'd actually considered sneaking off to school and sparing her my presence. I was probably the worst excuse for a brother that ever lived.

Of course, the problem was that I really didn't want to be her brother.

I looked at my clock. The minutes were ticking by. She hadn't knocked on my door. She was usually pretty punctual about getting in and out of the shower. Maybe this morning she absolutely didn't care if I had a chance to shower before school or not.

I stood and began to pace. Did I dare go into the hallway? What if she was in her underwear again? I felt like a prisoner in my own room.

On the other hand, maybe she was giving me the silent treatment—and maybe that treatment extended to not knocking on my door.

I was being ridiculous. I threw on some clothes. I'd just go into the hallway and if the bathroom was free, then I'd take my shower. I headed for the door and saw a slip of paper on the floor.

Bending down, I picked it up. It was from Robin.

Went to school early. See you there.
—R

She must really hate me, I thought, *if she fled the house at the crack of dawn just to avoid walking to school with me.*

Then an even more depressing thought hit me.

What if she and Richard arranged to meet early at school? Maybe they talked all night on the phone and she fell madly in love or something.

I suddenly realized that I had no idea how Robin felt about Richard. Maybe she'd liked him on the date. Maybe she was ecstatic that Richard asked her to the social.

What a mess I was in. Richard wasn't interested in Robin that way.

Now all I'd done was set her up with a guy who wouldn't ask her out again!

Her whole plan would backfire on her, all thanks to me.

Ugh! Why couldn't Robin have been a guy!

Fifteen

Robin

I WAS INCREDIBLY relieved when the first bell rang, signaling the beginning of the school day. I'd been hanging out in the school yard for the past hour in order to avoid having to walk to school with Kit.

As cowardly as it was, I simply could not face him. He wanted me to be what I couldn't be, what I absolutely loathed.

As I headed toward the building, I rounded the corner, and there was Brooke. The only person I wanted to avoid more than I wanted to avoid Kit. I stiffened when I recalled Brooke's nasty words from yesterday. But I knew I had to get beyond them. I'd no doubt see her at Kit's now and then. Right now, though, I wanted to ignore her, but durn my Texas upbringing. I just held my head up high and walked past her. "Howdy."

Inwardly I cringed. I'd meant to say something sophisticated like, "It's so wonderful to see you this bright and cheery morning." I imagined she thought *howdy* was about as hick as a person could get.

But then, what did I care what she thought.

"Robin!" she called out after me.

Against my better judgment, I turned and faced her. Let her toss out her insults. I'd just catch them and toss them back.

She looked really uncomfortable as she approached me. It was a strange sight to behold.

Then she cleared her throat, and her cheeks burned a dark crimson. "About yesterday," she began. "I'm really sorry for the mean things I said. I was jealous of a girl living with Kit, especially an exciting American, but then late last night I realized how stupid I was to be insecure about you, given how unexciting a foreigner you are."

"Thanks," I responded. "I'll take that as a compliment."

She gave me a funny look, then said, "I guess Kit's taking you to the social tonight."

She obviously thought I'd just fallen off the turnip truck and was trying to bait me. I chuckled. "Of course not. He's taking you, isn't he?"

At that moment Brooke looked like a feather

would knock her to her knees. "Kit broke up with me yesterday. Didn't he tell you?"

Correction. I'm the one who could have been knocked off her feet with a feather. Baffled, I shook my head. "When exactly did you break up?"

Brooke rolled her eyes. "After you went storming out of the house. He defended you, said you were so funny and so interesting and so kind." She waved her hand in the air. "Whatever. I stopped listening after a while. I'm surprised he didn't tell you."

I was too, but right now I felt like a cat had gotten hold of my tongue. Why hadn't he told me that he'd broken up with Brooke? And he'd done it before our argument in the gazebo.

"So who are you going to the social with?" Brooke asked.

"Richard," I told her.

She stared at me. "Incredible," she murmured.

I didn't know what to say. "So if you're not going with Kit, who are you going with?" I asked.

"I'm going alone," she snapped. "Not that it's any of *your* business."

Just before creative-writing class, I saw Kit in the hallway. He looked incredibly glum as he put his books in his locker.

I quietly came to stand beside him and leaned against the locker beside his. When he slammed his locker door closed, there I was. I could tell he was taken aback by my presence, which gave me the advantage.

"Why didn't you tell me that you broke up with Brooke?" I demanded. I couldn't believe how forlorn he looked. It actually hurt to see him looking like this.

"My breaking up with Brooke is my business and has nothing to do with you," he said in an incredibly clipped and British voice.

"You're wrong there, buddy. It seems y'all broke up because Brooke insulted me and you defended me," I pointed out.

Kit shook his head. "I broke up with Brooke because I don't have the feelings for her I'm supposed to. And I have those feelings for someone else. Or had them."

"Who?" I insisted.

Kit shifted the books in his arms and looked at me like he was searching for something he'd lost. "The girl I'd glimpsed in you when you were trying to hide who you were. That girl. But that girl doesn't exist, does she?" he asked hollowly just as the bell rang.

No, she didn't exist. *Or at least I don't want her to exist,* I thought as I followed him into the classroom.

I dropped into my seat, suddenly dreading the oral presentation more than I thought humanly possible. I pulled out my copious notes and my well-thought-out and written presentation. I'd printed it out using the printer in Mr. Marlin's office—in the dead of night when I was certain Kit was already asleep so our paths wouldn't cross.

But now the words on paper kept swimming in front of my eyes. I couldn't focus on them. Mrs. Lambourne was explaining the reason behind having us bare our souls, but I really wasn't listening.

I couldn't stop thinking about what Kit had said in the hallway. He had feelings for me? More than brotherly feelings? How could he possibly like that girl? She was loud, brash, pushy, goofy, not afraid to speak her mind, and had the worst Texas twang of anyone alive.

I turned around slightly and stared at Kit. He wouldn't be giving me any thumbs-up encouragement today when I gave my presentation. I remembered how he'd stuck up for me at the Tower of London when the snotty guard had made his Disney World comment. For a heartbeat I'd been myself, and he'd made me laugh. I thought about how I'd revealed my true accent later that night— and he'd sat beside me and we'd talked, really talked, for the first time.

And I remembered last night. When he'd held me while I bared my soul to him. He'd seen the real me then. He hadn't gotten angry until I'd asked him to help me get rid of that girl.

I turned back around. I missed that girl. The real Robin.

A little smile played at the corners of my mouth. I liked that girl too. And so did a lot of other people. Just one guy didn't, one guy who didn't deserve me.

"Miss Carter? Miss Carter?"

I snapped out of my reverie. People were looking at me and smiling indulgently. I figured everyone had pretty much guessed that I'd been daydreaming.

"Miss Carter, it's time for you to give your presentation," Mrs. Lambourne announced.

My presentation. I stared at the papers strewn on my desk. My well-thought-out, rehearsed-to-death, boring presentation. With a deep, shuddering breath I got up—and left the papers behind.

I walked to the front of the class. I wished that I had something to stand behind, something to hide a portion of myself. Mrs. Lambourne had said that speaking made us vulnerable. Speaking the truth would make me even more so.

I cleared my throat, met Kit's gaze, and began.

"My goal for this year is . . . to appreciate who I am, where I come from, and to be myself." Twang echoed around me. Out of the corner of my eye I saw Brooke's eyes widen. She was probably mortified to realize she'd spent time with a true country girl.

"I wanted to come to London for a year so I could turn into a sophisticated, demure girl. But a girl who has pet pigs, loves mud runs, won the hog-calling contest, and can outeat any cowboy in a baby-back-ribs contest isn't meant to be quiet and sophisticated. She's meant to be who she is."

Kit's mouth had dropped open, and he was staring at me intently. Not a good sign. But I couldn't turn back now. Besides, it felt good to finally reveal the real me and not to worry about my twang or my harsh voice or my ability to shove both feet into my mouth at the same time.

I took a deep breath and persevered. "My goal this year is not to be ashamed of my roots. Kit asked what my daddy does, and I told him he was into agriculture. Actually, he's a farmer. And me, I'm a farm girl. I get up at five-thirty in the morning to milk the cows before I leave for school. I also raise pigs and enter them in the county fair. I bought two pigs just before I left. I named them Jar Jar and Binks. I really miss them."

A couple of the kids laughed, but I didn't feel like they were laughing at me. They were laughing with me. If only Kit would. But he was just watching me with those intense blue eyes of his.

"I do have one last goal. I don't want to change so much as I want to learn how to talk to people better. See, on the farm there's just me and my animals, so I spend a lot of time talking to my mare, my cows, my pigs, my dog—and to be honest with you, they're not great conversationalists."

The whole class laughed then. Well, almost. Kit looked like he was on the verge of puking. Not that

I could blame him. I was revealing some pretty heavy stuff here.

I gave everyone a nervous smile. "I can pretty much say anything I want to my dog and he'll just lick my face, even if what I said is totally lame. So I want to learn to be me but around people. I figure if my pets like me—"

The bell rang. Thank goodness, because I knew I was starting to ramble.

To my surprise, a bunch of people clapped. Brooke rolled her eyes. No surprise there. And Kit . . . Kit just grabbed his books and stuff and headed out of the room without even giving me a backward glance.

Guess he didn't like what the real Robin sounded like after all, I thought miserably.

By the end of the day it seemed that the whole school had joined the YAS fan club. Only now people weren't just asking me questions. They were really talking to me.

They thought my life on the farm sounded great, and they adored my accent. Adored my twang. Knock me over with a spring breeze. Who would have thought that the thing I hated most was what would appeal to them?

"Robin?"

I turned as two girls approached me in the hallway. Bridget and Karen. They were in my creative-writing class.

"That was a marvelous presentation you gave

this morning," Bridget announced excitedly.

"Smashing!" Karen added. "I'm going to redo mine tonight. I actually lied about my goal."

I almost asked her why she'd done that, but I knew. It was just plain hard to make yourself vulnerable that first time.

"We're here on scholarship," Bridget explained.

"We actually live on farms in north England," Karen clarified. "We could really relate to what you said today."

Farm girls! I'd had no idea that someone just like me was sitting in class with me.

"Just like you, we felt like we had to hide where we came from," Karen continued.

"But now we realize how dumb it is to feel that way, thanks to your presentation," Bridget told me.

I smiled warmly. "It took me a while, but I finally realized it was dumb too. That's why I decided to speak so openly."

"That was incredibly brave," Karen commented. "You're an inspiration."

I wanted to laugh. I hardly felt like an inspiration to anyone, least of all myself, as I headed home. For all their kind words and enthusiasm for my presentation, I realized that I'd never get it right. I'd never be the kind of girl that any guy wanted.

Now that I'd exposed my true self, I was certain Richard wouldn't want to take me to the social.

And Kit's hasty retreat had made it perfectly clear that the real me sounded awful.

Sixteen

Robin

ON THE OFF chance that Richard had not yet heard about my debacle at school, I absently got ready for the social. It was possible that even if he had heard what the real Robin was truly like, he might still show up. And if he hadn't heard, he was gonna find out pretty durn quickly.

It wasn't a formal affair, but I did think jeans would be out of place. I selected a denim broomstick skirt, a red shirt, and a denim vest with Texas wildflowers embroidered down the front. And what was denim without cowboy boots? I thought about plopping on my hat but decided I didn't want to overdo the Texas image. If Richard was gracious enough to keep our date, I didn't want to send him screaming into the night as I put away my sophisticated image.

157

Although I had this vision of Brooke racing up to him and laughing uncontrollably about the girl he had really gone out with yesterday. Not that I was able to concentrate much on Richard and Brooke.

My thoughts kept turning to Kit.

It was incredibly obvious that he was avoiding me. I'd been unable to find him after school, and he had failed to join Mrs. Marlin and me for our afternoon tea.

A knock sounded on my door. My heart jumped. Maybe it was Kit. Maybe he just needed some time to adjust to the real me. That was perfectly understandable and cool with me.

But when I opened the door, Mrs. Marlin stood there, smiling warmly. "Your date's downstairs."

Unexpected relief hit me. At least Richard had shown up. Once he got a load of the real me, it would probably be the last time his shadow ever darkened Mrs. Marlin's threshold.

"Give me a minute to see if I can make this hair behave," I told her as I hurried back to the mirror.

Mrs. Marlin followed me into my bedroom. If she noticed that I was talking differently, she didn't say anything. "Well, I haven't much experience fixing daughters' hair," she said wistfully, "but I'll give it a go."

She took the brush and somehow managed to make the rebelling strands that wanted to poke out like rowels on spurs fall back into place.

I captured her gaze in the mirror and smiled. "Thanks."

When I turned, she gave me a big hug. I had needed that so badly that I almost cried. I didn't know how I was going to undo the disaster that this year was promising to be.

On my way down the hall I looked longingly at Kit's door and wondered if he was in there. If he wasn't taking Brooke to this social, then I figured he wasn't going. It would be the first time that I went somewhere without him there to offer me support and encouragement. But he'd wanted to see the real me. I'd warned him that he wouldn't like what he saw.

And yet, even though it had cost me his friendship, I knew that I wouldn't take back my presentation if I could. For the first time since I'd stepped off the plane at the airport, my stomach wasn't knotted up and my palms weren't sweaty.

I was me. And it felt good to be me again.

At the top of the stairs I came to an abrupt halt. Mrs. Marlin patted my shoulder. "There's your date," she whispered before hurrying down the stairs. She squeezed my date's shoulder before disappearing into the living room.

My date. Richard wasn't standing there. I stared in utter astonishment.

Kit stood there.

He wore khaki pants, a blue polo shirt that

brought out the shade of his eyes, and a navy blazer. And the warmest smile that I'd ever seen.

I was incredibly disappointed that Richard had decided to bail out. I'd really hoped that my true confessions earlier hadn't turned him off completely.

But I was so overwhelmed and grateful to Kit for stepping in. I honestly couldn't have asked for a better brother. I knew how he felt after my presentation. His hasty exit had made it abundantly clear. He didn't like me, but here he was, where he'd been from the moment he approached me at the airport—at my side, offering his support.

My heart rolled over, and I wished I could be the kind of girl who would appeal to him. But since I couldn't be that, I could be a good sister.

"Slide down!" he ordered.

I stared at him. Huh? I cast a quick glance at the banister. I'd been dying to slide down it since I got here.

"Come on," he prodded. "You know you want to."

It seemed my brother knew me all too well.

I hopped onto the banister, scooted to the end, and then shoved off. *"Wheeew!"* I cried out as I slid all the way down.

Kit caught me, and I held my breath. It felt so right to be here in his arms, gazing into his mesmerizing blue eyes, studying the way he smiled.

Very slowly he dipped down so I could straighten and my feet could touch the floor.

But his arms didn't leave me. They just moved lower until they circled my waist. I swallowed hard. "Where's Richard?"

"He's at the social with the girl of his dreams . . . Brooke," Kit explained.

Huh? So I had been right. Richard had been looking at Brooke more than a guy with no interest should. I nodded. "Guess I can't blame him for asking her after I revealed my true colors at school today."

Kit shook his head. "Your presentation had little to do with his decision to take Brooke. Actually I prodded, cajoled, and pleaded with Richard to ask you to the social because I knew how important it was to you to impress a 'proper English guy.'"

"I can't believe you did that!" I blurted out, trying to work my way out of his hold.

But his arms tightened around me. "Let me finish!" he insisted.

I stopped squirming. The only time I'd ever heard him yell was at the gazebo last night. He didn't strike me as someone who got upset often, but I sure seemed to put that side of him to the foreground.

He chuckled low. "I'm looking forward to you freaking out on me a lot this year, but right now, I want to talk."

"Okay," I said reluctantly.

"After creative-writing class today, I ran out to search for Richard so I could tell him that I didn't want him to take you to the social after all, that I wanted to take you. Richard was very relieved, especially when he heard that Brooke and I had broken up. Richard admitted he had a major crush on Brooke and was dying to ask her to the social. Which, I just learned, he did."

Kit was silent for a moment, and his brow did that cute little furrow. Then his hold on me loosened.

"Blast it all! I just realized that I might have acted way too hastily. Because maybe you like Richard and wanted to go with him. Maybe you don't want to go with me." He stepped back and slapped the heel of his hand against his head as if he was trying to knock some sense into himself. "Maybe I was way out of line—both in setting up your date with Richard and then undoing it!"

I laughed. I couldn't believe this was happening or that he would have such doubts about my feelings. I stepped forward and wound my arms around his neck. "It's amazing how keeping your real feelings to yourself ends up doing so much damage!"

"Don't I know that," he murmured as he slid his arms back around my waist. "I learned that lesson well enough."

I smiled warmly. "I couldn't be happier that you acted hastily. Because it worked out perfectly."

Kit lowered his mouth to mine and kissed me slowly, provocatively. My knees grew weak as my arms tightened their hold around his neck.

He drew back, his gaze holding mine. "I can't wait to spend this year with the real Robin Carter, the one who has pet pigs and won the hog-calling contest."

I groaned. "I still can't believe I admitted that in my oral presentation."

He kissed me again, a kiss as warm as a Texas summer.

I was breathless by the time we stopped kissing, breathless and so incredibly happy. And a little afraid that he would come to his senses.

"I'll be leaving at the end of the year," I reminded him.

"But we'll have the year," he said, "and who knows? Maybe I'll come to the States."

I hugged him. "My parents have a spare bedroom," I murmured. "I've always wanted a brother."

His laughter echoed around us. "Then you'll have to find someone else because there's no way I'll ever be able to think of you as a sister again."

When he kissed me this time, he left no doubt in my mind.

Epilogue

Robin

"YEEHAW!" KIT YELLED just before the mechanical bull sent him flying into the pile of hay.

Standing outside the corral that was inside the Texas Diner, Brooke, Richard, and I laughed. Kit had heard about this restaurant in London and suggested that we give it a go. Right now, I figured he was wishing he'd kept the place a secret. He slowly got to his feet and limped over to us. He rubbed his backside.

"I cannot believe Texans actually do that," he muttered.

"They don't do that," I pointed out. "They stay on the bull!"

Richard laughed loudly, and Kit glared at him. "Let's see you do it."

"No problem," Richard said before sauntering over to the bull.

Kit stepped out of the corral and slipped his arm around me. He moaned. "I won't be able to move tomorrow."

"Tell me where it hurts," I insisted.

He gave me a sly grin and pointed to his lips. Reaching up, I gave him a sound kiss.

We heard a yell and jerked apart. Richard was sprawled on the floor. He gave Kit a sheepish grin before working his way to his feet.

Brooke planted her hands on her hips. "Do you know how embarrassing it is for me that my boyfriend can't even stay on a machine for a single second?"

Richard jerked his thumb over his shoulder. "You want to give it a go?"

"Yeah, Brooke," I prodded. "Why don't you give it a go?"

She gave me an icy look, but it wasn't as chilling as the ones she'd given me three months ago. Ironically, we'd become good friends.

"I'll do it if you will," she dared.

Boy, howdy. She thought that she was going to get out of it. "Reckon you didn't know that back home they call me dare-me-to-do-anything Robin."

She rolled her eyes. "I was only joking."

"Too late!" I snapped. "Climb on the beast."

She did that familiar flip of her hair, roll of her

shoulders, but I could see the excitement brewing in her eyes. She really wanted to do this, but she had to pretend it was beneath her. She straddled the saddle on the mechanical bull and looked at me. "What do I do?"

"Just hold on for eight seconds!" I yelled right before the guy manning the bull pulled the switch.

Poor Brooke didn't last half a second. Her scream nearly shattered my eardrums, and her sophisticated backside landed hard in the hay along with her pride. Somehow she managed to get up elegantly, and she walked stiffly out of the corral. "Let's see you do it, Miss I'm Having a Hard Time Holding Back My Smirk."

"Aww righty," I drawled. I turned to Kit. "Kiss me for luck."

He obliged in a very warm way. Durn, I loved his kisses.

I sauntered toward the mechanical bull and threw my leg over the saddle. I grabbed the saddle horn and raised one arm in the air. I gave a sharp nod. "Do it!"

The bull bucked and turned, but I just let my body become fluid with the motions. It wasn't as easy as riding a horse or chasing pigs, but it was easier than trying to be something I wasn't. I'd learned a lot in the last three months. Mainly that I was the most interesting person these people had ever met. How small town was that?

The buzzer sounded, and the bull came to an

abrupt stop. I hopped off and gave the guy manning the bull a salute. I strolled cockily over to my mates, blowing on my fingers before buffing them on my shirt.

Kit creased his brow. "How did you do that?"

"Very successfully," I assured him.

He narrowed his eyes. "I'm going to give it another go."

"Marlin! Party of four!" the hostess called out.

I slipped my arm around Kit's. "Later—I'm starved right now."

We were escorted to a table covered with a red-and-white-checkered tablecloth. After we sat, the hostess—who wore Western garb—handed us the menus. I opened mine, settled back in my chair, and figured I was gonna eat more tonight than I had the entire time I was in London. My mouth started watering as I looked over the selections.

"Brisket?" Brooke murmured cautiously. "What is brisket?"

I looked over the top of my menu. The corner of her lip was curled up. I almost told her that I'd expected her to learn the cuisine of a country before she ate in its restaurant, but I knew too well how hard it was to know every little thing.

"Beef," I supplied, and went back to drooling over the menu.

I heard menus slap closed. I looked up.

Everyone was staring at me. "Y'all know what you want already?"

Kit shook his head. "Why don't you order for us?"

"All right," I said, really getting into the fact that I was in my element and they weren't. Who would have thought this would be so much fun? "I reckon we ought to get a sampling of everything and share."

"Share?" Brooke echoed. "Isn't that a bit much, even for friends?"

"This isn't a fancy restaurant, Brooke. You're gonna eat them baby-back ribs with your fingers," I pointed out.

Brooke rolled her eyes in disgust, and Kit laughed heartily. "I can't wait to see that."

I leaned back, queen of my domain. "I figure y'all need a good sampling of Texas fare, so we'll have baby-back ribs, brisket, pulled pig, potato salad, coleslaw, baked beans, corn bread, and lots of barbecue sauce. Then we'll move on to blackberry cobbler and apple pie."

I didn't think I'd ever enjoyed eating so much. Who would have thought that eating barbecue would make my friends look as clumsy as a three-legged calf? And talk about messy! They couldn't quite figure out how to get all the barbecue sauce off their face and fingers. I thought it was great!

After we ate, we went to the dance floor.

"Are we going to line dance?" Richard asked. "I've heard of line dancing."

"Not if you're getting a true taste of Texas," I explained. "Texas guys like to hold their girls close."

As if to prove my point, George Strait began crooning "I Cross My Heart."

Kit took my hand and led me to the center of the dance floor.

He smiled warmly at me. "So teach me how they dance in Texas."

I stepped close and put my hands on his shoulders. "Just put your hands on the small of my back and take small steps. I'll follow wherever you lead."

I fitted my head into the crook of his shoulder as we began to sway slowly in time to the music.

"Having fun?" he asked quietly.

I nodded and twined my arms more firmly around his neck.

"I love you, Robin," he whispered near my ear.

My heart did a little do-si-do, and I leaned back slightly to meet his gaze. "I love you too."

He smiled warmly and lowered his lips to mine. I could smell straw and barbecue. I heard the heartache of country music. I felt the thudding of Kit's heart keeping perfect rhythm with mine.

He'd heard my twang, my outspoken ways, my brash outbursts—and seen me freak out too many times to count.

And he still loved me. Small-town, farm-girl Texas Robin.

My parents were going to be here in a couple of weeks, and they planned to stay for a month. I couldn't wait to show them my school, introduce them to everyone, and take them around London.

I knew my daddy would be proud of me: He was going to see the same old Robin he'd sent to London. Only maybe now I was a little smarter.

Paris: Alex & Dana

One

Dana

I WAS AFRAID. Shaking in my boots afraid. The reality had finally hit home. Or I should say, it had hit Paris.

Paris, France! City of Light. City of romance. City of my dreams.

I hadn't realized until this moment as I stared out the window of my new bedroom how terrified I would be. Or how alone.

I, Dana Madison, born and raised in tiny Mustang, Texas, had never ventured beyond the Texas border, and here I was, thousands of miles from said border. It was beyond comprehension. Terribly exciting! And incredibly frightening.

I had been looking forward to this moment for so long that I was having a difficult time reconciling the terror gripping me. With a lot of cajoling, pleading, and promises never to ask for anything else as long as I lived, I'd managed to convince my parents to let me take part in the Year Abroad program. Paris had been my city of choice—for its art, but more important, for its romantic guys.

For a whole year I would go to a school in Paris—starting tomorrow. And that realization was what had me scared spitless.

I would attend a new school where I didn't know anyone! My best friend, Robin Carter, was spending the year in London. My other best friend—after all, a girl can have more than one best friend—Carrie Giovani was on her way to Rome. Maybe she was already there. I wondered if she was scared. I couldn't imagine Carrie being frightened of anything.

Of course, I hadn't expected to be frightened myself. I tried to draw comfort from the Eiffel Tower—outlined in lights—silhouetted against the night sky. The artist in me appreciated the view. The girl in me longed to see the vast Texas sky, feel the warm Texas breeze against my skin, and pick up the phone to call a friend. But long-distance phone calls were expensive and totally out of the question on a regular basis. Emergency only to friends. Once a week to parents.

I couldn't quite bring myself to classify these jitters as an emergency. Even though I thought I had a good chance of bringing up the foie gras I'd eaten for dinner. The French considered it a real gourmet item. Me, I hadn't been too thrilled when the meal was over to discover I'd wolfed down fatted goose liver.

Absorbing a culture was part of being a Year Abroad student. It required a strong stomach, a stout heart, lots of courage, and a desire for adventure. Robin, Carrie, and I had made a pact to e-mail each other at least once a day in order to keep our morale boosted—and to share these exciting moments.

I glanced around my room. The wallpaper was a mosaic of blues and purples. The host family had to guarantee that a YA student would have her own room. I couldn't believe that this one was so tiny. But that was typical for the French who lived in cities. Small houses or apartments were all this city of over two million people could find room for. Two million people. I could barely comprehend that number. My hometown bragged a population of ten thousand.

This small home had several balconies. Even my room had a balcony. I imagined a romantic French guy climbing the tree outside my room, clambering over the railing of the balcony, and reciting poetry.

Okay, so I was getting a little carried away, but it was hard not to. My bedroom had a canopied bed—so romantic! Even the poster of Justin Timberlake on the wall sent my romantic yearnings into overdrive. I had a small desk where I'd already set up my laptop computer so I could easily e-mail my friends.

My very own room. Back home in Mustang, Texas, I had to share a room with my younger sister. That hadn't always been the case. Before my parents got divorced, I had my own room, but everything changed with the divorce. My parents had to sell our family home in order to buy two houses—one small one for my mom, my sister, and me and one even smaller for my dad. I resented the divorce sometimes, felt like my parents should have tried harder to keep us together as a family. I thought of all the things we'd have if they'd pooled their money instead of having to purchase two of everything: house, furniture, appliances.

Their divorce had also added to the stress of my getting into the YA program. I'd ask Mom for permission to apply to the program, and she'd tell me to discuss it with my father. Before the divorce, she always called him "your dad." After the divorce, he became "your father." So unfriendly sounding.

When I'd ask my dad about being in the YA program, he'd tell me to talk to my mother. Same thing. Before the divorce, he called her "your mom." Then she became "your mother."

They weren't outwardly mean to each other, and I wasn't irreversibly scarred by the divorce or anything, but those small things told me they weren't in love anymore. And that sorta hurt sometimes.

I was a big believer in love. My first foray into the experience had been with Todd Haskell, and it had been a disaster. I think I wanted to be in love so badly that I convinced myself he was the one, and he turned out to be such a jerk. The final straw had been dumped in my lap the day after Valentine's Day, when he brought me a red-heart-shaped box of chocolates. I'm a sucker for chocolate, especially when it comes in a heart-shaped box with a plastic rose glued on top. But knowing that he'd waited until the day *after* Valentine's Day so he could get it half price made me feel . . . well, unloved. I figured if you really cared about someone, you didn't skimp on the things that counted—like making her feel special.

But Todd was out of my life now, and Paris was in, and with this city came the opportunity to meet, date, and fall in love with a romantic guy. I knew our time together would come to an end when I had to return home after I completed my year abroad.

But until that final moment came, I would know what it was to be loved and romanced. To have someone who was willing to pay full price for my chocolate. I could hardly wait to meet Mr. Romantic.

But before I met the perfect guy, I had to get down to the tedious task of unpacking my clothes.

A knock sounded, and I was grateful for the reprieve. I hurried across the room and opened the door. My host sister, Renée Trouvel, stood in the hallway.

"How's it going?" she asked with a wonderful French accent.

"Très bien," I responded. Very well. I hadn't taken two years of French at Mustang High for nothing.

Renée laughed. She had long, black hair and

5

dancing blue eyes. "You can practice your French on me, and I'll practice my English on you."

I sagged and smiled wearily. "I'm really too tired to concentrate on French tonight. I wish I'd had a few days to adjust before school started." But a few more days might have just made me more nervous. Besides, I'd enjoyed the layover in London. Carrie, Robin, her host brother, Kit, and I had gone to the Tower of London. And Robin had really needed the support of friends when she realized that Kit was a guy and not a girl. I was still a little worried about her. She had this crazy notion that she wanted to turn into Princess Di while she was in London—instead of just being her wonderful self.

"I haven't even started to unpack," I explained to Renée. "I was too busy admiring the spectacular view through my window."

"Do you not have a view like this from your bedroom at home?" she asked in halting English.

"Are you kidding?" I asked. "Trees, sky, and street-lights—that's about all I can see from my window."

"I thought you would see cactus and horses," she murmured, stepping farther into the room. "You know . . . cowboys."

I smiled warmly. "No cactus where I live. We do have a ranch or two outside of town, but it's probably nothing like you're imagining."

"I must go there someday," she said wistfully.

"Sure. When you visit, you can stay with me," I offered.

I walked to the bed and opened my suitcase. Renée squealed and pulled out one of my denim vests. It had ropes embroidered along the front.

"How cute!" she exclaimed. "A cowboy would wear this."

"I have a lot of western-looking clothes," I told her. "You can wear that one."

Her blue eyes grew really large. "Really?" She hugged the denim to her chest. "*Merci!* But I have nothing to let you wear."

I raised my brows. "Not true. I've been drooling over that miniskirt since I met you at the airport."

"This old thing?" she asked.

This old thing was a deep emerald green skirt that stopped at midthigh. Very chic. I had a lime green sweater that would be perfect with it. Back in Mustang, I'd be wearing shorts to class, but here the weather was already cooler than I was used to.

"Could you teach me how to tie that scarf around my neck?" I inquired. I had been admiring that fashion statement as well.

Renée touched the silk at her throat as if incredibly surprised. I worked part-time in a clothing store, and I figured I should really know how to add the little touches to items of clothing that made them seem so unique, but I'd never quite mastered it. Whenever I tied something, the bow or the knot always looked askew.

"*Oui.* I can teach you," she assured me, her eyes alight. She quickly untied the scarf and slid it from around her neck. "Come to the mirror."

I hurried to the dresser and stood before the mirror, which only showed me from the waist up. I could get to my unpacking later. Renée and I were almost the same height and build. She slipped the scarf around my neck, tied it with a tiny knot, and stepped back. *"Bon."*

Oh, it was *très bon.* With the knot on the side of my throat and the ends flowing over my shoulder, I looked sophisticated. "This is wonderful! Do it more slowly so I can watch."

Laughing, she untied the scarf and started over. She tugged on one end of the scarf. "This end goes on bottom, this end on top. The one on top goes over the one on bottom. Otherwise they both stick up like a bad-hair day."

I giggled. I'd been so afraid that I wouldn't have anything in common with my host sister, and here we were, discussing fashion accessories. She taught me several different ways to arrange the scarf. It was so exciting. Sometimes I even looked like a model. A short model, to be sure, but still a model.

"This will help me so much," I murmured, studying my stylish reflection in the mirror.

Renée wrinkled her brow. "Help you what?"

I hadn't planned to bare my soul so soon, but I felt incredibly comfortable around Renée. I spun around and met her gaze. "If I tell you, you have to promise not to laugh."

She pressed her palm over her heart. "I promise."

8

I took a deep breath and blurted out, "I want to fall in love while I'm in Paris."

"Fall in love?" she repeated.

I nodded quickly. "A year of romance like I'd never get in little Mustang, Texas. I want a guy who doesn't mumble one-word sentences like 'yep' and 'nope.' A guy who doesn't think that 'roses are red, violets are blue' is a romantic poem."

Her mouth fell open. "Are American guys like that?"

I dropped onto the edge of the bed and nodded balefully. "They are in Mustang."

"They know nothing of romance?" she asked, clearly unable to believe it. Her reaction reinforced what I'd already thought—Paris guys knew how to love right.

"They know absolutely nothing," I assured her. "It was a romantic date if my former boyfriend, Todd the Jerk Haskell, belched only three times during the meal."

Laughing, she fell across the bed and raised up an elbow. "I cannot believe this."

"Believe it," I retorted. "This year I want to experience what I will never find in Mustang. Someone who can whisper romantic French phrases into my ear. Someone who knows the art of romance."

I knew that dating a Paris guy would mean heartbreak at the end of the year when we had to say good-bye, but for this one year I would be romanced and cherished just as I had always dreamed.

Two

Dana

I STOOD IN front of the mirror the next morning, barely able to believe my eyes. My clothes were still packed, but I'd managed to find my lime green sweater. I was wearing Renée's emerald green skirt and my silver belt that I usually wore with denim, but somehow it looked right with this outfit. And the scarf was tied daintily around my neck. Renée had loaned me a hunter green felt beret. It sat jauntily on top of my red hair.

I'd applied my makeup to perfection so it hid the freckles that dotted the bridge of my nose and the rounded curves of my cheeks. My outfit of varying green shades highlighted the green hue of my eyes. I knew that I was going to turn heads today. By the end of the week Mr. Romance would be walking up to me and whispering those romantic French phrases in my ear.

A knock on the door broke into my fantasy. Renée peered into the room. "We need to eat breakfast and head to school."

I turned around slowly. "What do you think?"

"You look terrific," she assured me.

"I'm as nervous as a dog dreamin' of catchin' a rabbit," I confessed.

She laughed. "You Americans have the funniest sayings."

I smiled. "That's probably more Texan than American," I admitted.

"Even so, you don't look nervous," she told me.

I grabbed my backpack and followed her into the hallway. "I'm only going to be here a year, so it's important that I impress some guy right away," I explained.

"Love takes time," she muttered.

"I don't have time," I emphasized as we went down the stairs. Besides, I wasn't looking for an until-death-do-us-part kind of love. I only wanted romance.

"Bonjour!" Madame Trouvel said when we walked into the small kitchen. It looked much like our kitchen in Mustang. Tile-covered counters, cupboards, an island that resembled a butcher's block in the middle. *"Comment allez-vous,* Dana?"

How are you? *"Très bien,"* I assured my host mother.

"Wonderful! Sit down and eat," she ordered.

Monsieur Trouvel and Renée's sister, Geneviève, joined us. Geneviève was two years younger than Renée, and in a way she reminded me of my sister,

11

Marci. I hadn't expected to miss Marci. We fought more often than we agreed, but I guess that's what sisters are for.

I brought a blue bowl-shaped cup to my mouth and sipped café au lait. Basically it's coffee with a generous amount of milk. It warmed me, chasing away the chill of dread that was trying to creep over me. I dug into my food. If I concentrated on the moment and didn't think about the future, I thought I might make it to school without throwing up.

"Are you ready for your first day at Renée's school?" Monsieur Trouvel prodded.

So much for concentrating on the moment. My stomach knotted up at the reminder, and I knew I was finished with breakfast. I smiled kindly at Renée's father. He had dark hair like Renée and the same deep blue eyes. I hadn't expected it to be so hard to sit at a table with a complete family. "As ready as I'll ever be."

With apprehension mounting, I walked through the halls of the lycée—the French equivalent of Mustang High with a little twist. Only the top students attended. They were preparing to take the baccalaureate exams that would determine whether or not they could go to the university.

On my way to my first class I realized that I really wasn't ready for my first day at a Paris school. It was more than nerves and jitters. It was a complete lack of knowledge. I felt like I'd been dropped off on an alien planet and told, "Good luck!" just before the spaceship abandoned me.

Renée had taken me to the main office to get my schedule, my locker number, and a map of the school, showing where different classes were. Unfortunately, all the directions were written in French.

Yeah, sure, I'd had two years of French, and if someone spoke really slowly and had a slight Texas drawl, I could usually figure out what he or she was saying, but the people here didn't talk slowly, and they definitely didn't have a Texas drawl.

I don't know why I'd expected people to talk in English with a French accent. I couldn't figure out why I hadn't realized that they actually *spoke* French in France!

I guess that was the reason French guys could spout romantic French words. They talked French all the time!

I was beginning to wish I had studied more diligently in my French class back home instead of always doodling. But my hands had a life of their own, always drawing, always sketching. It was a given that if I had pencil and paper, I was going to draw something.

As I headed toward class—sculpting—I was a bit disconcerted to notice that people were paired up or grouped like friends. Renée had been wonderful showing me around, but she'd had to skedaddle to get to her math class, and it was obvious that they had cliques here—just like at home—and right now I didn't belong.

But I planned to belong and the sooner, the better. I could see guys checking me out, and I was definitely giving them a once-over.

I had developed a point system based on looks, attitude, cool clothes, smile, and a whole host of other attributes. Right now I was just making mental tallies because I didn't want to be obvious by pulling out my little notepad and taking copious notes.

With mounting anticipation, I spotted the doorway that led into my first class. This was it. The moment I had anticipated for months. I could hardly wait to sit beside the cutest French guy in the class, introduce myself in my practiced French phrases, and begin my journey toward romance.

Taking a deep breath, I stepped into the room and staggered to a stop.

No way! my mind screamed. *No way!* I was hallucinating. Having a flashback. Experiencing déjà vu. Or maybe my mind simply refused to accept that I was actually in Paris. It thought I was still in Mustang, Texas!

That was the only logical explanation. I blinked several times, but the tabloid remained unchanged. Horrifying. Excruciatingly painful, even. The last thing in the world that I wanted.

Blinking wasn't working to erase the image before me. Closing my eyes, I gave my head a quick shake. I thought of an Etch A Sketch. I just wanted to obliterate the image, wipe it from existence.

When I opened my eyes, to my profound disappointment, nothing had changed.

The room had tables, two chairs to a table. Only one chair was vacant. I couldn't believe this! One chair. The chair I would have to sit in.

One solitary chair—right beside a guy with brown hair. A guy I recognized! A guy from my high school back home.

What in the world was Alex Turner Johnson doing here?

Three

Dana

"TRYING TO CATCH flies?" Alex asked.

I snapped my mouth shut. To my absolute mortification I realized that I'd been staring at him, and he'd been rude enough not only to notice but to comment on it. So typically Mustang, Texas.

Because I had no choice, I walked toward him as if I was going to my execution. I absolutely did not want to sit by someone who spoke with a Texas accent. I dropped into the chair beside him. "What are you doing here?" I demanded.

He shrugged. "Waiting for the nude models to arrive."

I was afraid that the hinges on my jaws were going to lock up because of the way my mouth kept dropping open. I knew my eyes very nearly popped out of my head. *Nude models?*

I had expected school in Paris to be different from school in Mustang. Paris was renowned for its artwork. Much of that work involved people in what my grandmother referred to as their birthday suits, but I hadn't expected to jump into a project this intense on the first day. I felt heat suffuse my face, and I had to know. "Male or female?"

"Both," he replied in a way that made me think he was on the verge of yawning.

I couldn't believe how calmly Alex had responded. As if the most scandalous event in our young lives wasn't about to occur. I'd seen guys on the beach in skimpy swimsuits that didn't leave a lot to the imagination, but to see in the flesh what I hadn't even dared to dream about—and to see it for the first time in front of a whole class . . . with people I didn't know sitting around me. . . . No, wait, it was worse than that. I was sitting by someone who did know me, and for some reason that had my face burning even hotter. We'd both be sitting here side by side, gazing at . . .

Alex averted his face and pressed a fist to his mouth. His shoulders were jerking like a spastic chicken as he tried to contain his laughter. I narrowed my eyes, the anger roiling through me. "You're lying!" I accused.

He choked back his laughter.

"You believed me. You are so gullible," he chortled.

With my fist I pounded his shoulder, surprised

that it didn't have any give to it. The guy didn't play football on the Mustang High football team, so I'd expected him to be flab without an ounce of brawn.

"You creep," I retorted. His joking around was so typical of the immature guys in Mustang. Thank goodness I was going to be spared their presence in abundance this year. If only I'd had the good fortune to be spared his at this moment. "How did someone as immature as you get accepted into the YA program anyway?"

He stopped laughing and poked his finger into the mound of clay that sat on the table in front of him. "My parents pulled a few strings."

"I didn't even know you'd applied for the program," I murmured. I certainly didn't remember seeing him at any of the information meetings that had been held before and after the selections were made.

"It was a last-minute thing." He broke off a piece of clay and began to roll it between his fingers. He had really long fingers, and his nails were evenly clipped, not chipped or broken. I'd learned early on not to wear anything with threads that might get caught and snagged by one of Todd the Jerk Haskell's hangnails. His idea of a manicure had been to pull out his trusty pocketknife.

"You weren't on our flight—"

"Like I said, it was last minute," he interrupted, obviously annoyed. "That particular flight was already booked solid, so I had to take another one."

"Excuse me for pretending to care," I shot back.

He glanced at his watch and heaved a sigh. "This class is going to be over before it even gets started."

As if that was his cue, the teacher strolled into the room. His graying hair was pulled back into a ponytail that curled at his waist. Definitely not the style the male teachers at Mustang High wore.

And then my worst nightmare began. He began to speak—in French. Rapidly.

"Je ne comprends pas," I murmured. I don't understand. Panic seized me. I considered raising my hand and repeating myself, asking for a bit of leniency here, wanting him to issue his orders a little more slowly.

But as I glanced hastily around the room, it became obvious that I was the only one with a problem. Students were starting to work their fingers into the clay. I decided to take my cue from them. The clay had a really smooth texture. It was almost a sensual experience to knead the clay with my palms.

I darted a quick glance at Alex. He not only had long fingers, but he had large hands. They practically swallowed the clay as he shaped and molded it. His face was set in absolute concentration. It almost looked like he was trying to breathe life into the blob in front of him.

I imagined those hands caressing my cheek, massaging my neck and shoulders—whoa!

Where did that thought come from?

The last thing I wanted was for someone from

Mustang, Texas, to fulfill my fantasies for a romantic year in Paris. And I absolutely did not want Alex running his hands amok over my back.

No. I wanted someone else. A French guy.

As discreetly as I could because I didn't want Alex to know what I was up to, I studied the guys in the class.

Blonds, brunets, even a redhead. They all looked pretty serious about their project. That got them an extra point. Since art was my life, I wanted a guy who could relate, someone I could talk to about artistic endeavors.

There were a couple of really hot guys. I gave a total of twelve points for looks, and both of those guys got full credit. They were much cuter than dull Alex from Mustang. With his hair the color of mud and his soulful, brown eyes.

Tomorrow I would definitely have to get to class early so I could have the opportunity to sit by a Frenchie. This class had promise, lots of promise.

And none of those promises involved Alex Turner Johnson.

Four

Alex

DANA MADISON HAD the most delicate, elegant hands I'd ever seen. Just like a girl, she prodded the clay like she thought it would bite. Me, I was enjoying the texture of the clay and grateful for the opportunity to pound my fists into something, to squeeze and tear apart a blob. That gray goo represented my life. My life had no shape, no texture, no color.

I didn't usually have such a dreary outlook. As a matter of fact, until six weeks ago, when my parents announced that they'd enrolled me in the Year Abroad program, I'd say for the most part, I was a pretty happy guy. I'd dated a little, had good grades, and had plans for college that included a career path that would lead me straight into animated movies, working for Pixar.

Then my parents had dropped the bomb. They were getting a divorce and thought it would go easier on me if I wasn't at home while they "went through it." As if my being thousands of miles away would spare me the pain of our family falling apart.

I slammed my fist into the clay, and the table wobbled. Dana screeched and jerked back in her chair, her eyes wide.

"Gently, Monsieur Turner," the teacher scolded. I felt my entire face burn with embarrassment. "I realize that Americans are crude, but in my class you must pretend you are French."

Great, I thought. *A bigot.* I had discovered that Americans weren't real popular in Paris.

"What's wrong?" Dana whispered. "And why does he call you Monsieur *Turner* instead of Monsieur Johnson?"

I shoved the clay aside. "I'm going by my middle name while I'm here—three names is a lot in a foreign country." I didn't have to get into the whole divorce thing and how upset I was about it. "What's wrong is that this is a stupid class and a total waste of my time." I grabbed my backpack and stormed into the hallway. I turned the corner and pressed my back against the brick wall. I plowed my fingers through my hair. *That was real smart, Turner. I think your grades here transfer back home. You gotta make the best of this, dude, no matter how much you dislike being here.*

And making the best of it, in my opinion, meant getting heavily involved with a French babe.

Physical only. No emotion. No bonding. No declarations of love.

I stood in the hallway for a long time, trying to gain control over my anger and frustration. This year had barely begun, and already I hated it to the max.

The bell finally rang, and I began wandering the hall, heading for my next class. Oils. Nothing to punch, plenty to smear. For some reason, I thought of the finger painting I did as a kid. A mess of colors that made no sense, that represented nothing. Just like my life.

I shook my head to clear it as I walked into the class and took my place behind an easel. I didn't want to think about my life, or my parents' lives, or my older brother, Peter's, life. Peter was no longer living at home. He'd started going to the University of Texas last year. But my parents couldn't wait until I started college. Oh no. *Let's send Alex off to Paris so we can go ahead and get a divorce. So what if this decision ruins his last two years of high school?* My own personal way of acting out was to drop the Johnson, at least while I was in France. Three names *was* a lot to say to people who didn't speak your language. My parents didn't know—and they wouldn't have to know.

While I'd been brooding, the class had filled up quickly. And who should stroll in just as the bell rang?

Dana Madison. I couldn't believe it. Of all the schools in all of Paris, how in the world did she end up enrolled in mine? And worse than that, how had she managed to get herself into two of my classes?

Her presence here was a nightmare. I did not need—nor did I want—someone from my high school back home dogging my steps. And as fate would have it, she was late again and the only easel left was the one beside me. I'd hoped it would go to one of the French girls, but my thunderous scowl had probably chased them all away. I was going to have to watch that expression.

"Can't you get anywhere on time?" I chided as she came to sit on the stool beside mine.

"I'm having a hard time figuring out the French," she admitted, setting her backpack on the floor.

"Well, duh! This is France. What did you expect?" I retorted.

"Give me a break, will you? I don't want to sit beside you any more than you want to sit beside me," she snapped.

Ouch! That hurt. Normally it wouldn't have. Normally it would have washed right over me like the proverbial water off a duck's back. But nothing in my life had been normal since my parents' earth-shattering announcement.

I knew Dana didn't mean to reject my presence, to reject me—I didn't even know why I cared. Yes, I did. I just didn't want to think about it.

No matter how many times my parents told me that their divorce wasn't my fault, I couldn't help but think that it was. I needed a major distraction. I needed to get involved with a French babe, someone I couldn't understand, someone I wouldn't grow to love. A flash of passion, hot kisses; that's all I wanted. Nothing permanent. Just someone I could lose myself with so I could forget my parents' divorce. A French girl would be perfect for that ploy.

Sure, she'd be temporary, just for a year, but that was fine with me because the one thing I'd learned lately was that love didn't last.

The teacher, Mademoiselle Etiènne, was sweeping her paintbrush across the canvas, demonstrating the mastery of stroke. Her back was to the class, which I found incredibly convenient.

I allowed my gaze to wander around the room, weighing the merits of the female students. Eventually my gaze completed its circle and fell on Dana.

Shafts of sunlight streaked through the windows to highlight her red hair. Her hair was a shade that I couldn't describe, had never before envisioned. Did I even have that color available in my palette?

And her green eyes—like green in the spring. The gentle buds of a new leaf reaching for the sun.

She was so absorbed in what the teacher was saying, so totally captivated. And captivating.

She shifted her gaze to me. I jerked my attention to the teacher. The last thing I was interested in was having a relationship with someone from back home.

I headed for a nearby café as soon as I gathered my books from my locker after the four-thirty bell rang—signaling the end of the day. Apparently everyone else had the same plan. The line of patrons waiting to be served was half a block long. People were crammed inside the shop, and all the outside tables—with their bright red-and-yellow umbrellas open to shield the patrons from the sun—were full.

My stomach growled, and I patted it. "Sorry, old buddy," I mumbled. I was famished and figured I'd faint from hunger before I ever got a table. I'd have to seek out other means to tame this rabid starving beast.

Just as I turned to go, I saw a familiar face. Dana! Sitting alone at a table beneath an umbrella. Relief swept through me. My stomach was going to be saved from a fate worse than death after all.

I wended my way through the crowd and wove among the tables until I reached Dana. I dropped into the empty chair across from her.

"You finally got someplace early," I said as I snatched the menu from her fingers.

"You can't sit there!" she shrieked.

"Why not? I'm starving, and it's empty," I pointed out, my mouth already watering as I considered the options on the menu.

"I'm saving it for someone," she responded.

I scoffed. "Yeah, right." After only one day in school, who could she possibly know?

Leaning forward, she grabbed the menu from my fingers. "I'm meeting Renée," she insisted.

Renée? In France, Renée was a guy's name, wasn't it?

So what if it was? What did I care if she was

already dating? But oddly, it bugged me.

"Is this guy in one of your classes?" I asked, trying to sound uninterested, wondering why I had to try when I *was* totally uninterested.

Something that reminded me of the cunning look of a fox filled her eyes.

She tossed her head, the kind of move that a girl with long hair would make. I wondered briefly if she'd forgotten that her hair was short.

"No, I met Renée shortly after my flight touched down. We had an instant rapport. As a matter of fact, we were together last night until after midnight."

I really didn't want to hear about her date with some Frenchie. I figured I should probably move to a table with a Parisian girl, where I wouldn't have to worry about conversation. I glanced around. The place was packed like a can of sardines. It was either this table or the line.

I leaned forward and held out a hand imploringly. "Look, Dana, I'm starving. I missed lunch."

She quirked a delicate brow.

I grimaced. "All right. I'm having a hard time reading the French too. I couldn't find the cafeteria."

A bubble of laughter erupted from her throat. For some reason, it made me want to laugh, and I hadn't felt like laughing in over six weeks.

"Come on—just let me place an order," I pleaded, clasping my hands and shaking them in front of her. "I'll wolf it down and be out of here before this René guy ever shows up. Have pity. I'm a stranger in a strange land."

She laughed harder. She had a really pretty laugh. Light and airy. It kept washing over me in waves.

"Please," I begged. "Please." I began to gasp and rasp like a man crawling across the desert. "I'm starving. Food. I need food. *Le menu, s'il te plaît.*"

She thrust the menu at me. "You're pathetic. People are staring."

"*Merci,* mademoiselle." Triumphant, I leaned back and studied the menu. When the waitress came over, I ordered a couple of sandwiches. I wasn't certain what was in them and didn't want to drag out my English-French dictionary in front of Dana. I knew the bread was a croissant. I just hoped whatever fixings came in the middle weren't going to make me regret trying to act like I wasn't an ignorant tourist.

I watched Dana sip something that looked like lemonade but probably wasn't. I didn't remember her being so cute back in Mustang. I cleared my throat. "So how does Todd feel about you being all the way over here?"

Her green eyes popped open wide. "Why would I care?"

I felt the heat rush to my face. "I thought the two of you were an item."

"A discarded item," she responded.

"Hey, I'm sorry."

She held up a hand. "Don't be. When you start

at the bottom of the food chain, the only place to go is up."

I fought back a smile. I never had been able to figure out what she saw in the guy anyway. I mean, he wasn't an absolute loser, but the guy seemed more obsessed with riding bulls than dating. He was severely bowlegged.

"I didn't know you had an interest in art," I remarked. She'd been in my sketching class as well that afternoon. That gave us three classes together. Fortunately in the sketching class, though, someone had taken the chair beside me before Dana arrived, so I was spared her nearness as Madame Trudi explained the process of sketching and gave us our first assignment.

"I always took art as my elective at Mustang High." She furrowed her brow. "I don't remember having you in any art classes."

"Are you kidding?" I inquired. "And have the guys think I was a pansy?" I leaned forward conspiratorially. "So let's just keep my little foray into the art world between us when we get back home, okay?"

"No one would think you were a pansy," she insisted.

"Yeah, right. Most of the guys at Mustang think a smiley face is a work of art."

She giggled. Man, I liked that sound.

"That is so true," she responded.

"I mean, the guys are either into football or riding bulls, and the really macho guys do both," I explained.

"I can't see you on a bull," she commented. "But I could see you on the football team."

I sighed heavily. "My mom had a friend who played college football. He got tackled, snapped his neck, and was paralyzed. My mom forbid me or my brother to play football."

Dana furrowed her brow. "Her friend's accident must have been hard for your mom. I can certainly understand where she's coming from. Still, there's basketball, baseball, and track."

I shook my head. "No time for school sports."

"You make time for what's important," she pointed out.

"Exactly." I leaned back as the waitress set my sandwiches in front of me. "And school sports are not important to me."

Gingerly I lifted the top of one sandwich and peered at its insides.

"Don't know what you ordered, do you?" she teased.

"Yeah, I know what I ordered. Croissant sandwiches. I just don't know what's between the layers of bread," I confessed.

She laughed again, that remarkable laugh.

I bit into the sandwich, grateful to discover it was turkey.

"Uh, listen," she began hesitantly.

I finished chewing and swallowed. She looked really uncomfortable, and for one horrifying moment I was afraid that she knew about my parents' divorce. I'd been too ashamed to tell anyone, but in a small town like Mustang, gossip can spread like a brushfire.

With the tip of her elegant finger, she wiped the dew off her glass. "We had to put our clay projects on a table at the back of the room. I put yours away. It'll be easy for you to find tomorrow. It's the one that's not even beginning to look like anything yet."

Guilt pricked my conscience. "Ah, man, thanks. I really appreciate you doing that for me. I'm sorry I went postal——"

She held up a hand. "I understand completely."

Huh? How could she? Unless she knows about the divorce.

"I didn't expect it to be so hard to adjust to a new school, a new city, and a new family either," she added.

"Yeah." *A new family,* I thought. Once I adjusted here, I'd have to adjust back home. "I think all the classes are pretty good," I added, wanting to shift the subject away from my adjustments. I didn't know if I ever would adjust to my life A.D. After Divorce.

"I was surprised that we already have an assignment in sketching class," she admitted. "What are you going to sketch?"

"The Eiffel Tower," I said without hesitation.

She rolled her eyes. "That is so expected. So boring."

Before I had a chance to tell her my complete plans for the sketch, a girl with long, black hair and blue eyes dragged over a chair from another table and joined us.

31

"Hi, Renée," Dana said. "Meet Alex Turner from Mustang High."

Renée was a girl? I'd been deceived. Dana had knowingly let me believe Renée was a guy.

Dana looked incredibly cute with her smug expression. I had a feeling she was paying me back for my nude-model prank in our first class. She'd been cute then too and so obviously horrified at the thought of looking at a nude model.

I'd felt almost guilty about teasing her.

I could tell now that she had enjoyed my initial baffled expression, enjoyed more the fact that I realized I'd been had.

She'd tilted up her nose, and her eyes were challenging me to admit I'd fallen for her ploy, hook, line, and sinker.

I hadn't known Dana well back in Mustang, and now I was wondering why I'd paid so little attention to her there. She was intriguing.

Whoa! I didn't want to travel that route.

My goal this year was a French babe. Not some girl from Mustang High.

Five

Dana

I ABSOLUTELY COULD not believe the way Renée flirted with Alex—like he was something special!

Obviously it was a case of not realizing what you have. Renée was surrounded by romantic French guys all the time, so I figured she found Alex intriguing simply because of the fact that he was so utterly boring.

And a liar! He'd apparently forgotten his promise to wolf down his food and hightail it out of there. I really wanted to talk to Renée about the best place to meet guys. And I absolutely could not do that with Alex in attendance. No way.

I tapped my fingers impatiently on the table, but the guy didn't seem to be taking the hint. Dense. So completely dense.

I couldn't believe that he'd actually made me

laugh with his confession, reluctantly given, that he was having a hard time understanding the French and then the way he'd looked at that sandwich—fear clearly etched in his face.

I hadn't spent much time talking to Alex at Mustang. We'd had a class or two together, and we'd occasionally said hi when we passed in the hallway—if we weren't talking to someone else at the time.

But I really didn't know much about him. And didn't want to.

I certainly didn't want to spend my year abroad getting chummy with Alex Turner Johnson—or just plain Alex Turner as he wanted to be called—when there were romantic French guys to while away the hours with.

"Football games," he murmured, shoving his crumb-filled plate aside and smiling at Renée. "I think I'll miss the Friday night football games the most."

Was he trying to do a number on her, impress her with an athletic ability he didn't possess? "You don't play football," I pointed out.

He jerked his gaze to me. "I watch the games."

Oh, right. Why had I been so quick to jump on his case? Because he was interfering with my goal. Still, I couldn't stop myself from commenting, "I already miss the football games."

Alex looked at Renée, his eyes sparkling with excitement. "There's nothing like a game on a cold night."

"With a blanket draped around you and your best friends, all of you snuggling close," I added, thinking of all the Friday nights I had sat huddled between Carrie and Robin. We'd yelled at the top of our lungs until we were hoarse while the Mustang High Mustangs had made us proud. We'd drunk hot chocolate from a thermos.

"Remember last year's homecoming game?" Alex asked.

My heart actually began to pound, and I could hear the crowds. "Who could forget that?" I enthused. I touched Renée's hand. "The score was twelve to fourteen with forty-eight seconds left in the game. We were behind."

"And the opposing team had the ball," Alex said excitedly.

I couldn't believe how cute Alex was when he was talking about something he enjoyed. Something I enjoyed as well.

"And they fumbled!" I cried, trying to distract myself from the glow in his eyes.

"Jackson Lamont ran the ball down," Alex explained.

We both threw our arms in the air and yelled, "Touchdown!"

Heat suffused my face. Alex turned red and averted his gaze. People were staring at us. Renée was laughing.

"I can see why you miss it," she said.

"Uh, yeah . . . w-well," Alex stammered, reaching down and grabbing his backpack. "I gotta go. Thanks for letting me share your table."

He beat a hasty retreat, and was I ever glad. I was certain it was just shared memories that were causing this warm flood of feelings I had toward him. I couldn't like him—well, I could like him—but not in *that* way. Not like the image that suddenly hit me.

Alex Turner and I sitting on a cold metal bench wrapped in a blanket, snuggling close, at a football game!

The Musée du Louvre.

I was thrilled when Renée suggested that we visit the museum. I figured guys interested in art would frequent the place. Cute French guys. It was the perfect place to guy watch.

I was grateful that Renée had made the suggestion after Alex left the café. I was beginning to despair, afraid the guy would never finish eating. Three classes with Alex were enough—a meal with him almost too much.

Sure, I had enjoyed talking about home, but I didn't plan to spend the most monumental year of my life hanging out with someone from Mustang. I'd done that for sixteen years. Enough, already. Now I needed a break. And more, I needed a romantic Paris guy.

And where better to look than an art museum?

One of the most romantic things about Paris in my opinion was the abundance of gardens. They were beautiful and everywhere. Le Jardin des Tuileries surrounds the Louvre. French landscaping is an art form, and I realized these magnificent gardens were no exception as we walked through them on our way to the Louvre.

The museum itself was fascinating beyond my wildest dreams. It dated back to medieval times, and French kings had constantly renovated it and built onto it until it was huge: a myriad of buildings, 140 exhibition rooms, and eight miles of galleries.

As we wandered from room to room, I felt like I was in heaven—artist heaven. The art collection was incredible, the most important in the world. I found myself staring at original masterpieces like Leonardo da Vinci's *Mona Lisa* and forgetting my mission: to scout out the guys.

I imagined strolling through the Louvre with a guy who could actually appreciate all this. Todd's idea of artwork was stick figures.

Renée and I were engrossed in a sculpture titled *The Dying Slave*. A work by Michelangelo.

"I wouldn't mind meeting the guy who posed for this," I whispered to Renée.

"I think he is long dead," Renée whispered back.

"I'll settle for one of his descendants," I told her.

She smiled. "You think he would be romantic?"

"Well, let's see." I reached into my backpack and pulled out my notebook. "I have a ranking system. Zero is absolute loser in that area. Three is the best. So what should we give this guy for hair?"

She laughed lightly. "Since he seems to have plenty, I guess a three."

"I agree. Eyes, I'll have to give him a two because I don't know what color they are." The marble statue was all white. "I think blue is the most romantic."

"Eye color is romantic?" she asked, clearly amused.

"Sure. For physique, this guy definitely gets a three. Then I have personality broken down. Humor?" I allowed my gaze to wander over the statue.

"Well," Renée murmured. "He's not smiling."

What in the world would a dying slave have to smile about? Still, I thought he appeared stoic. "Okay. I'll give him a one. Intelligence?"

"Hard to say."

"Romantic?"

"Very!" we both said at the same time, and giggled. All in all, I knew I wouldn't be dating the statue. But this little exercise was demonstrating that using my point system wasn't going to be the perfect solution. A lot of things you didn't discover until it was too late—just as I had with Todd.

"Come on," I urged. "Let's find some real guys to evaluate."

We began walking toward the next room.

"I'm not sure love should be based on points," Renée explained.

"That's because you live in a world of romantic guys," I declared as we neared the doorway. "I only have this year to enjoy romance, so I have to find the best-possible guy. The one who can fulfill all my fantasies."

Out of the corner of my eye I saw a really cute guy. Tall. Blond. I made notations in my notebook, thinking he might be worth introducing myself to. I glanced back over my shoulder at him. Definitely hot.

Wham!

Someone rammed into me—or I rammed into him. My notebook and pencil went flying out of my hands, landing on the floor with a thud and a ping. Strong hands wrapped around my arms and steadied me. I jerked back my head.

To my horror, I was staring at Alex Turner.

"You okay?" he asked.

"Why don't you watch where you're going?" I snapped, even though I was the one who hadn't been watching.

"Sorry. I'm having a hard time dragging my gaze from the statues." He bent down and picked up my notebook and pencil. He furrowed his brow. "Why are you working a math problem when you're surrounded by all this exquisite artwork?"

I snatched my notebook from his fingers. "It's none of your business." His brow creased more deeply, and I didn't want him figuring out what my *math problem* really was. I decided to change the subject quickly. "Are you here to get ideas for your art project—something other than the predictable Eiffel Tower?"

"No, I'm definitely doing the tower," he insisted.

This guy was incredibly unimaginative. "That is so boring!"

"It's a Paris landmark."

"Exactly," I pointed out. "Don't you think it's been done a thousand times?"

"Not the way I'm going to do it," he insisted.

"What? Are you going to try and imitate Picasso?" I chided.

"No, it'll be an original Turner, which means it'll have a unique perspective."

"Oh yeah, right," I scoffed.

"Why don't you come with me tomorrow after school to the place where I plan to sketch the tower?" he challenged, a formidable glint in his eyes.

I love challenges, and for some reason, I really wanted to prove to this guy that he was as uninspiring as our hometown. I gave him a cocky smile. "Okay."

"Great," he replied, although he didn't sound like he really thought it was great. He was probably already having second thoughts because he realized how mundane his sketch would be—and I'd witness that revelation.

"I'll catch up with you tomorrow," he said just before he turned on his heel and walked away.

With a sinking feeling in the pit of my stomach, it hit me exactly what I'd agreed to do.

My first date in Paris was with an American, a boring American from Mustang!

Six

Dana

I TOSSED THE clothes from my suitcase into the dresser drawers. If I didn't keep my hands busy, I would pull out my hair. I couldn't believe that I'd actually agreed to go somewhere with Alex Turner.

What had I been thinking? Obviously I hadn't been thinking.

He was so smug about his desire to draw the Eiffel Tower. I guess I wanted to be present when he realized that I was right and he was so totally wrong.

That was a lousy reason. Why did I care what he drew? I didn't. I didn't care anything about him. I wasn't interested in him. If he flew home tomorrow, my life would be complete.

I slammed a drawer shut just as someone knocked on my door. Renée walked in and plopped onto my bed. "So tell me everything about Alex," she demanded.

I zipped up my suitcase and moved it to the floor so I could sit on the edge of the mattress. "What do you care? You have a boyfriend."

"Jean-Claude is wonderful, *oui,* but I am fascinated by this Alex," she commented. "He is the first American guy I have ever talked to."

My eyes almost popped out of my head. "Fascinated? He is so uninteresting."

She shrugged and flipped her long, black hair over her shoulder. "I thought he was cute. What scores would you give him with your rating system?"

"All zeros." But even as I spoke, I knew I was lying.

"Come on. Let's see how he rates," she prodded.

"It doesn't matter how he rates," I pointed out. "He isn't French."

"Afraid you'll discover he has a good score?" she challenged.

Sneering—half jokingly—I reached for my notepad and pencil. I stretched out on my stomach. Renée rolled over so our shoulders touched. For a brief moment I thought of Robin and Carrie—and all the times we'd lain on the bed together like this, looking through teen magazines or our high-school yearbooks.

"Eyes?" Renée asked.

"Well, as a rule, I only give a three to blue eyes. . . ." But Alex had eyes the color of melted chocolate, and I was a sucker for chocolate. So I generously gave him a three.

"Smile?" Renée prodded.

"It's imperfect," I stated, my pencil hovering over the paper. His smile was lopsided. The right side always went up higher than the left. It was kind of intriguing, made him look a little shy. I put a three in the smile column.

He had smothered his laughter in class, so I couldn't rate it fairly. Hair. Brown like the mud in a creek back home. Two. I erased the two. He wore it short, and it never looked messed up. Three. I thought of what it would feel like to run my fingers through it. I didn't like how much that thought appealed to me. I erased the three and put back the two.

"What are you doing?" Renée asked.

"Trying to be objective." But the task seemed almost impossible.

I had to give him a one for temper after his angry display in sculpting class that day. A three for manners since he'd included Renée in our conversation and he'd picked up my notebook and pencil when I dropped them. He liked art. Three. Intelligent. Three. It stood to reason that anyone who appreciated art was intelligent. Romantic. A big, fat zero.

I smiled triumphantly. Where it counted the most, he was an absolute loser.

"He'll never do," I commented.

"Are you looking for someone with perfect scores?" Renée asked.

"You bet," I confirmed. "And French."

"Want to double-date?" Renée suddenly asked.

I laughed lightly. "I haven't found Mr. Romantic yet, but when I do—"

"A practice date," she interrupted. "So you can get used to the French dating scene."

"I'm not sure who I'd ask," I confided.

"I could have my boyfriend ask one of his friends to take you out," she offered.

Quickly I sat up. "Do you think he'd do that?"

She grinned. "*Oui.* Jean-Claude is very romantic. He'll find someone good for you."

"This will be great!" I told her. "I really don't want to blow it when I discover the real thing, and Todd wasn't exactly good practice material for how a date should be handled."

As we began discussing possibilities, I turned over my notepad. It bothered me to look at Alex's scores, confused me to even think about him.

The next morning I arrived at sculpting class early. I quickly scouted the room and took a seat beside an absolute dream guy. Blond and blue-eyed, he was the complete opposite of Alex. So his score shot up before I'd even finished assessing him.

He didn't have Alex's broad shoulders or Alex's height, but that was okay. He was French.

He took my hand and kissed my fingers. "*Ma chère,* welcome to Paris."

I was melting. How romantic. *"M-Merci,"* I stammered.

Great going, Dana. Impress the guy with your lack of sophistication. There were times when I really resented coming from a small town.

"I'm Dana Madison," I told him.

He smiled, a three-point smile. "We all know who you are. I am Pierre Robards."

I repeated his name. It was fantastic, not dull sounding like Alex.

I glanced over my shoulder, and who should I see but the bane of my existence. Alex Turner was talking with a beautiful French girl, making the girl laugh like a hyena. Good, maybe he'd cancel on this afternoon. I was accustomed to guys bailing at the last minute. Todd had repeatedly done that. If one of the guys called with a better offer than a night out with his girl—like driving trucks through mud—he was there.

I knew instinctively that French guys would be too romantic to cancel a date—for any reason. Although I would be here for only a year, I knew whoever I settled my heart on would follow me back to Texas, would swim the Atlantic and the Gulf of Mexico in order to be with me.

So maybe I had an overactive imagination where love was concerned. I mean, I understood that he wouldn't actually follow me across an ocean. But he would be romantic, and he would give me a year that I could hold close for the rest of my life.

"Messieurs! Mesdemoiselles!" The teacher tapped his knuckles on the desk. Then he told us in perfect French that we had to sit in the chair we had sat in yesterday. His seating chart was made.

My stomach dropped to the floor. I wanted to stay where I was. I was on the verge of offering Monsieur Henri an eraser or some Wite-Out when he snapped, *"Vite! Vite!"*

Hurry! Hurry!

I trudged to the table where Alex sat and dropped into the chair beside him.

With a wide grin, he leaned over. He jabbed his thumb over his shoulder. "Pierre over there? Before class, I saw him in the hall with a lip lock on some girl—" He shook his head. "Man, they probably had to bring in the Jaws of Life to separate them so they could get to class."

Disappointment hit me hard. "He has a girlfriend?"

"Either that or they say howdy different over here."

"They do say howdy differently," I shot back, wanting to wipe that smirk off his face. "They say *bonjour.*"

I was fuming. Not so much because Pierre had a girlfriend, but because Alex had witnessed my mooning over a guy who was unavailable. I was allowed to make mistakes. I just didn't want Alex Turner to witness them—or more, to comment on them. For all I knew, the girl he'd been talking with might have been lip locked before class as well.

With anger still too close to the surface, I started to mold the clay, working to finish up the project

I'd started yesterday—a vase. Unfortunately, it looked more like a lopsided bowl.

"Hey, by the way," Alex whispered conspiratorially.

Startled that he had leaned close enough for me to feel his warm breath skim my neck and to have that same breath send a shiver along my spine, I crumbled one side of my project. Great! Just great. Now I'd have to rebuild. I hadn't planned to have someone from my school back home witness any mistakes I made.

"You're gonna need a bike for our excursion this afternoon," he added.

I glared at him. "Where am I supposed to get a bike?"

"Check with your host sister," he suggested calmly.

"Think you could have told me sooner?" I asked.

"I'm telling you now," he pointed out. "You've got all day to find a bike."

Just like a guy not to realize all that was involved in going out. They never got ready for things. They just went as they were.

Why in the heck couldn't Alex Turner have gone to London like my friend Robin or Rome like my friend Carrie? Why Paris, where he could torment me without even trying?

After school I went straight to my host home. I'd seen Renée at lunch, and she'd told me that I could use her bicycle. How typical of a guy to remember at the last moment that a girl needed to prepare for a date.

Whoa! I stopped that thought. This excursion, as Alex called it, was not a date. No way. We were just going to work on our project for sketching class. Hopefully I could find something other than the Eiffel Tower to sketch. I refused to be boring Dana from dull Mustang.

But before I went on the field trip to Ho-hum or wherever Alex planned to go, I needed to get psyched up. And my best friends were the greatest at helping me accomplish that goal.

We'd finally figured out how to get into a private chat room. It was almost like talking on the phone, only our fingers did all the work. I sat at my desk, turned on my computer, logged on to the Internet, and accessed our private room. They were there and waiting.

Dana: Hey, guys!
Robin: Dana! Good to see you! :)
Carrie: Dana, how is Paris?
Dana: Paris is beautiful. How is Rome?
Carrie: Interesting. I'm engaged in a little experiment with a guy named Antonio.
Robin: What kind of experiment?
Carrie: Teaching him a lesson. Unfortunately, the better I know him, the more I'm regretting this brilliant idea I had. He hates Americans. And he doesn't know I'm American.
Dana: What?
Robin: What?

Carrie: It's a long story. How's your host brother, Robin?
Robin: He has a girlfriend.
Dana: Bummer. :(
Robin: Her name is Brooke, and she's beautiful. :P

I laughed. Robin had just stuck out her tongue at me. I felt for her. I'd met her host brother while I was in London. Kit was really cute, and he had the nicest British accent.

Carrie: Dana, got any dates yet?

I groaned. I'd failed to mention my lapse of judgment when I e-mailed them yesterday. Carrie, of course, would ask. I debated what to tell them.

Dana: Not really. I'm going on an outing with Alex this afternoon.
Carrie: Alex Turner Johnson?
Robin: Thought he was boring.
Dana: He is. The purpose of our outing is to show him exactly how dull he is.
Carrie: Why bother?

Good question. Trust Carrie to get to the heart of the matter.

Carrie: Hello, Dana! Why aren't you answering? You don't like him, do you?
Dana: No way!

And I didn't like him. At least, not in the boy-girl kind of way that Carrie meant. My point system proved that Alex wasn't the one for me. I glanced at my watch. Yikes! Alex was going to be here at any minute.

I sat on the front steps that led into Renée's house. The houses on this street were all brick, very narrow in the front, and hemmed in by houses on either side. So different from my home back in Mustang, which had a relatively large yard and space between it and the other houses.

Renée's bike was leaning against the wall beside me. I'd thrown on a navy blue sweat suit because the weather was already cool in Paris. Pleasantly cool, but I figured it would be close to dark by the time we got back, and it would be much cooler then. I wore a baseball cap too.

I glared at the bicycle. I couldn't remember the last time I'd ridden a bike. I hoped that I remembered how.

I heard the whir of wheels, turned, and froze.

Alex brought his bicycle to a grinding halt only inches away from me. He wore an honest-to-gosh cyclist's outfit. The shorts and the jersey were hugging his body like a second skin. It looked like he'd probably had to melt down his body and pour it into those clothes to get them on. The muscles on his calves were well-defined—just like the muscles carved onto the marble statues I'd seen yesterday.

50

And his thighs looked rock hard—like granite. I swallowed.

"Don't you have a helmet?" he asked.

I snapped my gaze to his. Gosh. Even his shoulders looked firm. I remembered being surprised when I'd punched him yesterday. I was stunned. "You cycle for real, don't you?"

He removed his helmet. His brown hair was plastered to his head. "Yeah. As a matter of fact, we're going to cycle over one of the roads that Lance Armstrong rode when he won the Tour de France in 1999."

I had watched the Tour de France that year, amazed that a person who had recently conquered cancer had managed to win the most prestigious cycling race in the world. Lance Armstrong was an amazing individual. I would have gladly told Alex that I admired Armstrong if I weren't so upset with Alex.

"You told me that you didn't have time for sports," I reminded him indignantly.

"I said I didn't have time for *school* sports. Mustang doesn't have a cycling team," he remarked. He extended his helmet. "You can wear my helmet."

That action seemed a little too personal, and I definitely did not want to get personal with this guy. I backed up a step. "That's okay. I'll be fine."

"Dana, it's really dangerous to cycle without a helmet," he said seriously, like a parent lecturing a child.

"It's okay for you to be in danger but not me?" I shot back.

"This excursion was my idea. I'd feel bad if anything happened to you," he said quietly, as if he was embarrassed to admit it.

"I kinda like the idea of you feeling guilty," I said.

"And I prefer the idea of you not getting hurt. Let's switch headgear," he suggested.

If I were honest, I wasn't all that confident in my ability to keep the bike upright. I just hoped that before we were done, I wouldn't regret not having shin guards and elbow pads. I handed him my cap, took his helmet, and settled it into place.

He grinned, that lopsided, cute grin. "That's some stunning outfit."

"This isn't a date," I pointed out. But I wished that I had worn something a little nicer. I hadn't even bothered to freshen up my makeup. What was I thinking? What did I care? This guy was Alex Turner. American. Not French.

I watched while he shoved my cap into one of the pockets on the back of his jersey. Indignation ran through me. "Aren't you going to wear my cap?"

He shook his head slightly. "Pink really isn't my color."

"But it makes such a fashion statement," I exclaimed.

He blushed. "A fashion statement I can do without, thanks all the same. Come on. We've stalled long enough. Follow me," he ordered, and began pedaling.

I grabbed Renée's bicycle, hopped on, and started after him.

We cycled out of the city, alongside the lush green countryside. I was embarrassed because Alex had to keep slowing down so I could catch up to him. He'd even walked up a couple of hills with me, pushing his bike and mine. Of course, he'd only done that after he'd reached the top of the hill, glanced back, and realized I was fighting an uphill battle that I probably wasn't going to win. The guy was so totally in shape that I couldn't help but be impressed.

I remembered all the riders whizzing by during the broadcast of the Tour de France, and it was obvious to me that Alex was pretty durn close to being in their league.

By the time we arrived at the hilltop where he finally stopped, I was breathing hard, and my muscles were trembling.

He looked like he'd just taken a Sunday stroll.

"You took that curve back there awfully fast," I chastised as I took off the helmet.

He touched a little monitor on the handlebars of his bike. "Forty-two miles an hour."

"You are serious about this," I murmured.

"Actually, I'd like to ride in the Tour de France someday," he said as he took our bikes and leaned them against a tree.

I was still catching my breath. He removed

his backpack and took out a blanket, then spread the blanket over the ground. I slipped my backpack off my shoulders. I had my sketch pad and my pencil, but that was about it. I couldn't imagine trying to cycle while carrying anything else.

He glanced over his shoulder. "Sit down."

I dropped onto the blanket, grateful for the opportunity to rest my legs. Alex handed me a bottle of juice. Nothing had ever tasted sweeter as I squirted the liquid into my mouth. And it hit me that he'd put a lot of thought into this excursion—even though it wasn't a date.

"I've got some goat cheese here, some apples, a baguette, a few other things. Just help yourself," he offered as he spread out the snacks.

"You thought of everything," I murmured, breaking off a piece of the crusty bread and some cheese. To my great surprise, I was famished.

He gave me that lopsided grin. "I get hungry when I cycle."

I smiled back. "I can see why. You don't exactly do a leisurely ride."

His face burned red as if my observation embarrassed him.

"What do you think of the view?" he asked.

I looked past him, and the breath backed up in my lungs. It was the first moment I'd actually looked around to see where we were. "Oh my gosh."

From where we sat, I could see the Eiffel Tower, framed by trees and deep blue sky. "It's beautiful," I whispered in awe.

"Worth sketching?" he asked.

"Definitely," I responded without thinking. Then I shifted my gaze to him.

He looked so pleased with himself. He settled back against the tree and picked up his sketch pad. "Guess you could sketch a tree," he teased.

I took my sketch pad out of my backpack. "I could. But I won't."

"You're rare, Dana," he said quietly.

I snapped my gaze to his. My heart was pounding in my chest. I didn't like the way he was studying me. Too intently, intensely. "Rare?" I squeaked.

"A girl who admits when she's wrong." He gave me a cocky grin that broke the mood.

Thank goodness.

"I'm so seldom wrong that I don't have a problem admitting when I am," I responded haughtily.

He laughed then, a deep, booming laugh. It echoed between the trees, echoed around my heart. His laughter was a definite three. Warm and full of life. I wished that I hadn't realized that.

I turned my attention back to the Eiffel Tower. "We'd better get busy here. It'll be dark soon."

I started sketching like crazy. The sooner I finished, the sooner we'd leave. And the sooner I'd be out of the presence of Alex Turner.

I got confused whenever I was near him. He was

from Mustang. That fact, in and of itself, guaranteed that he would not be romantic.

And yet here I was on a hilltop outside of Paris, gazing at the Eiffel Tower, an unexpected picnic spread before me . . . and a helmet resting beside my thigh because he didn't want me to get hurt. Even though it meant exposing himself to the dangers of a head injury.

I knew guys from Mustang. Had dated one. Romance was foreign to them. Alex was a definite contradiction. I couldn't figure him out, and I kept telling myself that I didn't want to.

I drew lines and shaded and worked hard to concentrate on the drawing. Anything to stop me from noticing the guy sitting against the tree, sketching as well. I didn't want to notice the way his hand swept over the paper or the deep furrow in his brow.

Or the way the muscles beneath his jersey quivered. There should be a law against clothes that fit that snugly. They were too distracting.

An eternity seemed to pass before my sketch was complete. Relief coursed through me. This nondate that was closer to a date than anything I'd experienced with Todd was about to come to an end. I held up my creation for Alex to see. "What do you think?"

He grinned and took my pad. I watched him run a critical eye over the lines and shadows I'd drawn.

"Hey, this is really good," he said, his voice reflecting admiration.

My heart did a little somersault. It was the artist in me that longed for his approval, I told myself. Not the girl.

"Let me see yours," I prodded.

His face turned red, and he shook his head. He handed my pad back to me and closed his own. "Mine's not that great."

"Let me see," I insisted.

He shoved it into his backpack. "It's really amateurish."

"You have to expect that," I explained. "You haven't taken any art classes before."

He started to put away the remains of our picnic. I was really pleased with my sketch, but I felt bad that it had made him feel like his wasn't any good. "It takes lots of practice to draw well," I said kindly, encouragingly.

"I know." He moved closer as he gathered the last of the items and put them in his backpack.

I raised up on my knees, preparing to get off the blanket. My gaze fell on the horizon, and I stilled.

The majestic sunset cast a golden glow over Paris. I'd never seen anything so spectacular. Or so romantic. Picture-postcard perfection. I forgot to breathe.

I smiled warmly and turned to Alex. "Thank you for sharing this place with me," I said softly.

He was so close, his eyes so rich a brown, like

the most expensive chocolate imaginable. I felt like I was drowning in those eyes.

"Do you think a true artist could paint this view without imagining a couple kissing?" he asked quietly.

I slowly shook my head, captivated by his nearness. I couldn't remember Todd ever getting close to me and just hovering, waiting, creating an anticipation I couldn't explain.

Alex inched closer. "The kiss doesn't have to mean anything, but it should be there. Don't you think?"

I wasn't thinking at all. I was just immersed in his presence, the artistry of the moment. I nodded slightly.

He lowered his mouth to mine. His lips were soft and tender, not at all what I'd expected. Gentle, even. Todd had kissed like we were having a race, fast and hard, let's get to the finish line as quickly as we can so we can start over.

Alex kissed like there was no finish line, no rush.

If he gives this kind of kiss when it doesn't mean anything, I thought, *a real kiss from him . . . would be painted in colors so warm, deep, and vibrant that it would never be forgotten.*

Seven

Alex

I FLOPPED BACK on my bed in my small bedroom at Jacques's house. I stuffed my pillow beneath my head and glared at the ceiling. Kissing Dana had been a major mistake.

I couldn't figure out what had come over me. The artist in me had appreciated the view, the way the setting sun had cast a golden halo around her. . . .

But the male in me had been drawn to Dana as if there was no other girl on earth.

Stupid! Stupid! Stupid!

I'd been like a mosquito hovering just beyond a bug zapper, and then suddenly it's lured in and . . . zap! It's all over. In that one second everything changes.

The mosquito is burned to a crisp. I was a little more fortunate. But not by much.

Dana had definitely zapped me.

I jerked her pink hat off my head. I'd forgotten to give it back to her, and once I was safely hidden away in my room, I'd put it on. I couldn't explain why. It just made me feel close to her.

That closeness I definitely did not need.

Sitting up, I tossed the hat so it landed on the bedpost and did a little twirl. I grabbed my backpack from where I'd dropped it earlier at the end of the bed. I jerked open the zipper and pulled out my sketch pad. I shuffled through the pages until I found the sketch I'd drawn on the hilltop.

The lines were perfect, and not because I'd drawn them perfectly. They were perfect before I ever put them on paper.

The soft curve of Dana's mouth. The sweep of her thick, auburn lashes. The dozen freckles that dotted her nose and circled her cheeks.

Man, I'd never expected to think freckles were attractive, but on Dana they were like . . . highlights.

I knew that with art, it was often the smallest aspect of the work that made the difference. Details were important. Small details the most important.

So why was I becoming obsessed with little spots of brown that dusted the bridge of Dana's nose?

Because she had a cute nose.

And an adorable laugh. And eyes that sparkled constantly.

And a wonderful sense of humor. I couldn't remember when I'd last laughed. But when she had told me that she was so rarely wrong . . . Her comment wasn't that funny . . . but the way she'd said it as if she honestly believed it but understood that it wasn't true at the same time. I couldn't stop myself from bursting out laughing.

I had taken her to that hilltop to prove myself. From a particular vantage point, I could draw a captivating sketch of the Eiffel Tower. Instead I'd found myself enthralled with her.

To the extent that I had wanted to kiss her—desperately. I hadn't expected her lips to be so pliant. So warm. So welcoming. I'd become lost in her. Completely forgetting about my parents' divorce for the first time in weeks.

For the briefest of moments, I wasn't sad anymore. Or unhappy.

My life had been filled with all the colors on an artist's palette.

Whoa! These thoughts were definitely going beyond heavy. Dana was a girl from back home. The last one I wanted to kiss.

I did not want a relationship that involved feelings or a girl who managed to arouse fanciful thoughts. Dana was definitely not what I needed.

Relationships did not last, and I wasn't going to let a fun, smiling, artistic girl make me believe that they did.

Walking rapidly down the street, the cool evening air surrounding me, I knew the signs of panic. I'd felt them when my parents had told me that they were getting a divorce. My life as I'd known it until that moment sort of exploded like a supernova.

Leaving behind a black hole.

I felt like I was free-falling more deeply into that hole. All because I had kissed Dana—and more because she had kissed back. She had responded so sweetly. I needed to make sure that she understood that kiss on the hilltop—given to her during a moment of weakness or insanity or maybe both—meant absolutely nothing. *Rien.*

A sane person would have waited to talk to her at school the next day.

As a panicked person, I felt the need to talk to her that night, that moment, that very second.

She didn't live that far away, and it was close to eight o'clock when I knocked at her house. A woman who I assumed was her host mother opened the door. When I explained who I was, she invited me in, but I didn't want any witnesses to a possibly embarrassing situation.

Outside, I paced in front of the house while she went to get Dana. My heart was pounding like the bass drum in a band during a football-game half-time performance.

"Hey, what's up?" Dana asked as she stepped outside, closing the door behind her.

I halted in midstride. Man, she was cute. It was dark outside, but I could still see those freckles in my mind. *Forget the freckles,* I ordered myself. *Forget the feel of her mouth against yours.*

"I just wanted to make sure that you understood that kiss didn't mean anything," I announced.

She crossed her arms over her chest and leaned back against the closed door. I felt her eyes boring into me. Scrutinizing me.

"You explained that on the hill," she reminded me.

"That doesn't mean you understood what I was saying," I told her.

"I understood. The kiss meant nothing," she said softly.

I took a step closer. "I'm not interested in a relationship—not with you, not with anyone."

"That's good because I'm not interested in having a relationship with you," she blurted out.

I should have felt relieved. For some strange reason, I was disappointed.

"I plan to date a hundred girls while I'm in Paris," I said, striving to convince myself as much as her.

She uncrossed her arms. "I understand completely," she assured me. "My plan is to become involved with one guy—but a French guy. Not a mundane American." She took a step closer. "I want to be romanced by someone who invented the word. And the French did that."

"Good!" I snapped. "I'm glad to hear that."

"The kiss meant absolutely nothing to me," she reiterated.

Nothing? That's what I wanted, right? I wanted it to mean nothing.

"Excellent. So we can go on with our lives as if nothing happened on that hilltop," I told her.

"Absolutely," she stated.

I nodded, but my heart was thundering. I felt like an absolute fool as I turned on my heel and began walking home.

The kiss had meant nothing to her. I was apparently the only one affected by it. I couldn't figure out why I was so miserable.

Suddenly I was lonelier than I'd ever been in my entire life—and that was pretty dadgum lonely.

Private Internet Chat Room

Dana: Guys, I have a hypothetical question. Is it possible
to enjoy kissing a guy that you don't like?

Robin: I've never kissed a guy, but I guess it might be possible if he was a good kisser.

Carrie: If you don't like him, then why is his mouth close
enough to yours to even kiss?

Dana: I said it was hypothetical.

Carrie: Did Alex kiss you?

Dana: What are you, psychic?

Carrie: Oh my gosh. He did, didn't he?

Dana: It wasn't a real kiss.

Robin: Describe a false kiss.

Grrr. I wished I hadn't desperately needed help
trying to understand what I'd felt on that hilltop.

Dana: Okay. So maybe it was a real kiss. But it didn't
mean anything.

Carrie: But you liked it?

I took a deep breath. These were my two best
friends. I could admit anything to them.

Dana: Yeah.

Robin: What are you going to do?

Dana: Try to forget it. He's completely wrong for me. He's not
French; he's not romantic. And worse, he's from home.
He is most definitely not my goal for this year in Paris.

Eight

Dana

I LOVED MY sketching class. Where else but Paris could I have three art classes, each one so incredibly different and yet each teaching me fundamentals that eased over into the other classes?

I'd received high marks for my Eiffel Tower sketch. I glanced across the room at Alex. I couldn't understand why he hadn't turned in his sketch. I wondered if he'd become self-conscious when I'd shown him my sketch on the hill—just before he kissed me.

Three days had passed, and I still couldn't get the memory of that kiss out of my mind. It was always there, haunting me. Whenever my art teachers swept their hands through the air and said to put more passion into my work, I thought of that kiss. Its warmth, its power. The sunset. It was so amaz-

66

ing the way everything had woven together like a perfect painting to create a lasting memory.

Yet all of it, particularly the kiss, had meant absolutely nothing to him. He probably didn't even remember the incredible sensations created by our mouths touching. He'd certainly rushed over to my house quickly enough that night to make sure that I understood the kiss meant nothing. That had hurt.

I knew it shouldn't have. I mean, he'd been upfront before he ever touched his mouth to mine. It was the artist demanding the kiss.

Not the guy.

And I was glad. I really was because the last thing I wanted was to fill this year with memories of kisses given to me by a guy from Mustang High.

I had to drag my attention away from Alex when the teacher started talking. It was getting easier to understand what my teachers were saying. I figured by the end of the year that I'd be much more fluent in French.

Madame Trudi explained that she was going to pair us up for a special project. She began calling out names. Girl, boy, girl, boy. I listened intently for my name.

"Dana! Alex!"

I groaned and slid my gaze to Alex. He had buried his head in his hands. I figured he was as thrilled as I was that we'd been paired together. When Madame Trudi finished calling out the names, she told us to sit by our partners. Why would she pair the two Americans?

I watched Alex reluctantly trudge across the room. The glower on his face was almost comical.

"Can you believe our rotten luck?" he asked in a low voice. "I was hoping she'd pair me up with Shari."

"I wanted Luc," I whispered back.

"We are going to move on to the human form," Madame Trudi explained in perfect French. "First the ladies will sketch the gentlemen, and then at the end of next week the gentlemen will sketch the ladies. Gentlemen, you will stand before your partners and remove your shirts."

My mouth dropped open, and Alex's eyes went as wide as two full moons.

"She's kidding, right?" he asked in a low voice.

I heard chairs scraping across the floor and girls giggling. "I don't think so." I smiled. "After all, this is Paris."

Alex slowly stood. He jerked off his Longhorns T-shirt, depicting the sign of the bull's head. In stunned fascination, I watched Alex's muscles ripple.

Wow! His cycling clothes had given me an idea of his shape, but seeing the actual hardened muscles was something else. This guy obviously worked out. Who would have thought a cyclist would look so powerful? An artistic cyclist at that. Alex was a contradiction to everything I believed.

And he wore such a cute blush. It started at his neck and went right up into his hair.

"Will you start sketching?" he ordered. "The sooner you finish, the sooner I can put my shirt back on."

"Oh yeah, right," I responded as I sat up straighter, put my feet on his chair, and set my notepad against my bent legs.

Like all the other girls in class, I took a quick glance around the room, comparing the models. I had definitely, much to my surprise, gotten the best. Even Luc didn't have muscles as defined as Alex's.

With Alex glaring at the far corner of the room, I settled back to slowly, ever so slowly, sketch that amazing torso.

"In a million years, I never would have guessed that Alex Turner had a great body," I told Renée as we wandered through a very chic clothing store.

I wanted something special to wear for my practice date. I'd purposely saved all my money from my after-school job back in Mustang so I could buy something in Paris.

Because who could come to Paris and not shop for clothes! This city had set the fashion trends for hundreds of years, and I absolutely could not come here without buying at least one designer dress.

"Maybe he is your destiny," Renée said.

I almost tripped over my feet. "What?"

"Fate keeps putting you together," she explained.

"No, teachers keep putting us together," I mumbled as I lifted a straight black dress off the rack. I imagined it with a colorful silk scarf tied at the waist.

"I think he's cute," Renée offered.

I wouldn't admit that in a thousand years. It somehow seemed a betrayal to myself. "He's okay," I muttered. "What do you think of this?" I asked, wishing I'd never started talking about Alex.

I didn't want to think about him. Tonight was a special night. My first real date with a Frenchie.

Renée angled her head. "With the right accessories, it could be perfect."

The right accessories ended up being a necklace that was a wide band of silver. It looked like something Cleopatra might wear. Little silver studs for my ears. A silver belt that looped around my waist and draped down one side. And silver shoes with three-inch spiked heels. Classy.

As I stared in the mirror, I thought I looked quite sophisticated. So what if the outfit took half my spending money? I hadn't even been in Paris a whole week yet. I'd have to be very frugal with my wardrobe money. My mom and dad were sending me a monthly allowance, but my wardrobe money was hard earned through my explaining to obese women why they didn't want to wear horizontal lines and to tall women why they didn't want to wear vertical lines. Some women had no fashion sense.

I turned slowly in front of the three-way mirror and wondered what Alex would think of the outfit.

I rolled my eyes. I could care less what he thought. I really could. Still . . . I wondered.

*   *   *

During dinner with my host family, I could hardly contain my anticipation about the evening. I was going on my first date with a French guy: François Morolt.

The name even sounded romantic. Although this was a practice date, I had hopes that it might prove to be more than that. My first week in Paris was nearing an end, and I didn't want to spend much more time looking for Mr. Romantic. Every week that passed was one week less that I'd have with him.

"How are you enjoying school?" Monsieur Trouvel asked.

"It's so different from Mustang," I enthused. "Especially the art classes."

"In what way?" Geneviève asked.

"Well, for one thing, I can't imagine any teacher back home telling the guys to take off their shirts," I explained.

"It's important for an artist to understand the human form," Madame Trouvel told me. "Someone once told me that da Vinci studied cadavers."

A chill went through me. "I'd rather use live subjects," I admitted. "Although I'm not sure how I'm going to gather up the courage to remove my shirt during the class."

Renée laughed. "French schools aren't that risqué. You'll be instructed to wear a bathing suit that day beneath your clothes."

Relief swamped me. "Am I ever glad to hear that!"

71

As soon as we were finished eating, Renée and I hurried upstairs to get ready for our dates. I really liked the way the black dress looked on me. It was a simple cut, but it hung perfectly over my short frame. It actually made me look a little taller.

I applied my makeup. Nothing too heavy. My main goal was to cover the irritating freckles. The Texas sun had a tendency to draw freckles on pale skin.

Not that it had ever drawn a freckle on Alex. He was so bronzed—

Stop that thought! I ordered.

I couldn't figure out why Alex tripped through my mind every five seconds.

I was about to go out on a date with a real French guy.

So why wasn't I excited? And why did I keep thinking about Alex, boring Alex, from Mustang High?

Nine

Alex

M Y HOST BROTHER, Jacques Reynard, and I were prowling the nightlife in Paris. It was way different from cruising in Mustang. The popular spots in Mustang were the Hamburger Hut, Giovanni's Pizzeria, and the bowling alley. Except on Friday nights. And then it was the stadium in the fall and the gym in the winter. Football and basketball. Spring and summer, it was the baseball fields.

Dances were limited to the homecoming dance and the prom.

In Mustang we didn't really have any hot spots unless beneath the stadium bleachers counted. I'd never taken a girl there. I don't know. It just seemed . . . really unromantic. And since I wasn't a romantic guy, I imagined girls rated it as less than unromantic.

Paris was filled with lights. Dazzling. No wonder it was known as the City of Light.

And Jacques knew all the places to go. Where kids our age tended to hang out.

With luck, tonight I would meet Miss Take My Mind Off My Troubles. A Parisian beauty who spoke a minimum of English.

We walked into a place that would be considered a nightclub in Mustang. But here it was more along the lines of a dance club. It looked like it catered to the under-twenty crowd. A live band had music bouncing off the walls while the band was bouncing over the stage. Laser lights beamed through the darkness.

Tables surrounded the dance floor. I didn't see any empty tables, and there wasn't a lot of elbowroom on the dance floor.

"We should have gotten here earlier," Jacques stated.

"I don't mind standing," I practically screamed in his ear.

Then I spotted three empty chairs. But the table wasn't empty. It was occupied by a lone girl. A very classy looking girl dressed in black. I tapped Jacques on the shoulder and pointed toward the table.

He nodded, which I took to mean it was okay to ask to share her table. I wasn't really up on French dating etiquette. Somehow that aspect of French culture had never come up in the French class I took back at Mustang High.

Avoiding the gyrating bodies of the dancers and the elbows of people sitting at tables, I headed toward the lone girl and the three vacant chairs.

A few steps later I stopped short. Jacques rammed into me. I couldn't believe it. The girl was Dana.

She gazed longingly at the dance floor, her chin resting in the palm of her hand. If I'd been smart, I'd have turned around and head to the farthest corner of the room or, better yet, I would have beat a hasty retreat for the door. But apparently I had yet to unpack my intelligence.

I found myself striding to her table.

"What are you doing here?" I asked once I got close enough that a moderate shout would suffice in order to be heard.

She jerked back as if I'd woken her up. With disappointment reflected in her eyes, she pointed toward a guy on the dance floor, a guy dancing with two girls. "My date!" She leaned over and shouted above the loud music.

I couldn't help myself. I smiled broadly. "A very romantic guy!" I yelled back.

With a disgusted look she punched me playfully on the shoulder. I jabbed my finger over my shoulder. "This is my host brother, Jacques."

Without missing a beat or letting the introduction cool, Jacques took her hand and said, "Let's dance."

Dana looked the way a deer did when it began to cross the road and suddenly found itself staring into headlights. Her surprised expression quickly changed, though, and she looked pleased as Jacques led her to the dance floor.

I dropped onto a chair so we wouldn't lose the table. I was slightly annoyed that Jacques had asked her to dance before I got a chance. I guessed French guys worked fast. I also didn't like the way Jacques looked at Dana—with definite appreciation. Not that I could blame him. She resembled a model in that black dress. And she was wearing more makeup than I'd ever seen on that cute face of hers.

The makeup wasn't too heavy, but I'd noticed in the dim light that it covered her freckles. A shame since I liked those freckles.

The music finally stopped, and Jacques escorted her back to the table. I expected her date to return, but the guy was busy talking with another set of girls. Dana looked so forlorn.

When the music started up again, I grabbed her hand. "Come on."

She staggered after me. I stopped, stared at her, and suddenly realized why she looked like a model. She was wearing extremely high heels. They looked practically like stilts. "How can you walk in those things?" I asked.

"With a great deal of discomfort," she admitted.

I knelt down and slapped my thigh. "Come on. Let's take them off."

Her mouth gaped open. "I can't take off these shoes."

"Sure you can," I explained calmly, or would have if it weren't for the music. As it was, I was shouting calmly. "It's better than breaking your neck."

She put her foot on my thigh. I slipped the strap off her heel, the shoe off her foot. She had such tiny feet. I could see where the straps had cut across her arch. Unthinkingly, I rubbed her foot. It had to ache.

I stopped rubbing and glanced up at her. She was staring at me, her mouth slightly rounded. I figured I'd overstepped some unwritten dating code . . . like you can't touch a girl's foot unless she's your date or something.

"Other foot!" I yelled over the din of music and dancers.

She put her other foot on my thigh. I quickly removed the shoe and decided not to give this one the Turner treatment since she didn't seem too happy about it before. I stood and looked at the spiked heels. "Man, these could be used as weapons."

"But they're pretty, and they make my legs look pretty," she explained.

"Your legs looks pretty without them," I told her, and put the shoes on the table. Then I took her hand and led her to the dance floor.

The fast beat that had been playing suddenly dimmed into a slow song. I gave Dana an apologetic shrug, not certain if she would feel comfortable with our bodies pressing close after that kiss on the hilltop. "Go or stay?" I asked.

She hesitated for only one drumbeat before saying, "Stay."

Until she spoke, I didn't realize how badly I was

hoping that would be her choice. I drew Dana into my arms. I was unsettled by how perfectly she fit. It was as if the curve of my shoulder had been shaped for her face.

I was supposed to be searching for a French babe to spend the year with. Instead I was content to be exactly where I was for the moment. I wasn't thinking about my problems. I was concerned with hers.

How hard could it be to find a romantic guy in Paris?

The music drifted into silence. Dana stepped out of my embrace.

"Thanks," she said.

I shrugged. "Anytime."

We walked back to the table. Renée came over, a dark-haired guy in tow. She introduced him as her boyfriend, Jean-Claude.

"I'm so sorry," Renée announced. "I can't believe François is acting like a total idiot. Jean-Claude is very upset with him."

Dana waved her hand dismissively. "Don't worry about it. It was just a practice date."

Huh? Why in the world would Dana Madison need a practice date? She'd had a boyfriend in Mustang. Okay, so maybe Todd Haskell wasn't a good example. I couldn't remember ever actually seeing them in date mode.

"Want to leave?" I asked. "I'll take you home."

She smiled sadly. "I can't. I'm on a date."

"Do you really think François is going to notice?" I asked as kindly as I could.

She glanced at the dance floor, where François was gyrating like a scarecrow caught in the winds of a hurricane. "You're right. Let's go."

I grabbed her shoes and tapped Jacques on the shoulder. "I'm going to take Dana home. I'll catch up with you later."

I escorted Dana into the night. The lights of Paris surrounded us. We'd have to catch a bus to get home, but I hated taking her home when she looked so down.

"Let's walk along the Seine," I suggested.

Her eyes brightened briefly. "Okay."

"Do you want to put your shoes back on?" I asked.

She shook her head. "My hose will get ruined, but it feels too good to have them off. But I'll carry them."

"Nah, that's all right." I shoved one in each coat pocket.

"Don't forget to give them back to me," she commanded. "You still have my pink cap."

And it was still hanging on the post of my bed.

"I won't forget," I promised.

We strolled along the Right Bank, the north side of the river, known mostly for its dedication to art and the artistic. The river was beautiful. The lights from the Eiffel Tower, museums, and fantastic buildings reflected off it.

For reasons I couldn't explain, it hurt to see Dana disappointed in the evening. "François was a jerk," I announced.

She shrugged. "I know."

I couldn't believe the guy didn't realize what a great date he had tonight.

"Blind dates can be a bummer," I pointed out.

She gave me half a smile. "Tell me about it."

"Okay, since you asked, I will. A friend set me up with a girl this summer. She was a vegetarian. Not that there's anything wrong with being a vegetarian. But when I ordered a steak, she shrieked," I explained.

Her eyes widened. "You're kidding."

"No. Everyone in the restaurant turned to stare at us."

A real smile started to play at the corners of her mouth.

"Then when the food got there and I cut into my steak, she said I was cruel to animals," I told Dana.

Her mouth blossomed into a smile. I decided to exaggerate a little.

"When I began chewing my steak, she started crying and blubbering about the poor cow. How mean I was, how heartless. I didn't kill the cow. I was just eating it," I pointed out.

Dana started to laugh.

"The waiter had to bring an extra tablecloth over to dry her tears," I enthused, really getting into this tale of woe.

She laughed harder. Man, I liked her laugh.

"Did you stop eating the steak?" she asked.

"Are you kidding? I ordered another one."

She slapped my arm. "You did not."

"No, but I thought about it," I admitted.

"Did you ever see her again?" she asked.

"No, I just couldn't deal with the guilt. That night I dreamed that the ghosts of cows were haunting me," I teased.

She laughed until she had tears in her eyes. "Thanks, Alex," she said when she finally stopped laughing.

But it wasn't enough. Telling her a silly story about my vegetarian date. I didn't want her first date in Paris to be a bad memory.

I grabbed her hand. "Come on, let's take a *bateau mouche*."

We hurried along the bank of the Seine until we reached one of the pickup points for the *bateaux mouches*. I bought the tickets and we rushed onto the boat just before it pulled away from the dock.

Dana stood at the railing, gazing out on what I figured was the most romantic river in the world. I could certainly understand why she expected some French guy to sweep her off her feet. Paris had been built for romance. Even I could see that, and *romance* was a word that seldom strayed into my vocabulary. But I could see it all around us here.

Lovers strolled along the river in the moonlight. The horn of the boat sounded, an eerie echo that was romantic in its own way. We could see the Eiffel Tower, and I thought of Dana sitting on the hilltop with the sun setting over Paris.

And I thought of that kiss. I wasn't a novice when it came to kissing, but with Dana I'd felt like kissing her was all that mattered.

Definitely not what I wanted to be thinking about.

The breeze from the river was toying with her hair. I had a strong urge to play with it as well. Wrap a lock around my finger. My stomach was starting to knot up. I did not want to think of this girl as anyone important. She was just someone from home I was trying to be nice to.

But the lights of the city glistened off her hair, reflected in her eyes. I needed a distraction.

"I can't wait until you have to take your shirt off in art class," I announced, surprised by the huskiness in my voice. I'd intended the words to be a joke. Instead they'd ended up sounding like something I really couldn't wait for.

She slid that enticing green gaze my way. "I'll be wearing a bathing suit."

"No way!" I exclaimed. I feigned anger. "That's not fair. At least tell me that it's a two-piece."

Smiling sweetly, she shook her head. "One-piece."

"Man, how am I supposed to learn to draw the human form if I can't see most of it?" I inquired.

"Use your imagination," she challenged.

And that was my problem. I had way too much imagination. Heck, I already had her starring in my first full-length animated feature—and I wasn't even working for Pixar yet.

"Think I'll file a complaint with the school board," I muttered. "Unfair art practices."

She laughed softly. "Do they even have a school board here?"

I shrugged. "Who knows?"

She leaned over the railing and sighed wistfully. "I love this city."

I couldn't believe how much I wanted to kiss her again, but that one kiss had kept me up all night—no way could I make that mistake again. She was so sweet. So much sweeter than I wanted her to be. What would one more little kiss hurt? I leaned toward her.

"Somewhere out there, the most romantic guy in Paris is waiting for me," she murmured dreamily.

Reality came crashing back. Neither of us needed that kiss. She probably didn't even want it. Dana Madison wanted a French guy to fall in love with her this year.

And me? I didn't want anyone who might still be around when the year was over.

Private Internet Chat Room

Dana: My practice date was awful.

Carrie: What happened?

Dana: François was a party guy. Unfortunately, he wanted to party with everyone but me.

Robin: Sorry to hear that. I have a blind date tomorrow, and I'm not looking forward to it.

Dana: Hopefully it'll go better than mine did.

Robin: Kit set me up with one of his friends. The problem is . . . I wish my date was with Kit.

Dana: I understand completely. He is so hot, Robin.

Robin: Well, I'm sorry your night was a total bummer.

Dana: It wasn't a total bummer. Alex was there.

Carrie: What was he doing there?

Dana: He just showed up at the dance place with his host brother. He took me on a romantic boat ride along the Seine River.

Carrie: Romantic?

Dana: Very romantic.

I'd been unable to believe how romantic it had all been: with the lights reflecting off the river, him carrying my shoes, his nearness as I stood at the rail. I hesitated before confessing what would have made the moment perfect.

Dana: For a moment there, I thought he was going to kiss me again. And the worse thing is that I really wanted him to.

Ten

Dana

ON MONDAY MORNING I stared at the empty chair beside me in sculpting class. Where was Alex?

As my hands continued to shape the clay into what might pass, with a great deal of imagination, for a vase, I couldn't stop thinking about Alex. Or our romantic boat ride along the Seine River.

It had been incredible. He was fun to be with and had made me laugh. After he walked me home, I'd changed some of his scores on my rating chart. Not because I was considering him as a possible boyfriend. I definitely was not doing that. But since Renée had forced me to rate him to begin with, it seemed only fair to be honest about the scores.

I knew he'd hoped to meet a French girl at that dance club. Instead he'd sacrificed his night to

85

make me feel better. I didn't want to think about how romantic that was.

Plus it made absolutely no sense.

Alex was from my hometown, for goodness sakes. He shouldn't have a romantic bone in his body, and yet whenever I found myself with him, as corny as it sounded, I thought of violins, starry nights, and dancing at midnight.

As much as I fought it, I enjoyed being with him. If I could just tone down my enjoyment so it resembled friendship instead of something more . . . I might be okay. I definitely did not want any romantic involvement with Alex Turner.

But I couldn't get him off my mind. It was as if someone had painted his portrait at the back of my brain. And of course, I had to see him with that cute, lopsided smile.

That image followed me from class to class. Worse—disappointment hit me every time I got to one of my art classes and discovered he wasn't there. Where was he? Why wasn't he in class? Had he dropped the art classes because he realized he had no talent?

As much as I hated to admit it, by the end of the day I was actually desperate to see him. Just to make sure he was okay.

I had just gotten my books out of my locker when I spotted Jacques, Alex's host brother, walking down the hallway. I called out to him. He immediately stopped, and I rushed over.

"Alex wasn't in any of my classes today," I announced.

He looked at me as if he expected me to say more. Honestly, sometimes guys can be so dense. "Do you know where he is?" I asked.

Jacques shrugged. "Alex gets up and rides his bicycle at five every morning. This morning he wasn't back before I left for school."

My heart pounded against my ribs as I thought about how fast Alex rode his bicycle. What if he'd lost control, tumbled down a hill? "Don't you think you should be worried?" I demanded.

Jacques glanced around as if he didn't know what to say. Finally he met my gaze. "He's a big boy. I'm sure he can take care of himself."

"But what if something happened to him?" I insisted. "What if he's hurt?"

"I think my parents would have called the school if there was a problem," he explained.

"But what if they didn't know? What if—"

He laughed loudly, his laughter echoing between the lockers. "Do you Americans always worry so much?" He angled his head slightly. "Or are you just worried about Alex?"

I stiffened. "I'm not worried about him. . . . I just . . ." Was worried about him. Not because I cared about him romantically or anything. I mean, we came from the same hometown. That forced an unwanted bond between us. I slung my backpack over my shoulder. "Just call me if he's not home when you get there," I ordered.

*   *   *

The problem with being artistic is that I can see things in such vivid colors. Blood is a bright red. Bruises are a deep purple. Scrapes look like they hurt.

I kept having these horrible visions of a wounded Alex calling out to me for help. While I was sitting at the table in the Trouvel home eating *pain au chocolat*. The flaky pastry with a chocolate bar nestled inside was a popular after-school snack.

Madame Trouvel and Renée were talking quietly beside me. Madame Trouvel always wanted to know how our day at school went. It was nice sitting here after a grueling day of studies. Normally it helped me unwind.

Today I felt like one of those springs in a mechanical toy that gets wound tighter and tighter and tighter. Then when it's released, it hops over the table like crazy until it finally topples off.

"Dana, what's wrong?" Madame Trouvel asked.

I jerked out of my dire thoughts and announced, "Alex wasn't at school today. Jacques doesn't know why he didn't go to school. I don't even think he knows where he is."

"Maybe you should call him," Madame Trouvel suggested.

I balked at that idea. "I don't want him to get the wrong impression."

"What wrong impression?" Renée asked. "That you care?"

"I don't care about him," I insisted while a little

voice in the back of my mind called me a liar. "I mean, I don't care about him personally, but he is my model, and if he's not in class, I can't complete my sketch project." The little voice in my head yelled that was another lie. I had memorized every line of his torso. I could draw him in my sleep. And that was a very disturbing thought.

"He is far from home with no one to call him," Madame Trouvel reminded me. "I think you should do it as a courtesy, one American to another."

Relief coursed through me. "Right," I acknowledged. "One American to another." Nothing personal. I would be like an ambassador of goodwill.

I excused myself from the table and hurried to my room. Sitting at my desk, I located Jacques's number in the school directory and quickly dialed it. My heart was hammering. Jacques answered, and I asked to talk to Alex. An eternity seemed to pass before Alex finally came to the phone.

"Why weren't you at school today?" I immediately demanded, hating the concern clearly reflected in my voice.

"I didn't feel like going to school today," he replied.

Didn't feel like it? "You mean, you didn't feel well?" I asked. "As in sick?"

"Sure," he responded, but there was a strangeness in his voice, an emptiness I'd never noticed before. "Look, I gotta go," he announced.

Before I could respond, he hung up abruptly. I

stared at the receiver. I had allowed *this* guy to fill my head with romantic notions? Had actually thought he might be romantic? Obviously I was becoming so desperate for romance that I was seeing it where it had no possibility of existing.

Two days later I was sitting on the steps outside Jacques's house. Alex still hadn't come to school. Jacques would only shrug when I asked him about Alex. Some host brother he was turning out to be. I'd rung the doorbell, but no one was home.

Naturally my creative mind imagined Alex being rushed to the emergency room with a burst appendix or something worse. But my rational mind insisted that I stay put. Sooner or later someone would come home, and I'd get to the bottom of Alex's disappearance.

I didn't care about him personally—I repeated that litany over and over. I did not care about him. But his absence was affecting my sketch project, and that I did care about.

My mouth dropped open when I saw a cyclist whizzing along the street. I recognized the outfit. Heck fire, I recognized the body. He didn't feel well enough to come to school, but he felt well enough to cycle? If I wasn't so angry, I would have been relieved.

Alex brought his bicycle to a skidding halt and removed his helmet. "What are you doing here?" he asked, clearly annoyed.

Incredulous, I slowly rose to my feet. "Don't you realize that they'll send you back home if you . skip classes?"

He shrugged. "Let them send me home. It wasn't my idea to come here in the first place."

I couldn't believe his attitude. He seemed so different from the guy who had rescued me from the blind date on Saturday night. Had I done or said something to upset him? I stepped closer to him. "What's wrong?"

He started chaining his bicycle to the wrought-iron fence in front of the house. "Nothing."

"Nothing," I muttered. His attitude was really irritating. He made me feel like I was a pesky fly buzzing around his face. "Fine," I snapped. "If you don't want to talk about it, that's just fine with me. But I'm not going to fail my sketch class because you're suddenly homesick."

He bolted upright. "I'm not homesick!"

"Whatever," I said, with a wave of my hand. "I've got my sketch pad and a project to finish. You're taking off your shirt, buddy. Now!"

I couldn't believe that Alex had actually been cooperative. He'd invited me into his host family's home. We went to the den. It was a small room filled with bookshelves and a large fireplace. Right now, no fire blazed within the hearth, but I was way too warm anyway—just looking at Alex and that well-defined body of his. Mustang definitely needed a cycling team. I was actually considering heading a committee to push for one when I got home. Not that I wanted to win points with Alex. I had realized he was absolutely nonromantic.

He had removed his shirt. But he stood beside the hearth, glaring at a distant wall. Impatience shimmered off him like the noonday sun off hot asphalt.

Sitting on the couch, I remembered how he'd glared in class as well. The guy obviously didn't like to show off those amazing muscles. But there was something different about him this time.

I studied the portion of the sketch I'd done in class. I'd managed to do most of his face. I'd left off his mouth, hoping at some point before I was finished that he'd give me one of his lopsided grins. But I'd drawn in his eyes, shaded them . . . glaring eyes.

I glanced up at him, nearly taken aback by the difference in his eyes. Now I noticed what I hadn't before. His eyes contained a profound sadness. More than homesickness was involved here.

"What's wrong?" I blurted out.

He slid his gaze to me. "I don't want to do this stupid project."

I set my sketch pad aside and leaned forward, bracing my arms on my thighs. "I'm serious, Alex. Something is upsetting you."

"Will you just draw?" he demanded impatiently.

I honestly thought the guy was going to cry. I could see him swallowing repeatedly, and he was looking at every object in the room but me. A horrible thought occurred to me. "Is your host family abusing you?" I asked softly.

A corner of his mouth lifted in a sad sort of smile. "No, Dana, it's nothing like that."

But it was something. Without realizing it, he'd admitted *something* was wrong. "What is it, then?" I prodded gently. "Did someone die?"

"Not someone. Something. My parents' marriage died." He sank to the floor as if defeated. "My coming here was their idea. They thought it would be easier on me if I wasn't there while they went through the divorce proceedings—like it isn't my life that's being affected as well."

My heart went out to him. Although it had been years since my mom and dad had split up, I could still remember the raw edge of that pain. It lessened over time, but I wasn't sure if it would ever go away completely. Sometimes I even imagined that they'd get back together. My head knew it was an absolute impossibility . . . but my heart refused to believe.

I slid off the couch and sat beside Alex on the floor. "You seemed fine when we were together Saturday night. What happened?"

He sighed heavily. "My mom called on Sunday. She gave me my dad's new phone number. He's moved out, has his own place, and it just made the divorce more real. I can't bring myself to call my dad. It's strange. I don't have his number memorized. I have to look at a piece of paper to call my dad. Now you understand why I dropped his name for the time I'm here. I guess I'm pretty mad at him. At both of them, really."

I wanted to comfort Alex as I'd never wanted to comfort anyone. I took his hand, glad he didn't resist. His hand was so much larger than mine that I wasn't certain if my small hand could offer him much comfort. "When I was ten, my parents got divorced. The hardest part was realizing that their divorce wasn't my fault. I kept thinking if only I'd kept my room clean or been more polite or made better grades . . ."

He nodded slightly. "I keep thinking if I'd gotten involved in school sports or didn't spend so much time drawing, my parents might have stayed together. So many of the things I do, I do alone. Maybe if I'd involved my parents . . ."

I touched his cheek. "They fell out of love with each other, Alex. They didn't fall out of love with *you*. Nothing you did or didn't do caused their divorce to happen."

He took my hand from his cheek and laced our fingers together. He held my gaze, and I felt like I was swirling endlessly in those soulful brown eyes of his. I could actually see his pain, his frustration, and his doubts.

"What finally convinced you that it wasn't your fault?" he asked huskily.

"It wasn't any one thing," I explained. "Divorce is like death. You mourn, you hurt, and you start to heal. My parents are so much happier now. As difficult as it still is sometimes, I know it's a good thing that they didn't stay together."

"I'm a long way from feeling like this divorce is a good thing," he confided.

I squeezed his hands. "It was incredibly hard watching my dad pack up his things and carry the boxes out to a moving van. That tore me up inside. Maybe your parents are right. It'll be easier not seeing everything."

He shook his head. "No. When I left Mustang, I had a home and a family. When I get back, I'll have nothing."

Eleven

Alex

THE FOLLOWING MORNING Jacques and I were cycling just outside Paris. I really couldn't have asked for a better host brother. He'd told me that Dana had been asking about me at school, but he hadn't told her that I was in a "black" mood, as he called it. Jacques had left me to sulk, which was exactly what I thought I wanted.

Until Dana had shown up on the doorstep.

I started pedaling harder, feeling the burning in my calves and thighs that meant I was pushing myself. But I wanted to do more than push *myself*. I wanted to push away thoughts of my parents' divorce, but more, I wanted to push away thoughts of Dana.

Or more specifically, the attraction I was feeling toward her. It would have been incredibly easy yesterday afternoon to pull her into my arms and kiss her. I couldn't believe how badly I'd wanted to do just that. When she'd touched my cheek, I'd felt a jolt of electricity shock my system.

She was tender and gentle, with the sweetest smile and the kindest eyes. I hadn't meant to pour out my soul to her, but it had been the most natural thing I had ever experienced. She was kind and generous and really seemed to care.

"Slow down!" Jacques called after me.

But I couldn't. I was scared, scared like I'd never been scared. I hadn't been this frightened when my parents told me about the divorce. I was falling for Dana. Hard.

I knew that emotionally I was a wreck. The disintegration of my family had left me feeling hollow and empty. I needed something to fill that black hole. Dana was convenient but completely wrong. I needed a French girl. I had no intentions of hurting anyone, but with Dana, I would constantly worry that I might hurt her. Still, I liked her, and she seemed to like me. The way she'd looked into my eyes . . .

I slipped my water bottle out of its holder on my bike and squirted the water on my face. A little shock therapy to bring me back to reality. Dana wanted romance. Flowers, poetry, the whole nine yards. And she wanted a French guy. Heck, we were both only going to be here a year. We'd have no other time in our lives when we could get involved with a foreigner. It was this year or never. Frenchies for us both.

I slowed down, my heart hammering. I wasn't certain if it was thoughts of Dana causing that reaction or the way I'd barreled down the hill. Jacques caught up to me.

"Are you trying to outrace that cute American girl?" he asked.

"I don't know what you're talking about," I lied.

He laughed. "You can't get her out of your mind, and riding like a maniac won't help," he assured me.

"I have no interest in Dana. What I'm looking for is a French babe. I thought you were going to help me find one," I reminded him.

He began to peel a banana. When you cycle seriously, you learn to drink, eat, and water the flowers along the roadway without ever getting off your bike. Sports commentators often remarked on the lovely flowers that bloom along the Tour de France routes thanks to the many passing cyclists.

"Maybe I should date Dana," he suggested.

I almost lost my balance and tumbled off my cycle. Jacques was good-looking and nice. Intelligent. He had a sense of humor. Heck. He was probably even romantic. My mouth had suddenly gone dry, so I squirted water into it before I spoke. "Sure."

That sounded like I didn't care. Unfortunately, I did. More than I wanted to admit.

I glanced over at him. "But first you have to help me find a French girl."

He smiled. "A bunch of the kids from our

school are meeting at Euro Disney on Saturday. That would be a good place to start."

I'd been to Disney World in Orlando, but visiting the theme park in Paris would be great fun. "I'll be there," I promised.

And I vowed to find someone to make me forget all about my parents' divorce . . . and more, to make me forget all about Dana Madison.

Forgetting about Dana wasn't going to be easy. I finally returned to school on Friday. When I strolled into sculpting class, Dana's face lit up like the Christmas lights strung along Main Street in Mustang. I couldn't remember if anyone had ever looked so happy to see me.

And what made it worse was how glad I was to see her. Only two days had passed since our last meeting, but it felt like an eternity. These thoughts were exactly what I did not need—or want. I was spending way too much time thinking about her.

I dropped into the chair beside her. I tried to ignore her honeysuckle scent that reminded me so much of home.

"Decided you couldn't run from your troubles, huh?" she asked, her eyes twinkling.

I shook my head. "No, just wanted to see you in a bathing suit."

I laughed at the blush that crept from her chin to her hairline. It was such a deep red that it nearly obliterated her freckles.

But in sketching class I was the one who blushed when Dana removed her top. She wore a modest emerald green bathing suit. A halter style that tied around her neck and left her shoulders bare. Many of the French girls in class weren't nearly as demure. String-bikini tops were in abundance. Some were so skimpy that they were really nothing more than string.

Any normal American male would have appreciated all that this class offered in the way of bare skin. I figured that I was as normal as they came, but I couldn't take my eyes off Dana. She'd kept her jeans on because we were only supposed to sketch from the waist up. But I kept wishing we were on a beach somewhere so I could slather suntan lotion on her back and see her bare legs.

"All right, Turner, you've looked—now sketch," she commanded.

"It's not so easy being a model, is it?" I pointed out.

"Draw fast," she ordered.

I wanted to, just because she wanted me to. I really did. I didn't want her to feel uncomfortable any longer than necessary. But my hands wouldn't cooperate. They were shaking as I struggled to draw the slender lines and the dainty curves that made up her body.

It had been so easy to sketch her on the hilltop—but that was before I realized I was falling in love with her.

Twelve

Dana

EURO DISNEY! I couldn't believe I was at Euro Disney in Paris—a much better place than an art museum to meet guys.

A bunch of kids from my school were meeting at the entrance. I was waiting with Renée and Jean-Claude. Jean-Claude had apologized so many times for the guy he'd set me up with that it had become a joke. Still, I felt a little like a third wheel standing there with them. He'd offered to set me up with someone else, but I'd declined the generous offer. By being a "free" agent, I could check out all the guys, go on rides with different guys.

I realized it would be like going to the Tastes of Mustang—an annual event held back home where all the local restaurants have booths so everyone can taste their food. Only this event would be the Guys of Paris. I could have a sampling of conversation and time spent with several of them.

I recognized several kids from my classes when they arrived. Everyone was excited and in a good mood. This day was going to be great.

Even the arrival of Alex couldn't dampen my mood—although I wasn't real thrilled with how glad I was to see him. I'd been sweltering in class yesterday with his eyes focused on me as he drew my form for our sketch class.

My mouth grew dry as I watched him amble over. He was wearing jeans and a Buzz Lightyear sweatshirt. I was beginning to think his entire wardrobe consisted of shirts geared toward movies. He gave me that lopsided grin and leaned close.

"Checking out the Paris guys?" he asked in a low voice.

I smiled. "You bet. I'm sure Mr. Romance is here. What are your plans for the day?"

"I am definitely going to find my French dream girl," he assured me.

"Well, that shirt will definitely get you a *girl*," I teased. I'd worn jeans as well, but a denim shirt and a bright green vest completed my attire.

He glanced down. "You don't think Buzz is sexy?"

I burst out laughing. "Hardly."

"He's my hero. Besides, someday I'll be doing movies that star guys like this one," he explained.

I raised a brow. "Oh, really?"

"Computer-animated movies. That's my career

path." I could almost see his chest puffing out.

"I'm more of a purist," I explained. "I'm interested in true animation, not computer."

"Everything involves the computer these days," he pointed out.

"But it doesn't all begin with the computer," I insisted. "I'd like to get involved in animated movies that follow the old tradition . . . one drawing at a time."

He looked like I'd just blasted him with Buzz's stun gun.

"You're interested in making animated movies?" he asked.

"Why do you think I'm studying art? I'd love to work for Disney." It had been my dream since I'd first seen *The Little Mermaid*.

"Amazing," he murmured. "I want to work for Pixar."

"You're going to have to get over not wanting to show people your work," I told him.

He smiled. "You may be right."

They opened the gates at Main Street Station, the gateway into the theme park. People began to jostle each other, trying to get into Euro Disney. I was swept into the crowd and was being pushed forward. I glanced over my shoulder and yelled back at Alex, "Good luck with your search!"

Alex gave me a thumbs-up. Strange how I wished we hadn't gotten separated. And how I really wished he had no luck at all.

* * *

The kids from our school tended to travel together in clumps of a dozen or so. It made it convenient for getting to know people. While I stood in line for the Big Thunder Mountain ride, I spent a lot of time talking with Gérard. I'd barely noticed him in our literature class, and now I couldn't figure out why. He was cute and interesting to talk with. I thought it would be fun to ride the roller-coaster-type ride with him.

He shifted slightly, and I could see Alex standing in the line right in front of us. He was talking with a beautiful, dark-haired girl. And bestowing upon her that adorable grin of his.

Jealousy shot through me like a speeding roller coaster. For some strange reason, I wanted him to look at me, leave that girl's side, and go on this ride with me. I wasn't real fond of roller coasters—and even less fond of watching Alex flirt.

I gave myself a mental shake. I was not jealous. I most certainly was not.

"Dana?" Gérard asked.

I jerked my gaze to his. "What?"

"Where were you?" he asked.

I shook my head. "What do you mean?"

"You have not answered a single question I've asked in the last five minutes," he explained.

I felt the heat suffuse my face. "I'm sorry. I got distracted."

"Does this part of the park make you homesick? It is supposed to resemble the American West," he informed me.

I knew this area of the park had been inspired by the American West. I was a little of a Disney nut, admiring a man who encouraged people to follow their dreams. And my dream right now was to become involved with a French guy. I was blowing my chances because I couldn't keep my attention from wandering to an American guy. And thinking about his dream of finding a French girl.

"No, I'm not homesick," I assured him. I leaned close. "To be honest, roller coasters make me a little nervous. I don't mind the speed, but the drops—"

"I will protect you," he promised.

I smiled brightly. His words sounded so romantic. It finally came time for us to load into the train. Even though Alex had stood before us, because of the way they loaded the train, he was now sitting behind me. I was grateful. I didn't want to see him "protecting" that dark-haired beauty.

The train took off, swerved around a bend, and rattled up an incline. Then poor Gérard lost it. As we took the brief plummet, he screamed as if he were watching the shower scene in *Psycho*. He closed his eyes tightly and scooted down in the seat, his knuckles turning white as he gripped the bar across our laps.

I could have sworn I heard Alex laughing hysterically behind me.

When the ride ended, we clambered out of the train. Out of the corner of my eye I saw Alex take the hand of the girl who had ridden with him and help her out. Gérard left me to my own devices. He was so pale and sweaty, though, that I decided being a gentleman wasn't on his list of top priorities.

"Excuse-moi," Gérard said. "My breakfast is not going to stay put."

I watched him hurry away. So much for romance. But at least he'd been considerate enough to explain his hasty retreat.

Alex chuckled as he walked past me and said in a low voice, "Would love to see that guy on a real roller-coaster ride."

I couldn't stop myself from laughing. As far as roller coasters went, this one was really pretty tame. Maybe I'd have better luck at the next ride.

I just sorta followed the group from one ride to another, meeting a guy here and there but no one who really impressed me as Mr. Romantic. I was getting quite bummed out and thoroughly disappointed.

We finally arrived at the Pirates of the Caribbean, and as fate would have it, Alex ended up sitting beside me in the boat. I really didn't like the way my heart did a little dance against my ribs.

"Having fun?" he asked.

"How can anyone not have fun here?" I asked.

"It's magical, all right, whether it's in English or French," he admitted.

The boat left the dock, humming along. We watched robotic pirates plunder an eighteenth-century Spanish fortress in a crescendo of explosions. When we floated by a setting that included robotic women, I leaned toward Alex. "Maybe one of those is your French dream girl."

He laughed. "Any one of those robotic dolls comes closer to being what I want than anyone I've met today."

"What about the girl you were talking to at Thunder Mountain?" I inquired.

"The key words there are *talking to*," he explained. "She speaks English. I want someone who only speaks French."

I was dumbfounded. I knew we both spoke French, but neither of us was exactly fluent. We could get by. "How can you develop a relationship with someone you can't communicate with?"

"That's just it," he stated. "I don't want a relationship. I just want a warm body and willing lips."

As the day progressed into night, I was aggravated with myself. I'd spent way too much time thinking about Alex. I thought it was sad that he just wanted a French girl with willing lips and no emotional ties. Although I had to admit that my stomach knotted up every time I thought about those willing lips.

Still, his attitude seemed incredibly cold. But was what he wanted that much different than what I was after? I wanted a French guy, someone to romance me. But I did expect to care for him and to love him a little. I knew that without some semblance of love, there could be no real romance.

This French guy would be my first real love. As sad as it was, and in spite of all the time I had given him, Todd didn't count. I had liked him, but I never really loved him. It hurt to admit that, but it was also liberating because I could admit that what I'd had with Todd wasn't love. So maybe I deserved the half-price box of Valentine candy.

No. Even if you only liked someone, you didn't skimp on treating her special.

With Todd, I had just wanted to have someone to go steady with. I was in love with the idea of being in love.

Just like now. I was in love with the idea of being in love with a romantic French guy.

Now Alex, durn his hide, was making me doubt my goal for the year. I was *not* going to be using a French guy. We'd be friends, have fun . . . and then I'd leave.

I was standing on a bridge, gazing at Sleeping Beauty's Castle or, as it was known in Paris, Château de la Belle au Bois Dormant.

"Excuse-moi?" a deep voice echoed near me.

I glanced over my shoulder. A tall guy with blond hair smiled at me. "Remember me?" he asked. "Philippe. We have history together."

I smiled at him. "I remember."

I'd spotted him on and off all day. Every time I saw him, he was watching me; then he'd look away as if embarrassed. I figured he was a little shy.

"I thought you were with the other American," he explained.

"Alex?" I asked.

He nodded.

"No, we're just friends," I assured him.

"I am so glad to hear that. I was hoping we could go out next Saturday," he informed me.

My first real invitation from a French guy! I couldn't wait to tell Alex. Whoa! I didn't need to be thinking of Alex at a moment like this. I smiled brightly. "I'd love to go out."

"Bon," he added in a low voice, took my hand, and stepped closer to me.

With a glorious burst of color and a deafening crack, the fireworks began filling the night sky. Philippe put his arm around my waist and drew me near as the crowd closed in for a better look.

I wanted to find Renée, to let Renée know that I'd had a successful day after all. Philippe appeared to be very romantic as he watched the fireworks, his gaze drifting to me from time to time as if I was more important than the night sky.

Suddenly I spotted Alex nearby. He wasn't watching the fireworks. He was apparently creating his own. He stood beneath a nearby tree, planting a doozy of a kiss on a girl with long, blond hair.

I turned away, staring unseeing at the sky, my chest tightening until it ached.

Why did it hurt to know that Alex had found the warm body and willing lips he'd been seeking?

Thirteen

Alex

MONIQUE HAD A mouth that just wouldn't quit—which was exactly what I'd expected of a French girl. Oddly, though, images of Dana's kiss kept flittering through my mind. And worse, I kept seeing her smile, hearing her laugh, listening for the softness of her voice.

I recognized that initially Monique wasn't taking my mind off everything that I wanted her to, but I figured in time . . .

We ended the kiss. She used the tip of her finger to rub her lipstick away from the corner of my mouth.

"Samedi?" she questioned.

Saturday. *"Oui,"* I responded. We'd already agreed to have a date before she planted that kiss on me. I figured next Saturday would be filled with kisses exactly like that one. She certainly wasn't shy. But she did have to catch a ride with friends tonight.

"Au revoir," she purred, wiggling her fingers at me.

"Good-bye," I responded. I watched her stroll away, her hips swaying in invitation. She glanced over her shoulder, and I think she was a little sorry that I hadn't followed her. I couldn't explain why I hadn't. I was catching the bus home, had no one waiting on me.

I heard the fireworks burst overhead and glanced toward the castle. And that's when I spotted Dana standing beside some tall, blond guy whose arm circled her waist. She'd obviously found Mr. Romantic.

I watched as the guy leaned down, kissed her cheek, and then walked away.

I couldn't imagine that Dana would think it was romantic for a guy to abandon her in the middle of a fireworks display. I didn't even think it was romantic. I thought about heading home. After all, my mission had been accomplished.

But I enjoyed watching the way the fireworks reflected off her hair more than the way they brightened the night sky. Why did she intrigue me so much? She was cute, sure, but not beautiful like Monique. And Dana was totally, completely wrong for me. For one thing, she would definitely be there at the end of the year, back in Mustang, dogging my heels, wanting declarations of love.

Heck, she wanted more than declarations of love. She wanted flowers, candy, and poetry.

Romance. A seven-letter word that I tried to keep out of my vocabulary. But it sure had begun popping up a lot since Dana Madison had walked into sculpting class that first day.

I couldn't deny that I was drawn to her—against everything that was rational and made sense. As if I had no control over my legs, I found myself walking over to her.

I leaned close enough to inhale her honeysuckle scent. "I met with success," I announced.

She didn't take her gaze from the fireworks. "I noticed you playing tonsil hockey."

She sounded seriously aggravated. Was she jealous? Why did that thought please me?

"Just for the record," I began, "Monique kissed *me*." Then I wondered why I felt the need to explain. It irritated me that I did. It irritated me even more that I wanted to know about the guy who had kissed her cheek. "So, how did your day go?"

She turned to me then and smiled brightly. "Great! I've got a date for next Saturday."

"Congratulations," I said, but my voice didn't sound as enthusiastic as it should. And my chest felt hollow. "Was that your romantic guy who just walked off?"

"Yes. He had to head home."

A burst of fireworks filled the air. Someone bumped into me, and I bumped into Dana. My arms went around her, my hands grabbing the railing of the

112

bridge. "Sorry, I'm kinda wedged in," I explained.

"That's okay," she said in a low voice. "It's almost over."

She glanced back toward the sky. I figured since she didn't mind, I might as well enjoy her nearness. I edged a little closer to get away from someone's elbow. The top of Dana's head came right below my chin. Her back was against my chest. I liked having her so close.

What I found really strange was that I enjoyed just standing here with her more than I enjoyed kissing Monique. That made no sense. From a guy's perspective, kissing a girl should always rank higher than just standing beside one.

I heard Dana sigh in wonder as the final burst of red, green, yellow, and blue fireworks torched the sky. I smiled simply because I knew she'd enjoyed the sight so much.

People started heading for the exits, but it was a while before I could move back enough to give her room to move away. When she turned, I was surprised to see a sheen of tears in her eyes. She released a self-conscious laugh.

"I'm a sap when it comes to fireworks," she explained.

Why wasn't I surprised? I just smiled. She had such an endearing way about her, wanted romance so badly. I wished the guy who had originally been standing with her on the bridge had stayed until the end. I was a pinch hitter who really didn't want to play the game of romance. No matter what I thought I was feeling.

I'd never known seven days could be an eternity. But that week passed so slowly as I anticipated my date with Monique.

Now, at long last, I was on my dream date with her. She was blond, tall, and extremely beautiful.

I'd even put aside my usual cartoon-and-movie attire. I was wearing khaki Dockers and a light blue shirt. I'd forgone the use of a tie. If it were Dana sitting across from me, I probably would have pulled out my Disney villain tie. I figured she would have appreciated it.

But Monique wasn't Dana.

And that was good. I kept telling myself that was good as the maître d' led us to a table by the window. I'd brought Monique to La Tour d'Argent. The Silver Tower. It was one of the most luxurious and expensive restaurants in Paris. I figured if I wasn't going to offer the girl love, I could at least treat her to a decent meal and a good time.

And money wasn't a problem. I suspected because of the guilt they harbored at sending me away, my parents had been very generous with spending money. "So you can have a year you'll never forget," they'd told me. But I figured they really wanted it to help me forget what was happening on the other side of the ocean.

Besides, I figured there was a chance Dana's date

might bring her here. Mr. Romance. Where better? And I would be able to see for myself that she was having a good time.

I shoved that thought aside. Tonight wasn't about Dana. It was about me and Monique and willing lips.

Monique wore a slinky blue dress that hugged her body like a second skin. I should have been impressed. Instead I kept thinking about a simple black dress that had held my attention one night. I kept thinking about Dana.

My thoughts were insane.

Monique smiled. Man, she had a gorgeous smile. "Goofy!" she squealed, and laughed.

Nodding, I smiled back. Her English was limited to three words: Mickey Mouse and Goofy repeated in an adorable accent.

We'd discussed Mickey pretty much all the way to the restaurant. While waiting for our table, we'd begun the discussion of Goofy. It appeared she was ready to continue the discussion.

My knowledge of French wasn't so lame that I couldn't carry on a conversation with Monique. After all, I'd managed to communicate that I wanted to take her out and understood that she was interested in me.

But as the evening progressed, I realized that she laughed at everything I said in English. She didn't understand a word. She laughed when I spoke in French as well.

As the waiter brought our desserts, I realized that I hadn't thought about my parents' divorce in about . . . five minutes. And I had never expected to be so bored.

I had stupidly thought I would welcome the absence of conversation. . . . Instead I found myself looking forward to the end of the evening.

I knew that my feelings weren't fair to Monique. She was pretty and sweet.

But I couldn't tell if she was smart or interesting. Okay, I had to admit that I had learned a valuable lesson. I needed a French girl who could speak a little English.

Fourteen

Dana

R-O-M-A-N-C-E.
  I considered tattooing those letters across my forehead. Maybe then one of these guys would get the message.

I wouldn't classify my date with Philippe as awful. I was fairly certain that he was a wonderful conversationalist, but he spoke so little English that I couldn't be sure.

As we walked along the street toward my house, he kept pulling me close and telling me to listen to the language of the body. Unfortunately for him, my body was translating loud and clear—this guy was not the man of my dreams.

He'd taken me to a see a French film that contained no subtitles—and why should it? I was in Paris, for goodness' sake. But I just couldn't connect to the movie, so I sat there the whole time wondering how Alex's date was going. It was so totally uncool to be sitting in a darkened theater with one guy while thinking about another.

And then Philippe had pulled a Todd. Maybe it was even worse than a Todd. He'd taken me to McDonald's for dinner. Not that I don't normally like McDonald's. But in Paris? With a guy who I'm hoping is Mr. Romance?

The twin yellow arches just didn't set the mood that I wanted. I was more than ready for this date to end as I walked up the steps to my house. I turned to face Philippe.

"*Merci,*" I said softly. "*Le soir*—the evening was wonderful."

He pulled me into his arms and planted his mouth on mine as if he intended to lay down roots. My first kiss from a French guy. I had expected to be swept off my feet. Instead my mind wandered to Alex, and I wondered if Alex had kissed his date good night.

I knew a person's mind really shouldn't wander during a romantic kiss. It sort of defeated the purpose.

Philippe slipped his hands beneath the hem of my shirt. I felt his palms on my bare waist. I grabbed his wrists and jerked back. "*Non, non, non.*"

I laughed, trying to make light of the uncomfortable situation. I'm not a prude, but I didn't expect a guy to touch me intimately until I was ready for the intimacy. And it took a lot more than a movie and fries to achieve that goal. It took hearts as one and souls calling out to souls.

Philippe drew me back against him and whispered near my ear, "You are not listening to the language of the body."

I squirmed, trying to extricate myself from a place I definitely did not want to be. Panic began to settle in. I figured if he wouldn't get the message, I could scream. The Trouvels were home and would be certain to hear me.

Suddenly Philippe staggered backward, and I saw Alex standing there. His hand was gripping Philippe's shoulder, and I realized he'd pulled him back.

"She said no, and no in English or French is no," Alex declared in a tight voice.

I had this flash of a notion—I knew how damsels in distress had felt when the knight in shining armor saved them from the dragons.

"Americans!" Philippe spat as he jerked free of Alex's hold and walked away in a huff.

I looked at Alex. Maybe his armor was a bit tarnished, but I was still appreciative that he'd stepped in when he did. "Thanks."

He shrugged. "You okay?"

"Yes. I don't think he meant any harm. He was just a tad more enthusiastic than I wanted him to be." I furrowed my brow. "What are you doing here anyway?"

"I was just walking home after my date with Monique," he explained.

Ah, yes, Monique. I couldn't imagine her saying

no to a kiss from Alex. I was taken aback by the jealous pang that hit me, and I was determined to ignore it. Or at least make Alex think that I didn't care. I forced myself to ask lightly, "So, how did it go?"

"It went great." A corner of his mouth lifted, and he shook his head. "It was awful."

"I'm sorry to hear that," I said, although I felt like jumping with joy. What was wrong with me? "What happened?"

He shoved his hands into his pockets. "The only English word she kept repeating was *Goofy*. About halfway through the meal, I realize she thought that Goofy was my name."

I couldn't help myself. I burst out laughing—not so much because I thought it was funny. But because I was incredibly relieved. "You're kidding me, right?"

"I wish. She was sweet, but I don't think she was the brightest bunny in the burrow. Hard to tell, though, since she didn't speak English and my French is only passable," he explained.

Passable enough to get a date, I thought. *But not enough to enjoy the date.* I thought about Philippe's suggestion to listen to the language of the body. I was incredibly glad that Alex hadn't known about that advice.

I must have thought about him a hundred times while I was on my date—and that was so unfair to Philippe. How could any evening hold the magic of romance if I was thinking about another guy?

Alex jabbed his thumb over his shoulder. "Hey, just so this evening isn't a total waste, you want to grab something sweet to eat? There's a late night pastry shop around the corner."

The offer was tempting, and not just because of my love for chocolate. Alex looked terrific. He wore khaki pants and a light blue shirt beneath a dark brown jacket. I wouldn't have been surprised if he pulled a tie out of one of his pockets. It looked like he'd put as much thought into getting ready for his date as I had into getting ready for mine.

Yet, we'd both had a bummer evening. I put my hand on my stomach. "Yeah, I think these McDonald's fries could use some company."

His mouth dropped open. "Tell me that your date did not take you to McDonald's."

I grimaced. "Afraid so."

He took my hand. It seemed so natural that I wasn't even sure he realized that he'd done it.

"I always figured the French were romantic," he murmured as we began walking along the dimly lit street.

"Me too. I had visions of flowers, candlelight, and poetry; French words whispered in my ear," I confessed.

He glanced over at me. A corner of his mouth lifted. "Maybe you expect too much."

I shook my head. "But this is the city of romance, Alex. I'll only be here a year. I have to pack enough romance into this year to last me a lifetime."

121

"Don't you think any guys from Mustang know anything about romance?" he asked thoughtfully.

I raised a brow. "Honestly? No. At least not the kind of intense romance that I want. I want to feel like the guy can't live without me, that I'm the center of his universe."

"Sounds like you're looking for some serious love," he mused.

"All I want is the romance," I assured him. Serious love would mean heartache at the end of the year, and I definitely did not want that.

"Do you honestly believe you can have one without the other?" he asked.

"Sure," I replied confidently, although I really was no longer certain. Was that where things were going wrong? I thought I could have romance without a long-term commitment?

We stopped walking, and Alex shoved open the door to a bakery. The aroma of freshly baked bread and pastries teased my nostrils. He waited for me to walk in first. Then he followed me to the counter. I looked through the glass at the assortment of pastries. "Any one of these is going to go a long way toward helping me to forget about my quest for romance," I admitted.

I ordered a chocolate-coated éclair while Alex ordered *chausson aux pommes,* a pastry filled with apples. We both ordered large milks. At the cash register I reached for my purse, a thin strap anchoring it over my shoulder.

"My treat," Alex announced, without looking at me. I watched him dig the francs out of his wallet.

I considered arguing. After all, we weren't on a date, but I didn't want to chance ruining the rapport we'd established. Besides, how many people in Paris could understand why I was searching so badly for romance? Renée didn't understand because she could not comprehend how totally unromantic the guys were in Mustang.

Alex knew the guys. He knew that in Mustang, I would never find the romance that I craved. It was just inconceivable.

We settled into a corner booth. Beside us the large window looked out on the street. It was after ten o'clock, but lovers strolled by, arm in arm. I could tell some were whispering, probably words of love.

With a sigh I took my fork and cut off a bit of éclair. I closed my mouth around the rich filling, the creamy chocolate, and the flaky pastry. I moaned softly. "This definitely hits the spot."

Alex chuckled. I watched as he dug into his pastry.

"I can't resist the lure of bakeries," he confessed.

"We have a bakery in Mustang," I chided.

He narrowed his eyes at me. "Donuts 2B8 is not a bakery."

He was so right. Three varieties of doughnuts hardly compared with the delicious éclair that was now making my mouth water.

"I'll probably go home a hundred pounds heavier," he murmured.

"Not the way that you ride your bike," I teased.

He smiled. "True."

His gaze held mine, and it occurred to me that I knew more about Alex Turner than I knew about any other guy in existence—certainly more than I knew about Todd. I knew Alex's dreams: to cycle in the Tour de France, to work for Pixar. I knew all the self-doubts he was experiencing over his parents' divorce. I relished the sound of his laughter and loved that lopsided grin.

Loved? How could I love anything even remotely related to a guy from Mustang?

I quickly dropped my gaze to his plate. And there were those amazing hands of his resting on either side of it. Originally, hands weren't on my guy score sheet, but after watching him day after day in sculpting class shaping the clay . . . Well, I'd had to add it to my list of things about a guy to consider. And I'd given him a three.

"You can have some if you want," he offered quietly.

I jerked my eyes back to his. "What?"

"You're staring at my pastry. Thought you might want to give it a try," he explained.

"Sure," I stammered, or would have if I'd had to say more than one word.

I watched him jab his fork into a piece of the pastry that he'd already worked free. Holding the fork, he carried the pastry to my mouth.

Sharing our food seemed so incredibly intimate.

My stomach knotted up, and I wasn't certain how I was going to be able to swallow. My heart was pounding as I closed my mouth around his fork.

He slid the fork out of my mouth and grinned. "Well?"

The apple-filled pastry was delicious. "Yummy. Want to try the éclair?"

"Yeah, I would. I'm a sucker for chocolate, but apples are healthier."

I laughed. "Right. And I eat carrot cake for the vegetables," I teased.

"Really? Me too."

We both laughed, and it was such a memorable moment. I'd never laughed with a guy. It was like a meeting of souls or something.

I cut off a piece of éclair, hooked it with my fork, and extended it toward him. He hesitated, and I wondered if he suddenly realized—as I had earlier—how personal it was to share food. I watched him take my offering, chew, and swallow.

"That's good," he agreed.

I was actually enjoying the evening. The disaster of my earlier date was a fading memory. But I was spending way too much time thinking of Alex in a romantic context. I needed to bring us both back to earth.

"Did you ever call your dad?" I asked.

All the sparkle went out of his eyes, and he shoved his pastry aside. "No."

I wished I'd kept my mouth shut. I hated seeing him looking so incredibly miserable.

I glanced at my watch. Midnight. I set my éclair aside.

"Why don't you call your dad now?" I suggested. "I saw a pay phone around the corner, and it's only five in the afternoon in Mustang."

He shook his head. "I can't, Dana. I've thought about calling him a hundred times this week, but it just makes the divorce too real, and I guess I'm not ready to face it."

I reached across the table and wrapped my hands around his balled fists. I could feel so much tension in him. "You know, Alex, it's already very real for your dad."

"Are you saying that's my fault?" he demanded.

"No," I replied softly. "I just remember when my dad moved out that I was afraid he'd stop loving me because he didn't live with me anymore. Later my dad told me that he had been afraid *I'd* stop loving him. If you don't call your dad, he might think that you don't love him anymore."

"I hadn't thought of it like that," he said quietly.

"He's probably just as scared as you are," I continued.

"I don't see how he could be," he snapped. "After all, it's *my* world that's falling apart."

"And his isn't?" I prodded gently.

Alex looked like I'd just dumped a bucket of cold water on him.

"You know, Dana, I hadn't really thought about what he must be feeling." He moved one of his hands out from beneath mine and combed his fingers through his hair. "I've been so selfish."

I squeezed his hand. "You've been confused—and that's natural," I assured him.

"My dad's alone, just like me," he pointed out.

I jerked upright. "And what am I? A figment of your imagination?"

His face broke into a warm grin. "No, you're a very special girl."

He reached into his back pocket, pulled out his wallet, and dug out a scrap of paper. Then he met my gaze. "How do I say I want to make a collect call?"

"Let me look in my trusty pocket-size English-French dictionary." I pulled it out of my purse, riffled through the pages, then smiled triumphantly as I found the expression. *"Je voudrais faire une communication avec PCV."* I looked at Alex. "You need anything else?"

"You," he answered quietly.

My heart slammed against my ribs. I was certain that all the blood had drained from my face.

"Will you stay with me while I call him?" he pleaded.

I nodded, surprised by the warmth that flowed through me because he wanted me. My heartbeat returned to normal, but I knew that I'd never forget the way he looked at me after I nodded. Like I placed the stars in the sky.

The pay phone was anchored to a wall, not enclosed in a booth. Fortunately the street was quiet this time of night. I watched Alex drop some coins into the slot. I heard him mumble in French. Then he gave a deep sigh.

"The phone's ringing," he muttered in a shaky voice.

I moved closer and rubbed his back. He was so incredibly tense. He glanced at me, and I could see the apprehension in his eyes. Maybe this wasn't such a good idea. I was on the verge of telling him to hang up when he said, "Dad?"

I felt the tension between his shoulders increase. Then he released a strangled laugh. "Nothing's wrong. I just wanted to talk to you."

He turned slightly, and his voice became muffled, so I couldn't hear what he was saying to his dad. I continued to rub his back. Little by little, I could feel the tension easing away.

I heard thunder. A raindrop plopped on my nose. I glanced up. Even though it was night, the sky looked darker than it should. Another drop.

Lightning zigzagged across the sky. Thunder rumbled. And then a gush of water drenched me unexpectedly. I shrieked as the rain began to fall harder and harder.

Alex turned around. He was grinning broadly. "I gotta go, Dad," he said. "Me too."

He hung up and took off his jacket. He draped it over my head. Laughing, he ordered, "Come on, let's get you home."

I couldn't believe how quickly it had started to pour. We rushed down the street, our pounding feet causing the water to splash our legs. Just as suddenly the rain let up slightly but continued to fall.

We reached my house, and I hurried up the steps. I turned to face Alex.

His hair was plastered to his head. Drops of rain were rolling down his face. His clothes were soaked. Not that I was in much better condition.

"A lot of good my jacket did," he announced.

"It's the thought that counts," I admitted. He'd at least tried to shelter me. As the rain continued to bounce off him, I couldn't believe how thoughtful he was.

"Thanks, Dana," he said quietly. "Thanks for talking me into calling my dad. He was really glad to hear from me. He thought I was angry with him. Maybe I was, a little. I'm not so much now."

"I've been there, Alex," I explained. "It's hard, but you'll make it through this divorce thing okay. Trust me."

"I do," he said solemnly. His gaze darkened as it held mine. He dropped his jacket to my shoulders so he no longer had to hold it.

The rain began to patter gently against my cheeks. Alex cradled my face between his hands, tilted my face up slightly, and lowered his mouth to mine.

The night air was cool, the rain cold, and his mouth so warm. I stepped closer to him and twined my arms around his neck.

He deepened the kiss in that slow, unhurried way of his. My body grew so incredibly warm that the rain no longer mattered.

All that mattered was Alex.

Fifteen

Alex

DANA WAS INCREDIBLE. She was so giving.
I felt like she was pouring her soul into our kiss, pouring herself into me.

All the loneliness I had been feeling was melting away like a chocolate bar left out in the August sun.

Yet this was all so totally wrong.

I knew what I had to do. End the kiss now before she got the wrong impression. Before she realized that she was all I could think about.

Our lips parted. But my will was weak. I kissed one corner of her mouth. Then the other. Then the tip of her nose, where all her cute freckles were.

Then I drew back and met her stunned gaze. Her mouth was still open slightly, and I was tempted to again cover it with mine. Instead I forced myself to back up a step.

"Sorry," I muttered.

"Sorry?" she repeated, clearly dazed.

"Don't read anything into the kiss, Dana. It was just another one of those artistic moments. . . ." My voice trailed off. I couldn't complete the lie.

"Artistic moment?" she reiterated.

"Yeah, you know. Like on the hilltop. Only this was night. Rain. I could see the canvas, and it was just begging for a couple kissing." I usually wasn't a babbler. I just didn't want to hurt Dana. If she knew how much I was coming to care for her, she might feel the need to reciprocate. I didn't want her to put aside her dream of being with Mr. Romance this year.

But I also didn't want her to think that I was taking advantage—kissing her when I really had no right.

She nodded briskly. "I see." She removed my jacket from around her shoulders and extended it toward me. "Thanks for sheltering me from the storm."

She sounded so formal. I was really afraid I'd hurt her. I could only hope it was a small hurt, something that would go away quickly. If I told her what I really felt, I could risk taking away her dream. That thought sounded so egotistical. Like she would set aside her dream for me.

Maybe it was me that I was afraid would get hurt. Dana had never hinted that I meant anything more than a friend—unless I counted that kiss. It had gone way beyond friendship.

Yet she'd made it perfectly clear what she wanted this year in Paris—a guy willing to fulfill her romantic expectations. Other than "Roses Are Red," I really didn't know any poetry to recite. Knowing Dana, she was looking for a Shakespearean sonnet.

I took the drenched jacket. It really hadn't done a lot of good. She looked like a drowned kitten. An adorable drowned kitten. Man, did I want to kiss her again.

I backed up another step. The rain was still falling, but softly now. "See you at school," I announced.

"Yeah," she replied, sounding somewhat sad. "See you at school."

"About that kiss—"

She held up a hand to stop me from saying anything else. "I know. It meant nothing."

Turning, she opened the door. I watched her disappear into the house.

No, I thought with a sigh, *that kiss meant everything*.

Sixteen

Dana

O N MONDAY AFTERNOON I sat on the bed in my room, my legs folded beneath me. In the center of the bed was a flat package. Gift wrapped. The bow on top was crumpled. Like a cotton shirt that needed to be ironed. It looked like someone had used the bow over and over.

That someone was Alex.

I wondered if he'd wrapped the gift, changed his mind, unwrapped it, changed his mind, and wrapped it back up again.

I'd been so nervous about seeing him in our first class this morning. After that earth-shattering kiss that had meant absolutely nothing to him . . . I had seriously considered changing all my art classes. I just didn't know how I could face him again.

The moment I saw him in the hall, right before

133

our first class, my heart sped up. Then he spotted me, and I had difficulty breathing. My lips tingled as if they remembered that kiss we'd shared in the rain. A kiss I knew I'd never forget even if I lived to be a hundred.

It had been the most romantic moment of my life. Standing there with the rain falling on us, the warmth of our embrace, the heat of our mouths.

I stood in the hallway like a deer caught in head-lights as Alex walked toward me. A corner of his mouth lifted, but his lopsided grin looked sad.

"How are you doing?" he asked once he got close enough that he wouldn't have to shout.

I took a deep breath and lifted my gaze from that incredible mouth of his to his soulful eyes. "Great. I woke up this morning knowing that Mr. Romance was going to walk into my life today."

"I really hope he does, Dana. You deserve your dreams." He extended a flat package toward me. "Open this at home."

"What is it?" I asked.

His grin grew. "If I wanted you to know right away, I wouldn't have wrapped it."

"Why can't I open it now?" I insisted.

"Because I asked you not to."

And that was that. The gift had haunted me all day. I figured it was a silk scarf because the box was so flat. Although I couldn't imagine why he'd give me a fashion accessory. Actually, I couldn't deter-mine why he'd give me anything at all.

But here I was, staring at the thin box, wondering if I really wanted to break the spell it had cast over me. As long as I had the package, my thoughts drifted to Alex.

Who was I kidding? With or without the package, I'd be thinking of Alex.

I reached for the box, carefully removed the wrinkled bow, peeled back the wrapping paper, and lifted the lid.

I stilled. My breath backed up in my lungs. I could not believe it.

I was looking at a sketch. A sketch of me, standing on a bridge with Sleeping Beauty's Castle in the background. Fireworks filled the sky over my head. But it was my image that held me captivated.

I've never considered myself plain, but neither did I think I was any great beauty. But in this sketch, I looked . . . beautiful. Incredibly happy. Magical.

I stared in stunned disbelief at the signature scrawled in the corner.

Alex Turner
September 2000

Alex had drawn this? I'd never been more confused in my life. His attention to detail was amazing. He even drew my freckles. Why hadn't he turned in his sketch of the Eiffel Tower that he'd created that day on the hilltop? It certainly wasn't because my drawing had intimidated him. He was far more talented than I was.

I lifted the sketch from the box, and beneath was a scrawled note that read, *Thanks for Saturday night.*

What did that mean? Was he thanking me for

A. Going to the bakery with him?

B. Talking him into calling his dad?

C. Staying with him while he talked to his dad?

D. Kissing him as if I had a serious crush on him?

I shook my head. B. I heard a voice asking if that was my final answer. Without a doubt. My presence didn't seem to mean much to Alex whether it was at a bakery or a pay phone. And as for the kiss . . . I didn't want to think about how much it hurt that it meant nothing.

Reaching across my bed, I grabbed the phone off the nightstand. With a deep breath, I dialed Alex's number. His host mom answered and promptly went to fetch him.

"Hello?" His voice was so deep.

"Alex, it's Dana," I announced.

"What's wrong?" he asked, and I could hear the concern in his voice.

"Nothing," I assured him. I glanced at the sketch. "I just . . . I just opened your gift. It's wonderful."

"It's no big deal. Since the rain from Saturday night continued into Sunday, I couldn't cycle, so it was something to do," he explained.

Something to do? With the details, it must have taken hours.

"I plan to have it framed once I get home. It'll be a great souvenir." I didn't know how to tell him exactly how touched I was by his gesture. I might even send it to my mom so she could see how I was adjusting to life in Paris.

"I'm glad you like it. Listen, there's someone here who wants to talk with you. I'll see you at school."

With that, he was gone.

"Dana?" asked a deeper voice with an incredible French accent. "It's Jacques."

Alex's host brother. "Hey, Jacques."

"I was wondering if you'd like to go out Saturday night?" I heard him grunt. "With me. Go out with me. On a date. A romantic date."

He seemed so nervous that it was actually cute. "I'd love to."

"She'd love to," I heard him whisper. Alex mumbled something.

"Wonderful," Jacques muttered. "I shall count the hours."

After I hung up, I sat there, staring at the sketch. Disappointment slammed into me. I had felt such an incredible bond with Alex on Saturday night that I had hoped he might ask me out. I had sorta hoped that the sketch was—a prelude to a date.

Sure, he wasn't French, but I was suddenly beginning to realize that where a person was from wasn't as important as the person.

Dana: Well, guys, I have a date with a Frenchie. A really nice one at that, who is totally hot.

Robin: How did that come about?

Dana: Alex. He set me up with his host brother.

Carrie: Alex again? You can't seem to get rid of the guy.

The problem was, I realized that I didn't want to.

Dana: Enough about me. What's happening with y'all? Carrie, did you get things worked out with Antonio?

Carrie: No, it's such a mess. I've really fallen hard for the guy, and he cares about me. But that will end the minute I tell him I'm an American. :(

Robin: You might be surprised. I finally revealed my true self to Kit.

Dana: And?

Robin: :)

Dana: What does that smile mean?

Robin: He's not only my host brother . . . he's now my boyfriend!

Carrie: Way to go, Robin!

Dana: I knew that would happen once you stopped trying to hide your true self.

I was so totally happy for Robin. If only Carrie could resolve the situation with Antonio . . . and if only I could figure out what it was I really wanted this year while I was in Paris.

Seventeen

Dana

LATE SATURDAY MORNING, I was in the kitchen with Madame Trouvel, Renée, and Geneviève. We were preparing lunch in their small kitchen. Madame Trouvel was teaching me how to fix crepes, which are like pancakes—and are delicious. I figured that by the time my year in Paris was over, I would be a gourmet chef. I was already planning on cooking one meal for my family.

Like just about everything in France, cooking was an art. I loved watching Madame Trouvel move fluidly through the kitchen. With her dark hair and blue eyes, she reminded me of a graceful dancer.

The doorbell rang.

"I'll get it," Renée said, and headed out.

With a wide spatula I gently lifted my crepe off

the pan and placed it on my plate. I leaned low and sniffed. "That smells so good."

"You are a natural, Dana," Madame Trouvel stated.

I felt myself blush. "*Merci,* but you did most of the work. I just sorta followed along and did whatever you told me to do."

She laughed. "That is more than my daughters can often do."

"Oh, Maman," Geneviève whined. "That's not true."

Madame Trouvel leaned down and kissed Geneviève's cheek. "Sometimes, *ma chère.*"

Renée came back into the kitchen. She was holding a huge crystal vase filled with a dozen red roses and an assortment of tiny white flowers—baby's breath.

"Wow!" I enthused. "Those are beautiful."

She smiled brightly. "They're for you."

I felt like someone had knocked the breath right out of me. "For me?"

"*Oui.*" She set them on the counter, removed the card, and handed it to me.

My hand was actually shaking as I opened the card. It simply said, *Jusqu'à ce soir.* Until this evening.

I pressed my palm to my rapidly beating heart. *Oh, be still, my fluttering heart!*

I felt tears burn my eyes. "No one has ever sent me flowers before," I told them. And these were no leftovers with wilted petals. They were just buds, waiting to open up and blossom.

"No one has ever sent me flowers either," Renée said.

Dumbfounded, I stared at her. "Surely Jean-Claude has sent you flowers?"

She shrugged casually. *"Non."*

"He's given you boxes of chocolate, though, right?" I inquired.

She gave her head a quick shake. *"Non."*

I felt like I was in the middle of some bad joke. "He recites poetry to you."

Laughter bubbled out of her then. "Jean-Claude? Poetry? *Non. Non. Non.* He would never read a poem to me."

My legs felt weak. I dropped down on a stool at the counter. "I don't understand. You said he was romantic."

"He is. *Très* romantic," she assured me.

"I'm completely lost here," I confessed. "How can he be romantic when he doesn't do anything special for you?"

She looked taken aback. "What are you talking about? He is romantic because he knows me. He knows when I am sad without me telling him, and he tries to make me happy. When I am not sad, he tries to make me happier. When I am with him, my smile is bigger and my joy is greater. With him, I am complete."

"But he must do something?" I prodded. "Something special."

She shook her head. "He is just who he is. The one I love."

* * *

141

By early evening, as I began to prepare for my date, I was still swirling Renée's startling declarations about Jean-Claude through my mind.

I felt sorta betrayed. She'd repeatedly told me that Jean-Claude was romantic . . . and now she'd revealed that he didn't do romantic things. No flowers, no candy, and no poetry.

In essence, he was simply . . . *there*.

I thought about the times I'd seen them together. Jean-Claude always stayed close to Renée, holding her hand or putting an arm around her. At the dance club he'd danced every dance with her. They'd laughed and talked . . . and kissed.

They had looked so . . . well, in love.

She had told me repeatedly that Jean-Claude was a romantic guy, and yet in my opinion, he didn't do romantic things. I was so confused.

I glanced at the beautiful bouquet of flowers that Jacques had sent me. Their fragrance filled my bedroom as I got dressed for my date. As I applied my makeup, my gaze kept darting between my face, the flowers, and Alex's sketch. Flowers were definitely romantic. A sketch? In the annals of romantic history, sketches were probably just a footnote.

But I found that my gaze lingered on it more than it did the flowers. Not because it was a portrait of me, but because the lines had been so meticulously drawn.

Jacques arrived exactly five minutes early. Not early enough to interfere with my getting ready, but early enough to hint that he was anxious for this date. I thought of that old joke about the guy always waiting for the girl to get ready. With Todd, I'd been the one always waiting for him to arrive. Yet here was Jacques, early enough to make me feel special.

And ohmygosh, did he look hot! His black hair was kinda long, but it was combed back off his brow. He wore a black blazer over a lilac shirt. In Mustang a guy would die before he'd wear a pastel shade. White was pretty much standard for any shirt that buttoned. I thought of the blue shirt Alex had worn, but then, he really wasn't typical Mustang.

I turned my attention back to Jacques and his dancing blue eyes. He wore black slacks and had a killer smile. Nice and symmetric, both sides curling up evenly. So far, he was scoring perfect threes across the chart.

"Ready?" he asked in a husky voice.

"Wow," I whispered when I got a good look at his car. I felt like Cinderella stepping into the pumpkin turned coach as I climbed into his black Mercedes.

"I borrowed my parents' car," he explained as he started the vehicle.

And we were on our way to what had already begun as the most romantic evening in my life.

The restaurant—La Tour d'Argent—was the ultimate in luxury. Jacques had somehow managed to get us a table by the window, and we had a gorgeous, panoramic view. It was so romantic that it took my breath away.

The food was incredibly expensive. It should have made me feel special, but it made me feel a little guilty. Jacques was going out of his way to impress me, and all I could do was think about Alex.

I felt like I was in a library. Everyone spoke in hushed whispers. The ambiance was something I'd never find in Mustang. In the center of our table a tall, tapered candle flickered. At its base was a circle of orchids. We were even drinking wine.

Well, Jacques drank wine. I'd taken one sip and decided to go with hot tea.

"Any idea what Alex is doing tonight?" I asked.

"He took off cycling just before I left," Jacques explained.

"He really cycles a lot," I murmured.

"Every morning and most evenings," Jacques concurred.

"Do you cycle?" I asked.

"*Oui.* I can barely keep up with Alex, though," he confessed.

"He is amazing," I enthused.

He leaned forward, his blue eyes darkening. "You think so?"

"Absolutely."

Jacques leaned back. "Do you like the restaurant?"

I nodded enthusiastically. "It's gorgeous."

A corner of his mouth quirked up. "Alex thought you would like it."

"He did?" I inquired.

"*Oui*. He thought it would be a romantic place, and he said you liked romance," Jacques explained.

Somehow the restaurant lost some of its romantic edge. Knowing Jacques had brought me here at Alex's suggestion made it seem less special. Maybe I was selfish, but I wanted my date to take me someplace that he thought I'd like. That was so unfair to Jacques, who was paying a fortune for our meal.

I touched his hand. "I also want to thank you for the flowers."

He blinked, looking somewhat dumbfounded. "The flowers?"

"The roses you sent this afternoon," I reminded him.

"Ah." He nodded thoughtfully. "The roses. Of course. I forgot about them. They were nothing."

"Hardly nothing," I told him. "They were lovely."

"I am glad you were pleased."

I tapped my fingers on the table. We'd discussed the restaurant, the flowers, cycling. . . . This was the most romantic night of my life. Renée's words kept swirling through my mind.

And as nice as Jacques was, as attentive as he was, I couldn't help but wonder what Alex was doing this evening. Who had he gone on a date with?

I stood outside the door to Renée's house.

"I had a wonderful time, Jacques," I told him. And I had. Or at least I should have. He'd done everything right. Everything romantic.

145

"I'm glad," he whispered just before he leaned down and kissed me.

It was a sweet kiss. Much better than Todd's kisses, not quite as heavenly as Alex's. It was simply . . . pleasant.

He drew back and gave me a small smile. "*Bonsoir*, Dana."

"*Bonsoir*." I went inside the house.

Renée pounced on me. She'd been sitting on the couch with Jean-Claude, watching a movie. "So, how did it go?

"It was probably the most romantic evening I've ever had," I acknowledged. After dinner we'd walked along the Seine, hand in hand.

I turned and started up the stairs, wondering why the most romantic evening of my life had felt so terribly wrong.

Eighteen

Alex

WORRYING ABOUT STUFF was starting to get wearisome. In particular, worrying about Dana. Lying on my bed, I watched her pink cap go round and round as I twirled it on the end of my finger.

Earlier in the evening, right after I'd walked past the bathroom and seen Jacques shaving for his big date, I'd thrown on my cycling clothes and hit the road.

Fast and hard. I'd taken corners like a maniac. Pushed myself up hills and soared down at breakneck speeds. Stupid. Dangerous.

But I was trying to escape the image of them in the fancy restaurant Jacques had agreed to take her to—with me splitting half the cost of the meal.

But escape was impossible. I'd returned home exhausted, too tired to hold the images at bay.

I could envision the candlelight flickering over Dana's face, highlighting her hair, reflecting in her green eyes. I could see her sweet smile grow warm as Jacques charmed her with French and courtly grace.

As an all-American boy, the image should have made me gag, but I knew how much all those things meant to Dana, and I wanted her to have them. Even if I wasn't the one giving them to her.

I heard footsteps in the hallway. Jacques's footsteps. I glanced at my watch. It was only nine o'clock. He should have kept her out until midnight.

I bolted off the bed and rushed into the hallway. Jacques stopped dead in his tracks as I advanced on him. "What are you doing home so early?" I demanded.

He shrugged. "The date ended."

"What do you mean, it ended?" I insisted.

"We did all there was to do," he explained.

By nine o'clock? I was baffled and disappointed. "So, how did it go?"

Jacques sighed heavily. "It went well, I think. It would have been smoother if you'd told me that you sent her flowers."

"What do you mean?" I asked.

"She thanked me for the flowers, but it took me a minute to figure out what she was talking about," he explained.

"Oh, sorry. It didn't occur to me that you'd discuss the flowers. Guess it should have. How about everything else?" I asked.

"I did everything you told me to do. Dinner at Tour d'Argent, a stroll along the Seine, a kiss good night," he murmured.

"I didn't say anything about kissing her," I retorted.

He quirked a brow. "How can you have romance with no passion?"

Why did I have the feeling that he was baiting me? I took a deep breath, trying to calm myself. He was right. Dana would have expected a romantic kiss. I just didn't want to think about Jacques kissing Dana—or her kissing him. "Then she had a good time," I admitted.

Jacques shook his head slowly. "I don't think so."

I went completely postal. "What do you mean, you don't think so? Dana wants to date a romantic French guy. You're perfect for her—if you did everything that I told you to. So why didn't she have a good time?"

Jacques gave me a sympathetic smile. "Because, *mon frère,* I'm not the one she loves."

I heard a clock downstairs chime midnight as I lay in bed, thinking about Dana. Earlier, Jacques had explained that I'd been the main topic of conversation during his date with Dana. Dana talked about me so much that Jacques had felt like I was sitting at the table with them. As much as I cared for Dana, I knew that I was totally wrong for her.

I wasn't French, but more than that, I came

from a broken family. And so did she. Neither of us had an example of a lasting relationship to build on.

I'd thought that I did. Sure, my parents argued, sometimes my mom cried . . . but they had always managed to work things out. Or so I'd thought.

I remembered Dana telling me how much happier her parents were now. When I'd spoken with my dad, after he'd gotten over the shock of hearing from me, he'd sounded relaxed, more relaxed than I'd ever heard.

I thought about the way it had felt to have Dana rub my back while I talked with my dad. It seemed so natural to have her there.

But no matter how much I cared for her, I knew Jacques was wrong. She didn't love me. She couldn't possibly. We hadn't been dating. We weren't boyfriend and girlfriend. We were just friends. That's all we could be.

She wanted romance, and I was the least romantic guy I knew.

But within my chest, near my heart, there was a little spark of hope. What if I *was* what she truly wanted?

Much to my surprise, Dana called me the next morning.

"Hey," she said sounding slightly uncomfortable.

"Hey, back," I replied. I stared out the window. The sun was shining brightly. Jacques and I had planned to cycle a hundred miles as soon as we finished breakfast.

"I have a huge favor to ask," she announced softly.

I could hear the nervousness in her voice. I figured she wanted another date with romantic Jacques and the sooner, the better. Only she didn't know how to arrange it.

"So ask," I prompted when she didn't continue.

She cleared her throat. "Um . . . well, I was wondering if you'd mind spending the day with me. Today."

"Spend the day with you?" I repeated, clearly stunned.

She released a nervous laugh. "This is so awkward. Do you remember Robin Carter?"

I blinked. "From Mustang?"

"Yes. Well, she's one of my best friends, and she's spending the year as a student in London. Today she's coming to Paris, and she's bringing Kit."

"Who's Kit?" I interrupted.

"He started out as her host brother, but now he's her boyfriend. Anyway, they're going to take the Channel Tunnel rail service. It's only a three-hour trip, so they'll be here around ten o'clock. And we'll spend the day sight-seeing."

"And you want me there because . . ." I let my voice trail off. I wanted her to say that she wanted me there because I meant something to her. After all, I had a life, plans for the day too. You didn't just drop everything because some girl who meant nothing to you called. The problem was, though, that Dana

151

meant something to me. Much more than I'd ever expected her to. More than I wanted her to.

"So Kit won't feel like a third wheel. It's awkward when you have an odd number in a group," she explained.

Not as awkward as realizing that you wanted to be as important to someone as she was to you.

"Why didn't you ask Jacques?" I inquired.

She gasped. "I couldn't ask him. It's not like this is a date or anything, and I wouldn't want him to get the wrong impression."

My pounding heart settled down. It wasn't a date. "What impression?"

"That I cared for him more than I do," she answered.

"Didn't you have a good time last night?" I asked.

She hesitated. "It was really nice. He was really nice. He did so many romantic things."

"So you had your Paris romance," I announced, glad I'd given her what she wanted.

She sighed. "Not really."

"What do you mean, 'not really'? You said he was romantic," I reminded her.

"No, I said he did romantic things. I can't explain it, Alex. It should have been the most romantic night of my life, but it wasn't romantic." Her voice trailed off. She not only sounded disappointed, but sad.

"How could it not be romantic?" I demanded. "It cost me—" I snapped my mouth closed. She didn't need to know how much I'd spent on her romantic evening.

"What cost you?" she asked.

"Nothing," I replied, annoyed with Jacques. More annoyed with myself. "I'll spend the day with you."

"It doesn't sound like you want to." I heard the caution in her voice.

"I do. Honestly. Just tell me where and when." I could cycle anytime. Dana was more important.

"The Notre Dame cathedral at eleven."

"Great. We can take the Metro together. I'll drop by your house about ten-thirty."

I hung up and stared at the phone. Girls were completely illogical. She'd admitted that Jacques had done romantic things. So how in the world could the night have not been romantic?

Jacques's words echoed in my mind. "Because, *mon frère,* I'm not the one she loves."

And I wondered why it was that when either Dana or I needed something, we turned to each other. And more, I wondered why it was that I so quickly changed my plans to accommodate Dana.

And why I always felt glad that I had.

Private Internet Chat Room

Dana: Jeez, Carrie, I wish you could be here. The day just won't be the same without you.

Carrie: I wish I could be there too, but Paris is quite a ways from Rome.

Dana: How are things going with Antonio?

Carrie: Well, he found out that I'm an American, and basically he hates me.

Dana: Bummer.

Carrie: I deserved it. He had this unflattering impression of what American girls were like. I wanted to prove him wrong. Instead I showed him exactly how right he was. I deceived him, Dana.

Dana: I'm really sorry, Carrie.

Carrie: I need to go. Give Robin a hug for me.

Dana: Okay. Take care.

I sat there, staring at the empty chat room for the longest time. We'd all had such glorious plans for our year abroad. So far, only Robin had achieved her dream—and it wasn't her original dream.

I wished I wasn't finding it so difficult to identify what my dream was. I'd lost it somewhere between a kiss on the hilltop and what should have been the most romantic night of my life. And now I didn't know how to recapture the dream.

Nineteen

Dana

"DID YOU SEE Disney's *The Hunchback of Notre Dame*?" Alex asked me.

We were standing at the West Front of what I figured was the most famous cathedral in the world. In answer to his question, I simply arched a brow.

He gave me his lopsided grin. "Stupid question. You probably have it on video," he speculated.

I smiled brightly. "That's right. I own all the animated movies that Disney has released on video."

"You could have your own Disney film festival," he teased.

I shrugged, slightly embarrassed. "Most kids our age wouldn't be interested in animated movies."

"I am," he responded quickly.

And I knew he was. I was constantly amazed to discover how much we had in common. "Maybe when

155

we get home, I'll invite you over to watch them."

"Do that. I'll bring my Pixar collection."

Had I just set us up for a date? No way. I was not dating Alex Turner. Ever. Not here in Paris and certainly not in Mustang. Yet here I was, as always, enjoying his company. I thought about how much more I would have enjoyed that fancy French restaurant if Alex had taken me. The conversation wouldn't have been so stilted or forced. Jacques was nice. He really was, but I'd just never been able to relax.

I shoved my hands into my pockets and turned away from him. "Where's Robin?"

I scanned the sea of faces. So many people were coming to the cathedral today.

And then I saw her. Bouncing along. Her smile bright. She was tallish, with short, blond hair and blue eyes. Kit had blond hair and blue eyes and was also tall.

I remembered how horrified she'd been when we'd arrived at the airport in London and she discovered that her host sister was a host brother. But seeing them strolling toward me, her hand nestled in Kit's, it looked like they were getting along really well now.

I knew the moment she spotted me. Her eyes widened, she shrieked, and she released Kit's hand. She rushed up to me and hugged me tight. "Dana, I'm so glad to see you," she announced loudly with her deep Texas accent.

Laughing, I leaned back. "What happened to

156

whispering, Robin?" I asked. While I'd had a one-day layover in London, Robin had been trying desperately to keep her loud voice and heavy twang hidden from Kit.

"She took pity on me," Kit explained in a wonderful British accent that reminded me of Hugh Grant. "She finally decided to talk normally."

"Normally?" Robin slipped her arm around Kit's and shook her head. "Can you believe this guy likes my accent?"

"I don't just like it; I adore it," he told Robin.

I couldn't believe how happy they looked. Or how in love. It was incredible and wonderful to see. Robin had really been self-conscious about the way she talked. I was glad to know that to Kit, she was perfect.

Just like Alex. Alex with his love of art, cycling, and dreams to work for Pixar. And his dream to find the perfect French girl. He should be on his quest today, but here he was once again with me.

I felt slightly guilty as I turned to him. "Do you remember Robin?"

He stepped closer to me, and my heart sped up. "Sure do. We had English together last year."

Robin's eyes widened. "Oh, right. Alex."

I introduced him to Kit, and then I didn't know what else to say. I knew Robin was wondering why I'd brought him. Even I wasn't sure. The crazy thing was, I had just wanted to see him.

"You know, if we hurry," Alex announced, "we can

157

catch the eleven-thirty tour of the towers." He looked at me. "If you're interested in seeing the gargoyles."

"Definitely," I admitted.

"I'll get the tickets." He turned to go.

"I'll go with you," Kit said, and fell into step beside Alex.

As soon as they were out of hearing range, Robin grabbed my arm. "What is Alex Turner Johnson doing here?"

I shrugged. "Just Alex Turner. He dropped the Johnson for France. Too many names. Anyway, I invited him."

"Why?"

A good question. "I just thought it would be more comfortable if . . . we were an even number."

"No third-wheel sort of thing," Robin mused.

"Right." I jumped on that reasoning, had used it myself earlier.

"I didn't remember him being so cute," she murmured. "You seem to have been spending a lot of time with him."

"We're just friends," I told her. "Besides, you know my plan: to be romanced by a French guy."

She slipped her arm through mine. "Yeah, and you knew my plan. To get rid of this horrid Texan accent. You see how well that plan worked out."

"You've got Kit, don't you?" I questioned.

She grinned. "Yeah, I've got him. Just be careful that you don't get Alex."

*   *   *

Alex held my hand all the way up the staircase that led to the north tower. Three hundred and eighty-seven steps. Not that I counted.

But the view from the top made the journey worthwhile. We looked out on a magnificent view of Paris. Alex's hand tightened on mine. "Wow."

I stepped closer to him. "It's incredible, isn't it?"

"You know we really need to go to the top of the Eiffel Tower before we leave Paris," he said quietly.

He'd said it as if we were an item, planning to do things together. We weren't. I glanced over at him. "That's so touristy."

He raised a brow. "And this isn't? Dana, we're tourists. Who knows when we'll get back to Paris?"

"You're right. Maybe we could go today while Robin's here," I suggested.

"Sure."

"Do you have that much time?"

He shrugged. "I have as much time as you need."

That was so typical of Alex. Whatever I needed, he seemed willing to give me.

"Don't forget to let me know how much I owe you for the tickets," I told him.

"Don't be dense. I've been wanting to tour Notre Dame, just didn't want to do it by myself," he explained. "The tickets are on me."

"Hey, guys," Robin whispered loudly. "Come see the gargoyles."

"*Les chimères,*" I corrected her.

She jerked her head around. "What?"

"That's what the French call them," I explained.

She held up a hand. "Look, I don't need to learn French. I'm having a hard enough time learning to speak British."

"What are you talking about?" I asked. "The British speak English."

"Which isn't American. They use the same words, but they mean different things. Trust me, it's another language entirely," she retorted.

"And you're mastering it very well," Kit assured her.

She rolled her eyes. "Yeah, right. But enough about me. Why would someone put something that hideous on a church?" She pointed at the gargoyles.

"I think they're cute," Alex and I said at the same time.

I jerked my gaze to his. He simply shrugged and grinned. "Great minds think alike."

"Right," I murmured. It was scary—how much we thought alike. And how perfect it felt to still be holding hands as we looked at the gargoyles and out over Paris.

"Besides, they're rain spouts," Alex added. "When it rains, the rain pours out their mouths. Supposedly it sounds like they're talking then— '*glug, glug, glug.*'"

"I don't think I'd want to be up here while it was raining," Robin said.

I thought of standing in the rain with Alex the night he called his dad. I wouldn't mind being up here in the rain with him. Or anywhere in the rain with him. A troubling realization.

I didn't count the steps on the walk down. I figured they hadn't lost any during the time we were at the top of the tower. I did notice the way Robin and Kit kept smiling at each other. Robin looked so incredibly happy and content.

But then, why shouldn't she? Her boyfriend was British. He wasn't from boring Mustang.

I glanced over at Alex. Why couldn't he have been French?

Twenty

Alex

THE CATHEDRAL OF Notre Dame was incredible, with flying buttresses, stained-glass windows, incredible arches, and magnificent statues. I could have spent the whole day here. With Dana.

It was really funny. The way we oohed and aahed over the same things. We looked at everything through the eyes of an artist. We appreciated everything with the same intensity.

I couldn't imagine touring a Gothic cathedral with anyone else.

I also realized that if Dana hadn't brought me along, she would have been the third wheel—not Kit. He was majorly absorbed with Robin. And she with him.

I could tell that Dana was a little bummed by that. After all, she'd been friends with Robin for a long time, and I figured she'd hoped for some serious girl talk while Robin was here.

It was midafternoon before we finished our tour of the cathedral. We decided to head toward the Eiffel Tower. After we ate at a café along the way, we'd ride the elevator all the way to the top. A total day of being tourists.

On our way to the métro that would get us to the tower in about ten minutes, we passed street vendors and flower carts. I decided to buy Dana some flowers to cheer her up a little. She wasn't frowning or anything, but I knew that today wasn't all that she'd hoped it would be.

I tugged on her hand. "Come on, let me get you a flower."

She chuckled. "*A* flower? As in *one*? Solitary? Single?"

"Sure, you don't want to have to carry a dozen around all day," I explained. Besides, with one flower, I didn't figure I could be accused of being romantic or coming on to her. One flower was harmless.

The vendor's cart had a whole range of flowers: tulips, carnations, roses, and a slew of others that I didn't know the name for.

She looked over the blossoms. "Hmmm. One flower. Let me see. I like roses."

"Yeah, but I sent you a dozen yesterday. Seems like you'd want some variety." I cursed under my breath as it hit me what I'd confessed. I spoke quickly, trying to cover my blunder. "Roses are fine. What color?"

She snatched her hand out of mine. It was the first time we weren't touching in almost four hours. Strange how much I suddenly missed that loss of contact. She planted her hands on her hips. "You sent the roses?"

I shook my head. "I don't know what I was thinking. I meant to say that Jacques sent you roses." I quirked a brow, trying to look innocent. "Didn't he?"

She nodded thoughtfully, but she looked troubled. "Interesting that when the topic came up last night, he didn't remember sending them. Why is that, do you think?" she asked.

"The guy did so much to be romantic that sending the roses probably just slipped his mind," I lied, hoping she'd drop the subject. I didn't want to ruin whatever fond memories she had of her date with Jacques, even though they didn't seem to be many.

"A pink carnation," she said softly.

"The florist sent only a pink carnation?" I demanded. Those flowers had cost me a fortune.

She tilted her head slightly, still studying me. "No, I'll take a pink carnation now."

Relief swamped me. "Oh, right." I jerked one out of the cart, paid the vendor, and handed it to her.

I watched her sniff at it, all the while her eyes never leaving mine. I wished I knew what she was thinking. Hoped she thought Jacques had sent the flowers. How could I be so careless?

"Dana, look what Kit bought me," Robin announced.

Dana turned around. Robin was holding about two dozen flowers, all varieties, various colors. And Dana held one scraggly-looking carnation.

"Aren't they gorgeous?" Robin crooned. "Isn't Kit just the sweetest?"

Dana smiled. "He's the sweetest."

And I felt like a complete loser. Robin took Kit's hand, and they started walking away. I touched Dana's shoulder. She glanced back at me.

I jerked my thumb toward the flower cart. "You want some more? Giving you just one was so stupid and cheap. Pick out some others."

She shook her head slowly and looked at the flower. "This one's perfect." Then she lifted her gaze to me. "Thanks, Alex."

She reached up and kissed my cheek. Then she took my hand. "Let's go eat."

I fell into step beside her, and the most insane thought flashed through my mind. Why couldn't I have been French?

Twenty-one

Dana

ALEX GUIDED US toward a cozy little café with
outdoor seating. I don't know why, but it just
seemed when in Paris, I should eat outside beneath
the umbrella.

Robin shrieked when she saw the menu—all in
French.

I laughed.

"How am I gonna know what to order?" she
asked. "I was hoping for bubble and squeak or toad
in the hole."

I stared at her. "What?"

She tilted up her nose. "See? I told you it wasn't
easy to understand British."

"You eat those things?" I asked.

She nodded. "Every chance I get. So what
should we eat here?"

I glanced over at Alex. He blushed. "I can translate only about half the menu," he offered.

"That should be good enough," Kit said. "I fancy some sort of sandwich."

Alex began to translate, and by the time the waiter came over, we'd decided on four *croque monsieurs*—these really yummy ham and cheese sandwiches I couldn't get enough of. "We are really daredevils," I murmured when the waitress walked away.

"Hey, we crossed the Atlantic," Robin reminded me. "That was pretty daring."

"Yes," I had to admit. "It was."

The waiter brought over our drinks. Robin stared at the glasses and the pitcher.

"What is all this?" she asked.

"The closest thing I've found to lemonade," I explained. "They give you fresh lemon juice, and you mix it with water and sugar syrup."

Robin nodded. "Interesting."

We all mixed up a round, and Robin nodded again. "Not bad." She leaned forward. "You know, when I filled out my application for this program, I expected there to be some cultural differences, but I didn't realize how subtle some of them would be or how many."

I smiled warmly. "Me either."

"What have you found to be the hardest thing to do over here, Alex?" she prodded.

He glanced at me. The right side of his mouth tipped up, and for some reason, my heart played a tap dance along my ribs. His brown eyes twinkled. "Take off my shirt in class."

"What?" Robin asked.

"Our sketching class," I explained. "The guys had to remove their shirts so we could sketch . . . the body."

"Whoa. And I thought getting up in front of the class and revealing my goals for the year was hard," Robin told us.

"Did you have to remove your shirt?" Kit asked me.

I felt my face turn hot as I nodded.

"But she got to wear a bathing suit underneath," Alex muttered.

"No fair!" Kit exclaimed.

"That's what I said," Alex chimed in.

Thankfully, our sandwiches arrived and everyone was too busy stuffing their faces to talk much. My gaze continued to drift between the carnation and Alex. And the intense way that he studied the people at the table.

And I knew, knew in my heart that he was going to sketch this moment.

When we finished eating, we headed for the Eiffel Tower. As we got close, Alex asked Kit to run ahead with him.

"It *is* getting late," Kit said as he glanced at his watch. "I suppose we should go check on the line to the lift."

"The lift?" Alex asked.

"The elevator," Robin said. "We'll wait for you over there." She pointed to a spot under the tower.

"Gotcha," Alex said. He leaned toward me and

168

whispered, "We'll take our time so you can visit with Robin."

Then he and Kit went in search of the elevator, and I had what I'd wanted for so long—some time alone with Robin that would span more than a couple of minutes. And Alex had somehow known that's what I wanted, and he'd made an excuse to get himself and Kit out of the way.

"I don't remember Alex being so nice," Robin told me. I heard the bafflement in her voice.

I twirled my solitary carnation. "I've got a problem, Robin."

Her brow creased. "What?"

"I think I love him," I blurted out.

"And that's a problem because?" she inquired.

"He doesn't want a relationship. He wants a French girl. Someone who speaks only a little English. Someone with willing lips." I spat out the last part. It still irked me that he was looking for that.

"Did he tell you that?" she asked as a bunch of French schoolchildren paraded by.

"Yes," I admitted sulkily. "When I told him that I wanted a French guy."

"You told him that?"

I nodded. "Like I told you in the chat room, he set me up with his host brother. I think he may have even paid for some of the date. And he is definitely the one who sent me the flowers."

"You're kidding?"

I shook my head. It was crazy. I didn't know

whether to be happy or sad. Here was this guy doing all these things for me, and he wasn't my boyfriend. But suddenly I wanted him to be. Even if he wasn't French.

"Dana, he obviously likes you," Robin said quietly.

I snapped my gaze to hers. "As a friend."

"I think more than that," she told me.

I heard familiar English-speaking voices. First Alex's, then Kit's. So much for taking their time. I really needed Robin's advice on what to do.

But there wasn't time to ask her any more questions. The guys came over, and Kit looked really bummed.

"It's a two-hour wait to get to the top," he announced. "I'm terribly sorry, Robin, but we're going to have to head back home before that."

She shrugged. "That's okay. Maybe we can come back."

"I wish you would," I told her. I felt tears sting my eyes. It was always so hard to say good-bye to my friends.

She gave me a hug, and I hugged her back—tightly.

"Romance is in the air," she whispered.

For her, maybe. Not for me. All my dreams for this year were crumbling.

We broke apart. She cradled her bouquet of flowers and slipped her hand into Kit's. "Cheerio," she called out with a British accent.

"Au revoir!" I called back as she and Kit started walking away.

I turned to Alex. "Thanks for coming."

170

"It was fun." He shoved his hands into the pockets of his jeans. "So, did you still want to go to the top?"

I grimaced. "It's a two-hour wait."

"Yeah, but we aren't going anywhere. Unless you've got a hot date," he remarked.

I laughed. "No. How about you?"

He gave me that lopsided grin. "Nope." Then he took my hand. "Let's be tourists a little longer."

We waited in line for a little over two hours, and we talked the entire time. About everything. Home. Mustang. School. Paris. Dreams.

And we held hands.

Finally our turn came to climb into the double-decker yellow elevator and ride to the top of the tower. My hand tightened around Alex's as we began the ascent. Riding up the tower was not a good idea if you were afraid of heights. The third level, which houses the viewing gallery, was 899 feet above the ground.

That's a lot of feet, I thought as everything below us kept getting smaller and smaller and smaller.

When we reached the top, my heart was pounding a mile a minute. I glanced over at Alex. He seemed okay with the height. "We are really high up," I said inanely.

"Be glad it's not a hot day," he suggested. "On hot days the tower is six inches higher due to the metal expanding."

"This is quite high enough, thank you," I said as we stepped onto the platform.

And my breath nearly left my body. The sun was setting, painting a golden glow over Paris. We walked to the railing and simply stood. My back to his chest, his arms around me.

In silence. With no need to say anything.

We watched the sun disappear beyond the horizon and knew it would be another seven hours before our families watched it disappear. In a tapestry of colors the sky faded into black. And one by one the stars came out.

I sighed deeply. "That is so beautiful."

"Just like you," he said quietly.

I turned to face him. He kept his arms around me. I studied his face in the shadows of the night. "You're going to sketch a picture of me and Robin at the café, aren't you?" I asked.

"Probably."

I took a deep breath. "Alex, why didn't you turn in your sketch of the tower that you did that day on the hilltop?"

"Because I didn't draw the tower. I drew you."

"I can't believe you did that when you had all of Paris—"

"Dana, I want dibs on you when we get home," he blurted out.

Stunned, I stared at him. "What? Dibs?" How unromantic was that? "Like calling for the window seat on an airplane?"

He shook his head briskly. "No, nothing like that. It didn't come out right. I just mean that after this year is up and we get back to Mustang, I want to date you."

"You want to date me?" I repeated.

"Yes. You're driving me crazy. I think about you all the time. You're not what I want. Or at least, not what I thought I wanted." He plowed a hand roughly through his hair. "Look, I *know* I'm not what you're looking for right now. I'm not French. I'm not a romantic guy. But I thought maybe once this year was over, since whatever French guy you hook up with won't be in Mustang, that maybe you'd consider dating me."

I was floored and didn't know what to say to his crazy proposition. "You're going to wait a year to date me," I said tentatively.

"Yeah, I understand your dream, Dana. Paris. Romance. There's probably no other time in your life when you can have all that you'll have this year. That's why I set you up with Jacques, tried to make sure he did everything romantic. I want you to have the romance you're looking for," he explained. He released his hold on me and stepped back.

"I'd just like to know that you'd consider going out with me when we get home," he said.

I nodded, still unable to believe what he'd said. "A whole year," I reiterated.

"I'm not saying it'll be easy for me, watching some French guy romance you." I watched him swallow. "But I want you to have your dream."

I felt tears burn the backs of my eyes. "Are you still going to look for your French dream girl?"

He shook his head. "I was miserable with Monique. I wanted a temporary relationship with a French girl, someone who would make me forget about my parents' divorce. The only time it doesn't hurt is when I'm with you."

I couldn't believe this. I sounded like an echo as I asked again, "And you're going to wait a year to be with me?"

He nodded solemnly. "I understand your dream, Dana. I want you to have it. I'd just like a little spark of hope that once you've realized your dream . . . you might make some time for me."

My chest ached with all he was willing to give up for me. "I can't do that, Alex."

He gave me a sad smile. "That's okay. I understand. A year is a long time."

"Exactly. And I don't want to wait that long to be with you," I said quietly.

His eyes widened. "What?"

I took a step closer to him. "You're the most romantic guy I know."

"Hardly," he mumbled.

I looked at the carnation. He grimaced. "I should have bought you more."

I shook my head. "No, you shouldn't have. Don't you see? That's the point. I thought I knew what romance was, but I was wrong. It's not flowers, or poetry, or chocolate. It's someone you can talk with and feel comfortable around. With Jacques you tried to give me what I wanted. And now you're trying to step back so I can have my dream. When all I really want . . . is you."

"You want me?" he rasped. "Now?"

I smiled tenderly. "Now. Tomorrow. The day after that."

He slipped his arms around me and drew me close against him. "Dana, I don't want you to give up your dream."

"Alex, don't you get it? You're my dream."

The corner of his mouth lifted. "I am?"

Smiling warmly, I nodded. "Yeah, you are."

He lowered his head and pressed his lips to mine, so warm and sweet. I slid my arms around his neck. He deepened the kiss in that slow, lazy way of his. No hurry. No rush. Just heat, passion . . . and romance.

Because here I was at the top of the Eiffel Tower, a star-filled night above me, the dazzling lights of the city below me, and the willing lips of the guy I loved playing gently over mine.

It was strange how the realization that I loved Alex just wove itself into my mind. So easily. As if it was something my heart had always known.

Alex rained kisses along my cheek until he reached my ear. He whispered huskily, *"Je t'aime."*

I love you.

My heart melted.

"I love you too," I said softly.

He returned his lips to mine, and I thought this moment was the most romantic thing I'd ever experienced.

And the best part was . . . Alex would be there when my year in Paris came to an end.

Rome: Antonio & Carrie

One

Carrie

BUZZING ALONG THE bustling street on a borrowed Vespa scooter, I had an incredibly strong urge to shout, *Ciao! Everyone, look at me! I'm here at last!*

Here was the most awesome of cities: Rome. The Eternal City. As I wove in and out of traffic, I, sixteen-year-old Carrie Giovani, felt like I'd come home. But home was really Mustang, Texas. A little town on the far side of nowhere. My mother had grown up there, and unfortunately, so had I. Not that I disliked Mustang. My best friends—Robin Carter and Dana Madison—lived there. We were constantly together. My oldest brother, Marcus, referred to us as The Three Stooges, but I always thought of us as The Three Musketeers—always willing to embrace adventure.

But I digress. In Mustang, I worked in my dad's pizzeria. I enjoyed school, was popular, and got the leading roles in school plays. But a part of me had wanted more. Something deep inside me had always longed for the romance of Rome. I'm not talking kissy-face romance here. I'm talking grandeur, history, art, and vibrant people who know how to enjoy life.

Rome. The city where my father had been born and raised. He'd told me once that in his youth, he'd been restless. I could certainly relate to that feeling. I always wanted to go places, do things, be in the center of it all. Absolutely no sidelines for me.

I figured that my mom must have had a bit of a restless streak in her as well. She'd gone to Europe during the summer after her graduation from college. She'd met my dad while she was touring Rome. And the rest, as they say, is history. They fell in love. He'd proposed marriage before she returned to Mustang. They'd had what gossip columnists discussing Hollywood types always refer to as a whirlwind courtship.

Pretty romantic, huh?

I always thought so. Anyway, my dad said goodbye to his family and immigrated to the States. He moved to Mustang, married my mom, and established Giovani's Pizzeria. The business thrived, but not to the extent that he'd been able to afford to take his family of seven children to Italy. But many a night he told us about his homeland, and I fell in love with a place I'd never visited.

Now I was here, puttering along those very streets, waving at people I didn't know. Grinning like a fool—a fool in love with all that surrounded her. I couldn't have been happier or more excited. I believed that the whole world was a stage and that we should play as many roles as we can. Daughter. Student. Friend. Waitress—my least favorite role. Explorer. Adventurer was my latest, greatest role. Of course, I didn't know any of the scenes yet, and all my lines were ad-lib. No rehearsals. It was sort of like being an improv actress.

I was going to attend a school in Rome for an entire year. I'd been accepted into the Year Abroad program—just like my two best friends. Dana was spending the year in Paris. Her goal was to find a cute French guy to romance her. Robin was spending the year in London with one incredibly hot host brother, Kit Marlin. I'd met him during a one-day layover in London. I'd considered changing places with her, but with five older brothers in Mustang, I was looking forward to a year without guys hogging the bathroom and the television. My host sister, Elena Pietra, was an only child. In her home I would have peace and quiet—and a bedroom all to myself. No sharing with my younger sister, Maria.

Like my friends, I had a goal for the year: to get in touch with my Italian side. To become one with my heritage. Not that I was far from that goal. I had long, dark hair and an olive complexion. In Mustang, I stood out as an Italian. But I knew that

3

there really wasn't an Italian "look" to speak of. People in northern Italy tended to be fair, those in the south dark. But as I sped along the *via*—the street—I saw blondes *and* brunettes.

I knew I'd fit in here. I had the added advantage of speaking Italian fluently. So fluently, in fact, that in my mind I always heard English when anyone spoke Italian. My mind was simply set for automatic translate. Back in Mustang, my dad spoke Italian, my mom English. Yet I never got confused. Like a heavy-duty sponge, I simply absorbed both languages. When I spoke English, I had a Texas drawl, and when I spoke Italian, it was pure Italian. I could, when the situation warranted, even speak English with an Italian accent—something that had impressed my hometown when I had played Juliet in our school's production of *Romeo and Juliet*. After all, fair Verona was in Italy. Of course, our Romeo had spoken his lines with a bit of a twang . . . but his failure had only served to make my star shine more brightly.

I figured my fluency in Italian was going to come in handy this year. I'd been with Dana when she'd bought her English–French dictionary. She had taken French for two years at Mustang High but wasn't taking any chances. I didn't need an English–Italian dictionary. As a matter of fact, once my plane had touched down in Rome yesterday and my host sister had met me at the airport, I hadn't spoken a single word of English.

I had become totally immersed in Italy! Tomorrow

4

I would become immersed in an Italian school. But right now it was time to become immersed in family. I'd suggested staying with my aunt and uncle for my year in Italy, but my parents had thought the familiarity of family would take away from the experience of living in a foreign country with people I didn't know.

I'd promised my father that I would visit his sister as soon as I got settled in. Aunt Bianca and her family owned a restaurant. I'd looked it up in my guidebook. Yes, as much as I knew about Rome, I didn't know everything. A guidebook was a must for a girl who came from a town so small that you could see all of it just by driving down Main Street.

I had been pleased to discover that my aunt's restaurant wasn't that far away. I'd borrowed Elena's Vespa scooter—or, as most Italians referred to it: her wasp. It sounded like a bee buzzing along the street, but it was the easiest way to get around. Rome's streets were narrow and crowded. Plus the city had been built on seven hills. Riding a bicycle was out of the question for me—I hadn't ridden a bike since I was ten. There was also no way that I was going to risk driving a car. The Italians were lethal! They loved their little cars and sped along the streets pretty much like maniacs. Everyone had a cell phone because they were more reliable than the regular phone service, and everyone talked on the phone when they drove. And it was no myth that Italians talked with their hands; here they were, holding the cell phone with one hand, gesturing wildly with the other—and what was holding the steering wheel? A pair of knees, maybe? I didn't know. Didn't want to know. I just knew that it made me nervous. Slow traffic and congestion were also rampant. Another reason that the scooters were so popular. I could weave in and out of the stalled or stopped vehicles.

The Eternal City had recently been cleaned of pollution, the buildings scrubbed down until they revealed their original colors. Every now and then I saw a small electric bus humming along. I guessed the improvements were all part of Rome's desire to be shiny for the new millennium.

I finally arrived at my destination. I read the words engraved on the stone building: *La Sera*. Evening. I thought that name was romantic. It was my aunt Bianca and uncle Vito Romano's trattoria. A trattoria was a family-owned restaurant with good home cooking. A *ristorante* was usually more elegant and much more expensive. On either side of the door of the trattoria was a mosaic of clouds, stars, and a moon. Mosaics were very popular in Italy and adorned many of the buildings that I'd passed. I hadn't seen any yet, but I'd heard that mosaics often decorated the floors as well.

I brought the Vespa to a halt and moved it to the side of the building, where several others were already parked. I figured most belonged to the employees. Patrons would no doubt show up at this nice establishment in a cab.

I removed my helmet and pulled the red scrunchie out of my hair to release my ponytail. My brown hair fell like a curtain past my shoulders. I ran my fingers quickly through the thick strands. I was going to meet my father's sister and her family for the first time. I wanted to make a good impression, but I didn't want to overdo it, or I'd have something to live up to the next time we visited. I figured it was best just to be me.

The Romanos lived in an apartment above the restaurant. I climbed the stairs, my heart pounding. This moment was the most exciting of my life. I was going to meet the woman my father had probably teased while he was growing up. Taking a deep breath, I knocked on the heavy oak door.

It flew open as though the woman standing in the portal had been waiting for me. She was well-rounded, her black hair streaked with silver pulled up into a bun on top of her head. Her cheeks puffed out as she smiled broadly and held out her arms. "Carrina!"

"Aunt Bianca!" I stepped into her hearty embrace. Carrina is my real name, but only my dad calls me that—and my mom when I've done something wrong. To the rest of the world, I'm Carrie. But I loved the way my name rolled off her tongue in such a rich Italian accent.

She took my arms and pushed me back a little. "I would know you anywhere," she said in halting English. "You look just like your papa." Actually, except for the coloring, I looked mostly like my mom—but if she wanted to see her brother in me, hey, that was fine. I knew my father had sent them school pictures and family photos every year. And they had done the same, sending us family photos that included their five sons. So I felt like I was meeting someone I already knew, for the most part. Still, seeing someone in the flesh made it all the more real.

She beckoned me inside. "Come, meet the rest of the family."

The living room was quite small—or maybe it just seemed small with six guys standing in its center. Uncle Vito looked exactly like his photos. He was a big bear of a man with a shiny bald spot on top and tufts of white hair on the side just above his ears. My five cousins reminded me too much of my brothers. They were tall and dark, with only a year separating them from the one who was next in line. Roberto was the oldest and closest to my age. We made the round of introductions, and then my cousins dropped on the couch or the floor, and I sat in a plush purple chair.

I was amazed at how comfortable I felt around them. My aunt bustled in and gave me an orange juice. Freshly squeezed juices are popular drinks in Italy.

"So what is your host family like?" Aunt Bianca asked in English.

"Wonderful," I told her. "Elena Pietra is an only child. It's a little strange. The house is very quiet."

"I know Elena," Roberto told me, also in English. "She is very nice."

"We hit it off," I assured him. "And I have my own room. At home I have to share my room with Maria." My younger sister by one year. A slob who always borrowed my clothes without asking.

Aunt Bianca wagged a pudgy finger at me. "You will miss your sister and all your brothers before the year is out."

"I seriously doubt it," I responded, but deep down inside, I had a feeling she was right. Although I had a habit of never revealing the good side of any of my siblings, I loved them beyond measure.

Uncle Vito glanced at his watch. "We must get to the restaurant. You can eat there, Carrina, if you do not mind eating alone."

"But don't expect fast service," Roberto announced. He shook his head. "Two of our servers are sick tonight, and we are always extremely busy."

Uncle Vito waved his hand. "My boys always help me in the kitchen. Tonight I will have to let one of them serve the customers, or food will go out cold."

I eased up in my chair. "I could wait tables for you," I offered. During my year in Rome, I had planned to come as close to having a vacation as possible, but they were family, after all. What would it hurt to work one night?

Aunt Bianca fluttered her fingers. "Don't be silly, Carrina. You are a visitor."

"I'm family," I pointed out. "Besides, I wait

tables in Dad's place, so I have the experience."

Uncle Vito looked uncomfortable. He moved both hands as though he were juggling invisible balls. Robin and Dana always teased me because I spoke with my hands constantly in motion. I'd always told them it was the Italian in me, and here I was discovering exactly how true that statement was.

"You see, Carrina," Uncle Vito said, "we have so many tourists that it's important we create an authentic Italian atmosphere."

"I'm Italian," I began. Then I realized that we'd been speaking in English from the moment I walked through the door. In perfect Italian, I said, "I speak Italian fluently. And I can speak English with an Italian accent."

Uncle Vito laughed. Aunt Bianca beamed. "Your papa, he taught you Italian?"

"*Sì,*" I assured her.

Uncle Vito slapped his hands on his thighs. "Then tonight, you can work for us. We even have a uniform you can wear."

I stood up and smiled. "*Grazie.*" I held up a hand, caught up in the moment. "But don't tell anyone I'm your American relative. Tonight I want to be a true Italian."

It was a role I'd never played before—but I could hardly wait.

Two

Carrie

I'D FORGOTTEN EXACTLY how much I missed waiting on people—about as much as I missed raw, oozing blisters on my feet. And wearing a black pleated skirt, a stiff white starched shirt, and a black bow tie didn't increase my affection for the job. The uniform for Giovani's Pizzeria was a bit more laid-back—T-shirt and jeans.

Almost all the tables were occupied. Uncle Vito had introduced me to a few of the staff as the evening shift began, but many of his workers arrived a little later—with the crowds. All the workers spoke only in Italian—even to the customers.

Not only did tourists enjoy the restaurant, but so did a good many Italians. It was definitely to my advantage that I understood Italian. I wasn't exactly being a waitress. I was more of an all-around helper.

Clearing tables, getting second drink orders, putting fresh tablecloths on the tables, and setting out new silverware.

I glanced toward the front of the restaurant. Aunt Bianca looked calm as she explained to someone that it would most likely be a half-hour wait for a table. In Rome, evening meals usually didn't get seriously under way until around nine.

I glimpsed a dirty table and headed over. I stacked the plates, then the glasses, and lifted the whole thing. I hooked the rim of the top glass with my chin to prevent the tower of glasses from tumbling over.

I heard a couple of gasps as I passed some tables. I imagined I looked like a juggler in a circus. A balancing act on the verge of catastrophe. But I'd cleared too many tables for too long to think that I didn't know what I was doing.

Carefully I wended my way around the tables and headed for the kitchen. A swinging door kept the inner workings of the kitchen hidden from patrons. It occurred to me that tourists at least might enjoy watching the show that went on in the kitchen.

I pressed my shoulder to the door and swung it open. A guy with four plates running up one arm and a plate in his other hand jumped back.

"Mi—Mi scusi," I stammered as I regained my balance and caught my breath.

"Va bene," he replied in a deep, rich voice that reminded me of hot syrup dripping over pancakes.

I lifted my gaze from the plates he was expertly

balancing to his face—and lost my breath again as I stared into the most incredibly deep blue eyes that I'd ever seen. His eyes held me captive. The guy was tall, his blond hair combed back off his brow.

"Antonio!" Uncle Vito yelled. "Get the food out while it's hot."

Of course, Uncle Vito was yelling in Italian, but as usual, when it reached my brain cells, I heard in English.

Antonio gave me a charming smile, shrugged, and eased past me. I watched him stride through the restaurant with confidence. I appreciated the view of his broad back. And I liked the way his black trousers hugged his narrow hips.

With five brothers who constantly eyed girls and had no qualms about assessing their attributes out loud, I'd learned early on to pay as much attention to guys and not feel self-conscious about it.

And Antonio was definitely hot. I walked into the kitchen and deposited the dirty dishes near the sink. But I couldn't stop thinking about the guy I'd just seen.

Working here as a pinch waitress was going to pay off in ways I'd never imagined.

I hadn't come to Rome looking for romance, but when a romantic opportunity knocked—I wasn't foolish enough not to open the door.

Around eight-thirty I watched as Antonio began lining up empty tables. I really liked the way he moved—totally efficient. I could see the muscles rippling beneath his shirt. He wore a uniform like mine—almost. He wore black pants instead of a pleated skirt. But he had the starched white shirt and the black bow tie. I pictured him in a tuxedo, going to a prom—with me as his date, of course. That was a fantasy that would never come true. I wasn't even certain if they had proms in Italy.

My father had been more interested in discussing the Forum and the Pantheon than the social functions at the schools he'd attended. I assumed that was a typical male preference.

Aunt Bianca walked over to where Antonio was working. She began pushing the chairs against the tables he was arranging. "Carrina? Come here, dear," she said in Italian.

Okay, calm down, I ordered my heart. I was going to be able to get another close-up look at Antonio instead of watching him from afar—and hoping that no one noticed I was watching him.

"Yes, ma'am?" I said in perfect Italian.

She nodded toward the front, where a group of people had gathered. "Carrina, there are twenty people in this party. I want you to help Antonio serve them."

Help Antonio? Could I have asked for a better assignment? I wanted to hug Aunt Bianca. Throw my arms around her neck, kiss her cheeks, and promise her my firstborn child. Okay, I knew I was getting carried away, but this waiter was definitely

14

the cutest of the bunch, and now I'd have a legitimate excuse to be near him. On the outside, I remained amazingly calm, while on the inside, I was doing a victory dance.

I shifted my gaze to Antonio. He was watching me speculatively. I felt myself grow hot under his perusal. "What do you want me do?" I asked in Italian.

He smiled warmly, shrugged, and responded in Italian, but of course, my automatic translate was working. "They are Americans, so they'll need menus. If you could get those—"

"Sure," I blurted out. "No problem." I'd already handed out menus to several Americans who had requested them. Few tourists understood that in Italy the waiters usually told patrons what foods could be ordered. Of course, waiters spoke in rapid Italian, and if a tourist wasn't familiar with the foods or the language, there was a good chance that the waiter was simply wasting his breath. Still, when in Rome . . .

"Then I'll take their orders," Antonio continued, "and you can help me bring out their food. Americans usually leave a tip. We'll split it evenly if this group does."

I knew that Italians weren't generally in the habit of tipping. My father had explained some of the social graces, although he'd been more concerned about teaching me how to keep my money out of the hands of pickpockets when I browsed through the open-air markets. My dad knew me well enough to know that I wouldn't be able to resist the lure of the marketplace.

I grinned at Antonio. "Sounds fair." I jerked my thumb over my shoulder. "I'll get the menus."

"Carrina," he said softly.

I turned around to face him.

His gaze touched me like a caress. "A beautiful name," he murmured.

Then he strode toward the kitchen, leaving me standing there with a song of love humming through my veins. No one had ever told me my name was beautiful, and no one had ever spoken it with such a harmonious cadence.

I thought that I could definitely fall for this guy fast and hard.

I was accustomed to handling entire baseball and soccer teams at Giovani's Pizzeria. My dad's place was where all Little League sports teams assembled after beating each other—to create a show of good sportsmanship.

So helping Antonio with this group of Americans was a breeze. It was funny to watch the older girls giggle every time Antonio neared their table. It was so obvious that they'd developed crushes on him while he'd taken their orders. A couple of the guys at the table tried to flirt with me, but I pretty much nipped their amorous intentions in the bud when I told them that I had an older brother who wrestled bulls for fun. I whispered it in

English with an Italian accent so they couldn't mistake that I was *not* interested.

Antonio seemed to be enjoying the girls' attention, though. I guessed that I couldn't blame him. They were pretty much goggling at him like he was some movie star they'd spotted. I was surprised by how much it bothered me. I'd only just met the guy, and for all I knew, he could have a serious girlfriend. Guys this hot usually did.

We divided up the orders so we each made two trips, carrying five plates each. I could tell Antonio was a little impressed that I could carry four plates on my arm, one in the other hand—just as he did. My arms were tough. I was used to balancing pans of pizza and hauling pitchers of root beer.

All in all, Antonio and I made a good team. We didn't get in each other's way. I shadowed his moves. I let him lead. After all, he was the real employee here. And I simply followed, making sure everyone's order was perfect and everyone had a good time. It was actually a lot of fun. I thought of these people as my audience as I played to perfection the role of the Italian *cameriera*—waitress.

When they walked out of the trattoria, they left behind a tip that was the equivalent of forty American dollars.

"I can't believe this," Antonio said quietly as he handed me half the money. "I've never had anyone leave this much money."

"My papa always told me that great service equals

17

a great tip," I told him as I pocketed the money.

"Your papa," he repeated. "Lucky you."

Huh? What did he mean by that? He reached for a plate. We were still really busy, and I knew we didn't have time for idle chitchat. I'd have to pursue that avenue later.

"I'll clean the table," I offered. "You still have customers to serve, and I'm just a helper tonight."

"Thanks, Carrina."

I watched him head back toward the kitchen. I wondered why mentioning my pop seemed to bother him. Or maybe it was just my imagination. Maybe he was simply tuckered out. After all, we'd just worked together for an hour to keep this table of twenty—not to mention his other patrons— happy.

I was sure my dramatist imagination was going into overdrive because I too was a little worn out. Jet lag was beginning to take its toll. Only two days earlier I'd been in Texas, calling Dana and Robin to see what all they were packing.

I glanced at the table of dirty glasses, plates, and silverware. I groaned. Thank goodness, my waitress days were about to be behind me—at least until I returned to Mustang.

I looked toward the kitchen. Antonio came out, bearing an armload of plates loaded with spaghetti. Filling in tonight had definitely paid off. I'd met one hot and interesting guy.

18

Now I just needed to find out if he found me equally fascinating.

By the time the last customer walked out, it was close to eleven o'clock. And I had school tomorrow! But I wasn't tired. At home it was late afternoon. I was going to have to adjust to the time difference in a big way.

Aunt Bianca had tried to persuade me to leave when the crowd had begun thinning about half an hour ago, but I'd never left a job unfinished. My father had a really strong work ethic—an hour's work for an hour's pay. My brothers and I always rolled our eyes when he said it, but that didn't stop us from following his teachings.

Leaning over, I blew out the flame in the candle that adorned one of the tables. I loved the atmosphere that all the tall, flickering candles sitting in wine bottles had created. The wax dripped, flowing along the sides of the bottle until the wax hardened. I could see the drippings from so many other candles—a history of sorts. I wondered at all the people who might have sat here while the flame melted the wax.

I removed the tablecloth and wiped down the table, glancing casually over my shoulder to catch a glimpse of Antonio. Our paths had crossed several times after we'd waited on the group of twenty together. We hadn't had time to talk, but the more I saw him, the more he intrigued me. My heart sped up every time we passed. He had the nicest smile and a way of making me feel like he was giving it to me as a special gift.

I couldn't explain it. He was so totally hot. I knew I was being shallow, judging the guy mostly by his looks and his ability to carry an armload of plates. But I had plans to expand my horizons where Antonio was concerned. Before I walked out the front door, I was determined to discover if he had a girlfriend. With five brothers who had way too many male friends, I wasn't exactly shy around guys. I'd learned early on how to hold my own.

I finished wiping the table. I leaned back, trying to work the kinks out of my lower back. My feet were swollen. Waiting on people was hard work. But the dining area looked clean now, so I figured my evening as staff at La Sera was about to come to an end.

I headed into the kitchen. And there was Antonio—and several of the other waiters—mopping the floor. Smiling, I pressed my shoulder to the wall and simply watched the way the muscles in Antonio's back and arms flexed beneath his shirt as he moved the mop over the floor.

"Americans," he spat, talking to the guy working next to him. "The girls, they are so stupid, so selfish. I hate waiting on them. They giggle like hyenas."

Stunned, I felt my mouth drop open. I couldn't believe what he'd said. What a loser! Had I actually spent most of the night drooling over this guy? He hated Americans. He thought we were stupid and selfish. Anger surged through me. As an American, I was neither stupid nor selfish.

Hadn't I sacrificed my evening to help out?

How small-minded to judge an entire group of people based on a few individuals. Boy, did I have a few choice words to toss at this guy. Hearing his comments had totally cooled any interest I had in him.

Hands balled into fists at my side, I took a step toward him—and halted.

Confronting him was way too easy. Telling him he was an idiot wasn't nearly enough. He needed to be taught a lesson he'd never forget. Someone needed to bring this arrogant Italian down a notch or two.

And I knew I was just the girl to do it.

Drama was my life back at Mustang High. So now I would have a larger stage—even if it was a smaller audience.

Antonio didn't know I was American. Why tell him I was?

I could get to know him a little better, give him the opportunity to get to know me. And when the time was right, when he was under my spell, I'd break the news to him that I was an American.

And gain retribution for all American girls everywhere!

Three

Antonio

I FELT THE hairs on the back of my neck prickle. Someone was staring at me. Hard. Intensely. A shiver traveled down my spine.

Or maybe I was just exhausted from a grueling night of waiting on people who had way too much money. Still, I looked over my shoulder.

And there was the new girl. Carrina.

Man, was she cute. And so exotic looking. She'd pulled her long, brown hair back in a ponytail, but I wanted to see it hanging loose around her face. And what a face. Her oval eyes were a dark brown—like expensive chocolate.

Tonight was the first time she had worked at La Sera, yet I had been amazed at the ease with which she had handled customers. Even the bratty Americans did not seem to bother her. I had seen her laugh with some of them as though they shared a private joke.

She fascinated me. And judging by the way she watched me, I thought that maybe I intrigued her. I wanted to get to know her better, but approaching girls was foreign to me. Ever since my papa had died, my life had narrowed down to work, school, and taking care of my sisters. Still, I did not want to let this opportunity to speak with her pass me by. Besides, I had a perfect excuse. She'd helped me out tonight. What would it hurt to thank her again? She wouldn't be able to read anything into that.

I took a deep breath to calm my nerves and repeated beneath my breath that girls were people too. Then I strode over to where she was standing near the wall.

I tried to give her a warm smile, but I had a feeling that my mouth probably looked like I'd just bitten into a lemon. Why couldn't I relax? After all, she was just a fellow worker. "I . . . I . . . uh . . . really appreciated all your help tonight." Now that I was really aware of her, it seemed that my tongue had forgotten how to form words.

She flashed a beautiful smile. "No problem."

Of course, it was no problem. She was paid to help. Now what should I say? Something clever would be good.

"I didn't catch your whole name," I confessed. Okay, not clever, but true. "I'm Antonio Donatello."

"Carrina Gio—Gio. Carrina Gio," she stammered.

Was she nervous as well? Briefly that made me feel better, but then I started to worry that maybe I was coming on too strong. I was most definitely nervous. I wiped my sweating palms on my trousers and tried to think of something else to say—something to fill the yawning abyss of silence stretching between us.

"Have you worked here long?" she asked.

I could have kissed her for that one. I was better at answering questions than asking them.

"Two years now." Two long years. Hard years. I did not want to think about them. I wanted to think about her. And I wanted to get to know her better. Much better.

"Listen, I know we just met, but . . . would you like to go have a cup of coffee at a nearby café?" I asked. I had a little extra spending money thanks to that generous tip the Americans had left. I held my breath.

Her mouth opened slightly. Her brow furrowed.

"I have a hard time unwinding after a hectic night," I explained quickly.

"Um . . . ," she began.

"The café is just around the corner," I assured her. "We can walk." I knew some girls were nervous about going places with guys they didn't know. Or maybe she had a boyfriend and was trying to decide whether or not he'd beat me up if she had coffee with me.

She nodded. "Yeah, sure. I would like to clean up a little first, though."

"Okay. It'll take me about twenty minutes to finish up here. I'll meet you out front," I told her.

She nodded quickly. I watched as she slipped through the swinging door, barely opening it.

I could only hope that she didn't have a boyfriend. Girls as cute as she was usually did.

I paced outside the restaurant. My nerves were a wreck.

Had I, Antonio Donatello, actually asked a girl out on a date?

No, no, this wasn't a date. We were just going to get something to drink and chat a little bit. Friends, maybe we would become friends.

I could certainly use one.

But a girlfriend? I had no time and very little money. It would be years before I could impress a girl enough to have a girlfriend.

The resentment rose up in me, and I shoved it back down.

Chill out, Antonio, I commanded myself. *There is nothing you can do about the past.*

And because of the past, it would be a long while before I could have the future I dreamed about. A future that included the one thing I wanted most: a girlfriend.

But what girl would settle for the little that I had to give right now?

The answer was obvious. No girl. Girls required time, attention, gifts, dates. . . .

The door to the restaurant opened. I watched Carrina step outside. Immediately I regretted asking her to join me. Usually I went to the café alone to unwind. Having someone with me tonight would only make it harder to go there alone tomorrow.

I was surprised to see Signora Romano hug Carrina. But then, Signora Romano had a tendency to treat everyone like one of her children. And Carrina was a new employee. I figured she just wanted to make sure Carrina felt good about her first night at work.

Carrina smiled brightly as she hurried down the steps. She wrapped her arm around mine. "Lead the way," she ordered.

Her flawless Italian carried an intriguing accent. I almost felt like it was a shadow over something else. I couldn't explain it. And I'd never known a girl to be so bold as to touch me like this. Especially after she'd seemed so hesitant to join me. Carrina was incredible. Totally relaxed, as though she were used to being around guys. Not a good sign. She probably had a bunch of boyfriends. I started walking toward the corner. "Tell me about your family," I prodded.

She groaned. "Boring. Five older obnoxious brothers, one younger spoiled sister." She looked up at me. "You?"

I smiled. "Four younger sisters."

She shuddered. "Italians always have such big families."

And the fact that she had so many brothers

might explain why she was so comfortable around me. Her brothers probably had lots of friends, and she was used to being around guys.

Unfortunately, except for my sisters, who were much younger than me, I was not used to being around girls. My heart was pounding. I was afraid she'd be able to hear it.

But if she did, she didn't say anything.

We rounded the corner. My mouth went dry when I saw the café. It was so plain. Suddenly I wished I'd offered to take her to a real restaurant.

"Is that it?" she asked, pointing toward the tables and chairs that lined the sidewalk in front of the café.

"Yes," I admitted.

"Awesome! I love eating at an outdoor café." She beamed at me.

"You do?" I asked.

"Truthfully, I've never eaten at one before, but I've always wanted to," she enthused.

I couldn't imagine how she'd avoided eating at a café. Maybe her family had to watch their money as carefully as mine did. Maybe they seldom ate out. For whatever reason, I was grateful for her enthusiasm.

I guided her toward a table away from the street. I wanted to be able to talk to her without having to shout over the roar of passing vehicles. Even though it was late at night, the streets were filled with people going places.

I ordered an espresso, and Carrina ordered a

caffè latte. I decided to splurge. I ordered us each a *tiramisú*. Her eyes brightened when she heard me order. I didn't very often spend money on myself. But then, neither did I ever find myself sitting at a table at a café with an exotic-looking girl.

She leaned forward and crossed her arms on the table. "I'll pay for mine."

I was seriously insulted. "I invited you. I'll pay."

She hesitated a moment before settling back in her chair. "Okay."

"Is working at La Sera your first job?" I asked. I wanted to know everything about her.

She looked slightly uncomfortable. "Uh, no. I worked at a pizzeria."

"Which one?" I asked.

She waved a hand in the air. "It was just a little one. You've probably never heard of it."

I nodded. "You're probably right. I don't eat out much."

"Do you like working at La Sera?" she inquired softly.

"I like working for the Romano family. They are good to me, fair to their workers," I admitted. "But I hate waiting on the rich Americans. They're such snobs."

She gave me a smile that seemed a little false. "I never noticed Americans were snobs."

"You probably haven't been around very many," I explained.

"Oh, I've been around quite a few," she assured me. "They seem nice to me."

"Nice?" I repeated. "Nice?" I raised my voice to a squeak. "'I want a vegetarian lasagna, but take out the peppers, and the onions, and the tomatoes.'" I returned my voice to normal. "How do you take tomatoes out of lasagna?"

She pressed a hand to her mouth, hiding a smile. A genuine smile this time. I knew because it touched her eyes.

"And then there's the pasta," I continued. "Americans call everything pasta. They don't understand that there's conchigliette, cappelletti, fusilli, farfalle, and a hundred others."

"Some understand," she protested.

"Not enough. An American couple orders cappelletti. I bring out the pasta that looks like little hats. The woman squeaks like she saw a mouse."

Carrina's smile broke free.

"You know this American woman?" I asked.

She shook her head.

"Be glad. Because like I said, she squeaks, 'Ah! Ah! That's not what I ordered!' Then she starts fluttering her hands, waving her arms like she wants to fly," I explained.

Carrina laughed. The sound was so lovely. I wanted to hear more, so I exaggerated the tale a bit.

"'I want butterflies,' she tells me. 'The pasta that looks like butterflies.' Then she gets out of her chair and starts floating around the room, dipping here, dipping there."

Shaking her head, Carrina laughed fully then, so

vibrant, so alive. Her eyes sparkled. "No, she didn't," she insisted.

"She did. You can ask Signora Romano. She disrupted everyone's meal. All because she wanted butterfly pasta."

The waitress brought over our pastry and drinks.

Carrina was still chuckling. "That's not being a snob," she argued. "That's simply trying to ensure that you get what you want."

"I have to take the pasta back and toss it in the garbage because she ordered the wrong thing. I have new pasta made—then her food is cold. All night I am going back to this one table, trying to please this one woman. My other customers get angry. Then no one is happy," I explained.

Carrina nodded slowly. I watched as she bit into her *tiramisú*.

"Maybe La Sera needs a place on the menu with photos of the actual pasta so the customers can point to what they want," she suggested.

I stared at her. "*We're* supposed to bend over backward because *they* are ignorant."

"They don't know they're ignorant. I don't think they mean to be trouble. They spent a lot of money to come here. They want authentic Italian cuisine—" She touched her fingers to her lips, kissed them, and then spread her fingers apart. "What's wrong with helping them have it?"

Pondering her question, I sat back and drank my espresso. I'd never considered the dining experience

30

from an American's point of view. It troubled me to think she might have a valid point.

She leaned forward, moving aside her empty plate. "Enough talk about work. What do you do for fun?"

I lifted my cup—indicating I was doing what I did for fun—and gave her a half grin. "I'm a very exciting guy."

She laughed again, that remarkable laugh.

"I know you do more than drink coffee," she chastised.

"Let me see. For fun." My mind was an absolute blank. When was the last time I had fun? Right before my father was killed and I had to become the man of the family. "Honestly, Carrina, just sitting here talking with you has been more fun than I've had in a very long time."

"Then you definitely need a life," she stated, but not unkindly. Her eyes were sparkling as though we were sharing some inside joke.

I grinned. "I was thinking the same thing earlier this evening." And I was definitely thinking now that I wanted my life to include her.

Four

Carrie

ANTONIO DONATELLO WAS an arrogant Italian. I repeated the litany over and over as I sat at the breakfast table with my host family.

That he'd asked for my full name last night had caught me off guard and had me stammering like a novice actress. For all I knew, my aunt and uncle had mentioned to the staff that their American niece, Carrie Giovani, would be coming for a visit. Then when he'd asked me to join him at the café . . . ad-libbing, I'd quickly discovered, was not my forte. I was much more comfortable with script in hand. Still, once we'd gotten to the café, things had gone well—too well.

I didn't want to think about how much I'd enjoyed being with him. Or the way he'd made me laugh. Or the way he'd looked so deeply into my eyes that I felt he could see my soul. Heavy thoughts, but at the time they'd seemed so true. There was a sadness in his deep blue eyes. *From what?* I wondered.

Had he been feeding me a line when he said that talking to me was the most fun he'd had in a long time?

What if he hadn't been? It didn't matter. I couldn't let his words or his eyes distract me from my goal. I had gone out with him just to get even with him and his small-minded attitude toward Americans.

Granted, I could have told him at any time that I was born and bred in the United States. He'd given me plenty of opportunities—every time that he put down Americans. But I figured that the longer he thought I was Italian, the more stunned he would be when he learned the truth.

At least that was what I told myself. It was better than doubting my plan.

I found the silence at the Pietra table unnerving—I could actually hear myself think. I was accustomed to having meals with nine people talking at once, each louder than the other, fighting to be heard. Signore and Signora Pietra were very polite and reserved as they sat, drinking their coffee and eating a sweet roll. Italians usually had a light breakfast, unlike the plate of scrambled eggs, bacon, sausage, home fries, and toast that were heaped on my—and everyone else's—plate back home.

Their home was small, typical of Italians. Next to the tiny kitchen was the *tinello,* a medium-sized room where we ate our meals at a large table. Since my arrival I'd spent most of my time in this room or my small bedroom. The house also had a *salotto*—which was the equivalent of a living room—but it was used only for formal entertaining. And occasional television watching.

"Nervous about your first day of school?" Elena asked, pushing a strand of silky, dark, short hair behind her ear.

Actually, until that moment I hadn't thought about it.

"A little," I confessed, now that it was on my mind. I would be attending the *liceo,* a secondary school that offered courses specializing in the languages, the arts, and the sciences. I planned to take at least one drama class. I was considering looking into a music class as well. Opera was big in Italy, and although it was considered a geek thing, I loved opera. Again, it was the Italian in my blood. Opera called out to me. "I can't believe your school days are so short," I admitted. School started at eight-thirty and ended at one-thirty. Everyone went home for lunch. No cafeteria food, no lunchrooms. A definite plus in my book since I never could figure out exactly what the food at school was made of.

Elena's pretty brown eyes twinkled. "The teachers give you enough assignments to keep you busy in the afternoons. And don't forget we have school on Saturdays too."

I groaned at that revolting thought. "A total bummer."

She laughed. "You Americans are spoiled."

Antonio had said the same thing, but it wasn't true. "Not really," I was quick to explain. "Our school days are longer. I think it all evens out."

"Did you enjoy meeting your relatives yesterday evening?" Signora Pietra asked me.

I smiled warmly at Elena's mother. "I loved meeting them. As a matter of fact, I'm going to be working in their restaurant for a while."

Signora Pietra furrowed her brow. "But I thought foreign-exchange students weren't supposed to work during their year abroad. Won't a job take away from traveling or having fun?"

"Maybe a little," I said. "But no matter what, family is family, and right now some of their staff is sick." Besides, the only way to see Antonio and finish teaching him a lesson was to work at the restaurant. It was the only place where our paths would cross. I couldn't very well just show up on his doorstep every day. I really wasn't looking forward to working regularly. After all, I had sort of envisioned this year as a vacation. Sure, I had school to attend, but that was nothing compared to my usual schedule at home.

But working would be worth it in the end. I couldn't wait to see the shock on Antonio's face when I finally told him the truth. Once he knew he'd misjudged Americans.

I was so excited as I walked the hallways of my new school. All around me I heard the rich cadence of

Italian. The school, housed in a white, one-story, meandering brick building, wasn't that different from my school back home. Students roamed the halls, talking, laughing, hanging out. Through the open doors I could see desks similar to the ones I sat in back at Mustang High. The only major difference was that the chalkboards were freestanding in many of the rooms.

I felt like the starship *Enterprise,* going where no Giovani had gone before. I was totally new at this school—the first Giovani in my family to grace its classrooms.

No teacher would say to me, *Miss Giovani, your brother Marcus was an ace at math. Why are you having problems figuring out the logarithm?*

No girl would try to be my best friend just so she could weasel a date with one of my older brothers. I'd learned early on to suspect any girl who complimented me or wanted to join me for lunch or acted like we were best buds when I didn't even know her name. Most were just striving to get information on my brothers.

Except Dana and Robin. My two best friends in the whole world. I treasured their friendship simply because they had absolutely no interest in my brothers. They cared about *me.*

Already I missed them. I'd spent a day with them in London before heading to Rome. I wanted to call them, but phone calls weren't cheap. We'd agreed to e-mail instead and if possible meet in a private chat room on the Internet. That would be fairly close to a phone call. Not as satisfying, to be sure, but better than nothing.

I'd checked my e-mail before heading to school. Carrie and Dana had sent me letters, explaining how nervous they were about their first day in a foreign school. I understood their nervousness. But I didn't share it. Sure, I was in uncharted territory— but I welcomed the adventure. The thrill of it all. I knew absolutely no one—and no one knew me.

Except Elena, of course. And a couple of my cousins who also went to school here. Like Roberto. Other than them, I wouldn't run into anyone I knew. It was a liberating thought. No one would judge me according to the low standards that my brothers had set.

I turned the corner and staggered to a stop. *No way!* the silent scream echoed in my head. I couldn't breathe. My heart hammered. A guy stood in front of a wall of lockers. Tall. Blond. I'd recognize him anywhere.

Antonio!

No, no, no. Not at *this* school. He couldn't be a student at *my* school!

But clearly he was. I watched him open a locker. He put something inside and slammed it shut with a metallic echoing. Then he turned in my direction.

Oh my gosh! I couldn't let him see me! I was supposed to be an American at this school. I couldn't be Italian as well!

Backing up, feeling my way along the hallway with my hand, I never took my eyes off him. A horrid thought flashed through my mind. What if we had a class together? He'd learn the truth way before I was ready for him to know. I'd have to reveal my true nationality because every teacher knew who the Year Abroad student was. How would I explain the situation to Antonio with people standing around us? What would his reaction be?

Maybe he wouldn't care. Yeah, right. After he'd put down Americans to my face? After I didn't tell him who I was? I felt pretty confident that he would care a great deal when he discovered I was an American.

Students kept weaving in and out between us, but soon it would just be him and me. Face-to-face. He was closing in on me. I had to escape and fast. I felt the smooth wood of a door. I jerked my head around. A bathroom. Great! A place to hide until he'd walked past. I pushed open the door and ducked quickly inside.

Realizing much too late that it was the boys' bathroom.

Five

Antonio

TODAY HAD BEEN the longest first day of school that I'd ever experienced. For the first time in a long time, I couldn't wait to get to work. Although it wasn't work that I was truly anxious for.

I was anxious for a glimpse of Carrina. So eager, in fact, that I arrived early at the trattoria. I opened the front door quietly and stepped inside. She was already there. Her back was to me as she stood at a table, filling salt-and-pepper shakers.

She was more elegant than I remembered. And so efficient as she filled the shakers, as though she'd done it for a lifetime. No one else was in sight. Quietly I tiptoed across the room until I was close enough to smell her perfume. A soft, flowery scent.

I leaned close to her ear. "Where have you been all my life?"

Carrina shrieked. She jerked back, her arms went up, and pepper rained over us. And when her arms came down, they hit the tray, and all the shakers took flight.

They showered the table, the floor, and us with salt and pepper.

Carrina sneezed. *"Achoo! Achoo! Achoo!"*

It was a cute sneeze. Small, tiny. She spun around. Her eyes were watering. She sneezed again. "What did you think you were doing?" she demanded.

I felt incredibly silly. I'd wanted to be romantic, and instead I'd been stupid and caused her to create a mess. I knew so little about girls, but I should have known I'd startle her. "I'm sorry." I bent down and began picking up the shakers. "I'll get these if you'll get the broom."

She knelt beside me and sneezed again. "I don't know where the broom is. I'll get these. You get the broom."

I hurried to the kitchen. Roberto raised an eyebrow at me. "What happened out there?" he asked. "I thought I heard Carrina scream." He was preparing the grill for tonight's crowd.

"I startled Carrina, but she's fine," I assured him as I opened the door to the closet and grabbed the broom and dustpan.

I rushed back into the main dining room. Carrina had picked up all the shakers. I watched as she tossed a pinch of salt over her shoulder.

"Superstitious?" I inquired as I neared.

She turned to look at me. Such deep brown eyes.

"You bet. You'd better take precautions as well," she advised. She held out the salt container.

Normally I was not superstitious, but right now I thought I could use some good luck with this girl. I wanted to get to know her so much better, and I didn't really know how to accomplish that goal. I extended my hand, and she poured a little salt into my palm. I tossed it over my shoulder. *Let her like me,* I wished silently.

I didn't even know if you were supposed to make a wish when you tossed salt over your shoulder, but I thought it couldn't hurt. Then I realized how selfish the wish was because I still had no more to offer her today than I had last night.

She took the dustpan and knelt on the floor. "I'll hold the dustpan; you sweep up the mess you made," she ordered.

"Me?" I scoffed. "I'm not the one who threw everything in the air."

She peered up at me. "You're not going to blame this on me."

I smiled. She was not easily intimidated. She no doubt was always arguing with her five brothers. Perhaps if my sisters were older instead of younger, I would know more about girls.

I swept up the grains of salt and flecks of pepper until the floor was spotless. Carrina stood and sneezed again. I took the dustpan from her. "You didn't answer my question."

41

She gave me a coy smile. "What question?"

"Where have you been?" I repeated.

Her smile blossomed. "Right here."

"But where? We don't go to the same school, or I would have seen you. Where is your family? Who are your friends?" I asked. I wanted to know everything.

She sighed and began refilling the shakers. "My two best friends are in the Year Abroad program this year. One is in London, the other in Paris."

"What a coincidence. My school is hosting a student in the Year Abroad program—an American." I started laughing. "I heard she went into the boys' bathroom today."

I expected Carrina to laugh. Instead her face turned red as though she were embarrassed. Was she shy about discussing bathrooms? I wanted to put her at ease.

I shook my head. "So typically American, to go to a foreign country where you don't know the language, to expect everyone to cater to you and put up signs in English. I hope my path crosses hers someday just so I can tell her how silly I think she is."

She looked like she might be ill. "Excuse me, will you? I need to get some more salt."

I watched her hurry into the kitchen as though she couldn't wait to get away from me. What had I done wrong?

Later in the evening, as I gathered the dirty dishes from one of the tables where I'd waited on patrons, I darted a quick glance around the dining room. No Carrina.

I had the distinct impression that Carrina was avoiding me. She somehow managed to be in the dining room when I was in the kitchen. In the kitchen when I was in the dining room. It was quite an elaborate little game of hide-and-seek. Sometimes she would even disappear for a while. Then I'd spot her talking with Signora Romano at the front. Tonight she was taking orders and serving customers. But she didn't seem as energetic as she did yesterday. Maybe she was simply nervous with the added responsibility.

The only other possibility was one I didn't like to acknowledge. I'd definitely done something to upset her. But what?

Carefully balancing the dishes, I crossed the dining room, pressed my shoulder against the swinging door, and shoved it open. Carrina stood on the other side—impressively balancing five plates on her forearm. We'd been like this when we'd first met last night—only in opposite places. She started to edge past me.

"I need to talk to you," I whispered.

"I'm busy." She averted her gaze.

"After work," I insisted.

She gave me a brisk nod, then marched into the dining room.

Never before had I felt so attracted to a girl. It was more than the beauty of her face. She worked hard. She had a nice laugh and a beautiful smile.

And there was something . . . different about her. I couldn't explain it, couldn't put my finger on it. But whatever it was, I liked it.

It was crazy for me to want to spend time with her based on absolutely nothing but a feeling. But I did. And in a few hours I would.

I went into the kitchen and deposited the dishes by the sink. We had two guys who washed all the dishes. I was glad that wasn't my job. I washed enough dishes at home.

Roberto was dipping a big ladle into a pot of steaming spaghetti sauce.

"What do you know about the new girl?" I asked him.

He stilled. "What?"

"Carrina. Do you know anything about her?"

Roberto looked me directly in the eye. "I know that my parents would *not* be happy if someone hurt her."

Wow! That was a heavy answer. Why would anyone hurt Carrina? I only wanted to get to know her, make her smile.

"Do you know if she has a boyfriend?" I prodded.

Roberto poured the thick sauce over the meatballs and noodles. "Look, Antonio . . ." His voice trailed off.

My heart sank. She did have a boyfriend. Last night she'd simply been nice. A friend. A fellow worker needing to unwind as much as I did. No wonder she was avoiding me. I had begun flirting with her the moment I came into the restaurant. I started to head back into the dining room.

"She doesn't," Roberto snapped as though he were seriously irritated with me.

I spun around and looked at him, hope sparking. "Doesn't what?"

"She doesn't have a boyfriend, but . . ." Again he seemed reluctant to continue.

"But what?" I prompted.

"But if you break her heart, my parents will kill you."

"Antonio!" Signore Romano yelled. "Don't you have customers?"

"*Sì!*" I shouted back.

Sì! Sì! Sì! She didn't have a boyfriend!

Carrina was sitting on the steps outside the trattoria by the time I finished helping close up. She stared at the vehicles whizzing by on the street. I wondered what she was thinking.

How did a guy figure out what a girl was thinking?

I dropped down beside her. She twitched as though I'd startled her again. She looked at me and smiled warmly. "No salt or pepper to spill this time," she said.

"I'm sorry that I startled you earlier," I admitted.

"No big deal," she assured me as she stood up, shoving her hands into the pockets of her pleated skirt.

"If you live near here, I thought I could walk you home," I suggested.

She smiled again. "Sure."

As we began walking, all I could think of was that I didn't get it. Had I done something wrong earlier today or not? Now she didn't seem to hate my guts. Granted, she wasn't exactly bursting with joy at the sight of me, but she had smiled at me twice. So why the cold shoulder all day? And why was she still being so quiet now?

I wished I'd spent more time with girls my own age. Yes, I'd had girlfriends; well, a few dates, a few weeks of dates, but the way girls' minds worked remained a mystery. The only girls I knew well were my sisters—and they still played with dolls. The silence stretching between Carrina and me was driving me crazy.

Every time we walked beneath a streetlight, I could see her face. Then the shadows moved in, and I could only guess at what she might be thinking. I figured the best approach was to just blurt out my concerns. "Did I say something to upset you?"

She glanced at me. I watched her nibble on her bottom lip as though she were trying to figure out exactly what she wanted to say. And in that moment I knew I'd blown it. I'd lost any chance of another date—if last night even counted as a date.

She sighed. "I've been thinking about that poor American student at your school. Trying to put myself in her place."

"Why would you want to do that?" I asked. She'd withdrawn from me because of the American?

Honestly, Americans were more trouble than they were worth.

"Because it helps me understand people if I try to imagine what it's like to walk in their shoes." She stared straight ahead, her expression serious. "So I'm seeing this girl walking through the halls of a school she's never been in before." She peered at me. "Do you remember how you felt the day you went to your school for the first time?"

Unfortunately, I did. I'd been terrified, petrified, afraid I wouldn't fit in. My friends had already dwindled down to just a few. Most didn't know what to say to me now that I had no father.

"I remember my first day at a new school," Carrina murmured, breaking into my thoughts. "I was excited but nervous. I knew only two or three people. I figure this Year Abroad student probably felt the same way, but I bet she was a little frightened as well. Even if she was unwilling to admit it to herself."

"Frightened?" I asked. *And who cares anyway?* I thought. *Why the big interest in the American?*

She held my gaze. "Frightened. She isn't sure what people expect of her. She's special. She has a role to play. She's representing her country, a country she loves, with a heritage she's proud of. Yet she's equally proud to be here, and she loves all that she's seen of Italy so far. But she has to project the image of the confident American. And maybe she's not quite as confident as she thought she would be. Maybe she worries about things. She studied

47

Italian. She can read Italian, but she gets nervous and goes into the boys' bathroom by mistake."

I raised my eyebrow. Whatever. I was much more interested in asking Carrina questions about herself than in talking about the scared American. Carrina's compassion was a surprise. That she cared so much about the silly foreign-exchange student was nice. Very nice. I don't think I'd be so silly as to go into the girls' bathroom if I were a Year Abroad student in the States, but . . . "Okay," I conceded. "Maybe that's what happened. Maybe she wasn't looking for signs written in English."

"Can you imagine how embarrassed she was?" Carrina prompted.

Okay, okay, enough already about the American! I was about to change the subject by asking Carrina why she felt such a kinship with the Year Abroad student, but she'd beat me to a question.

"What is your most embarrassing moment?" she asked softly.

I felt the heat burn my face. That I did not want to discuss with the girl I wanted to like me! "What does it matter?"

"Mine was walking into a boys' bathroom," she confessed. "Just like the American did today."

I stopped walking and stared at her. Ah. So that's why she felt so much sympathy for the girl.

She looked down as though she couldn't bear to meet my gaze. "It wasn't that long ago. I can remember the moment vividly. Seeing those guys standing there when I'd expected to see girls putting on makeup. The worst part, the absolute worst part, was how quickly everyone heard about my faux pas. I could see people pointing, hear them laughing and snickering whenever I walked by. So I understand how your American student felt."

Idiot! I yelled at myself. I could kick myself in the shins so hard! *That is what you get for being so quick to judge people and for being so interested in your own ends, Antonio! You were so busy thinking about getting to know Carrina that you didn't even pay attention to her when she was trying to share something with you.*

I took her hand. "Carrina, I'm sorry. I didn't know. When I laughed about what the American did, when I said she was silly . . ." I sighed deeply, then realized that I was holding her hand. Worried that I'd been too forward, I pulled my hand away, supposedly to run it through my hair. No wonder Carrina had been upset with me. She must have felt like I was laughing at her when I'd joked about the American earlier. I had to undo the damage—no matter what the cost to my own stupid ego. "I told jokes with my fly open," I blurted out.

Now it was her turn to stop and stare at me. "Come again?"

"My most embarrassing moment," I admitted. I could still remember the sting of humiliation. "I was twelve. My friends and I approached a group of girls. I wanted to impress them, so I told a joke. They laughed. I told another joke. They laughed harder. Only later I discovered that they weren't laughing at my jokes. They were laughing because my jeans were unzipped."

She slapped her hand over her mouth, but still I heard a bubble of laughter trying to escape.

"You think it's funny?" I asked, trying to hide my smile. I was so relieved to see her laugh—to hear her laugh—and to see those brown eyes of hers sparkling again.

Carrina shook her head. Then she nodded and laughed. "Yes, I do." She held up a hand. "I'm sorry. But it is funny."

I smiled. "Maybe a little. And you know what? The American walking into the boys' bathroom is funny too. And when she goes back home to the States at the end of the year, it'll be the first story she shares with her family and friends, and she'll smile when she tells it."

"You really think so?" she asked, looking up at me thoughtfully.

"Definitely," I assured her, touched by how much she really did care about the girl. "In fact, if that were the kind of American that she was, perhaps I could like her," I admitted.

"Really?" she asked softly.

I nodded. "But Americans aren't like that. On second thought, she'll never think it's funny. I've worked at La Sera for two years. Americans—with their fancy clothes and their fancy cameras—complain, complain, complain. Nothing's funny to them. They don't know how to laugh at themselves. Hey, I have a great idea—why don't we forget Americans?"

She glanced at me, then stared straight ahead. "Most people are like that, Antonio. Not just Americans. I'll bet when you realized your zipper had been open while you were telling jokes to those girls, you didn't laugh about it right away."

She had me there. "Okay, maybe you're right."

She smiled. "Fine, so now that we're agreed on that, we can definitely stop talking about Americans."

We started walking again. I liked having her so close. I couldn't believe that I'd told her that embarrassing story about my zipper, but there was something about Carrina that made me feel I could tell her anything. I wanted to walk and walk and walk, ask her all about herself, where she lived, what she liked to do with her spare time. I wanted to know everything about this new girl who'd come into my life.

With a deep breath I slipped my hand back into hers. "Carrina, I want to be honest with you. Just tell you something outright."

She glanced up at me, clearly surprised.

"I really like you," I said, surprising even myself. "I've never felt this comfortable around a girl before."

Abruptly she stopped walking. She slid her hand out of mine. "Antonio, I . . . I . . . I'm sorry. I left something at the trattoria. I have to go back for it."

"I'll go with you," I offered.

She shook her head quickly. "No, please. I don't want to inconvenience you. Thank you for walking me this far."

I watched in stunned silence as she tore away and dashed up the street—never once looking back. Had I frightened her with my declaration? We only met yesterday. Had I moved too fast? I was being the only way I knew how to be. But perhaps that was not the way with Carrina? I thought girls liked guys to be strong and romantic.

Groaning, I started walking toward the bus stop where I would catch the bus home. I didn't understand girls. I didn't know what they wanted or what they expected.

All I knew was that I had opened up to Carrina, and it had meant nothing to her.

Six

Carrie

MY HEART POUNDED as I ran around the corner and headed back to the trattoria.

Antonio liked me. This very evening had been one of my dreams when I'd thought about living in Italy for a year. Walking down the beautiful, old streets of Rome, hand in hand with an Italian guy, soaking up the culture of my ancestors. But now . . . everything was a mess.

And the worst part was—I liked him. I hadn't expected that. He had such a warped view of Americans, but somehow I understood his position a little better than I had when I'd first heard him put down the people of my country. As someone who worked in a restaurant that catered to tourists, what he knew of Americans was limited to what he saw of Americans: the ones who visited the trattoria and complained, making his job even harder than it was already.

But instead of telling him that he was wrong, that not all Americans were like that, that I, in fact, was American and if he'd get to know me, he'd see how wrong he was, I had decided to play a game.

Not a role. A *game*. Like I was in middle school. Like I was a child.

How in the world was he going to feel when he discovered I was an American? And not just any American? *The* American.

Suddenly I felt mean and spiteful.

I'd deliberately started our walk in a direction that wouldn't lead to my home. So I could add deceptive to the list of my awful traits. But I couldn't risk letting him know where I lived. What if he knew Elena? What if he knew Elena was hosting his school's Year Abroad student? I'd been surprised enough today to realize that my aunt, uncle, and cousins hadn't mentioned my background to the staff of La Sera. I knew they wanted to project the image that only native Italians worked there, so perhaps the Romanos hadn't shared my nationality with their employees just to make sure the secret didn't leak.

What if Antonio realized that the YA student was me?

I'd known at some point—as we walked in the wrong direction—that I was either going to have to blurt out the truth about myself or find an excuse to leave him standing there. Once he'd told me he liked me, blurting out the truth was no longer an option.

I'd wanted to teach him a lesson. I hadn't wanted to hurt him! And telling him the truth would only make it seem like I'd been making a fool out of him.

I arrived at the trattoria and found Elena's scooter where I'd locked it up earlier. Slipping the helmet on my head, I straddled the scooter, then turned the ignition and rolled onto the street. The scooter sounded like an angry bee buzzing around me.

Oh, how I longed for the quiet of Mustang so I could think. Sure, it was noisy at home, but I could always go to Robin's farmhouse for quiet since she was an only child and lived outside of town. I needed to talk to my friends—desperately.

What would they think? Would they think I was cruel?

This farce had gone on long enough. I needed to end it—and soon!

But how? How could I end it without causing him to hate me?

When I arrived at the Pietras, my host parents were just finishing a cup of tea. After I'd assured the signora that I didn't want a single thing, she and her husband kissed me good night and went into their bedroom. Elena must have been sleeping already. I rushed up to my bedroom, grateful for the solitude.

My room was tiny, but I loved it. The bed had a brass-railing headboard, which I thought was incredibly romantic. The small wooden desk held my laptop computer and a telephone, and beside the desk was a white miniature dresser with gold paint etched along the edges. It looked ancient—like everything in Rome. And I adored it.

I sat on the edge of my bed and stared at the phone. Who should I call? Dana? She was Miss Practical. She would *not* understand what I'd done or why I'd done it—but she would have a reasonable solution to my dilemma. She looked at everything with the broad strokes of an artist.

Or maybe I should call Robin. Dare-me-to-do-anything Robin would certainly understand my need to trick Antonio. She would also approve. Be Daring was her motto; well, at least until she'd arrived in London and decided she was going to change her personality from outgoing to demure. Robin thought the English wouldn't approve of her unless she acted—and even spoke—differently. In a way, Robin was being her usual daring self by pretending to be quiet. I just hoped she reverted back to her great self once she realized that people would like her just as she was, no matter what country she was in.

After all, I was a perfect example of what could happen when you pretended—no matter what the reason—to be someone you weren't.

I needed both my friends for advice. But I couldn't afford to call both of them. Heck fire, I couldn't afford to call one of them. I crossed my small room and opened the double doors that led onto the balcony. I wrapped my fingers around the black wrought-iron railing. I felt like Juliet from *Romeo and Juliet*, like a star-crossed lover.

Rome. Roma. Romance. It was a city meant for romance, and I'd unexpectedly fallen under its spell. No tall office buildings or skyscrapers marred the skyline. It looked as it had for centuries, with Corinthian columns and the cupolas of baroque churches silhouetted against the sky. The view was breathtaking. And it made me feel insignificant and wondrous at the same time. I couldn't explain it.

Although my balcony was bare, I could smell the flowers from all the other balconies. When a city had three million people, it didn't leave a lot of room around houses for gardens, so many people had created little gardens with pots and pots of beautiful flowers and lush plants.

My head throbbed. I rubbed my temples. Antonio liked me. Isn't that what I'd wanted? Snare him. Get him to like me and then, with the perfect smirk, announce: *But how can you possibly like me? I'm an American.*

The words had been on the tip of my tongue. . . . If only he hadn't been so apologetic when I told him that I'd walked into a boys' bathroom. He didn't know I'd been talking about that very morning, but I had described to him exactly how I'd felt when I'd seen guys standing in the white-tiled room. It had been without a doubt the single most embarrassing moment of my life.

A couple of the guys had laughed. The other four had simply stared at me with mouths agape. And I'd stared back before dashing out, my hair covering my face, just in case Antonio had been there. So I'd waited until the guys cleared out and the bell rang. I'd been late to my first class. By the time I got to my last class, the rumors had circulated throughout the school. The female Year Abroad student had gone into the boys' bathroom. I heard them whispering about it and giggling. They didn't seem to be laughing at me in a mean-spirited way, but that hadn't made me feel any better.

Yet I knew someday I *would* laugh about it. Just like Antonio said I would. Certainly the story would have my brothers rolling on the floor. That thought made me smile.

"Carrie?" a soft voice whispered.

I turned to see my host sister, standing in the doorway of the balcony. "Hi, Elena. I thought you'd already gone to bed."

"No, I was reading a magazine," she said in English. "Are you all right?" She stepped onto the balcony. Elena had told me she wanted to speak English with me as much as possible in order to practice. She spoke English almost as well as I spoke Italian.

I sighed. I was far from okay, but I didn't want to worry Elena. "Just thinking."

"I heard that your first day did not go as smoothly as you'd hoped," she murmured.

I looked at the black sky. "Nothing is going as I'd hoped."

"Everything will be okay, Carrie," she consoled me. "Just give it some time."

I turned around and smiled at her. "I know you're right. It's just hard right now, I guess." I felt guilty.

We were talking about two different things, but I so appreciated the kind words, even if she thought I was referring to the infamous Bathroom Episode.

"How did you manage to go into the boys' bathroom?" she asked, clearly baffled. "You can speak and read Italian better than some Italians I know."

I sighed again. "It's a long story." I crossed my arms over my chest and leaned back against the railing. "Do you happen to know Antonio Donatello?"

"Sure, I know him," Elena said. "He works at La Sera. But since I don't work there, I don't know him too well."

"Don't you know him from school?" I asked.

"Not really," Elena replied. "Antonio doesn't have a lot of time for hanging out or after-school events."

"Why?" I asked. Probably because he worked at La Sera. A part-time job didn't allow for much socializing or school activities.

"Because his papa died," Elena explained. "He has to be so responsible for his family."

I gasped and felt my heart tighten. I remembered how quiet he'd gotten our first night at the café when I'd mentioned my father. Had it made him think of his own father? "His papa died? How?"

"An automobile accident," Elena said solemnly. "A drunk driver." She shook her head. "It's such a sad thing. Antonio is the oldest, the only boy. When his mama works, he takes care of his four younger sisters. When his mama isn't working, he is."

"Oh gosh." I pressed my arms against my chest,

trying to ease the ache I felt. Poor Antonio. "When did his papa die?"

"Two years ago," Elena told me.

Two years. That was exactly how long Antonio had been working at La Sera. In light of this new information, my ploy to teach him a lesson seemed incredibly petty now. What had he really done? Taken a dislike to Americans because they were rude and impatient and mean when they came into the restaurant.

Wouldn't he dislike them a whole lot more when he found out that I was an American and had been taking him for a ride?

Stupid plan, Giovani, I chastised myself. I had to tell Antonio the truth right away.

And suffer the humiliation and the consequences that would follow.

The next day at school I felt like I was constantly playing dodgeball—only I was playing dodge Antonio. I peered around every corner, scoped out every hallway. I'd gone from boldly going where no Giovani had gone before to *sneaking* where no Giovani had sneaked before.

If my new classmates thought me strange yesterday, they must have found me downright bizarre today. I was grateful when the school day ended, as it always did, at one-thirty. Since all the kids went home for lunch with their families, I didn't have to worry about a cafeteria confrontation—with my classmates about how weird I was . . . or with Antonio.

After my last class I decided to drop by the school library. In my history class we'd been assigned a research paper on a famous artist. We were studying the various churches in Rome, and they all had some amazing artwork. I'd chosen to write my paper on Michelangelo.

As I wandered down the aisles between bookshelves, it was a kick to see all the books with Italian titles—books I'd read in English. The classics, like *Tom Sawyer* and *Charlotte's Web* and *Hamlet,* plus the ones Robin, Dana, and I traded, like the Harry Potter books.

Suddenly my heart stopped. I heard Antonio's voice—asking for the biography section. He had to be standing at the front desk. I heard the librarian's voice but not her response. Footsteps echoed over the wooden floor. Nearer, nearer. Panic hit me.

I ducked around the corner. Straight into a dead end. Bookshelves on either side of me but no exit—except the opening through which I'd come. This was almost as bad as ducking into the boys' bathroom. Would I never learn to look before I ducked?

The footsteps came closer, closer. My heart pounding, I grabbed a book, opened it up, and held it in front of my face.

The footsteps stopped. I barely breathed. *Dare I lower the book?* I wondered.

"Have you seen any other biographies on Raphael?" Antonio asked.

I nearly jumped out of my skin. What was he talking about? I peered at the chapter opening I had the book open to: "Raphael's Early Works." Oh.

I'd grabbed a book on the very artist he was researching! "No," I replied in a falsetto voice.

"Excuse me," he said. "I need to get to those books on the other side of you."

I pressed my back to the shelf while he edged past me. Out of the corner of my eye I could see him crouching, searching the books. He pulled a book off the shelf and riffled the pages.

"I have to do a research paper on an artist for my history class," he said conversationally. "But it looks like you've got the only book on Raphael. Guess I'll do it on Botticelli." All the junior-year history classes must have the same assignment, I realized.

I brought the book closer to my face as he stood up.

"Raphael is one of my favorite artists," Antonio added. "Don't suppose you want to do your report on Botticelli?"

"No," I whispered. "Sorry."

"I didn't think so, but it never hurts to ask." Unfortunately, I heard the disappointment in his voice.

I listened to his footsteps echo as he walked away. Fainter, fainter. I pressed the book against my face. A close call. Too close.

Because of me, because of my stupid plan and my stupid need to hide from him until I could bear to tell him the truth, Antonio couldn't do his paper on Raphael. How could the library have only one biography of Raphael? With his work schedule Antonio probably didn't have much access to the Internet to do school research. Sneaking in some reading during breaks and before bed was probably his only time to study.

When I heard him leave the library, I grabbed a book on Michelangelo and strode to the counter, the Raphael biography still in hand. The librarian smiled at me. "How do you like going to school in Rome?" she asked.

"It's definitely not like attending school in the States," I told her. In Mustang, I walked the halls like I owned them. I'd pretty much planned to do the same thing here. Instead I was creeping through the hallways in *Scary Movie,* waiting for the guy wearing the distorted white mask to jump out at her. "But I sure do like it here," I added, placing the biography of Michelangelo on the counter. "Especially getting out so early."

She smiled as she stamped the book for me. "Ah, but you Americans are not used to school on Saturdays."

"I will be after this year," I told her with a smile. "Could you do me a favor?"

"*Sì,*" she told me. "If I can."

I slid the book on Raphael toward her. "The guy who was just in here—"

"Antonio Donatello?"

I nodded. "He was looking for a book on Raphael but couldn't find it. I found this after he left. It was shelved in the wrong place," I whispered as though I intended to keep this horrible alphabetical offense between us. "Could you send a note to him in class tomorrow and let him know that this book is available?"

She smiled and took the book. "Yes, I'll do that."

I leaned forward. "Don't tell him that I found it. I'm sure some student put it back on the shelf carelessly."

She gave me an appreciative smile. "I'm used to that."

I took the Michelangelo biography, shoved it into my backpack, and walked out of the library. At least now Antonio could do his report on Raphael. I felt a little better knowing that, but not much.

After all, I'd let the perfect opportunity to reveal myself pass me by. All right, I'd let it pass me by because it was not so perfect. That wasn't quite the truth either. It wasn't quite the perfect spot for me. I wanted to tell Antonio the truth, but preferably someplace with no witnesses. I figured his home turf would be best. And chicken that I was, I was thinking about waiting until Saturday to talk to him so we'd have Sunday—a whole day without our paths crossing—to lick our wounds.

Besides, I needed to figure out the best way to announce my deception. Every line that I ran through my head sounded like it came from a bad play. Perhaps I had better just tell him the truth in as straightforward a way possible. I supposed I could start with my name. Carrina Gio. That was what he thought my name was!

Antonio wasn't a slouch in the intelligence department. I knew it was only a matter of time before he realized how close Carrina Gio and Carrie Giovani were. What had I been thinking when I'd come up with that lameoid variation of my name?

Obviously I hadn't been thinking. My emotions had been dictating my actions. And my emotions apparently weren't real bright.

I'd never in my life been so angry with myself. Because the truth was, I liked Antonio. I liked him a lot. He was an interesting guy, complex. He'd been honest and open with his feelings, whether about Americans or me, a girl he thought he liked and wanted to know. When he wasn't putting down Americans, he was easy to talk with. And he was so totally hot to look at.

When I got home from school, I called Aunt Bianca to ask if she needed me at the trattoria. Score! The guys who'd been sick were now fine, so I wasn't needed for the rest of the week! I told Aunt Bianca that was great news since I had so much schoolwork to do that I would have trouble working and keeping up with my studies. In fact, I added, if anyone at La Sera asked why I wasn't working, she could just tell them that I was taking the week off to work on my school projects. That way, I knew, Antonio wouldn't think my sudden absence had anything to do with him, and he wouldn't ask questions that might reveal who I really was.

That settled, I logged on to the Internet. First I typed Antonio's name into a search engine and prayed. Bingo! There he was. His name and address. He didn't live very far from La Sera. I copied the address, then entered the private chat room that Carrie, Dana, and I had learned how to access.

We'd agreed to meet at a certain time every few days to chat, vent, get advice, and feel like we were together. Yesterday I'd told them a little about Antonio. Dana had told us that Alex Turner Johnson, a guy from Mustang, was in Paris and most of her classes. She was annoyed because she was attracted to him, a regular guy from home, when her dream was to find a French boyfriend.

Robin had discovered that her gorgeous host brother, Kit, had a girlfriend. A total bummer. She had a major crush on the guy, and I couldn't blame her. She was still hiding her real personality.

Our year abroad was off to a bad start for each of us. We all needed each other more than ever—and we were in different countries.

Carrie: Hey, guys. How's it going?

Dana: Other than the fact that I can't seem to escape Alex Turner Johnson—it's going great. Why does he have to be so cute when I only want to be attracted to hot French guys?!

Robin: It's hard living with a guy when you really like him—especially when he treats you like a sister! I wish he didn't have a girlfriend.

Carrie: Looks like we have guy troubles all the way around.

Dana: What's happening with Antonio?

Carrie: I have to tell him the truth. That I'm an American. I'm just not sure how to do it.

Dana: Uh, Antonio, I'm really sorry I didn't tell you this before, but, um, I'm an American. No, not just an American. The American you made fun of for walking into the guys' bathroom. The American you assumed was silly and stupid.

Robin: Yeah, but guess what? I'm not after all! See, Americans are great! Um, you forgive me for lying to your face, right?

Carrie: Come on, I need real help here! I can't just say all that. Can I? What am I going to say?

Robin: Did you ever actually tell him that you were Italian?

Carrie: No, I just did my best to make sure he assumed I was.

Dana: What's the worst thing that could happen when he learns the truth?

Carrie: He could hate me.

Robin: So you like him.

Carrie: Way too much.

By the end of the week I was a wreck. I'd spent most of my time at school hiding out in the girls' bathroom . . . which really limited your social life and the "Italian experience." So far, most of my conversations had revolved around makeup, hairstyles, fast food, and television shows—not that I minded discussing any of those topics. But there quickly came a point where you'd said all you cared to about eye shadow, McDonald's, and *Lost*. And I'd also done absolutely no sight-seeing. My parents had asked for details about Rome's architecture and ruins and street life, and I'd been embarrassed to report back that I hadn't had time to do any sightseeing yet. I'd been so obsessed with the stupid lie

67

between Antonio and me that I'd gone straight from school to the Pietras'. I'd spent a lot of time on the balcony outside my bedroom.

There was no way I could complain, however, about my limited social life or sight-seeing schedule. After all, Antonio's very existence was limited and for a very sad reason. Whenever I saw him in the hallways, he was alone. Always alone. He didn't hang around in cliques. I didn't see him laughing hysterically with guys. I didn't see him lounging against his locker, looking the girls over as they walked by—which a lot of the guys did do.

Between school, work, and caring for his sisters, he obviously had no time for friends; he'd probably lost the ones he used to have. The guys at La Sera were probably the only acquaintances he had.

He'd reached out to me—not knowing that I planned to betray his friendship.

I felt like a complete and absolute jerk.

When Saturday arrived, I absolutely could not bring myself to go to school one more day. I couldn't play dodge Antonio one more minute. I couldn't risk our paths crossing before I'd told him the truth. I explained to Signora Pietra that I wasn't feeling well, which was true. Then I sat on my balcony, running words through my head, trying to come up with a way to explain to Antonio why I, Carrie Giovani, wasn't exactly as he thought Americans were— selfish and spoiled, only interested in myself.

Seven

Antonio

I STOOD IN the tiny kitchen and glared at the slab of butter that was slowly melting in the pan.

My mama was at work. My sisters were playing in their rooms. And I was fixing lunch. Typical Saturday afternoon routine. Dull, boring. Not at all the way that I'd planned to spend my teenage years.

I had never resented that my papa died in an auto accident— until now. Certainly I had despised the driver who had gotten behind the wheel of a car after drinking too much wine—but I'd never blamed my papa.

But suddenly I was tired. Tired of being the oldest. Tired of working. Tired of going to school. Tired of being alone.

Sure, I had family, but family wasn't a girlfriend. And I wanted a girl in my life. A girl like Carrina.

I had tried to stay angry with her after she had run off. But if I was honest with myself, I couldn't blame her. We hadn't spent enough time together to really know each other. Yet I'd announced that I liked her and expected her to respond with equal fervor.

Stupid, Antonio, I berated myself. *Stupid. You have to take a girl out, treat her special, show her that you care.*

Not announce it like an advertisement.

But dating was out of the question. My mama needed every lira that I could hand over each night. Even if she didn't, where would I find the time? Perhaps it was best that I'd ruined my chance with Carrina. She simply wasn't interested. She'd been so eager to avoid me that she'd even taken the week off from work; Roberto had mentioned that she needed some extra time to study. I was sure she simply needed extra time away from me. From me and my stupid mouth.

I tossed diced onions and peppers into the skillet and listened to them sizzle. The gray smoke rose.

No, I'd never blamed my papa. But then, never before had I craved some time that was mine alone, time that wasn't taken up with school, work, or watching over my sisters.

If only Carrina did like me back. I'd find a way, find the time, to take her on a real date or just a walk home after work. I'd show her how much I truly wanted to get to know her. And maybe she'd see that I wasn't just being a romantic type when I'd told her how comfortable I felt with her. When I was with

Carrina, whether watching her those two days at La Sera or walking her that short distance from the trattoria, I felt like my troubles didn't exist anymore.

I heard the doorbell ring. Who could that be? Probably one of my sisters' friends. I really wasn't in the mood to have a bunch of laughing, giggling, talking girls in the house. But I wanted my sisters to be happy. Even if I wasn't. So I'd quietly suffer through the invasion of their friends.

I wiped my hands on the flowery apron I wore. My mom's apron. She liked bright colors and flowers and combined the two whenever possible. The doorbell chimed again. I jerked it open, prepared to be run over by five giggling preteens.

But the girl of my dreams stood before me, staring at my apron, her lips twitching as though she was fighting not to laugh.

I felt the heat of embarrassment burn my face. I jerked off the apron and balled it up. I was mortified that I had been caught wearing it, but the longer I kept my jeans clean, the less laundry I had to do.

"What are you doing here?" I asked. I was stunned. How did she know where I lived? Why was she here? I'd thought I totally turned her off.

Carrina bit her lower lip and stared at the ground. "I just wanted to talk to you."

I studied her. Now that I was looking at her, I could still feel the sting of her rejection the night I started walking her home. Was she here to tell me she wanted me to leave her alone at work?

71

"You didn't seem so anxious to talk to me the other night," I reminded her.

She blushed. A pretty blush. I wished that I hadn't noticed. I wished I could stay irritated with her. But I was really incredibly glad to see her—after what seemed like an eternity since we'd last talked.

She held up her right hand, and I saw a pewter ring on her finger. "I'd left my ring at the trattoria that night—it's what I'd had to go back for."

She took it off and shook it. It broke apart into several thinner rings, all dangling from one main ring. "This is a puzzle ring," she explained. "It took me forever to figure out how to put it together when it came apart. I didn't want to risk it disappearing and having to get another one. Each ring goes together differently."

I watched as she put it back together. She had such delicate hands. She slid the ring onto her finger and looked at me expectantly.

"You haven't been at work this week," I pointed out. "Roberto said you had a lot of school-work to do and wouldn't be keeping a regular schedule at La Sera."

She scuffed the toe of her sneaker into the ground. "Yes, um, I did have a lot of school projects this past week."

I leaned against the doorjamb, drinking in the sight of her. I couldn't believe how glad I was to see her. But I definitely could not invite her into the house. I didn't want her to see the mess. My sisters had been little terrors this morning, and the house looked it.

"What did you want to talk about?" I prodded.

She stood on her tiptoes and looked over my shoulder. I shifted to block her view of dolls, puzzle pieces, and crayons.

She furrowed her delicate brow. "Is something burning?"

I cursed under my breath. My onions and peppers!

I rushed into the kitchen and groaned at the sight of black smoke spiraling toward the ceiling. Too late!

I turned off the stove and lifted the pan. I glared at the charred remains that were now burned to the bottom of the pan. I'd used the last of the onion and pepper. So now my sisters would complain because the spaghetti sauce I'd planned to feed them for lunch would be bland. I could hear them now.

"Blah!"

"Antonio, what's wrong with this?"

"Don't you know how to make spaghetti sauce?"

"Why don't you get a girlfriend who can come over and cook for us?"

My sisters were always harping that I needed to get a girlfriend. I don't know why they cared.

I dropped the pan into the sink, turned on the water, and heard the hiss as it hit the hot pan. I'd have to scrub it. I tossed the apron I'd balled up earlier onto the counter. Then I remembered why I'd taken it off.

I glanced over my shoulder. Carrina stood in the kitchen, watching me. "Lunch," I announced dejectedly.

I heard pounding footsteps. My sisters skidded

into the kitchen, barely missing Carrina.

"What's that stink?" Gabriella asked. She was six. Her crayons littered the living room.

"Did you burn lunch again?" Isabella asked. She was eight. Her dolls were strewn over the living room.

"I'm gonna tell Mama," Luisa announced. She was ten. She dropped puzzle pieces everywhere, so her hundred-piece puzzles were never finished.

"I'm hungry," Mara whined. She was twelve and hinted more than the others that I needed a girlfriend— someone who could show her how to apply makeup.

"Who are you?" Gabriella asked. She was staring up at Carrina.

Carrina smiled warmly. "I'm Carrina."

"Are you Antonio's girlfriend?" Luisa asked.

"No, she is not my girlfriend," I stated quickly.

"Antonio's never had a girlfriend before," Mara announced.

"Out!" I shouted. I didn't need my sisters to reveal the whole history of my dull and boring life. I waved my arms in the air. "Get out!"

"But I'm hungry," Isabella cried.

"Then get out so I can fix lunch. Go!" I yelled.

They turned to leave. Luisa giggled. "He just wants us to leave so he can kiss her," I heard her say as they walked out of the kitchen. I wanted the floor to crack open and swallow me. Where was an earthquake when I needed one? Or a volcanic eruption? Pompeii had been obliterated. Why not me?

I gave Carrina an apologetic shrug. "I'm sorry.

74

Right now is not a good time. I have to fix lunch for my sisters and finish cleaning."

A bubble of laughter erupted from her throat. It was such a pretty sound even if she was laughing at me.

"What?" I demanded.

She pointed toward the arched doorway where my sisters had shuffled out. "They remind me so much of my brothers. If a guy stopped by the house to borrow a schoolbook, my brothers would give him and me a hard time—make kissing sounds. Guys learned real quick to avoid my house or suffer the consequences."

I smiled and leaned against the counter. "Really. So only a brave guy would date you."

She laughed as though completely comfortable with herself. "Right. And most don't stay brave for long."

"I would." I glanced at the murky water in the pan. I hadn't meant to admit that. I realized that I would face her brothers for an opportunity to go out with her—but even that wasn't enough for us because I still didn't have time, and I didn't have money.

I turned my attention back to her. "I've got to fix lunch. What was it you needed to tell me?"

"Uh . . . it can wait." She pointed her thumb over her shoulder. "I noticed a pizzeria around the corner on my way here. Why don't I treat you and your sisters to some pizza?"

"No way. Girls don't pay—"

"They do when they're responsible for you burning your lunch," she explained.

"No," I declared adamantly. I really wanted to

spend time with her and wondered if the money in my pocket would cover a pizza.

She took a step closer. "Antonio, it's my fault your lunch is ruined. Please let me take you and your sisters out. Otherwise I'll feel guilty for the rest of my life." She pressed the back of her hand to her forehead and looked up at the ceiling. "Forever, it will eat at me," she crooned dramatically. "The guilt, the guilt will destroy my dreams. I'll have no chance for happiness—"

I laughed at her dramatic display. "All right," I conceded. "But I don't think you truly understand what you're getting yourself into—hauling my four sisters around."

"It can't be any worse than traipsing after five brothers," she assured me.

Carrina was amazing. I could not believe the way she handled my sisters. Or should I say the way she *bribed* them. If they wanted pizza, they had to help clean the house. I'd never seen my sisters so enthusiastic about cleaning. No whining. No pouting. They were willing to do whatever Carrina asked because she promised them a reward.

She even helped me clean the kitchen.

I was putting away the ingredients that I'd taken out earlier for my sauce when I heard Carrina shout, *"En garde!"*

I turned around. She was brandishing a celery stick. She tossed one at me. She held hers out and placed her other hand on her hip. "Defend your right to clean the charred remains from the pan," she ordered.

Dumbfounded, I stared at her. What was she doing?

She bounced toward me, waving the celery stick in the air.

"Fight, Antonio!" She slapped her celery stick against mine.

I couldn't believe she wanted to have a fencing match in the kitchen using celery sticks as rapiers.

With the flowery end of the celery she poked my chest. "Defend yourself!" she commanded.

"Carrina," I began.

She tilted her head at me and smiled, then hit my celery stick. This was crazy. Totally insane! I, always amazingly calm, straight-as-an-arrow Antonio, struck back. Her eyes widened before she pounced again.

The next thing I knew we were thrusting and volleying and darting around the kitchen. Feinting here, striking there. I'd never done anything so . . . incredibly childish.

Or had so much fun!

Carrina was laughing, her wondrous laugh. But even so, she never lost sight of her goal. To beat me. Our celery sticks clashed high, met low.

Suddenly she struck mine, and it went sailing across the kitchen.

"I won!" she shouted. She tossed her celery stick to me. "I'll clean the pan."

"But it's a mess," I pointed out.

She raised an eyebrow. "Then you should have

fought harder to defend your right to wash it."

I watched as she rolled up her sleeves and attacked the pan with the same enthusiasm that she'd had when she attacked me with a celery stick. The winner shouldn't have to wash the pan. The loser should have to, but I didn't want to argue with her. I just wanted to enjoy her presence.

I wiped down the counters while she scrubbed the burned onions and peppers out of the pan and made it shine. Then she dried it. When she was done, she flicked my backside with the towel. "Come on, Antonio, work faster!" she urged.

"Come on, Antonio," my sisters cried from the living room. "Work faster!"

And I did. And so did they. I thought the house had never looked so nice as we walked to the pizzeria. And then Carrina revealed her true genius.

When we arrived at the pizzeria, Carrina said in a devilish voice, "I think your sisters are big enough to sit at a table by themselves, don't you, Antonio?" She batted her eyelashes at me.

My sisters giggled.

"They want to be alone," Luisa whispered.

So alone we were. Or as alone as we could be with my sisters sitting at the next table, leaning over, trying to hear what we were saying. I took Carrina's hand. My sisters snickered. Self-conscious, I released her hand and smiled. "I can't believe they do anything you want," I announced.

"I have a younger sister," Carrina whispered. "I

78

learned long ago how to make her do what I wanted while making her think she was doing what she wanted."

"How much younger is she?" I bit into a slice of pizza.

"A year younger and a holy terror. She's always getting into my things. She's a real pain sometimes. I can't believe how much I miss her," she said.

"Miss her?" I asked. I wondered if her sister had died—like my papa.

Carrina choked on her peach tea. I was about to worry that she wasn't okay when she slapped herself on the chest and took a deep breath. "Sorry, I think the tea went down the wrong way. I meant that I miss my sister this minute. She's a sweetie." She looked toward the marble slab where the workers flattened the dough. "I love the aroma of fresh dough," she murmured.

"Tourists like to watch them work," I mused.

"I'll bet."

Using a long-handled peel, the cooks whipped the pizza in and out of the wood-burning oven. The pizzas came out thin and crunchy with an assortment of ingredients to tempt any customer.

"My papa used to manage a pizzeria," I said quietly.

She jerked her gaze around to me. "He did?"

I nodded. "Sometimes I'd help him, but not often. He wanted me to study, to do well in school. To go to the university. He was killed in a car accident. A couple of years ago now."

She placed her small hand over my larger one. "I'm so sorry."

I turned my hand over and intertwined our fingers. I heard my sisters giggle again, but I was determined to ignore them. I decided I needed to be honest with Carrina. "I don't have a lot of time. I don't have a lot of money. If I did, I would want to date you."

She touched my cheek, and I felt the warmth shoot through me.

"What are you doing now?" she asked.

"This isn't a date," I assured her. "You're buying. My sisters are here."

"But we're together. I like it," she said softly.

"Do you?" I asked, needing the reassurance. I had so little to offer.

She smiled warmly. "Yeah, I do." She leaned toward me. "I have an idea. Let's play tourist this afternoon. All of us, you, me, and your sisters. There's plenty to do that doesn't cost money."

"Tourists?" I echoed. "Why?"

"Most people never look at their hometowns. Today let's pretend that we've never seen Rome— and let's see it together," she suggested.

Her idea appealed to me. I couldn't remember the last time that I'd taken a moment to look at my city. Nor could I think of a single girl I'd ever known who would want to spend the day with four giggling kids just to be with me.

A tourist in my own city. Interesting. And I knew that with Carrina beside me, everything would look different anyway.

Eight

Carrie

I WAS LIVING on the edge, flirting with danger. I was also flirting with Antonio.

I knew that I was just putting off the inevitable, but I wanted to have some warm memories of time spent with him before he hated me.

And hate me he would once he learned of my deception.

Why couldn't he have been the obnoxious jerk that I first thought he was? Why did he have to be sweet and lonely?

Why did he have to make my heart flutter like the wings of a captured butterfly every time he looked at me? Perhaps because he was capturing my heart.

Crazy, I know. I barely knew the guy, but I knew him well enough to know that my plan to teach him a lesson had turned on me. I was the one being taught something.

That intolerance worked both ways—and before I judged, I should probably walk in the other guy's shoes.

Piazza di Spagna—Spanish Square—was crowded when we arrived. Not surprising since it was one of the most famous squares in Rome. Within the center of the square was the true lure of the area: the Spanish Steps.

"Antonio, can we go to the top of the steps?" Gabriella asked.

"Yes, but hold hands," he ordered. "And wait at the top for us."

I watched his sisters run up the steps. I was glad he'd let them go. I wanted a little time alone with Antonio here.

The square reminded me of a crooked bow tie. Beige-, cream-, and russet-colored houses lined the square, some with their shutters closed, others with the shutters open.

"Let's go look at the fountain," I suggested.

Antonio gave me a smile. "Okay."

He took my hand. His hand was larger than mine and so warm.

"Is there a reason you waited until your sisters were out of sight?" I asked, holding up our joined hands.

"My sisters would tease you," he explained, his face turning red.

I tightened my fingers on his. "Antonio, with five brothers my life has been one long series of jokes, teasing, and general aggravation."

His smile deepened. "I'll remember that." He glanced away briefly before meeting my eyes. "Actually, Carrina, since my papa died, I haven't had much time for girls. I'm not always certain what's appropriate."

"Just do what feels right. If I don't like it, believe me, I'll let you know," I assured him.

He laughed warmly. "You aren't shy."

"Nope. I believe you have to grab every moment of life and ride it for all it's worth." I tugged on his hand. "The fountain."

The fountain at the base of the Spanish steps—the Fontana della Barcaccia—was far from spectacular. So many people sat on its rim that it was almost hidden. The pressure from the aqueduct that fed the fountain was extremely low, so it had no grand spurts of water or spectacular cascades. Still, the shallow pool was worth viewing.

Especially with Antonio by my side.

"If I remember my history, Spain's ambassador had his headquarters on this square in the seventeenth century," Antonio muttered.

"That's what the guidebook said," I concurred.

"The guidebook?" he asked.

I refrained from rolling my eyes. I was going to give myself away if I wasn't careful. I'd almost blown it earlier when I'd confessed missing my sister.

"Yes, guidebook. Like I mentioned earlier, people don't pay a lot of attention to the sites of interest in their hometowns, so . . . I bought a guidebook, and my hobby this year is to see all the spots mentioned in the book," I explained—without actually lying. The one thing that I did not want was for Antonio to think I'd lied to him. Deceived him, yes—by omission. But I didn't think I'd ever actually lied. Well, except about my name.

"I think it would take more than a year to see everything in Rome," Antonio stated.

"I'll just see what I can," I said.

"And see the rest next year," he told me.

"No," I said quietly. "I just want to see as much as I can in a year. . . . That's my goal. If I don't see it then, I don't know if I ever will."

He paled and pulled me away from the fountain. "Are you dying?" he asked in all seriousness.

I saw the fear in his eyes, the worry, and the concern. He knew only too well that a life could be short. I rubbed his arm, trying to reassure him. "Oh no. No, nothing like that."

"Then why do you only have a year to see Rome?" he asked.

I began to weave an elaborate story through my mind—then ordered myself to stop. I couldn't lie. He was going to despise me as it was. I didn't need to add more fuel to the fire. "Next year I'll be going to school in America."

His brow furrowed. "You've been accepted into the Year Abroad program?"

I didn't say anything, didn't nod, didn't shake

my head, didn't say, *Well, yes, and I'm in it now.* But my silence and sudden need to tie my sneaker left the false impression that I was going to be a Year Abroad student next year. Perhaps he thought I didn't answer because I was sad to be thinking of leaving Rome for a year just when I'd met him. Or maybe I was getting too ahead of myself—or even flattering myself that he'd care. Still, I comforted myself that my answers couldn't be construed as lies—even though they were misleading. I had to guide us away from a potentially dangerous topic.

"Yes, I'm in the program, but let's not talk about that. I won't be leaving for a whole year."

That was the truth.

We started walking up the Spanish Steps. "Why would you want to leave Italy?" he asked. "Especially Rome. It's so amazing. The city, the sights, the food, the people."

I couldn't deny that I loved the fast-paced life of Rome. People here never seemed to slow down.

"It's not that I *want* to leave," I tried to explain. Then I decided to give up. I sighed. "Oh, Antonio, my leaving is a whole year away. Let's just enjoy now."

He gave me a hesitant smile as he quickened his pace so we could catch up to his sisters. "Maybe I will give you a reason not to go."

And I realized I was afraid that might happen. Knowing Antonio better would give me a reason to want to stay in Rome—but once he learned the truth, he would definitely want me to leave. He'd probably buy the airline ticket himself—with what little money he had.

The exuberance and vitality of Rome shone in the outdoor markets. We had left the Spanish Steps and soon found ourselves immersed in a bustling area where vendors displayed the most unassuming vegetable as though it were a work of art. Stallholders called out their wares, luring Italians and tourists alike. Everything was brightly colorful and incredibly exciting. I loved listening to the hum of conversation and watching people haggle with the vendors over a price.

"I don't know how people do that," I said to Antonio as we walked along, watching a vendor gesturing frantically with his hands while a potential customer did the same.

"It's an art," he admitted. "I usually just pay whatever they ask."

"Looking at all these ripe fruits and vegetables is making me hungry," I announced.

He laughed. "I'll have to keep you away from the celery so we don't have a sword fight in the middle of the square."

I blushed, remembering our little joust in the kitchen. I don't know what had possessed me to tease him with a stalk of celery—I just knew I wanted to see him smile. "Why stop at celery?" I inquired. "I can turn any stalk into a handy weapon."

"Antonio, I'm hungry," Gabriella muttered.

Antonio rolled his eyes. "We just ate a little while ago."

"I'm thirsty," Luisa stated.

"Me too," the other sisters chimed in.

I could tell that Antonio was about to protest. I wanted to keep his sisters happy so he could enjoy the day. "I saw someone walking by with some gelato," I told them. "Why don't we see if we can find the shop?"

His sisters brightened up and started searching for the shop. Gelato—Italian ice cream—was a little different from American ice cream. I was becoming a bit addicted to it.

"The gelato will be my treat," Antonio said quietly beside me.

"Okay." I squeezed his hand.

"There's a shop!" Gabriella shouted, pointing toward a *gelateria*.

The inside of the ice cream shop looked pretty much like the ones at home. Inside a huge glass bowl various types of cones were stacked one inside another. A cylinder held spoons for those who wanted their gelato in a cup. The guy behind the counter wore a paper hat.

Antonio's sisters danced up and down in front of the glass display that revealed all the flavors of gelato.

"I don't know what kind I want," Gabriella stated.

"Me either," Luisa chimed in.

"We'll be here forever," Antonio muttered.

I decided it was time to take over. "First things

first. Everyone tell me what kind of cone you want." Once cones were selected, I quickly moved them on to the gelato. We had two chocolates, two vanillas. Antonio ordered coffee flavor, and I ordered rum and raisin. Sounded weird, but I'd become hooked on it. We walked out of the shop with everyone smiling brightly, licking their double scoops of gelato.

"Have you ever tried this flavor?" I asked Antonio.

He grimaced. "Frozen raisins? No."

I shoved my cone toward him. "Try it."

He shook his head.

"Come on, chicken," I taunted. "Cluck, cluck, cluck."

He narrowed his eyes. "I don't want it."

"Just one little taste—be adventurous," I insisted.

"One taste," he agreed.

I watched as his mouth neared my cone. He had a really great looking mouth. His lips appeared soft. I watched his tongue dart out to touch the gelato before his mouth closed around the pointed tip I'd created with my constant licking.

A warm sensation shimmied through me as I wondered what it would feel like to have those lips touch mine.

Dangerous thought, Giovani, I warned myself. *Those lips will never kiss you. All they'll do is tell you to get the heck out of Rome.*

Antonio straightened, and I watched as his face showed mild surprise. Then he licked his lips. "Very good."

"Want some more?" I asked. My voice sounded like I'd just lined my throat with sandpaper. What was wrong with me?

I watched him take another bite—and then I put my mouth right where his had been. Probably the closest thing to a kiss I'd ever experience with him. And it was cold.

But I was certain it wasn't as cold as his kiss would be once he learned the truth.

Nine

Antonio

I COULDN'T REMEMBER when I'd enjoyed an afternoon so much.

Carrina was incredible. So full of life. She had so much energy. And she knew how to handle my sisters.

When they started to whine, she made them laugh. When they grew tired of walking, she created games that made them forget they were walking. How far can you travel without stepping on a crack? Not far on the cobblestones, but still, the game distracted my sisters.

Distracted my sisters but kept my attention focused on Carrina. She'd pulled her dark hair back in a ponytail, and it bounced against her back as she walked. She did everything quickly as though she was afraid she would run out of time—and still have so much left to do.

She intrigued me as no one else ever had.

Through her eyes, I was seeing Rome as though for the first time.

We arrived at the Trevi Fountain, the largest and most famous fountain in Rome. I couldn't remember when I'd last been here. Waterfalls cascaded over huge stones. The main statue was Neptune, flanked on each side by a Triton with a sea horse. I had forgotten how magnificent the sculptures were at the Trevi Fountain.

My sisters squealed with delight and ran to the rim of the fountain.

"Look, Antonio," Gabriella yelled. "There's money in here!"

Holding Carrina's hand, I walked to the edge of the fountain. Coins littered the bottom.

"Legend says if a visitor tosses in a coin, he will one day return to Rome," I explained.

Carrina dug her hand into her pocket, turned her back on the fountain, and tossed a coin over her shoulder.

"Why did you do that?" I asked. "You're not a visitor."

She blushed and shrugged. "I was making a wish. You don't have to be a visitor to do that."

"What did you wish?" Mara asked.

Carrina touched the tip of Mara's nose. "I can't tell you, or it won't come true." She handed each of my sisters a coin. "Make a wish."

My sisters' coins plopped into the water and

floated to the bottom of the blue fountain.

Carrina held my gaze and pressed a coin into my palm. "Make a wish, Antonio."

"I haven't wished in a long time," I said quietly.

She smiled warmly. "Then you're long overdue, and it's bound to come true."

I grinned at her. Whenever she looked at me like she was daring me to step out of my shell—I wanted to do whatever she wanted. I sighed deeply. "One wish. I could wish for money. I could wish for power. Or I could wish for—".

"Don't say it, Antonio!" my sisters shrieked.

I turned and tossed the coin over my shoulder.

"What did you wish for?" Carrina asked.

I laughed and took her hand. "I thought it was supposed to be a secret."

"You can tell me," she whispered.

"I don't think so." How could I tell her my wish when it revolved around her?

"People at school have been talking about the American Year Abroad student," I told Carrina as we neared my house. I felt her hand tense inside mine.

"Oh, really," she mused. "I suppose she's still using the boys' bathroom."

I chuckled. "No. I think you were right that she was just nervous. No one mentions that mistake anymore. Those who have met her really seem to like her."

"Is that so?" she inquired.

"I'm thinking that maybe I judged her too harshly," I admitted. "Like you told me."

"Sometimes it's just hard when we don't know people. I don't know why, but we tend to think the worst of them," she explained.

"You're right. That's why I've decided that I want to meet her," I stated.

Carrina came to an abrupt halt. Her dark eyes were wide, her brow furrowed. "You want to meet her?"

I nodded. "I only catch a glimpse of Americans when I serve them at the trattoria. I think it would help me understand Americans if I met the student at my school."

Carrina shook her head. "I doubt that. I hear that she's very quiet and that she keeps to herself at school and barely lifts her head when she walks down the halls."

"Maybe she's just shy," I pointed out. Weird. Now I was defending the American? "Anyway, people at school seem fascinated by her."

Carrina smiled. "That's very nice. I won't worry about her so much anymore."

I smiled back, and we started walking again. My sisters rushed ahead and got to the house first. I wished that I didn't have to go to work that evening. I wanted to spend more time with Carrina.

As we reached my house, I remembered that she'd originally come over to talk. There hadn't been a spare moment of awkward silence all day between Carrina and me. I wasn't surprised that I hadn't remembered until now. "You said you came over to talk to me about something."

"We talked plenty today," she said with a laugh. "I'll see you, Antonio."

I wanted to ask her when and where and how and what. But I figured I'd see her soon at La Sera, or perhaps she would surprise me with another visit at the house. I had a feeling I shouldn't crowd her.

"Is Carrina your girlfriend now?" asked Gabriella, hands on her little hips.

"It's looking good," I told her with a smile.

Happy shrieks and giggles emanated all over the house.

Private Internet Chat Room

Carrie: I spent the afternoon with Antonio. We toured parts of Rome. This city is so beautiful and old and amazing. I hope you guys can come over during the year.

Dana: Hey, so he took the news okay that you're the American?

Carrie: I didn't tell him.

Robin: Oops! Carrie, you have to tell him.

Carrie: I know. I was going to tell him today, but I just couldn't.

Dana: You really like him, huh?

Carrie: Yeah. I like him a lot. Maybe even more than a lot. He hasn't spent a lot of time around girls because he works so much and has to take care of his sisters. When he learns the truth about me, it's going to be a double whammy. Not only did an American betray him—but the first girl he ever trusted deceived him as well.

Dana: That's a little melodramatic, Carrie—even for you!

Carrie: I don't know about that. I really think he's going to hate me.

Robin: Maybe he'll surprise you and be completely understanding.

Carrie: Yeah, in my dreams.

Robin: So what are you going to do?

Carrie: Haven't a clue. I don't have a script. How I wish I did.

Dana: Tell him the truth, Car. It's the best way and the only way. The longer you put it off, the worse it'll be.

Carrie: Don't I know it.

Ten

Carrie

I STRETCHED OUT on my bed and opened the book on Michelangelo. Perhaps I should have told Antonio that I was the Year Abroad student when he'd mentioned he wanted to meet her.

But as my brothers would say—I'd choked. Bonked. Blew it.

All I'd had to say was, *You're holding her hand and looking at her like you really like her.*

Yeah, that would have gone over well. He would have stared at me in shock and horror and told me I'd played him for a fool. And how could I have done that in front of his sisters?

Excuses, excuses.

Watching Antonio with his sisters had warmed my heart, reminded me of my brothers, my family. Reminded me of what was real, what really mattered, what was important. My own stupid ego, my own stupid lie was pathetic in the face of everything Antonio had heaped on his young shoulders.

I closed the book. So much for working on my research paper. I'd rather work at La Sera. I could help out, spend a little extra time with my aunt and uncle and Roberto, and see Antonio.

I arrived at my uncle's restaurant two hours later. Aunt Bianca was happy to have me for the day. I talked to my aunt and uncle in the back room for a little while, mostly about school and about the e-mails I'd gotten from my parents, and then I put on an apron and headed into the dining room. Antonio was serving a table for two. A guy and a girl. I wondered if he was thinking that he wished he could be that guy, taking his girl out on a real date to a trattoria. The thought made my heart squeeze for him.

Every time Antonio and I passed each other, he'd smile warmly at me—and my heart would do this crazy kind of flutter.

Not good, Giovani, I thought. *Not good at all.*

I was incredibly torn. I needed to tell him the truth. I wanted to keep my secret.

I thought of the gladiators who had fought in the Colosseum in Rome. I'd seen pictures that showed a gladiator with one arm tied to one horse, another arm tied to another horse. He was supposed to be strong enough to keep them from tearing him apart.

I figured terror had gripped him at that moment as he hoped he was strong enough. . . . I always imagined that he had been. I was a sucker for courage.

And sadly lacking it.

Antonio, I'm American. Three little words. How hard could they be to repeat, to acknowledge? Pretty dadgum hard when saying them meant that Antonio would never again smile at me.

Antonio had offered to walk me home. I was waiting for him out front. I had a plan. A stupid plan, but a plan all the same.

I was going to let him take me home. All the way home. To Elena's. Then he'd realize who I was. I wouldn't have to speak the words. He would just . . . know.

I'd pulled Elena's scooter out from beside the building. She was a great host sister, letting me borrow it all the time.

The front door opened, and the moment I had been dreading had finally arrived. I turned and faced Antonio.

He walked down the steps, his brow furrowed. "You have a scooter?"

I nodded jerkily. "It's a friend's. I just borrowed it. I thought you could ride in front and I could ride behind."

He smiled. "Okay. But you have to wear the helmet."

I worked it onto my head. He started to turn the

scooter around. I put my hand on his arm. "Actually, I live in that direction."

He stared at me as though I'd lost my mind. "But the other night we went in that direction." He pointed behind me.

"I know. I got confused." I released a stupid, silly girl laugh. "I didn't realize it until I came back for my ring."

Don't question me here, I pleaded silently.

He nodded and swung his leg over the scooter. I got on behind him and put my arms around him.

"Where do you live?" he asked.

I gave him Elena's address.

"Do you mind if we take a detour?" he inquired.

I welcomed the reprieve—a few more minutes before he hated me. "No, I don't mind," I assured him.

He turned on the scooter. It made its little buzzing sound. I tightened my hold on him. Then we were churning along the street, heading into the night.

"My papa used to bring me here," Antonio said quietly as we stood by one of the huge columns on the steps of the Pantheon.

Visiting hours were over, and we couldn't go inside. But the building didn't lose its majesty with the coming of night. Its huge, domed roof simply reflected the moonlight and the lights of Rome.

"I had forgotten," Antonio added. "Until today, when we pretended that we were tourists."

He took my hand and intertwined our fingers.

"Always be proud of your heritage, Antonio." He sighed. "That is what he always told me . . . and what I forgot."

Even in the darkness of the night I could see his sad smile. I didn't think he really wanted me to comment. I thought he probably just wanted someone to listen.

"Inside the Pantheon, the only light comes from a hole in the center of the dome," he explained. "My papa would show me everything. Explain everything. He didn't need a guidebook."

His fingers tightened on my hand. "I miss him, Carrina. I had forgotten how much. Today you helped me remember."

"Oh, Antonio." I touched his cheek and felt the dampness where a tear had fallen.

He turned away his face, and I could see him wiping his face in the shadows. Why did guys have to think that tears were a weakness? My mom cried, and she was the strongest person I knew.

"My papa loves his heritage too," I said softly.

Antonio smiled. "I would like to meet your papa."

My heart rammed against my chest. Impossible. But I did wish that Antonio could meet my dad. He'd like my father. I knew it. Family was incredibly important to my dad, and he always made time for us—no matter how busy he was, he was never too busy for us. Just like Antonio seemed to be with his sisters and mother. I smiled at Antonio. "Maybe someday you will meet him," I said.

Antonio squeezed my hand, then sighed heavily. "I don't know why I came here."

"To feel close to your father," I explained. "We all have a special place for remembering those we love."

"I didn't want to come alone," he confessed. "I hope you don't mind that I brought you."

"No. It means a lot to me that you wanted to share this place with me," I told him.

"You mean a lot to me, Carrina." He tugged on my hand.

I stepped closer. Antonio drew me against him, lowered his head, and kissed me.

I melted, from the top of my head to the tips of my toes.

And Antonio tasted wonderful. He felt wonderful . . . and I knew how Pinocchio had felt when the fairy had touched her wand to his head and turned him into a real boy—that nothing would ever be as wondrous as this moment.

Eleven

Carrie

ANTONIO APPARENTLY HAD no idea that Elena lived in the house that he'd dropped me off in front of last night. I was as relieved as I was tormented. And left with the searing memory of his kiss. He'd kissed me again before he left to walk the half mile to his own house. I watched him until he disappeared into the night, my fingers caressing my lips in awe and wonder.

Now, Sunday afternoon, I stretched out on my bed with Elena beside me. She'd brought in a stack of pop magazines, including *Uno* and *Tutto*. They were pretty much like the magazines I read at home. Music, movies, and rock stars.

"Isn't he a heartbreaker?" Elena crooned in English.

Heartbreaker? That sounded like something my mom might say—twenty years ago. Elena was taking

English in school. In Italy it was considered a foreign language, of course, but it still seemed so odd to me. I mean, I found it strange that anyone would think of English as a foreign language. It just seemed like it should be at least everyone's second language if not their first. I heard a little voice inside my head, chastising me for escalating the significance of English. The little voice sounded a lot like Antonio's.

But that aside, Elena wanted to practice her English—slang and sayings. She was already far advanced in grammar and proper usage.

I glanced at the glossy photo of the dark-haired guy. "We'd say *hot* instead of *heartbreaker*," I told her.

"*Hot?* Hot. Isn't he a hot?" She smiled at me. "Like that?"

I grinned at her. "Without the *a*. Just *hot*. Totally hot."

"Isn't he totally hot?" she repeated. *"Grazie."*

"Thank you," I corrected.

She laughed. "I forget to always speak English when we get going in conversation."

She turned the page, and I went back to reading an article on Madonna, of all people. There were more Americans in this Italian magazine than Italians.

I gave up on the article. I couldn't keep my mind on it. I just kept thinking about Antonio. Last night when he'd brought me to Elena's house, I had expected him to confront me—to know I was the Year Abroad student. My heart had been pounding so hard, I was afraid he could hear it. With Antonio's schedule, it made sense that he wouldn't be up on where everyone in his school lived or who was hosting the American. He clearly didn't pay much attention to who was who or who was doing what with whom.

Last night at the Pantheon had been incredible. Not just the kiss, but the whole moment of closeness. Antonio had revealed some pretty heavy stuff about his feelings. I was willing to bet that he'd never opened up to anyone like that before. A wounded soul reaching out. A kindred spirit seeking shelter. He'd confided in me, turned to me for comfort. Me, the one person who had betrayed him—he just didn't know it yet.

"Carrie, what's wrong?" Elena asked.

I snapped to the present and looked at her. "What?"

She furrowed her brow. "You looked sad totally."

"Totally sad," I said, gently correcting her. Then I shook my head. "Only I'm not sad." *Devastated* was a better word, but I couldn't admit that without explaining what I'd done. How quickly my plot for revenge had turned on me. "Italy has been an adjustment I wasn't expecting."

"In what ways?" she asked.

"I just thought I knew everything about Italy and Italians . . . and I'm learning that there's a lot that I didn't know." The explanation sounded stupid. I wasn't learning so much about Italians as I was learning too much about me.

*   *   *

Being a Year Abroad student didn't mean that you were the host family's guest. Rather, it meant you became part of their family—which meant, unfortunately, chores. Groan.

Keeping my room clean, doing my laundry, helping with meals, cleaning up after meals—pretty much life as it was lived back home. Of course, there was a lot less to clean up after a meal at the Pietra table because they didn't have my five brothers eating like pigs at a slop trough.

There was also a lot less food served. And shopping for it was kinda fun because I didn't go to a grocery store. I simply went to the market. It was like walking through a never ending produce section of the grocery store back home—except I was outside. Huge open tents marked off the vendors' areas and provided some shade. Of course, for a girl accustomed to one-hundred-degree days, I wouldn't have minded the sun.

But I loved the atmosphere. Local produce like grapefruit was packed into carts. And imported fruits like pineapple were also available.

Signora Pietra had given me a list of what she needed to prepare her meals for the next few days. She'd told me to pick up anything else that I thought I might like to try. I had several hours to myself before my host mother expected me back with the groceries. That meant I could explore to my heart's content all day.

I'd come alone. Elena's chore had been to head

to the meat market. We'd agreed to switch off next week. I wanted to experience every part of Rome that I could. No task was too menial, no chore—regardless of how much I complained—beneath me.

It was all part of this exciting adventure called being a Year Abroad student.

Uncharacteristically I walked slowly from stall to stall, examining the produce. The area was a potpourri of aromas. I picked up something that looked like a melon. I brought it to my nose, closed my eyes, and sniffed.

It smelled sweet and ripe. My mouth watered.

"Restocking your arsenal?" a deep voice asked.

My eyes flew open. I recognized that voice. My heart patted my ribs as I turned and faced Antonio. He looked incredible. He was wearing a black T-shirt and jeans.

I moved my hand up and down as though gauging the weight of the melon. "I recently acquired a cannon. Now I need some ammunition."

He laughed, deeply and richly. It was a really nice laugh. My gaze dropped to his lips, and I remembered the kiss he'd bestowed upon me. My body grew warm. Maybe it was one hundred and five degrees in the shade after all.

I had to get my mind off that kiss, off that night of intimacy when he'd shared so much of himself with me. "What are you doing here?"

He grinned. "I need some onions, peppers." His smile grew. "Celery with stronger stalks."

Now it was my turn to laugh. "I guess you've figured out that I have a flair for the dramatic."

"You do have a way about you, Carrina Gio," he admitted.

My stomach lurched at the butchering of my name, a name I'd given him. A reminder of the lie that created a chasm between us. A chasm only I was aware of. I could tell him the truth now—even though the arsenal was at his disposal. I could imagine him searching for, finding, and throwing rotten tomatoes at me.

He took my hand, and I shoved all thoughts of revealing the truth to the back of my mind. The middle of a produce market was not the place.

"What are you shopping for?" he asked.

I put the melon back, reached into my pocket, removed the list, and flicked it open. "Boring stuff. Small knives." I winked at him. "Carrots. Bullets." I gave him a pointed look. He was grinning. "Grapes." I shrugged. "Just a few things."

Suddenly shopping for produce really did seem incredibly boring. I laced our fingers together. "I have a crazy idea."

He shook his head as though reading my mind. "I have to leave for work in a few hours. I don't have time to play tourist."

"How about lazy bum?" I prodded.

His eyes widened. "What?"

Excitement was thrumming through me. I knew it was dangerous to spend more time with

Antonio. The more comfortable I became around him, the less I kept my guard up. The easier I let little slips of the tongue reveal what I needed to tell him up front. But he was here, unexpectedly, and so was I.

And what could a couple more hours together hurt?

"I saw a park on my way over here. Some kids were playing soccer. I was thinking of going over there and watching."

"Every Sunday there are professional soccer games—"

"No," I interrupted. "I like to watch people play for the love of the game, not money. They still have the dream of being something. Too many professionals just dream about how much money goes into their bank accounts."

"What about your shopping?" he asked.

"I can do it later." I tugged on his hand. "Let's be wild and crazy."

Wild and crazy was a relative experience. Holding hands, we walked toward the park I'd seen. We passed one of Rome's many drinking fountains.

"Thirsty?" Antonio asked me.

"A little."

We backtracked and stopped at the elaborate fountain, where the water poured out of the mouth of a stone image—some mythical god, I assumed; Juno, maybe. I sipped the water. It was naturally sweet and really good.

"Every time I drink this water, I'm amazed at how good it tastes," I remarked.

"Another gift from the ancient Romans," Antonio responded. "Don't you know that the water is piped down from the hills through a series of pipes and aqueducts that have changed little over the centuries?"

I'd somehow overlooked that little fact in my guidebook, but a true Italian would know. "Of course I know, and knowing just makes me appreciate the water all the more."

But more than the water, I loved the fountains. Etched in stone. So much more interesting than the electric water fountains we had in Mustang—where the water always tasted like rust.

Antonio carried a bag of oranges that I'd picked up at one of the stands before we'd begun our trek to the park. I had decided that a makeshift picnic was in order.

We reached the park and sat at the top of a knoll where we had a clear view of the playing field. Antonio sat on the ground with his back against a tree. I sat in front of him, my back to his chest, his arms around me.

Content. Incredibly content.

The kids playing soccer were probably around twelve. They wore uniforms, so I figured they were part of some organized league. Soccer was extremely popular in Italy.

My brothers and I played constantly. I was tempted

to go down to the field and help out, but I was too happy where I was. In the circle of Antonio's arms.

I heard his stomach growl. I laughed. "I know that sound."

I reached for the bag beside us, pulled out an orange, and began peeling off the rind.

"You always add special touches to our excursions," he murmured.

"I believe in living life to the fullest," I commented as I tore off a section of the orange. I twisted around slightly. "Open your mouth."

He did, and I slid the orange into his mouth. I watched as his tongue licked the outer edges of his lips. So much for trying not to think about the kiss. I slipped an orange section into my mouth. I needed to keep my mouth busy—otherwise it was going to lean forward and kiss Antonio.

Would that be so bad? a tiny voice inside my head asked.

No, it would be wonderful, but until I knew if his feelings for me could withstand the truth, I thought it was best if I didn't make any advances. Oh, what a tangled web I'd woven, so tangled that I was now caught in it.

I wanted Antonio to be my boyfriend. In a way, I felt like he was. I wasn't seeing any other guys in Rome. I wasn't even flirting with any guys at school. As far as I was concerned, there was only one Italian for me—and I was with him right now.

What would it hurt if I never told him the

truth? Plenty. It would hurt plenty—him and me. Him because our relationship would be a lie. And me because I would be hiding my heritage—a heritage I was very proud of. And with every day that passed, I knew that I increased the risk of him finding out about me from someone else. I had to be the one to tell him.

But the perfect moment just never seemed to be here. I fed him another section of orange. It was such an intimate thing to do—almost as intimate as kissing. But it didn't send warm shock waves through my system the way his kiss had last night.

When we were finished with the orange, I snuggled back against him and tried to watch the soccer game, but all I could think about was how wonderful it was to be here with Antonio. I wanted to share every moment of this year with him.

"Where do you go to school, Carrina?" he asked abruptly. "It's so crazy that I just realized I don't know."

My heart bounced against my ribs. Oh gosh, there was no way that I couldn't *not* lie.

"I mean," he continued, "you don't live that far from me, we shop at the same market. . . . It just seems like we should be going to the same school."

I knew that in Italy, students had a choice between the *liceo,* a technical institute, or a teacher-training college. I cleared my throat. "My mom's a teacher. I thought I'd follow in her footsteps." That wasn't a lie. I was planning to major in drama and get a teaching certificate when I attended college

111

back in Texas. And my mom was an English teacher at Mustang High.

"So you're already working on your teacher training," he murmured.

I felt terrible. I hated lying. I hated it so much! How I wished I could turn back time to that first day when I'd heard him putting down Americans. How I wished I'd marched up to him and told him he was wrong, that I would prove to him how great Americans were.

I wondered what would have happened. Perhaps he wouldn't have given me the chance to prove anything. Perhaps he would have written me off as a rude, silly girl.

I sighed and nodded slightly in answer to his question as I snuggled closer against him. Let him take that nonanswer for a yes. If he thought that, he wouldn't expect to run into me at his school. But how—how, how, how—was I going to explain my lies when he learned the truth? One lie perhaps he could deal with. But all of these half-truths? All I was doing was digging myself in deeper.

But what else could I do? Telling him the truth meant losing him. And that I couldn't bear.

We sat in silence for several long moments. I enjoyed the peacefulness of it. I didn't know how much longer I'd have.

"My father and I used to play soccer," Antonio said quietly.

I burrowed my head against his shoulder. It

was another moment when I thought my silence was needed more than any trite words I could offer.

He brushed his cheek against mine. "Have you ever lost someone you loved?"

I shook my head. "I've been lucky."

"Carrina, turn around," he urged gently. "I have something for you."

A kiss. He was going to kiss me. I licked my lips. I tasted like orange. But then, so would he.

I turned around until I could face him. He reached behind his neck and lifted a chain over his head. On the end of it dangled a gold medallion. He slipped the necklace over my head. I cradled the medallion in the palm of my hand and studied the man who appeared to be hiking.

"It's Saint Christopher," Antonio said solemnly. "He is the patron saint of all travelers."

I lifted my gaze to his. "Antonio, I can't accept this."

He closed his hand around mine, pressing the medallion against my palm. "Please, Carrina. For when you travel to America."

I touched his cheek. Tears burned my eyes. "I'm not leaving for a whole year."

"Then let him protect you wherever you travel. Even in Rome it can be dangerous. I don't want you to get hurt."

I knew it was wrong to accept so precious a gift. But Antonio looked at me with such hope in his eyes that I absolutely couldn't say no.

Nor did I want to. The gift was precious to me. So, so precious.

Later that evening, in my room at my host family's house, I sat on my bed and leaned against the brass-railing headboard. I held the Saint Christopher medallion in my palm.

Was this how teens in Rome indicated that they were going steady?

Antonio and I hadn't even had what I'd consider a real date. But somehow that didn't matter. When I was with him, I was incredibly happy—except for that little voice at the back of my mind that kept nagging me. A little voice that kept reminding me that I wasn't the girl he thought I was.

Would he have given the medallion to an American girl? Probably not.

I knew that I had no business accepting his gift. But I'd been powerless to say no. I didn't want to hurt him, and I could tell that he would have felt rejected if I hadn't taken the medallion.

All that aside, I wanted it. I wanted something that had once belonged to Antonio.

I slipped the chain over my head and felt the medallion grow warm just below my throat. I pulled my small jewelry box closer. I needed to find something to give him.

I lifted the lid. A ballerina dressed in pink sprang upright and began to twirl as music tinkled into the room. Corny, I know, but I'd had the jewelry box since I was eight. When you were eight, twirling ballerinas were romantic. At sixteen they were a reminder of exactly how much you'd matured.

I'd brought only my favorite jewelry (not that I had so much in the first place). I picked up a charm bracelet. I couldn't quite envision Antonio wearing a charm bracelet, and the charms, which included the state of Texas, the Alamo, and a longhorn, revealed more about me than I wanted Antonio to know at this moment.

I set aside the bracelet and picked up a necklace. The silver chain was thick, but the heart-shaped locket that dangled from the chain—I really couldn't see that around Antonio's neck.

What was I thinking to even consider giving Antonio something in exchange for the Saint Christopher? I was going to have to give it back to him. When he learned the truth about me, he was going to demand that I give it back to him.

I would understand completely.

I stretched out on my bed and shoved my pillow beneath my head. I watched the ballerina twirl— and thoughts swirled through my head.

Tell Antonio the truth—and lose him.

Keep my secret—keep Antonio.

But did I truly have Antonio when he didn't know everything there was to know about me?

Twelve

Antonio

ON WEDNESDAY NIGHT Carrina and I sat at the café near the trattoria. Our shift had ended, and we'd come here to unwind. We had our usual order. . . . Only this time we shared the *tiramisú,* one of my favorite desserts.

I'd never shared anything with a girl until Carrina had made me sample her rum-and-raisin gelato. I liked how close it made me feel to her. I thought I could tell Carrina anything, and she would understand.

"I have decided that the Year Abroad student is a myth," I announced. I sipped my espresso and gazed at her over the rim of my cup.

She stilled, her piece of *tiramisú* halfway to her mouth. "What?"

I set down my cup and leaned forward.

"People tell me about her, but I never see her—not in the hallways, not in any classes, not in the boys' bathroom."

A corner of her mouth tilted up. "I thought she'd stopped frequenting boys' bathrooms."

I shrugged. "That's what I heard. So where is she? You said two of your friends were in the Year Abroad program. Don't they have to go to class?"

"Of course they do," she admitted, but she seemed a little agitated.

I wondered if she missed her friends. To have two friends go away. "Do you miss them?" I asked.

"Who?"

"Your friends," I prodded.

She smiled softly. "Yeah, I do."

At that moment I realized that I knew so little about Carrina. I'd never met her family. Had never seen her with any friends. Was she as lonely as I was? "What are they like?"

"Well . . . Robin is the one in London. I call her dare-me-to-do-anything Robin. But she doesn't really like herself, and she wants to change while she's away," she explained.

"What does she want to change?" I inquired.

"The way she talks. She wants to be sophisticated." She shrugged. "But I like her the way she is."

"And your other friend?"

"Dana." Her smile grew. "She wants to fall in love while she's in Paris. She dated a totally unromantic guy for a while, and she's determined to have an all-out romance while she's in Paris. Unfortunately she keeps running into a guy from our school who's also in the program. He's driving her crazy."

"Why?" I asked. I wasn't sure it was a bad thing for a guy to drive a girl crazy. Didn't that mean she was always thinking of him?

"Because he's interfering with her plans to fall for a French guy," she stated.

"Only if she lets him," I pointed out.

She glanced around the restaurant as though she was looking for spies. Then she leaned forward, a conspiratorial glint in her eyes. "Truthfully, I think she likes him. And she doesn't want to. He's not French. He's Am . . . uh . . . a guy that we went to school with."

"You are very close to them," I murmured.

"Extremely." She leaned back. "I can tell them anything—the very worst thing about me—and they'd still be my friends."

"You're lucky. A lot of my friends didn't know what to say when my papa died. I still have a few friends, but it's hard to lose friends," I surmised.

"Well, I haven't lost Dana and Robin. They're just gone for a while. But in a year we'll be back together," she said.

"Until you leave for America," I reminded her.

She nodded. "Right."

I slapped my hand on the table. "I need to meet this American student at my school."

Carrina eyed me. "Why?"

"I want to know that they are nice in America. That they will treat you right while you are away," I told her. She would be so far from home, away from all that she knew. I could not imagine the courage that would take—to leave everything you knew and loved to experience another culture. That was part of the reason I'd given her my Saint Christopher medallion.

Carrina was looking at me with a strange expression, an expression that told me she thought what I'd just said was nice and sweet. "Americans are nice, Antonio. Maybe not all of them, but I've met some Italians who weren't nice," she told me.

"Like who?" I asked.

"Like the pedestrian who stepped onto the street in front of me this afternoon because she was too busy talking on her cell phone to pay attention to where she was going," she said. "I had to swerve to miss her and almost lost control of the scooter." She touched my medallion and smiled warmly. "Thank goodness I had this to protect me."

I was also glad that she had it. "Maybe it was the American," I suggested.

Carrina laughed, and I laughed too.

"I really want to meet this American," I told her. "How do I find her?"

"You'll find her eventually," she said.

"I hope so. I feel like I've been unfair to Americans, so I want to talk with one when I'm not serving her food," I explained.

She smiled. "You know, Antonio, if you're not careful, you might make me jealous."

I laughed. "If you are jealous, then you must like me."

She placed her hand over mine. "I do like you, Antonio. Very much."

She removed the puzzle ring from her third finger. Then she took my hand. I held my breath while she slid it onto my little finger.

She gave me a wry look. "It won't protect you from anything."

I lifted my hand and studied the ring. It wasn't delicate. It could actually be a guy's ring. It looked like several figure eights woven together. "I don't know what to say, Carrina. I thought this ring was important to you."

"You're more important," she assured me.

The next afternoon I sat on my bed at home, turning the ring on my finger over and over. Was Carrina my girlfriend now? I didn't know how to know if I had a girlfriend. Were we supposed to announce it—or did it just happen?

I wasn't sure, but I did know that I felt the need to celebrate. She didn't just like me. She liked me very much! And I was important to her.

Her acknowledgment called for a celebration of great magnitude. Fireworks. A national holiday. And if I couldn't get that—at least a night off from work. A night off with Carrina.

If she was willing. She'd given me her phone number. I stared at the phone. I'd never had a real date with a girl. Even though I was certain Carrina would say yes, I was still nervous.

Sweat beaded my brow. And my hand was actually shaking slightly as I picked up the phone and dialed her number.

When a girl answered, my mouth went dry. Why hadn't I thought to have a glass of water nearby?

"Uh . . . uh, is Carrina there?" I asked.

"Just a minute."

I heard the phone click as she set it down. That must have been her younger sister. Funny how she sounded older than I would have expected. I guessed that I was just so used to my younger sisters that I expected all girls who weren't my age to sound silly on the phone.

"Hello?"

My heart slammed against my ribs as I heard Carrina's voice.

"Carrina, it's Antonio."

"Antonio! How are you?"

"Well. I . . . uh . . . I was wondering if you'd like to go out on a date—a real date—Saturday night. We could both ask off from work," I suggested.

"A date?"

"I was thinking the opera. There is an open-air showing at some of the Roman ruins. I thought you could check it off your list of sites to see this year." I was rambling. I knew I was rambling. Why was I so nervous when I knew that she liked me? We'd exchanged tokens of affection—or were they just tokens of friendship?

"The opera," she said softly. "I'd like to see the opera."

"So you'll go with me?" I asked. I wanted to make sure she was saying yes to the date.

"Yes," she responded.

I closed my eyes tightly and pressed my fist against my chest. Yes! She'd said yes.

She agreed to call the Romano family and ask for Saturday night off. Since I was working later that evening, I decided to ask in person.

I arrived at the trattoria more than nervous. What if they said no?

Signore Romano was setting huge pots of water on the stove when I arrived. I figured we went through a ton of pasta every night.

I rubbed my damp palms on my trousers. "Signore Romano?"

He turned and raised a brow. "Antonio, you're early tonight."

"Yes, sir. I wanted to ask you if I could have Saturday night off," I told him. Then added, "This Saturday."

He slowly ran his gaze over me as though he wanted to get a measure of the kind of person I was. He nodded. "Yes, you can have Saturday night off." He quickly held up a finger. "But you take care with Carrina's heart."

I jerked my head back as though he'd slapped me. "You know that I'm taking Carrina out?"

He jabbed two of his fingers toward his eyes. "I have eyes! I see the way you look at her, the way she looks at you. Then she calls and tells me she is to go out with you. I don't want to see her get hurt."

"I would never hurt her," I announced adamantly. "I like her. A lot."

"Sometimes, Antonio, that is not enough," he said quietly.

Did he want me to love Carrina? I couldn't figure out why he cared. After all, she was just an employee here—like me. I didn't know what to say to him.

Signore Romano suddenly smiled brightly and slapped my shoulder. "Have a good time Saturday."

He turned back to his boiling water. Strange. He'd almost acted like I was taking out his daughter.

Private Internet Chat Room

Carrie: I don't know whether this goes under the heading of getting better or worse. But I have a date—a real date—with Antonio on Saturday night.

Dana: Cool!

Robin: Awesome!

Carrie: Here's what I'm thinking. We'll have this one night of perfection, and when it's over, I'll break the news to him that I'm American.

Dana: You'll ruin the evening.

Carrie: But if we have a good time, maybe he'll be more forgiving.

Robin: I think you're asking for trouble.

Carrie: I know. I probably should tell him before we go out. . . . But I want this night with him.

Dana: Maybe you'll never have to tell him. We're only going to be abroad for a year. Tell him before you go back home.

Carrie: Easier said than done. I'm playing dodge Antonio at school, and it's growing wearisome. Sooner or later he'll learn the truth, and I want him to hear it from me.

Robin: Then tell him the day after your date. After all, I was honest with Kit . . . and now he's my boyfriend.

Robin had told us a couple of days ago that Kit had broken up with his girlfriend and declared his serious like for Robin. I was totally happy for her. But her situation was way different from mine.

Carrie: But you didn't deceive Kit. You just hid your accent from him. Not your identity.

Thirteen

Carrie

A REAL DATE with Antonio required something special. Something definitely Italian.

With Elena in tow, I headed to the Mercato di Via Sannio. It was an open-air market where random stalls were set up to sell all sorts of wares inexpensively—including clothes and shoes. My budget was horrifyingly limited.

Department stores—*grandi magazzini*—were rare in Rome. The city had two shopping centers. As for malls—forget it. If they existed within the city limits, neither Elena nor I knew the whereabouts. And that was fine with me. I thrived on the open-air markets. The bustle, the bickering, the vendors trying to draw you closer so they could sell you something that you probably didn't really need or truly want.

Browsing was a totally cool experience. Even with all the noise and excitement in the air, I didn't feel the need to rush. I just wanted to find the perfect outfit to wear for Antonio.

"So who is this mystery guy?" Elena asked as she picked up a dress, then put it back on the stack resting on the table.

I hadn't told her that I'd been seeing Antonio. I was afraid she might say something to someone at school who might say something to someone else, and eventually Antonio would hear that he was dating the Year Abroad student. Wouldn't that just thrill him to death?

I picked up a colorful, flowing skirt and held it against my waist. The hem touched me at midcalf. Red and black designs swirled over the cloth. "I'm not ready to talk about him yet, Elena. I'm afraid to jinx it."

She smiled. "I know what you mean. Okay, you'll tell me when you're ready. You can tell me what he looks like, though, right? Is he totally hot?"

I laughed, clutching the skirt to my chest as I thought of Antonio. I knew I had a dreamy look on my face. I just couldn't help it. He did that to me. "Totally, totally hot. He's tall. Dirty blond hair, blue eyes. He's so cute. And so very nice."

She squealed. "I can't wait to meet him when he comes to get you tonight."

I'd been thinking about that problem, wondering how I was going to avoid her seeing Antonio.

Or worse, him seeing her. I'd considered walking to the end of the block and waiting for him there, but I was afraid I might miss him or he might not see me. There was no way around this. I was going to have to come clean.

I put the skirt aside. "Elena, I'm going out with Antonio."

Her eyes nearly popped out of her head. "Antonio Donatello?"

I nodded.

"That's wonderful. I remember that you asked me about him, but I didn't know you wanted to date him," she exclaimed.

"Elena . . ." I felt tears sting my eyes.

She took my hand. She looked worried. "What's wrong?"

"He doesn't know I'm American," I blurted out.

Her mouth dropped open. She snapped it shut. She waved a hand through the air. "How could he not know?"

"This skirt is your color!" a man's voice announced.

I jerked around. The heavyset vendor was clutching the skirt I'd been looking at. "You want?" he asked.

I shook my head. "I'm still thinking about it." Of all the places to explain my stupidity. I grabbed Elena's arm and led her away from the stalls. People brushed by us.

"It's been awful," I finally admitted. "I overheard Antonio putting down American girls, so I decided to teach him a lesson. I was going to let him think I was Italian, flirt with him a little, get him to like me . . . then tell him I was an American. Only it backfired."

"Backfired?" she repeated.

"Turned on me," I tried to explain. Sometimes no language had the right words.

"Because you ended up really liking him," she stated with understanding.

I nodded. "A lot. And I know that it's going to hurt him when he learns the truth."

"He goes to our school," she pointed out.

"And that has been an absolute nightmare. I'm constantly peering around corners, ducking into classrooms where I don't belong. A couple of times he's come so close to seeing me. I'm just grateful we don't have any classes together," I admitted.

"Ah, so that's why you have the reputation for keeping to yourself! I can't believe you managed to avoid him."

"Neither can I." I wrapped my hand around her arm. "Elena, I didn't tell you about him because I was afraid you might accidentally mention what I'd done to someone—and he'd hear about it. I have to be the one to tell Antonio what an idiot I am."

She moved her fingers across her lips as if she were zipping up a dress. "My lips are sealed."

"Grazie," I said with meaning.

"When are you going to tell him?" she asked.

"I don't know. I've tried a couple of times, but I

129

just don't know how to say it," I confessed.

"You'd better be the one to open the door tonight. If he sees me or my parents—I don't know him well, but he knows who I am," she told me.

"He brought me home one night. I was afraid then that he'd figure it out," I told her.

She shook her head. "We have a class together, but I don't think he knows where I live."

I sighed deeply. "I know I have to tell him soon. The longer I put it off, the worse it's going to be."

As we walked back to the stalls, though, I was afraid I'd waited way too long already.

I was determined that tonight would be the night when I told Antonio the truth. I could see the moment so clearly in my mind.

We would be standing outside Elena's house. The aria from the opera still circling on the air around us.

Antonio, I would whisper softly. *This was the most incredible night of my life, and I want to give you something that you've wanted for a long time.*

He would lean closer and say, *You know what I want?*

Yes, I would admit. *You want to meet the American Year Abroad student.* I would throw out my arms. *Ta da! I'm her!*

At which point I somehow ended up with a pot of spaghetti sauce dumped over my head, and Antonio was nowhere to be seen.

I groaned as I stared at my reflection in the mirror. "It's not going to be pretty."

But, I thought with a little satisfaction, *I* looked pretty. Pretty good anyway. My trip to the market had paid off. I'd returned to that first stall and purchased the red-and-black skirt. Then I'd found a red top with spaghetti straps and sheer shirt to go with it. I'd discovered the most adorable belt made out of ancient-looking coins. They were linked together, and when I hooked the belt, a chain of coins dangled down my side.

I was wearing my hair loose, like a curtain flowing past my shoulders. On one side I'd clipped a barrette that had tiny red flowers. I thought it made me look . . . well, exotic. I'd used powder on my nose and a touch of shimmery pale eye shadow on my lids and a little mascara.

I wanted to give Antonio a night to remember. Because it might very well be our last.

Fourteen

Antonio

CARRINA LOOKED . . . incredible. I could hardly take my eyes off her as we sat among the Roman ruins. At the front was a stage, and behind it was what remained of columns. It created a magnificent backdrop to the opera.

Sitting in the audience, Carrina and I held hands. I'd been disappointed that I hadn't been able to meet any of her family. When I arrived to pick her up, she'd told me that they'd gone out for the evening. Carrina's life had so many pieces that I didn't know anything about. Her family, her friends, her school, her hobbies and interests. I did know she enjoyed opera. Her expression was one of . . . rapture.

She was totally absorbed in *Aida* as the hero sang of his love for an Ethiopian slave. And I was totally absorbed in Carrina. She was the main piece of the puzzle—and even without knowing everything about the other aspects of her life, I knew that I cared for her deeply.

I'd never felt this way about a girl. I wanted to see her every day. I loved talking with her. Her voice was music, her smiles were sunshine, and her laughter touched me as nothing else ever had.

Okay, heavy thoughts. I'll admit I was a little frightened that I was having them. I knew guys who let girls wrap them around their little finger. I'd never expected to be one of those guys.

But whatever Carrina wanted to do, I wanted to do. Be a tourist? I'd be a tourist. Understand Americans? I'd try.

I just might do anything for the girl.

My mama had refused to purchase a car after my papa was killed—not that we could really afford one. So my traveling was usually using the underground system—the Metropolitana—or the city buses. Tonight I wished that I did have a car.

Although Carrina didn't seem at all bothered by the fact that we had to use the Metropolitana, then a bus, and then our legs to get to her house. True, the bus had dropped us off only a block or so from where she lived, but I would have preferred being able to drive her to the front door.

Still, there was something romantic about the night. It was late, and the streetlights cast a hazy glow over everything. It seemed the most natural thing in the world to hold Carrina's hand—as I had for most of the evening. I loved the way her small hand fit inside mine. So trusting. It made me feel complete.

"You know, it's the funniest thing," I began.

She peered over at me. "What is? My hair? My outfit?"

I smiled. "No, your house. A girl from my school—Elena Pietra—used to live there. When I picked you up earlier, I realized that was why the house looked familiar to me from the outside. I'd passed it a few times, and the people I was with pointed out that was where Elena lived. I didn't know she'd moved. But then again, I know so little about my classmates."

"Were you and Elena friends?" she asked.

I shook my head. "No, we have a class together this year, but that's all."

Carrina squeezed my hand. "I really enjoyed the opera."

"Is that the reason I have a soggy handkerchief in my pocket?" She'd cried when the hero and heroine had died together. Although saying she cried was putting it mildly. More like sobbed her heart out.

Carrina sighed deeply, and I knew she was still thinking of that tragic ending. Strange how I understood that even though there were so many things that I didn't know about her.

"I'm still getting shivers running down my back," she said softly.

"The air is cool. Maybe you're just cold," I teased.

She glanced over at me and eyed me thoughtfully. "Oh, Antonio, it's the night, all right, but it has nothing to do with the temperature." She squeezed my hand. "Everything was just wonderful."

"I'm glad," I admitted. "I was so nervous about tonight."

She smiled warmly. "Why?"

I ran a hand through my hair. Dare I reveal the truth? I dared. "This was my first date." My first real date anyway. I didn't count walking girls home from school before my papa had died. Or sitting in the library with a girl with our noses in textbooks.

Her smile withered, and she stopped walking. A sadness touched her eyes. "Then that makes tonight extra special."

"You made it extra special, Carrina."

I hadn't planned to kiss her so soon. I'd planned to wait until we reached her house—but if being with Carrina had taught me one thing, it was to seize the moment.

I placed my hands on either side of her face. Her eyes were such a deep brown. I felt like I was swirling within the chocolate depths.

"I like you so much," I said hoarsely.

Then I pressed my lips to hers. She stepped closer to me and wound her arms around my neck. The kiss took on a life of its own.

135

All my senses burst into life as they never had before. I tasted the sweetness of Carrina's lips—more flavorful than the most expensive truffle. I inhaled her flowery sent. My fingers skimmed along her silky cheek. I heard her soft moan.

And even though my eyes were closed, I could see her so clearly—this girl who had touched my life and changed it in ways I'd never thought possible.

Fifteen

Carrie

I LAY ON my bed, curled on my side. Psychiatrists call it the fetal position. People go into it when they're afraid, they miss their mothers, or the pain is too great to bear.

I was experiencing all three, but most of all, I hurt.

Hot tears streamed along my cheeks. My chest ached as though someone had managed to put a tight rubber band around it. My head throbbed. And my heart . . . my heart felt like it was breaking.

Five of the most beautiful words in the world. *I like you so much.*

Only Antonio didn't know that he didn't mean them.

He couldn't possibly feel that way about me because he didn't know who I really was. He thought I was a quirky Italian girl who was obsessed with sightseeing. He thought my family lived in this house. He thought the Romano family was my employer.

He didn't know that the reason he'd never seen the Year Abroad student at his school was because she—or rather I—was wearing myself out trying to avoid him. In the last week I'd had too many close calls. Coming out of the girls' bathroom one second after Antonio walked by the door. Turning to find my nose almost touching his back.

It was getting harder and harder to hide from him at school because he was becoming more insistent on finding me. Why did he care so much about finding a girl that he'd admitted he thought was stupid? Curiosity?

I couldn't help but think I'd brought his obsession with the YA student on myself—blathering about how great Americans were and how important it was to walk in their shoes—well, right now the shoes were pinching my toes.

I squeezed my eyes shut. Tears leaked between my lids. Why hadn't I told him the truth about me sooner? I'd never been chicken. I'd never been afraid. I'd never been mean. Now I was all three.

After he'd declared his feelings, there was absolutely no way I could reveal the truth. And after that incredible kiss that had melted my bones, I wasn't certain that I could have spoken if I'd tried.

But it was more than that. I didn't want to see the soft look in his blue eyes turn hard.

When he spoke my name—Carrina—my name just rolled so provocatively off his tongue. It sent warm shivers along my spine.

What was I going to do?

I'd fallen for Antonio—and I knew if I told him the truth now, I'd lose him . . . forever.

On Monday morning I was called into the main office at school. The academic adviser wanted to see me. I couldn't figure out why. My grades were good. I was turning in all my assignments. I liked my classes. I wasn't having any problems with the teachers. All in all, her summons made no sense whatsoever. At least this was one thing American schools and Italian schools had in common. Kids got called to the office and didn't have a clue as to the reason.

The receptionist sat behind a huge counter, clicking away at her computer. I stared at plaques on the wall—totally uninterested in their significance. As I waited for Signorina DiMitri, the academic adviser, I reflected on the decision I'd made the night before.

Sunday I hadn't gone to work at La Sera. Neither had Antonio called me. That had bummed me out a little. After his declaration Saturday night, I figured he'd want some contact. I didn't want to sever all ties with him. I wanted to hear his voice. But I thought seeing him in person would be too incredibly hard.

I had spent Sunday doing a lot of soul searching. Not exactly what I'd planned when I decided I wanted to spend a year in Rome. By the time I crawled into bed, I'd gathered my courage.

Today after school I was going to tell him the truth about me. I was going to go to his house and confront my fears, face my misgivings, and deal with his anger.

Signorina DiMitri stepped out of her office and smiled broadly. "Thank you for coming, Carrie."

I held up the note she'd sent to my first-class teacher. "Back home when we get a note from the office, we don't have a choice."

She laughed. "It's the same here."

"So what did you need?" I asked.

"Well, I have a special favor to ask. As you know, English is a foreign language here. We teach formal English, but Signora Calendri wants to take advantage of your presence in our school. She was hoping you'd consent to teach her students some of the American phrases that you wouldn't find in a textbook."

A whole slew of phrases went through my mind. None of them would be in any textbook—American or Italian. I shrugged. "Sure."

"Wonderful!" She gazed past me, and I heard footsteps as someone else came into the office. "Here's your escort."

I turned, and my heart slammed against my ribs. Antonio!

Joy lit his face momentarily. Then he furrowed his brow as though he suddenly realized that I shouldn't be here at his school.

"Antonio, have you met our Year Abroad student?" Signorina DiMitri asked.

His mouth dropped open, and he stared at me. The color drained from his face. "No," he replied hesitantly, his gaze never leaving my face. I knew all the blood had drained from my face too. I probably looked like a ghost. "I have wanted to . . . but our paths have not crossed," he added stiffly.

"Well, then, let me introduce you. Antonio, this is Carrie Giovani, from Mustang, Texas. Carrie, Antonio Donatello is in Signora Calendri's English class during this hour. We thought it would be easier for you to find her class if someone walked you there."

I heard a phone ring in the distance.

"Excuse me," Signorina DiMitri said. "I have to get the phone, but you can go on to the class."

She walked back into her office, but neither Antonio nor I moved. He looked like he might be close to barfing.

"Carrie?" he rasped. I heard the disbelief in his voice.

My chest ached. My mouth was dry as I responded in English. "Carrie is short for Carrina."

"You're the Year Abroad student?" He looked like he was in pain. I wanted to put my arms around him and comfort him. "You're American?"

I nodded. My stomach roiled. "I can explain."

"You can explain?" he repeated. "You can explain? You can explain making a fool of me?"

"I didn't mean for it to be like that—," I began.

"I never want to see you again!" he shouted. "Ever!"

I watched him storm out. Then I heard the sound of my heart shattering, and I knew what it was to lose someone you loved.

Sixteen

Carrie

I PUTTERED ALONG the street on Elena's scooter. Destination: La Sera.

I had explained to Signorina DiMitri that I needed a couple of days to come up with some examples of American slang. She'd been thrilled with my enthusiasm for the project and had immediately gone to tell Signora Calendri of the change in plans.

I hadn't seen Antonio since he stalked out of the office. After school Elena had told me that Antonio had never returned to English class. I remembered that they had one class together. Why hadn't it occurred to me that it was English? Why hadn't I asked Antonio what classes he took? Why hadn't I asked Elena what class they shared?

Would that knowledge have made a difference? My head said no, but my heart was searching for ways I could have altered this morning. Oh, to have a time machine . . . to go back just twenty-four hours. If only I'd gone to his house yesterday. He'd probably never believe now that I had planned to tell him the truth.

I'd waited too long. Now I had so much more to explain. If only he'd hung around long enough to hear what I had to say.

I parked the scooter outside the restaurant. As I removed my helmet, I realized that my hands were trembling. I took a deep breath and marched up the steps as though I were going to an execution. No matter how many different ways I ran the story through my mind, I was the bad guy.

I, who usually played the heroine. Juliet. Maria in *The Sound of Music*. Eliza Doolittle in *My Fair Lady*.

Now I truly felt like the only villain I'd ever played: Cruella De Vil.

I opened the door and peered into the restaurant. Aunt Bianca was placing white starched tablecloths over the tables. She turned and smiled brightly. "Carrina!"

She held out her arms, and I went into her embrace. I needed to feel the love of family. I wrapped my arms around her and hugged her tightly.

"Ah, Carrina," she crooned. "I did not think you were going to work this week."

I leaned back and met her gaze. "I'm not. I just need to talk to Antonio."

She wrinkled her brow. "Antonio quit."

143

Shocked, I stepped back. "What?"

She moved her hand through the air as though she couldn't explain. "He just called your uncle Vito and said he would not work here anymore."

"Oh no!" My heart sank. I dropped into a nearby chair and buried my face in my hands. I knew Antonio couldn't afford not to work. How he must hate me to give up what he so desperately needed.

Aunt Bianca sat beside me and rubbed my back. "What is wrong, Carrina?"

I raised my gaze. "Oh, Aunt Bianca, my brilliant plan turned out to be not so brilliant. Antonio liked me. I liked him. But he thought I was Italian. And today at school he found out I'm American."

"Ah," she said on a soft sigh.

"He hates me," I blurted out. "I guess he quit because he doesn't want to see me anymore." I touched her arm. "You have to let him come back to work here."

"Not if he hurt you, Carrina," she stated adamantly.

"He didn't," I promised her. "I hurt him."

I remembered the first time I ever had a lead in a play. I was in the sixth grade, and I was Joan of Arc. I was totally nervous, shaking so badly that my armor—paper clips linked together to form my chain mail—rattled. I'd called myself the Maid of New Orleans instead of Orléans . . . I think because we'd gone to New Orleans for vacation that summer. Everyone had laughed. I'd been mortified.

I wanted to share these embarrassing moments with Antonio. Make him smile; more, make him laugh.

But I didn't think he'd give me a chance to share much before he went postal at my presence.

Taking a deep breath, I knocked on his door. I was hoping one of his sisters might answer it and I'd have a bit of a reprieve. Then I wished that he would open it so I could get the worst moment of my life over with.

Antonio answered the door. Well, one wish had come true.

My breath backed up in my lungs. I'd never seen so much hurt reflected in a pair of eyes before.

Anger flared in his eyes briefly, and he started to shut the door. I slammed my palm against it. "Antonio, I have to talk to you."

"Carrie, isn't it?" he asked, saying my name as though it were repugnant. "I don't think we have anything to talk about."

"You don't have to quit working at La Sera," I blurted out.

He narrowed his eyes. "Are you quitting?"

I swallowed. "I never really worked there. Signora Romano is my father's sister. I was just helping out that first night."

I saw the fury roll over his face. "They knew? They knew the trick you were playing?"

"No!" I responded quickly. "They told me to keep the fact that I'm American to myself because the tourists like the real thing to serve them. So I kept quiet."

"Why, Carrina?" he rasped. "Why did you deceive me?"

Tears stung my eyes. The moment of truth had come, and it sounded so . . . so lame. "I overheard you putting down American girls that first day we met. You said they were selfish and silly. I thought if you got to know me—thinking I was Italian—that when you discovered I was American, you'd realize that you were wrong about Americans."

"Instead I learned that I was absolutely right," he said harshly.

I nodded. "Yeah. You were right. I shouldn't have done what I did. I wanted to tell you—I tried a hundred times. I just couldn't because I was afraid I'd lose you. I fell for you, Antonio."

I had hoped my confession would soften him. Maybe allow him to forgive me. It didn't.

"Tell your *family* that I'll be back at work," he said in a tight voice. "I need the job, as you know."

Then he slammed the door in my face.

"Mea culpa," I whispered as tears stung my eyes. *I'm so very sorry.*

But it was too late.

Seventeen

Antonio

B ETRAYAL!
    Standing in our kitchen, watching butter melt in the pan, I felt like my life had turned into a tragic opera. Just when it was beginning to be all that I wanted.

I was seriously angry. I had never felt this betrayed. Not even when my papa died.

I had been totally wrong about Americans. Yes, they were rich, selfish, spoiled—but more, they were deceptive!

I tossed onions and peppers into the pan. If Carrie—Carrie. How American that sounded! If Carrie had waited five more minutes to knock on the door, we might have had a repeat of her first visit to my house. My burning the vegetables I had meant to sauté.

I thought about the way she'd helped me clean

the house—a house she didn't live in. The way she had handled my sisters.

I remembered her working in the restaurant. I had thought she was such a hard worker. But it was all games. Games designed to teach me a lesson. Well, I'd learned a lesson, all right. I'd never again trust another American.

"Antonio, when will supper be ready?" Mara asked.

I stirred the onions and peppers. "Soon."

Mara hopped onto a stool. "When is your friend coming back to see us?"

"What friend?" I asked.

"Carrina! I really liked her," she announced.

"Her name is Carrie, and she's never coming back to see us," I responded.

"Why?"

"Because she's an American," I explained. Because she was dishonest. Because she had stabbed me in the heart.

"What's wrong with Americans?" Mara asked.

I glanced at Mara. Most Italians didn't mind Americans. They loved tourists, loved showing off their country. If I didn't have to wait on them, I probably wouldn't mind them either. I didn't want Mara to dislike them.

"There's nothing wrong with Americans." I moved to the counter and sat on the stool beside her. "The problem is Carrie. She made me think she was Italian."

"How did she *make* you think it?" Mara asked.

Ah, to be young and unable to understand so much. "Well," I began, "she didn't really make me think it, I suppose. I just assumed she was Italian because she spoke Italian, she looks Italian, and when I told her that I wanted to meet the Year Abroad student, she didn't tell me that she was the Year Abroad student."

Mara's blue eyes widened. "Carrina's the Year Abroad student?"

"Yes," I admitted.

She giggled. "So you wanted to meet someone you already knew."

"Sort of. Only I didn't know that I knew her."

She stared at me. "So if you wanted to meet the Year Abroad student and she was the Year Abroad student, why can't she come over?"

I slumped on the stool. "Because she lied to me—by omission. By not telling me, she deceived me."

"Oh." Mara stuck out her bottom lip. "I liked her," she repeated.

"I liked her too." Had fallen for too, as a matter of fact, but she wasn't the girl I thought she was.

"Antonio, what's that stink?" Mara asked.

I groaned and rushed back to the stove. My diced onions and peppers were burned to a crisp. Fortunately I had more this time that I could cut and cook.

My gaze slid to the celery stalk. I thought of my fencing match with Carrina—Carrie. Funny how I suddenly realized that "Carrie" suited her. Short and quick. Energetic, even.

149

Just like Mara, I liked Carrie too. But it wasn't enough. Not when she'd betrayed me.

School became a nightmare.

Everywhere I looked, there was Carrie.

I must have been the only person in the entire school who hadn't met her. Only I *had* met her. I just hadn't realized that I'd met her.

Whenever our paths crossed, our eyes locked. Mine hard. Hers . . . sad. I should have felt glad about that. Felt a measure of satisfaction, but I didn't. When I couldn't stand it any longer, I approached her in the hallway.

"Are you deliberately getting in my way now?" I demanded.

"No, before I was deliberately avoiding you." She gave me a wry smile. "You know. By ducking into boys' bathrooms."

"You went into the boys' bathroom to avoid seeing me?" I asked.

"I didn't realize it was the boys' bathroom. I just knew it was a door and you were getting close. At the time I didn't think anything would be worse than you finding out that I was American," she explained.

"And now?" I insisted.

"I was right. There was nothing worse."

I should have felt a measure of satisfaction. Instead I wanted to draw her into my arms and find a way to get that sad look off her face.

I turned on my heel and headed for my next

class. No way was I going to comfort her. No way would I ever forgive her.

I would despise her as long as I remembered her.

Unfortunately, I feared I would remember her forever.

Eighteen

Carrie

EVENING WAS BEGINNING to descend. I sat on the balcony outside my bedroom and stared—at nothing. Not even the incredible sunset could stir me. Being miserable was not how I'd planned to spend my year in Rome. How had my whole world crashed?

I was staying away from La Sera. I'd stopped dodging Antonio at school. There was no point in doing that anymore. Except that it hurt so much to see him. Our paths crossed constantly. I absolutely couldn't believe that I'd managed to avoid him for so long. *I'd make a great spy,* I thought.

I'd e-mailed Dana and Robin about the situation; their advice was to keep trying, to keep apologizing and explaining myself and pray he'd forgive me. I wasn't sure he would forgive me. In fact, I was sure he wouldn't.

I propped my bare feet on the wrought-iron railing and tapped my pencil against the legal pad resting on my thighs. I still had to come up with a "lesson plan" for the English class. Then I'd have to go into the class—where I knew Antonio would be waiting—stand up in front of everyone, and explain what *hey, dude,* and *going postal* meant. I really wanted to give them an American experience, but the experience encompassed so much. Where to begin? I hadn't a clue.

I heard a shuffling sound and glanced over my shoulder. Elena stepped onto the balcony and dropped down. She folded her legs beneath her and leaned back against the brick wall. She peered up at me. "Are you avoiding my English class?" she asked in English.

I smiled. "Yep."

She wrinkled her nose. "*Yep.* Is that like *yes?*"

"Yep," I repeated. "Sometimes we say *yeah* or *uh-huh* or *you bet.*"

"But *no* is just *no,* right?" she inquired.

"Nope. No could be *uh-uh* or *nah* or *no way,*" I explained. I rolled my hands one over the other. "And American is more than just words. How do I explain chicken-fried steak, home fries, and Texas toast? Pictures are so boring—I wanted students to see the real thing, but how am I going to take food to school? If there was a kitchen at the school, I could offer to cook for the class." I drew a big *X* on the yellow paper. "No matter how I try to present

153

this information, it's going to put every student in that class to sleep."

Elena sat up straighter. "What if we had a party here?"

I stared at her. "A party."

She smiled brightly. "Yep. Saturday evening. We could invite all of the students in Signora Calendri's classes. She probably has about fifty. It would be crowded, but I think it would be great fun. Then you could cook your fried-chicken steak," she said, her eyes sparkling.

I laughed. "Chicken-fried steak." I gnawed on my lower lip. The idea really appealed to me. And with all of the English classes here, I wouldn't have to stand in front of a room, trying to avoid looking at Antonio. "We could have a Texas theme," I suggested, really getting into the idea. "I could make invitations that say, 'Y'all come see us, ya hear?'"

Elena giggled. "When you don't talk Italian, you really sound funny."

"You mean my Texas drawl?" I asked, really emphasizing my twang.

"Yep," she said, beaming.

"You should hear my friend Robin," I told her. "She has a really heavy accent." Unless her time in London had tempered it. But I couldn't really see that happening. How could a few weeks erase sixteen years of good-ole-boy talkin'?

I ripped off the top sheet of paper—my X'ed paper. I started to make a list. "I have some home videos I can show." I glanced at Elena. "Seeing my brothers will really give the students a taste of Texas life."

"I think you should wear one of your Texas outfits that I've seen in your closet. Maybe I should wear one too," Elena hinted. "Just to give everyone a true feeling for Texas."

"Good idea," I admitted. My list grew. Food, exhibits, videos, music. I'd brought some Dixie Chicks and Clay Aiken CDs. Some Shakira and Black Eyed Peas as well, but I figured I should really play country music. Everything I wanted to do was snowballing.

"Do you think Signora Calendri would mind if I put the lesson off for a week?" I asked. "There's so much I need to do to have everything the way I want it."

"I think she will think it's worth the wait," Elena stated.

"I'll talk with her tomorrow," I murmured. But my excitement was mounting. I could share a part of my culture . . . and maybe when Antonio got a true taste of Texas hospitality, he might forgive me a little.

The next week at school, when I saw Antonio in the hallway, I called out to him. "Antonio!"

He stopped walking and turned. My heart pounded as I approached him. I couldn't help but think that he looked so totally hot. And so totally still angry.

"Did Signora Calendri give you an invitation to

the Deep in the Heart of Texas party?" I dared to ask.

"Yes, but I have to work Saturday," he said without emotion.

"We'll be partying late. You could come by after work—you know, to unwind," I suggested.

I watched as his jaw clenched.

"You wanted to learn about Americans," I began.

"You've already taught me everything I need to know about Americans," he interrupted.

He turned on his heel and walked away.

No, I thought, *I didn't teach you anything about Americans. I only taught you something about me.*

Nineteen

Antonio

LATE SATURDAY AFTERNOON I arrived at La Sera, not at all in the mood to work. I stood at the back of the kitchen, looking at the invitation to Carrie's party.

She'd drawn a Texas flag on the front. Inside she'd written, *Y'all come on over for a good time and good food—Texas style.* The party started at seven at Elena's. At Elena's. I shook my head. How had I managed to miss the fact that Elena Pietra was hosting this year's Year Abroad student? I felt like I had buried myself in a cocoon—until Carrie with her exuberance had made me want to do things again.

It had taken a lot of courage for her to approach me in the hall. I hated to admit that fact because it made me feel like I should admire her. She had looked sad when she'd talked to me. I was glad she

157

was suffering. It was only fair that she should hurt the way I hurt.

No, I thought, I really didn't want her to hurt. I just wanted her to stay out of my life.

"Antonio?"

At Roberto's summons I stuffed the invitation into my pocket and turned. It was time to get to work.

"Good news." Roberto smiled. "Papa just called, and we're closing the restaurant for the night."

"Closing?" I sounded like an echo.

"Yep, but you'll still get paid as though it had remained open," Roberto assured me. "Carrina's having her party tonight, and Mama and Papa want the family to be able to go over there. Apparently Carrina thought it would be nice to cook a meal for everyone. Mama and Papa went to help." He grinned. "She's giving them a crash course in cooking Texas cuisine. So let's close up, and you can ride over there with me and my brothers."

I shook my head. "I'll help you close up, but I'm not going to the party."

"Why do you have such a problem with Carrina?" he asked.

I thought my eyes were going to pop out of my head. "I can't believe you asked me that. Don't you know what she did?"

Roberto shrugged. "Sure, I know. We all know. As far as I'm concerned, though, you deserved what she did."

"Deserved it? Are you out of your mind?" I cried.

"No. I'm very sane. You, however, have a chip on your shoulder the size of a Roman hill. You come very close to being rude to our American customers. Is it any wonder they're rude back?"

"I'm rude?" I asked.

"Yeah, you're always looking down on them. The only reason Papa doesn't fire you is because he knows you need the job. You liked Carrina just fine when you thought she was Italian. She's the same girl."

"No, she's not. She's an American," I pointed out.

Roberto glared at me. "Antonio, she was an American all along."

I did not want to see Carrie. But I had to admit that I was a little curious about what she would share with everyone.

All right. Maybe I wanted to see her a little bit.

With Carrie's cousins, I arrived at Elena's. Elena opened the door. Smiling brightly, she said in English, "Y'all come on in."

She ushered us into the house and closed the door behind us. Her eyes widened slightly when she spotted me in the group, but she didn't say anything about my being there.

"Come on into the kitchen," she said. "We're cooking bebarcue chicken."

I heard Carrie's laughter. "Elena, that's barbecue chicken!" she shouted from the kitchen.

Elena waved her hands in the air. "Whatever. Y'all come help."

I hung back as Carrie's cousins followed Elena into the kitchen. I heard cries of hello and then Carrie's voice as she rapidly gave orders.

Slowly I approached the kitchen and peered inside through the open arched doorway. What an incredible mess!

All except Carrie. She wore tight-fitting blue jeans, a cowboy-looking shirt, boots, a cowboy hat, and a vest. Did she really wear those clothes back home?

"What is this?" Roberto asked as he lifted a ladle and poured thick white goo back into the pot.

"That," Carrie told him, "is white cream gravy. You pour it over the chicken-fried steak that Uncle Vito is cooking. If it's made right, it's guaranteed to clog your heart."

She looked so happy with her family. So relaxed. She hadn't spotted me yet. I didn't know if I really wanted her to. She was just like the girl I'd fallen in love with—only she wasn't.

I heard a knock on the door. Everyone in the kitchen was talking at once, so no one else heard it. I figured it was probably students from class arriving early. I thought it would be all right if I let them in.

I crossed back to the door and opened it. Four people stood there. I'd never seen them before. A tall, English-looking guy with blond hair had his arm around a blond girl. Beside them was a girl with short red hair and a tall, dark-haired guy. All four were smiling like lunatics. None of them looked Italian.

"Ciao!" the blond girl said with an accent that could have come right out of an American western.

"Robin, I thought *ciao* meant 'good-bye,'" the redhead said with an accent similar to her friend's but not quite as bad.

"Actually, Dana, I believe it means both," the blond guy said. I'd been right: The guy was British.

"Kit, are you telling us that Italians have one word that means two different things?" Robin asked.

"I believe so," Kit said.

"Just hold on a minute," Dana said. "Let me pull out my trusty English–Italian dictionary." She reached into her purse.

"I speak a little English," I told them.

The girls' eyes widened. "Wonderful!" they both said at once.

"I love Italians!" Dana said. "You're so much friendlier than the French."

Things were starting to click. Carrie had told me that her two best friends were in the Year Abroad program. One in London. One in Paris. It didn't hit me until now that they were Americans and not Italians.

"That's because the French don't like Americans," the dark-haired guy said. It was the first time he'd spoken. Definitely American.

"Alex is right about that," Dana said. "But right now that's not important. What is important is that we're Carrie's friends, and we're here!" She glanced quickly around. "If this is the right house."

I don't know why I smiled. "It is. Come in."

"Grazie," Robin said with such a twang that she mutilated the word. She held up a hand. "That means 'thank you,' and that's all it means."

They walked into the house.

"I smell barbecue!" Dana yelled.

I closed the door and turned just in time to see Carrie dash out of the kitchen. Her mouth dropped open, and tears filled her eyes. "Oh my gosh! What are y'all doing here?"

Y'all? Did they really say y'all in Texas? I wondered. I figured Carrie had written it on the invitation as some sort of joke and Elena had been in on the joke.

Robin and Dana rushed forward, and the three girls hugged.

"I can't believe y'all are here!" Carrie leaned back. "How did you get here?"

"Well," Robin began, "Kit and I took the Channel Tunnel rail service from London to Paris. There we met up with Dana and Alex. And we all took the French train. It goes one hundred and eighty-five miles an hour." She snapped her fingers. "We were out of France in no time."

"We arrived in Italy," Dana continued. "Got on an Italian train, and, as they say, 'All roads lead to Rome.' We knew you were nervous, and we wanted to be here to offer moral support."

Nervous? I couldn't imagine Carrie nervous.

"Nervous?" Carrie questioned. "Try terrified. A week ago this sounded like such a good idea . . .

162

and now . . . now . . ." She gave them a smile that transformed her face into one of rare beauty. "Now I know I can pull it off."

She looked past them to the guys. "I can't believe y'all came too."

"I wouldn't miss an opportunity to see Robin charm people with her accent," Kit said.

Carrie hugged him. "Some big brother you turned out to be."

"I fancy the role of boyfriend more," he admitted.

Then she turned to Alex. "Alex Turner Johnson. We were in Mr. Martin's math class together."

He gave her a crooked grin. "Right."

Then she hugged him too. "It's good to see a familiar face."

When she stepped back, her gaze fell on me. The sparkle left her eyes, and her smile withered like a flower that went too long without water. "Antonio," she rasped. "I didn't know you were here."

I shrugged. "I came with your cousins."

She pointed to the people surrounding her. "You met my friends."

I nodded.

"Everyone, this is Antonio," she said softly.

"Jolly good to meet you," Kit said.

"Yeah, nice to meet you, dude," Alex said.

But Dana and Robin apparently knew more about me than either of the guys did because they were just staring at me as though I were a bug they were considering squashing and they couldn't figure out why I was here. Even I wasn't sure why I was here.

"Carrina!" Signore Romano yelled. "I don't know what to do with this food."

Carrie jumped and then looked at her friends. "Kitchen duty awaits."

"We'll help," Dana said.

I watched Carrie and her friends disappear into the kitchen. I leaned against the door. Signore Romano had closed the trattoria so his family would be here to help Carrie. Sure, she was his niece, but not having the restaurant open tonight was going to cost him a fortune. Her friends had traveled from two different countries to be with her during this event. She apparently instilled loyalty in family and friends.

Maybe I needed to take another look at Carrie Giovani.

Things got really crazy after all the students in Signora Calendri's English classes arrived. I figured there were close to fifty people crowded into the Pietra home.

The restaurant had the capacity to hold 160 patrons. But fifty people crammed in a house weren't nearly as organized as 160 people sitting in a restaurant. For one thing, the Pietra family had only one table and four chairs.

So people stood around in the kitchen and the front room. Eating, talking, laughing. I'd sampled chicken-fried steak smothered in cream gravy—according to the folded card in front of it—home fries, Texas toast, barbecue chicken, baked beans, and corn bread. I thought the chicken-fried steak was especially good. I even considered getting the recipe so I could make it sometime for my sisters.

Of course, the person with the recipe was the person who I really didn't want to talk to. I certainly wouldn't ask her for anything.

Carrie's extravaganza had one rule. Everyone had to speak English. Made sense. After all, we were here because we were taking English as our foreign language. It was funny listening to people stammer and stutter with unfamiliar phrases.

But Carrie never laughed. Sometimes her smile was a little brighter when she corrected people or told them an alternate way to say what they wanted. And she made them laugh with words and phrases that we'd never heard in class: *boot scootin', yeehaw, heck fire.*

Her friends were teaching as well. They all had incredible accents. And they really did say y'all. I heard them saying it constantly, and it was obvious that it just slipped out. It wasn't part of any grand scheme to make us think they said words that they didn't.

"Okay," Carrie announced. "I've got my video camera set up in the *salotto* so I can show you Texas. It's gonna be a tight squeeze, so be sure you sit by someone you like."

Everyone laughed as they made their way into the *salotto*. As I had most of the night, I held back. I thought about going home, but unfortunately my curiosity was stronger.

I crept to the doorway and peered into the room.

Carrie stood at the front beside the television. She'd hooked her video camera to the television and was playing the video so everyone could see it.

"This is my high school's football team," Carrie explained as guys in purple uniforms started running toward guys in white uniforms. "The Mustangs. Friday night is football night, and in Texas football is everything."

The camera zoomed in on the people watching the games. There was Carrie sitting between Dana and Robin. I wondered if she'd ever had a boyfriend. If maybe he was on the football team. She jumped up and started yelling for some guy named Biff to go.

I didn't like the jealousy I felt at the thought that this guy might mean something to her—now or in the past.

"My dad closes down the pizzeria during the game—but after the game!" Carrie's voice trailed off, and the scene changed. "My dad's pizzeria," she explained. "My brother Marcus has the camera— anything to get out of work."

I watched her carrying pitchers of soft drinks to tables. Every now and then she'd stop by a table where Robin and Dana were eating pizza. They'd talk for a while, and then she'd rush off to get someone else's pizza or drinks. The scene changed to the kitchen, and the camera zoomed in on a rotund man flipping pizza crusts in the air.

Signora Romano shouted, "That's my brother!"

There was a little break in the video, and we were looking at another stadium, but it looked very different from that of the football game.

"Now, this is a rodeo," Carrie explained. "My dad has the camera." The camera swept along the seats. Dana and Robin were there. Then she pointed to her sister and four of her brothers. "Now, believe it or not, this is how guys in Mustang have fun. You're going to see my oldest brother, Marcus, riding a bull."

"Riding a bull" seemed to be giving her brother a lot more credit than he deserved. The bull crashed out of the gate. It did a couple of kicks. Marcus hit the ground, scrambled to his feet, ran to a fence, and climbed over.

"The whole family is hoping someday a bull will knock some sense into him," she explained, and everyone laughed.

The video continued to play, and Carrie continued to explain life at her home, but I'd seen enough. I'd seen that her enthusiasm wasn't something that she'd discovered in Rome. I'd seen that she worked hard and played hard. Whether she was in Texas or Rome, Carrie Giovani embraced life to the fullest. That was one of the reasons I'd fallen so hard for her. She did everything with such excitement.

Except now when our paths crossed, the excitement was missing. I wasn't going to feel guilty about that. I wasn't the one who had decided to teach someone a lesson. I wandered back to the front room.

Carrie had set some things on the table. A book that seemed to be a history of her school. Pictures of students, students in class, students engaged in sports. She had a map of Texas showing Mustang, her hometown. It was just a dot on the map.

A CD player was playing music low. Some women were singing that Earl had to die. The sentiment seemed strange, but I liked the beat of the music. I guessed this was the kind of music Carrie listened to at home.

"I didn't think you were going to come," a soft voice said behind me.

I stiffened. Then I forced myself to relax, turn around slowly, and face Carrie. "I was just curious."

"If you have any questions, I'll be happy to answer them," she murmured, but she looked anything but happy.

I considered blowing her off, telling her again that I had all the answers, but watching that video had caused me to wonder about a few things. It would be silly to let my disappointment over what she'd done interfere with my learning. Besides, who knew what questions might appear on my English exam?

"Don't you resent that your friends don't have to work?" I asked, remembering how they'd been laughing and eating pizza while she'd been rushing around her dad's restaurant.

She laughed. "Robin lives on a farm. While I'm sleeping, Robin is milking cows at five in the morning. I'm a night owl. I wouldn't trade places with her for the world. And poor Dana works in a clothing store. The stories she tells about women squeezing a size-sixteen body into a size-eight dress. No thanks. I'll take my dad's restaurant any day."

"The guys who came with them," I began.

"They're Robin's and Dana's boyfriends," she interrupted. "Kit is Robin's host brother while she's in London. They sorta decided they weren't really interested in a brother-sister relationship. Alex is from Mustang. He's a Year Abroad student as well. He's in Paris. He and Dana hooked up. I'm sure he'd be happy to answer your questions if you'd like to know America from a guy's point of view."

I shook my head, but I was curious about something else. "You told Robin and Dana about me."

Her cheeks burned bright red as she nodded. "Yeah. Like I told you before, I can tell them the worst thing about me . . . and right now that just happens to involve you."

"Why didn't you tell me that you were an American?" I asked.

I watched as she gnawed on her lower lip and the sadness in her eyes increased. "I wanted to teach you a lesson, but by the time I realized that you didn't deserve the lesson—I liked you too much and knew if you found out the truth, you'd stop liking me."

"I told you that I wanted to meet the Year Abroad student," I reminded her.

"Yeah, and you also told me that Americans were silly and selfish. And as it turns out, you were right. I'm really sorry about that." She slipped her fingers underneath the chain at her throat and lifted the necklace I'd given her over her head. "I'm sure you want this back."

I really didn't want it back. But I let her drop it into my palm, and I closed my fingers around it. I could feel the heat from her body on the medallion. I still wanted it to protect her, but I didn't seem able to find the words that would allow me to give it back to her. I tugged on the ring she'd given me. She touched my hand, and I stilled.

"Keep it," she ordered. "Maybe it'll remind you that life is a puzzle, and it isn't always easy to figure out how it works." Then she pointed toward the kitchen. "There's some apple pie on the counter in there. Give it a try. It's as American as you can get."

I watched her walk back to the family room. Someone stopped her, and they started to talk.

Carrie had said she was sorry. I was sorry too. More than I would have thought humanly possible. Because the truth was, in spite of everything, I still adored her.

Twenty

Carrie

"**I** STILL CAN'T believe that y'all are really here!" I exclaimed.

I was sitting on my bed, my back against the headboard, my knees pressed to my chest, and my arms wrapped around my legs. Dana and Robin sat at the foot of my bed—just like they had a hundred times before in Mustang.

Dana shrugged. "We just thought that you needed us."

They were definitely the best friends in the whole world. Once the party had ended and everyone had left, I'd discovered that they'd been in contact with Aunt Bianca. She'd helped them arrange things—getting here in time and finding Elena's house. Aunt Bianca had even talked with Signora Pietra, and she had agreed they could spend the night here. An American slumber party in Rome. We'd invited Elena to join us, but she said she'd had enough Texas for the evening.

Alex and Kit were spending the night with my cousins. They would no doubt have stories to tell on their trip home tomorrow.

But tonight I was happier than I'd been in a long time.

"You both look so good in love," I teased, butchering a line from a George Strait song. "I can't believe that Alex and Kit came too."

Dana blushed. "Well, actually, Alex came because he wants to see the Colosseum tomorrow before we leave. He has this thing about the movie *Gladiator,* and he just thought it would be awesome to see the arena."

I smiled. "I don't know, Dana. I saw the way he looked at you all night. I think he would have come even if there was no Colosseum." I shook my head. "I didn't remember Alex Turner Johnson being so cute."

Dana grinned like someone who was completely in love. "He turned out to be quite a surprise."

"Even if he isn't French?" Robin asked.

"Especially since he isn't French," Dana confirmed.

"And what about you and Kit?" I asked Robin.

"It's kinda neat having your boyfriend living right across the hall," Robin admitted.

Dana cleared her throat. "I was surprised Antonio was here."

172

"Yeah, he told me that he wasn't going to come." I wrinkled my brow. "Well, he said he had to work, but my uncle closed the trattoria, so . . . I don't know. I guess Antonio decided what the heck."

"He's really hot looking," Robin pointed out.

"Tell me about it. That's one of the reasons I fell for him—a major mistake."

"I don't know," Dana said thoughtfully. "Every time I looked at him, he was watching you."

"Not the way that Alex watches you, though. For Antonio it's more like, how do I hate thee, let me count the ways." I'd just butchered the lines from a poem. Seemed like I was butchering everything in my life: songs, poems, my love for Antonio, his for me.

"I don't think what you did was so awful," Robin stated.

"Yeah, it wasn't so awful," Dana seconded.

That was what best friends were for.

On Sunday afternoon I felt like a fifth wheel as we toured the Colosseum. Kit and Robin were so obviously in love. So were Dana and Alex. They held hands and sneaked kisses whenever they thought no one was looking.

I was 110 percent happy for my friends. I really was. But I had no hand to hold. No one to share this monumental Colosseum with. No one whispering in my ear and making me laugh.

The design of the Colosseum was truly amazing. I'd

always thought it was circular, but it was actually shaped like an ellipse. We were walking along an internal corridor. It was wide, designed to allow large, unruly crowds to get to their seats within ten minutes. We could use these corridors at the stadium in Mustang.

We'd just been to the underground area where animals had been kept in days of old. Their cages were actually elevators that lifted them to the arena level when it was their turn to fight. Pretty impressive—if you were into the gory sports of our ancestors.

We walked through an arched entrance. There were eighty that had allowed spectators into the seating area. We followed another path until we reached the arena.

"I can actually hear the clash of swords," Alex said quietly.

I had to admit there was an eerie cadence in the air.

"I can see the bright red blood," Dana whispered in awe.

"I can envision the madness of the crowds," Kit admitted.

Robin looked at me. "I see sand and stone."

"Same here," I concurred, not wanting her to feel unimaginative. Although I could also see the emperor sitting in the podium with his wealthiest and most loyal subjects. I briefly pictured myself sitting there. Nah, I decided I'd rather be a female gladiator. Although rare, they had existed. I thought of my fencing match with Antonio. Celery had worked well as a rapier, but I wasn't certain what vegetable I'd use as a broadsword.

"I see Antonio," Robin murmured.

I leaned forward, certain I'd misheard her. In London, Robin had taken to talking really softly so no one would detect her accent. But I couldn't figure out why she was doing that here. "What did you say?"

"Antonio," she repeated, barely moving her lips. "One hundred and eighty degrees."

"My Antonio?" I rasped.

She nodded slightly.

"What's he doing here?" I whispered.

"Watching you," she muttered.

My heart pounded as I slowly turned. My gaze clashed with Antonio's. I could hear the hiss of steel sword sliding against steel sword. Only I didn't want to fight with him anymore, or argue, or apologize.

He stood within an entrance, his arms folded over his chest. Watching. Waiting. For what?

He started walking toward me. I thought I knew how those in the arena had felt when the lions were let loose.

"Kit, let's go explore," Robin said. Out of the corner of my eye I saw her take Kit's hand and stroll away.

I wanted to call her back. *Don't leave me,* my mind screamed.

"Oh my gosh," Dana declared. "What's he doing here?"

"I don't know," I answered.

"Well, Alex and I are just going to tiptoe out of

earshot. Holler if you need us," she told me.

It took every ounce of willpower I possessed not to grab her arm and jerk her to my side. Some friends they were turning out to be . . . leaving me alone.

I thought about retreating. But Italians had stood within the center of the Colosseum and faced things more frightening than an angry guy.

I took a deep breath, squared my shoulders, and decided I'd apologized enough.

"Sight-seeing?" I croaked when Antonio stopped inches away from me.

A corner of his mouth lifted. "Not exactly. I overheard Alex tell Kit last night that he planned to come here today. I assumed you'd welcome the opportunity to check off the page in your guidebook."

I nodded. "Yeah, I haven't been doing much sight-seeing lately, so I figured today would be a good day to start catching up."

I realized that he'd figured out I would be here— but that still didn't explain what he was doing here. I wrinkled my brow. "So what are you doing here? I know that you hate me, so why in the world would you come here, knowing that I was going to be here?"

"I don't hate you, Carrie," he said solemnly.

"I don't hate you" was a long way from "I still like you so much" . . . but still, it gave me a spark of hope that we could at least be friends.

"I'm glad you don't hate me, Antonio," I confessed. "I truly never meant to hurt you. I just thought . . . I don't know; I just thought—"

"That I had misjudged Americans," he interrupted.

"Yeah. I mean, if you could get to know Dana and Robin, you'd realize that some Americans are the most wonderful people to be around," I explained.

He took a step closer. "You're right. I noticed last night. Your friends. Their boyfriends. Doing everything they could to help you."

Now I understood. It was like a lightbulb was suddenly turned on in my head. He'd mentioned countless times that he wanted to get to know an American, and I had three great examples right here.

"They're only going to be here a couple more hours, but if you want to get to know them better, I'm sure they won't mind if you join them. And I'll even bug out—"

"Bug out?" he repeated.

"Leave. Since you dislike me, I don't want to interfere with you getting to know them," I responded.

"I don't dislike you, Carrie. That's the problem. I want to dislike you, I really do . . . but I just can't."

A spark of hope filled my heart like a star shooting across the vast Texas sky.

"Maybe we could start over," I suggested.

He shook his head. "If we start over, I'd have to forget everything."

My heart plummeted as I realized that Antonio wanted to gnaw on my betrayal like a scroungy dog with a bone. I blinked, trying to stop the tears from stinging my eyes. "I understand."

"I don't think you do." He lifted the chain from around his neck and slowly settled it around mine until the medallion rested at the base of my throat. "If we started over, I'd have to forget the way your hand feels in mine. The sound of your laughter, the warmth of your smiles."

My heart was pounding a mile a minute as he took my hand and pulled me toward him. "I think it's better to remember so I don't forget that American girls are smart, work hard, and aren't self-ish. And that I'm a little stupid."

"You're not stupid," I said breathlessly.

"Yes, I am. I listened to my pride instead of my heart—and almost lost you."

He lowered his mouth to mine and kissed me deeply. Ah, I liked the way his heart spoke.

I wound my arms around his neck, and he pulled me closer. The kiss was fantastic. I allowed myself to accept it and fall into it, like diving into the deep end of a heated pool.

This time there was nothing between us but the truth. My knees grew weak. Antonio was kissing Carrie—the American. My heart soared.

He drew back and met my gaze. "I like you so much, Carrie. So much."

My smile was so big that I thought my jaws would crack. "You know, Carrina is my real name. And I sure like the way you say it."

"Carrina," he repeated in a low voice.

I pressed my hand against his chest and felt the

rapid beating of his heart. "I like you so much too, Antonio. I have for so long. Honestly, I didn't mean to deceive—"

He touched his finger to my lips. "The only thing that matters is that you love me." He trailed his finger around my face. "You're a puzzle, Carrina, and I intend to spend the next year figuring you out. And if a year isn't long enough, I have a pocketful of coins that you can toss into the Trevi Fountain to ensure you return to Rome."

Joy shot through me. Antonio settled his lips against mine, and I became immersed in the kiss. Totally. Completely.

I was vaguely aware that within the shadows cast by the Colosseum, Robin was kissing Kit, and Dana was kissing Alex.

Our year abroad had only just begun. But already I knew that it was going to be the best year of my life.

Elizabeth Craft
Coauthor of *Bass Ackwards and Belly Up*

Prom
Season
Three Novels

*H*ow will three best friends spend the biggest night of their lives? Find out in *Prom Season*—three irresistible novels about the highs and lows of getting the perfect date and meeting the perfect guy: whichever comes first!

"Hey, the guys are here," Max declared, gazing over my shoulder. "Jane, this is a perfect opportunity for you to try flirting."

I barely heard what Max said after the words *guys* and *here* sank in. Every hair on the back of my neck stood up, and I couldn't breathe. I knew, I just *knew*, that Charlie Simpson was heading our way. This was it. Charlie was going to notice me, talk to me, think, Hey where's she been hiding for the past four years?

I used every ounce of my considerable willpower to restrain myself from turning around to confirm whether or not Charlie was one of the "guys" Max had spotted.

"Yo, Max," Brett Richmond called. "What's up?"

"Not much," Max answered. "Jane and I are chillin' with some chili fries."

Three, two, one. The guys reached our table. Brett Richmond. Jason Frango. Pitter-pat. Pitter-pat. *Charlie Simpson.*

"Hi, Jane," Brett greeted me. His voice was friendly . . . but confused. There was no doubt about it.

"Jane and I are brainstorming for one of our classes," Max explained. "And hanging out," he added, ever mindful that I not think of myself as just a study dork.

"Hi, guys." *Did those words actually come out?* I wondered. I was so nervous that my throat was totally constricted.

"Hey." Jason clearly had no idea who I was. But

I *did* notice (unless I was temporarily insane) that his eyes lingered on my face for a few more seconds than necessary. Score!

But Jason wasn't the guy who was making me feel like the laws of gravity had gone by the wayside. I looked at Charlie, willing him to talk to me.

Ideally he would pop the prom question right now, on the spot. If that didn't happen, I would have settled for a request for a date. Or a how-are-you. Or hello. *Okay, I'll settle for a nod and smile.*

"Hey," Charlie said, nodding at me.

My heart skipped several beats as all the blood in my body rushed straight to my cheeks. *You're cool. You're confident. Yet you're also flirtatious.* "Hi, Charlie."

I waited for him to say something else. *Anything.* Instead his eyes sort of glazed over and he turned to Max. "You watching the game tonight?" he asked.

"Maybe," Max answered. "I'll call you later."

Oh, to be able to casually announce one's intentions to pick up the phone and dial Charlie's number. It would be heaven! *555-6174.* I had memorized the digits almost four years ago, hoping that someday I would have a reason to use it.

"Have fun, you two," Brett said.

As the guys moved away from the table, I felt oddly deflated. Here I was, sitting with one of the most popular guys in school. And I had been acknowledged by his friends as more or less an actual person. But Charlie didn't even notice me! I might as well have been wallpaper.

The more I thought about the way Charlie's eyes had skimmed over me, the worse I felt. Even Jason hadn't really been looking at me, now that I went back over the sequence of events. He had probably been reading the big printed menu over my head.

I was, in a word, crushed. If Charlie hadn't paid any special attention to me now, he never would. The transformation was a big, fat failure.

Max probably knows I'm hopeless, I decided. He'd been flattering me for one reason and one reason only. He wanted to spare my feelings.

And why *wouldn't* he want to be nice to me? After all, I was the girl who was freeing up his time by writing two huge term papers for him. In theory, Max was helping transform me. In reality—he was just humoring me.

I blinked back tears. This experiment had been a joke. And I was a fool.